An Armada

The Three In

Armada
An Imprint of HarperCollinsPublishers

*All the mysteries solved by the Three Investigators
are available in Armada*

1   Terror Castle
2   The Stuttering Parrot
3   The Whispering Mummy
4   The Green Ghost
5   The Vanishing Treasure
6   Skeleton Island
7   The Fiery Eye
8   The Silver Spider
9   The Screaming Clock
10 The Moaning Cave
11 The Talking Skull
12 The Laughing Shadow
13 The Crooked Cat
14 The Coughing Dragon
15 The Flaming Footprints
16 The Nervous Lion

Contents

The Mystery of the Magic Circle   7

The Mystery of the
Scar-Faced Beggar   159

The Mystery of the Blazing Cliffs   313

This Armada Three-in-One was
first published in the UK in 1992

Armada is an imprint of
HarperCollins Children's Books,
part of HarperCollins Publishers Ltd,
77–85 Fulham Palace Road,
Hammersmith, London W6 8JB

Printed and bound in Great Britain by
HarperCollins Book Manufacturing, Glasgow

THE MYSTERY OF
THE MAGIC CIRCLE

The Mystery of the Magic Circle was first published
in the USA by Random House Inc in 1978
First published as a single volume
in the UK by Armada in 1981

I

Fire!

"EXACTLY WHAT are you boys up to?" demanded Horace Tremayne. He stood in the doorway of the mail room of Amigos Press and scowled at Jupiter Jones, Bob Andrews, and Pete Crenshaw.

"Up to?" said Pete. "We're ... we're just sorting the mail."

"Don't give me that!" snapped Tremayne. His face, which was usually quite pleasant, looked threatening. "You've got some nerve, pretending to be mail clerks when you're really private detectives!"

With that, Tremayne—the young man who was publisher at Amigos Press, and who was called Beefy by everyone on the staff—relaxed and began to chuckle. "You *are* private detectives, aren't you?" he said.

"Hey," said Pete, "you really scared me!"

Bob Andrews smiled. "The private detective business is slow this summer," he said. "We thought we'd get some experience with office work."

"How did you find out about us?" asked Jupiter Jones, his round faced filled with curiosity.

"Last night my uncle Will hired a limousine to take us to a premiere in Hollywood," said Beefy

Tremayne. "It was a gold-plated Rolls-Royce, driven by a British chauffeur named Worthington."

"I see.". Jupe laughed, for Worthington was an old friend. Some time before, Jupe had entered a contest sponsored by the Rent-'n-Ride Auto Rental Company and had won the use of the gold-plated Rolls for thirty days. Worthington had chauffeured the car for the boys, and had become fascinated with their detective work.

"Your names came up when Worthington started telling me about his regular clients," Beefy explained. "When he heard that you three had summer jobs here, he said I was in for a lively time. He said that trouble just seems to happen when you're around."

"It doesn't just seem to happen," said Pete. "Jupe stirs it up!"

"Then we all help settle it," put in Bob.

Jupiter took a card from his wallet and handed it to Beefy. It read:

THE THREE INVESTIGATORS

"We Investigate Anything"

?   ?   ?

First Investigator — JUPITER JONES
Second Investigator — PETER CRENSHAW
Records and Research — BOB ANDREWS

"Very professional," said Beefy. "What are the question marks for?"

The stocky First Investigator looked smug. People always asked about the question marks. "They're the universal symbol of the unknown," said Jupe. "The unknown is always intriguing."

"Yes, it is," agreed Beefy. "If I ever need a private detective firm, I might call you. Worthington says you're very clever."

"We've been able to solve a number of interesting cases," said Jupe. "We think our success is due to the fact that we believe almost anything can happen."

"You're young enough not to be prejudiced, eh?" Beefy commented. "That could be a great help in an investigation. Too bad there's nothing around here that needs investigating—besides why the coffee machine makes such lousy coffee!"

The boys heard footsteps outside the mail room. Beefy stepped back into the hall and looked towards the front of the building. "Uncle Will, what took you so long?" he called.

A second later, a tall, thin man with sandy hair and a small moustache appeared beside Beefy. He was Mr William Tremayne and, as usual, he looked very elegant. He wore beige slacks and a linen jacket the colour of cocoa. He glanced into the mail room but didn't bother to speak to the boys.

"They didn't have a spare car to lend me when I left the car at the garage," he told his nephew. "I had to call a cab. It's so tiresome. Nothing is really properly organized these days."

"I suppose not," said Beefy in his cheerful way. "Say, listen, Uncle Will, today's the day Marvin Gray's coming in with that manuscript. Do you want to see him about anything when he gets here?"

"Marvin Gray?" William Tremayne looked both bored and puzzled.

"Oh, come on, Uncle Will, you remember him," said Beefy. "He's Madeline Bainbridge's business manager. He negotiated the contract for her book."

"Ah, yes," said William Tremayne. "The chauffeur."

"He *used* to be her chauffeur." Beefy sounded irritated, but he took a deep breath and kept his voice level. "He's Bainbridge's business manager now, and that manuscript he's bringing could be terrific. Madeline Bainbridge knew everybody who was anybody in Hollywood when she was a star. Just wait till the news gets out that we're going to publish her memoirs!"

"I'm sure it will cause a sensation," said Will Tremayne disdainfully. "I do not understand this fascination with has-been actresses, but there is no reason why we shouldn't make money on it."

"Bainbridge isn't a has-been," said Beefy.

"Then what is she?" demanded his uncle. "She hasn't made a picture for thirty years."

"She's a legend," Beefy declared.

"Is there a difference?" asked William Tremayne. He turned away without waiting for an answer. A moment later the boys heard him on the stairs that led up to the first floor, where he had his office. Beefy stood looking unhappy, as he often did after an exchange with his uncle.

"Have you actually met Madeline Bainbridge?" Jupe asked.

Beefy blinked. "You know about her?"

"I'm a student of films and the theatre," Jupe explained. "I've read about her. She was beautiful, and supposedly also a fine actress. Of course, it's hard to judge today, when her films are never on release or on television."

"I haven't actually met her," said Beefy. "She's a recluse. She doesn't see anyone. She does everything through Marvin Gray. He seems a very competent business manager, even if he did start out as a chauffeur. Bainbridge bought the negatives of her films from the producers when she retired, and they're in storage in a special vault on her estate near Malibu. Marvin Gray hinted that she may sell them to television soon. If she does, her book could be the bestseller of the year."

Beefy grinned at the thought, and left the mail room. The boys heard him start up the stairs and stumble. He recovered and climbed to the first floor, whistling cheerfully.

"He's a nice guy," said Pete, "but he's got no co-ordination."

No one argued with this. The boys had been

working in the offices of Amigos Press for three weeks, and they knew that Beefy Tremayne tripped on the stairs every morning. He was as broad shouldered and muscular as any athlete, but he gave the impression of being made of slightly mismatched parts. His legs were just a bit too short to go with his barrel chest. His feet were slightly too small, and so was his nose, which he had fallen on and broken at some time in his life, so that now it was flattened and slightly crooked. His fair hair was cropped close, yet it managed to seem untidy. And although his clothes were always fresh and starched, they were also always somewhat rumpled. He was homely, and yet very pleasant looking. The boys liked him.

Pete and Bob began sorting the mail into neat stacks on the long table that ran along one side of the room. Jupe was just opening a big canvas sack stuffed with letters when a withered-looking grey-haired man came bustling in.

"Good morning, Mr Grear," said Jupiter.

"Morning, Jupe," he replied. "Morning, Bob. Pete."

Mr Grear, who was the office manager, went into the small room that adjoined the mail room and sat down at his desk. "Have you seen Mr William Tremayne this morning?" he asked.

"He went upstairs a few minutes ago," said Jupe.

"I have to see him," said Mr Grear. He sighed. Mr Grear was not fond of William Tremayne.

12

Indeed, no one on the staff seemed to care for him. William Tremayne was regarded as a usurper. Amigos Press had been founded by Beefy's father, and Beefy was heir to it. A tragic boating accident had made Beefy an orphan when he was nineteen, but according to the terms of the will left by Beefy's father, William Tremayne was president of Amigos Press and would control the business until Beefy was thirty.

"I guess Beefy's father only meant to protect Beefy and his inheritance," Mr Grear had said one day. "He was such a clumsy boy. No one suspected that he'd show a flair for publishing, but he did. He's got a real nose for a saleable manuscript. Now in spite of that, we're all stuck with William Tremayne—at least until next April, when Beefy turns thirty. It's a great trial. He's the only one who can make any decisions about money, so every time I need new supplies—even a box of pencils—I have to get his permission to order them!"

Mr Grear always looked outraged when he told the boys about William Tremayne. He looked outraged now, but he did not speak again. He was still in his office, staring unhappily at the papers on his desk, when Pete set out to deliver the mail to the other offices in the building.

Amigos Press was located in the Amigos Adobe, a historic two-storey structure that was sandwiched between more modern commercial buildings on busy Pacifica Avenue in Santa Monica.

The adobe dated back to the days when California was ruled by governors from Mexico. The walls were thick, as adobe walls always are, and even though the summer sun blazed outside, the rooms were cool. Decorative iron grilles on all the ground-floor windows added to the charm of the building.

Pete stopped first in the accounting department, a big room across the hall from the mail room. A dour, middle-aged man headed this department, supervising the work of two sullen women who laboured there with adding machines and heaps of invoices.

"Good morning, Mr Thomas," said Pete. He put a packet of envelopes down on the man's desk.

Thomas scowled. "Put the mail in the box on that table over there," he ordered. "What's the matter with you? Can't you remember a simple thing like that?"

"All right, Thomas," said a voice behind Pete. It was Mr Grear. He had come out into the hall and was watching Mr Thomas. "I'm sure Pete understands. Just remember, *I* supervise the mail room. If the boys get out of line, you tell me and *I'll* talk to them."

Pete scooted out of the accounting department. As he passed Mr Grear in the hall, he heard the office manager muttering to himself. "Troublemaker! He won't last a year here. I don't know how they put up with him at that pharmaceutical company for five years!"

Pete didn't comment. He had several letters for the receptionist, whose desk was in the big front room of the adobe. He delivered these, and then went up the stairs to the first floor. The editors, book designers, and production people had offices there.

Mr Grear and Mr Thomas did not speak to each other again until mid-afternoon. Then the copying machine that stood in a corner of the mail room jammed. This caused a fierce argument between Mr Thomas, who insisted that the machine be fixed immediately, and Mr Grear, who declared that the repair man couldn't come until morning.

The two men were still exchanging angry words when Jupiter went upstairs shortly before four to collect outgoing mail from the staff there. Mrs Paulson, Beefy's assistant, looked up and smiled when Jupe stopped at her desk. She was a smooth-faced, plump woman many years Beefy's senior, who had previously been assistant to Beefy's father. She handed a couple of envelopes to Jupe. Then she glanced past him at someone just coming up the stairs.

"He's waiting for you," she said, pointing to the open door of Beefy's office.

Jupe looked around. A thin, dark-haired man in a light gaberdine suit went past him and into Beefy's office.

"That's Marvin Gray," said Mrs Paulson softly. "He's delivering Madeline Bainbridge's manuscript." Mrs Paulson sighed. "He's given his whole life to looking after Madeline Bainbridge. Isn't that romantic?"

Before Jupe could comment, Beefy came out of his office with a sheaf of papers in his hands. "Oh, Jupe, I'm glad you're here," he said. "Take this manuscript down to the copying machine and make a duplicate of it right away. It's handwritten, and there's no copy. Mr Gray is concerned about its safety."

"The machine is out of order," said Jupe. "Shall I take the manuscript out and have it copied elsewhere?"

Gray appeared in the doorway beside Beefy. "No, don't do that," he said. "It would be safer just to keep it here."

"We'll take good care of it," promised Beefy.

Gray nodded. "Fine. And now that you have the manuscript, if you'll give me the cheque, I'll be on my way."

"The cheque?" Beefy echoed. "You mean the advance?"

"Why, yes," said Gray. "According to the terms of the contract, you are to pay Miss Bainbridge twenty-five thousand dollars upon delivery of the manuscript."

Beefy looked flustered. "Mr Gray, we usually read the manuscript first. The cheque hasn't even been made out yet?"

"Oh," said Marvin Gray. "I see. All right. I'll look forward to receiving the cheque in the mail."

He went off then, down the stairs.

"He's certainly in a hurry for the money," said Mrs Paulson.

"I guess he doesn't understand publishing contracts," said Beefy. "He missed the phrase about how the manuscript has to be acceptable."

Beefy went back into his office and Jupe returned to the mail room.

"Want to work overtime tonight?" Mr Grear said when Jupe came in. "The printer just sent over the brochures for the mailing on the songbird book. We can stuff the envelopes in a couple of hours, and I can take them to the post office first thing in the morning."

The boys were glad to put in the extra time, and they called their homes in Rocky Beach to report that they would be home late. They were busy folding circulars and putting them into envelopes when the rest of the staff left, singly and in groups. At a quarter to six, Mr Grear set out to take the last of the mail to the main post office. "On my way back I'll pick up some fried chicken at the shop down the street," he promised.

The boys toiled on after he left. A breeze came up and blew through the open window of the mail room. It caught the door and slammed it shut. The boys jumped at the sound, then resumed work.

It was six-fifteen when Bob stopped working and sniffed. "Do I smell smoke?" he said.

Pete looked around at the closed door. In the silence, the boys heard the hum of traffic on Pacifica Avenue. They heard another sound, too—

a low, crackling roar that came to them muffled
by the thick adobe walls.

Jupe frowned. He went to the door and put his
hand against it. The wood felt warm. He put his
hand on the knob, which felt even warmer, and
very cautiously pulled the door open.

Instantly the roar became almost deafening. A
great billow of smoke gushed into the room and
overwhelmed the boys.

"Good grief!" shouted Pete.

Jupe threw his weight against the door and
slammed it shut. He turned to face the others.
"The hall!" he said. "There's fire all over the
hall!"

The smoke was seeping in around the door now,
thickening the air as it wafted towards the open
window, which looked out on a narrow walkway
between the adobe and the building next door. He
leaned on the iron grille covering the window and
pushed. "Help!" he shouted. "Help! Fire!"

No one answered and the bars didn't budge.

Bob snatched up a metal chair and shoved it
through the bars. He and Pete tried to prise the
metal grille away from the building. The chair
only bent in their hands, and one leg snapped off.

"It's no use," called Jupe from Mr Grear's
office. "The telephone is dead. And there's no one
around to hear us yell."

He hurried back to the door that led to the hall.
"We've got to get ourselves out, and this is the
only way."

He went down on his knees, and again he edged the door open. Again the smoke gushed in through the opening. Bob coughed, and Pete's eyes began streaming. The two boys knelt behind Jupe and peered out into the hall. They saw smoke that looked almost solid. It seethed and glowed red with the light of flames that danced up the walls and licked away at the old staircase.

Jupe turned his face from the fire for an instant. He took a breath that was almost a sob. Then he started forward, holding his breath. But before he could get through the doorway, a gust of hot air pushed at him like a giant hand. He flinched, drew back, and slammed the door.

"We can't," he whispered. "Nobody can go through that fire! There's no way out! We're trapped!"

2

The Bleeding Man

FOR A MOMENT no one spoke. Then Pete made a choking sound. "Someone's got to see the smoke and call the fire department," he gasped. "Someone's just *got* to!"

Jupe looked around wildly. For the first time he saw something that might give them a chance. There was a trap-door under the long table that the boys used for wrapping and sorting.

Jupe pointed. "Look! There must be a cellar. The air's bound to be better down there."

The boys ran to pull the table away from the wall. Pete prised open the trap-door, and they looked down into a brick-walled cellar. Its dirt floor was more than eight feet beneath them, and they smelled air that was heavy with damp and decay. The boys didn't hesitate. Pete swung down through the trap-door opening, holding on to the edge of the floor, then let himself drop the few remaining feet. The others followed. When they were safely in the cellar, Bob stood on Pete's shoulders and pulled the trap-door shut.

The boys stood in the darkness and strained to

listen. They could still hear the fire. They were safe, but for how long? In his mind's eye Jupe pictured flames mushrooming through the first floor and eating away at the roof. What if the roof caved in? Would the floor above them hold if flaming timbers came crashing down on it? Even if it did hold, would anyone fight through the fire to find them hiding in the cellar?

"Hey!" Pete grasped Jupe's arm. "Hear that?"

There were sirens in the distance.

"It's about time!" said Bob.

"Hurry up, firemen!" pleaded Pete. "We haven't got all night!"

The sirens came closer and closer. Then there were more sirens and still more. Then, one by one, the piercing mechanical wails stopped.

"Help!" cried Pete. "Help! Hey, you guys!"

The three waited. After what seemed an age, they heard a wrenching sound and a crash above them.

"I'll bet that's the window!" said Bob. "They're yanking the grille out of the window!"

Water thundered and gushed on the planks above them. Jupe felt wetness on his face, and on his shoulders and arms. Rivulets of dirty water spattered down all around him.

"We'll drown!" Pete yelled. "Stop! We're down here!"

The sound of rushing water ceased.

"Open the trap-door!" Bob cried.

There was the protest of wood scraping on

wood. The panel above them opened and a fireman looked down.

"They're here!" he shouted. "I found the kids!"

The fireman leaped into the cellar. An instant later Bob was being boosted up through the trapdoor to a second fireman, who seized him and sent him staggering towards the window. The iron grating was gone and two hose lines ran into the mail room. Bob scrambled over the sill and out on to the narrow walkway.

Bob had gone only a few steps when he heard Jupiter behind him. Pete followed, and the firemen who had pulled the boys from the cellar came after them. "Keep going!" ordered one of the men. "Move! Fast! The roof's going to cave in any second!"

The boys ran until they reached the open street. It was blocked with fire engines. Hose lines lay in tangles from kerb to kerb.

"Thank heaven! You're safe!" Mr Grear ran forward, clutching a paper sack of fried chicken.

"Hey you, get back!" shouted a fireman.

Mr Grear retreated towards the crowd that had gathered across the street. The boys went with him. "They wouldn't let me go in after you," said Grear. "I told them you were in there, but they wouldn't let me go." He seemed to be in a daze.

"It's okay, Mr Grear," said Jupiter. "We're safe." He took the sack of chicken from the old man and helped him sit down on a low wall in front of a little shopping centre.

"Mr Grear! Mr Grear!" The boys looked round to see Mr Thomas hurrying towards them. He was dodging this way and that to get through the crowd of onlookers. "Mr Grear, what happened? I saw the smoke. I was having dinner at a place near here and I saw the smoke. Mr Grear, how did it start?"

Before Mr Grear could comprehend that Thomas was questioning him, Beefy Tremayne came dashing around the corner on to Pacifica Avenue. His uncle trailed him, with Mrs Paulson bringing up the rear.

"Mr Grear!" cried Beefy. "You okay? Hey, are you boys all right?"

"We're okay," Pete assured him.

Beefy crouched beside Mr Grear.

"I would have called you," said Grear, "but I was too concerned about the boys."

"We saw the smoke from our apartment and came running," said Beefy.

A shout went up across the street. Firemen scrambled to get clear of the adobe. Then the roof of the building fell in with a roar.

Flames leaped up against the sky. The thick walls of the old building still stood, but the firemen ignored them now. Hoses played steadily on the roofs and walls of buildings up and down the street.

Jupe looked at Mrs Paulson. She was crying.

"Please don't," said Beefy. "Please, Mrs Paulson, it's only a building."

"Your father's publishing house!" sobbed Mrs Paulson. "He was so proud of it!"

"I know," said Beefy, "but it *is* just a building. As long as no one was hurt . . ."

The young publisher stopped talking and looked at the boys in a questioning way.

"We were the last ones out," said Bob. "Nobody was hurt."

Beefy managed to smile. "That's what's important," he said to Mrs Paulson. "And Amigos Press isn't wiped out—not by a long shot. Our inventory of books is safe in the warehouse and our plates are in storage. Why, we've even got the Bainbridge manuscript!"

"We have?" said Mrs Paulson.

"Yes. I put it in my briefcase and took it home. So things aren't that bad, and . . ."

Beefy broke off. A man with a hand-held camera had stepped on to the street and was walking towards the fire.

"Uh-oh," said Beefy. "The television stations are covering this. I'd better find a phone."

"Why?" asked William Tremayne.

"I want to call Marvin Gray," Beefy explained, "to tell him the Bainbridge manuscript is safe. If he watches the news and finds out that Amigos Press burned down, he'll think the manuscript went with it unless I tell him differently."

Beefy headed for the filling station on the corner, where there was a pay telephone. At that moment, Jupiter became aware that there was a

24

man approaching from across the street—a man whose face was ghastly white. He was bleeding badly from a wound on his scalp.

"Oh, gosh!" exclaimed Pete.

The blood coursed down the man's cheek and soaked the front of his shirt.

"What on earth?" said William Tremayne.

Jupiter started forward as the man collapsed in the street. A fireman ran to bend over the fallen man, and two policemen hurried to help him. Gingerly they turned him over on his back, and one of them looked quickly at the wound on his head.

"Say, I know him!" A stout woman pushed her way out of the crowd and went to the policemen. "He works in that film place there." She pointed towards Film Craft Laboratory, a solidly built brick building which was next to the ruins of Amigos Press. "I've seen him come and go lots of times," said the woman.

One of the policemen stood up. "I'll call an ambulance," he told his partner. "Then we'd better check out that film lab. Doesn't look as if this guy's going to be able to tell us anything. He might not wake up for quite a while!"

3

The Double Disaster

THERE WAS a brief account of the fire on the late news that night. Jupiter watched it with his aunt Mathilda and uncle Titus, with whom he lived. The next morning, he was up in time to see the *Los Angeles Now* show.

"Haven't you had enough of that fire?" said Aunt Mathilda as Jupe put the portable TV on the kitchen counter. "It could have killed you!"

Jupe sat down and began to sip his orange juice. "Maybe there'll be news about that man," he said.

"The one who collapsed in the street?" Aunt Mathilda sat down to watch, and Uncle Titus poured himself a second cup of coffee.

On the television screen, newscaster Fred Stone looked grave. "There was a double disaster in Santa Monica yesterday," he said. "Fire broke out in the historic Amigos Adobe on Pacifica Avenue at approximately six o'clock. The building, which housed the offices of Amigos Press, was empty except for three young mail clerks. They were trapped by the flames, but were rescued unharmed by firemen."

26

The image of Stone faded from the television screen. It was replaced by scenes of the smoking ruins of Amigos Press. Stone's voice went on narrating. "The adobe building was completely destroyed. Damage is estimated at half a million dollars.

"As the fire burned, police discovered that a robbery had taken place at Film Craft Laboratory, immediately adjacent to the adobe. At some time between five and six, thieves entered the laboratory, which specializes in the restoration of old motion pictures. They made off with almost one hundred reels of film, the negatives of motion pictures made by actress Madeline Bainbridge more than thirty years ago. Miss Bainbridge, who was once a leading star, had just sold the motion pictures to Video Enterprises, which owns this station— Station KLMC—and its affiliates."

Stone appeared again on the screen. "There is a possible witness to the unusual robbery," he said. "Film technician John Hughes was working over-time at the laboratory. He was apparently beaten by the thieves in the course of the crime. He managed to make his way to the street, where he collapsed. Hughes regained consciousness briefly at Santa Monica Hospital this morning, and he is believed to have given a statement to detectives."

There were footsteps on the front porch and the doorbell chimed urgently. Jupe went to the door and admitted Pete and Bob.

"You watching the news?" said Pete. "I saw the

early show. Whoever bopped that guy on the head yesterday also swiped a whole bunch of movies from that lab in Santa Monica!"

"And they were Madeline Bainbridge's movies," said Bob. "How's that for a coincidence?"

"Much too coincidental," declared Jupiter.

The boys followed Jupe to the kitchen. On the television, Fred Stone was reporting a late development in the Bainbridge case. "This morning, a telephone call was made to Charles Davie, president of Video Enterprises," he said. "Mr Davie was told that the Bainbridge films would be returned to Video Enterprises upon payment of two hundred and fifty thousand dollars to the persons who are holding these films. Mr Davie made no statement as to whether or not Video Enterprises would ransom the pictures, which are considered irreplaceable."

"What a gimmick!" exclaimed Pete. "Swiping old movies and holding them for ransom!"

Fred Stone went on with his newscast. "Following the robbery at the Santa Monica film laboratory last evening, Station KLMC was able to arrange an interview between Jefferson Long, veteran crime reporter for the station, and Marvin Gray, who has been Madeline Bainbridge's business manager for many years. We now bring you a broadcast of that taped interview."

Fred Stone turned to look at the television monitor to his left. A second later, Jupiter and his friends saw a sun-bronzed man with wavy white hair on the screen. He sat on a straight wooden chair in front of a fireplace and held a microphone. A clock on the mantel behind him showed the time as half-past nine.

"Good evening, ladies and gentlemen," said the man. "This is Jefferson Long, your KLMC crime reporter, at the Bainbridge estate near Malibu.

"Tonight Marvin Gray, Madeline Bainbridge's long-time friend and confidant, has consented to talk with us about the films which were taken earlier this evening in the robbery of the Film Craft Laboratory. Perhaps Mr Gray will also tell us something about Miss Bainbridge and her work, which many still remember."

The camera pulled back away from Jefferson Long, and the watchers saw Marvin Gray. He appeared grubby and insignificant next to the impressive Jefferson Long. He was smiling in a superior manner, however, as if Long amused him.

"I'm sure you remember Miss Bainbridge very well, Mr Long," he said. "If I recall correctly, you were an actor once yourself. You had the role of Cotton Mather in Miss Bainbridge's last picture, *The Salem Story*. It was your first picture, wasn't it?"

"Well, yes," said Long, "but—"

"Also your last," said Marvin Gray.

"How unkind of him to put it that way," said Aunt Mathilda. "You'd think he didn't like Mr Long."

"Perhaps he doesn't," said Jupiter.

Jefferson Long looked flustered, and he hurried into his interview. "I'm sure that Miss Bainbridge was very upset when she learned that her films had been stolen," he said. "We had hoped to see her in person."

"Miss Bainbridge doesn't see reporters, ever," said Marvin Gray, "and she's resting this evening. Her doctor prescribed a sedative. As you say, she *is* upset."

"Of course," said Jefferson Long smoothly. "Mr Gray, none of Miss Bainbridge's films have been seen by the public since she retired. What influenced her to sell them to television at this time?"

Marvin Gray smiled. "Thirty years ago, studio executives didn't realize that feature motion pictures would become valuable television attractions," he said. "Madeline Bainbridge did. She had a lot of faith in the future of television—although she doesn't care for the medium."

"She doesn't watch television?" asked Long.

"No, she doesn't. But thirty years ago, she knew how important it would be, and she purchased all the rights to the pictures she had made. She decided three weeks ago that the time was right. She signed an agreement with Video Enterprises, releasing the films to them. Video Enterprises took possession of the negatives this morning and had them moved to Film Craft Laboratory for inspection and repair."

"Then it's really KLMC's loss if the films aren't recovered," said Long.

"Yes, but it's a loss to the world, too. Miss Bainbridge is a great artist. She played memorable roles—Cleopatra, Joan of Arc, Catherine the Great of Russia, Helen of Troy. The portrayals will be lost forever if the films aren't recovered."

"Certainly that would be a calamity," said Long, "and all due to a crime that is unique in a city that has seen many bizarre crimes. I am sure we all wish for the prompt apprehension of the two men who broke into the laboratory, and for the speedy recovery of the stolen films."

The camera moved in close to Jefferson Long, who looked at his audience with great sincerity. "Ladies and gentlemen, this is Jefferson Long, coming to you on videotape from the estate where Madeline Bainbridge has lived for many years as a recluse, the beauty which helped make her a star hidden from all but a few close friends. Ladies and gentlemen, I thank you."

The screen went blank. Then Fred Stone was on camera again. "And now for other news . . ." he began.

Jupiter turned off the television. "It sounds like a publicity stunt, but it can't be that," he said. "That film technician was seriously hurt. And Marvin Gray overlooked a great opportunity to mention the Bainbridge memoirs. He would have mentioned them if he were looking for publicity."

Just then there was a crash on the verandah.

31

"Oh, blast!" exclaimed an exasperated voice.

Jupiter went to the door. Beefy Tremayne was standing on the porch.

"I knocked over a flowerpot," said Beefy. "Sorry."

He stepped into the living-room. "Jupe, I need help," he said. Jupe saw that there were circles under his eyes. "I need The Three Investigators. Worthington says you're good, and maybe you'll help me out. Uncle Will won't pay to hire a regular detective."

Pete and Bob had come in from the kitchen. They looked at Beefy with curiosity.

"What's the matter?" Jupiter asked.

"The Bainbridge memoirs," said Beefy. "The manuscript has disappeared. Somebody stole it!"

4

A Case of Witchcraft?

"OKAY, I admit that I'm clumsy," said Beefy Tremayne. "I drop things and knock things over. However, I do pay attention to business, and I'm good at my business. I do not lose manuscripts!"

"Nonsense!" said William Tremayne.

Beefy had driven The Three Investigators from Rocky Beach to the high-rise building in West Los Angeles where he shared an apartment with his uncle. It was a modern security building; the garage doors were opened by a sonic device and the door from the lobby to the inner court was monitored by closed-circuit television. The boys had found William Tremayne lounging on a sofa in the living-room of the apartment. He was smoking a long, slender cigar and staring at the ceiling in a disinterested way.

"I refuse to waste time and effort fussing about that manuscipt," he announced. "You've misplaced it in your usual blithering fashion, and it will show up. We don't need any aspiring juveniles to snoop around with magnifying glasses and fingerprint powder."

33

"We left our fingerprint powder at home today, Mr Tremayne," said Jupe stiffly.

"I'm delighted to hear it," declared Tremayne. He continued to gaze at the ceiling. "Beefy, while you were out, the insurance adjustor was here. He asked a lot of idiot questions, and I didn't care for his tone. Just because I look after your financial interests, and just because the money from the insurance company will come to me for disbursement, there's no need for anyone to take the attitude that I had anything to gain from that fire."

"Uncle Will, they have to ask questions," said Beefy.

"You mean they have to make it look as if they're earning their money," snapped William Tremayne. "I only hope there's no delay in settling our claim. It's going to cost a fortune to relocate the offices and start operations again."

"I can start operating right now if I can just get my hands on that manuscript!" said Beefy.

"Then look for it!" said his uncle.

"I have looked. It isn't here!"

"Beefy, do you mind if we look?" asked Jupiter. "If you say it isn't here, I'm sure it isn't, but it won't hurt for us to double-check."

"Okay. Go ahead," said Beefy. He sat down and glared at his uncle while the boys searched the apartment. They looked behind every piece of furniture and into every cupboard and bookcase. There was no sign of a manuscript that could be the memoirs of an ageing movie star.

"All right, Beefy, it isn't here," said Jupiter at last. "Now let's begin at the beginning. When did you last have the manuscript?"

Bob sat down near Beefy, took a small pad from his pocket, and prepared to take notes.

"Last night," said Beefy, "about nine-fifteen or nine-thirty. I'd taken the manuscript out of my briefcase and started to go through it. But after the fire, and seeing that man bleeding the way he was, I was too shook up to read. I felt as if I had to do something physical. So I put the manuscript down on the coffee table, and I changed into trunks and went down to the pool for a swim."

"Were you here?" Jupiter asked William Tremayne.

The older man shook his head. "I played bridge with friends last night. I didn't get home until nearly two."

"And when you got back from the pool, the manuscript was gone?" Jupe said to Beefy.

"Yes, it was. I noticed it the minute I came in."

"Could the apartment door have been left unlocked while you were in the pool?" Jupe asked. "Do you ever go down and leave the catch off?"

"Never," said Beefy. "And I'm sure it was locked last night, because I forgot my keys when I went down to the pool. The manager had to come up and let me in with his pass-key."

Jupiter went to the apartment door, opened it, and looked closely at the door-jamb and the lock.

"There's no sign of forced entry. And the lobby door is always locked, isn't it? And this apartment is twelve storeys above the street. Someone must have a set of keys."

Beefy shook his head. "There isn't a spare set, unless you count the master key that the manager has. And that's ridiculous. We've had the same manager for years. He wouldn't take a toothpick!"

Bob looked up from his notebook. "Your set and your uncle's set are the only ones?" he asked.

"Well, there was a set in my desk at work," said Beefy. "I kept them there in case I lost mine. But they would have been destroyed in the fire."

"Hm!" said Jupe. "So it would seem." He closed the apartment door and went to stand at the open window and look down at the pool, many storeys below. "Someone came into this building, which is not easy to enter," he said. "Someone then got into this apartment, found the manuscript on the coffee table, picked it up, and took it away. How was that done?"

Pete came and stood beside Jupe. He didn't look down towards the pool. Instead he looked up towards the sky. "They flew in over the roof and came through the open window," he said, "in a very small helicopter. It's the only answer."

"How about a broomstick?" said Uncle Will sarcastically. "That would do nicely if someone wanted to come in through the window, and it narrows our field of suspects. The manuscript was taken by a witch."

Beefy started as if he had been struck. "A witch?" he exclaimed. "That's . . . that's weird!"

"Why?" said his uncle. "Do you like the helicopter theory better?"

"It's just that it's strange that you mentioned a witch. I read some of the manuscript before I went down to the pool, and it had bits of really crazy gossip about Hollywood people. Bainbridge described a dinner party given by Alexander de Champley, the director. She said he was a magician and a black witch, and he wore the pentacle of Simon Magus!"

Beefy took a pen out of his pocket and began to sketch on the back of an envelope. "There was a drawing of the pentacle in the manuscript," he said. "A five-pointed star in a circle. Bainbridge said it was gold with a circle of rubies on the outside. Now, I've heard of Simon Magus. He was a wizard back in the days of ancient Rome, and people believed that he could fly."

"Marvellous!" said Uncle Will. "This old friend of Madeline Bainbridge put on the pentacle of Simon Magus and flew in here and took the manuscript so that we wouldn't find out that he's an evil wizard."

"If anyone flew in, it wasn't Alexander de Champley," said Jupe. "He died more than ten years ago. But were there other scandalous stories in the memoirs?"

Beefy shook his head. "I don't know," he said. "I only read that one anecdote. It's certainly possible that Madeline Bainbridge knew the secrets of lots of prominent people."

"Then that could be it," said Jupiter. "That could be the reason the manuscript was taken. Some person she knows wants to prevent the publication of her story!"

"But how could that person know the manuscript was here?" asked Beefy.

"Easily!" Jupe began to pace back and forth. His eyebrows were drawn down in excited concentration. "Beefy, last night you called Marvin Gray after the fire and told him the manuscript was safe. Of course he told Madeline Bainbridge. Then Madeline Bainbridge called a friend—or perhaps Gray did—and that friend told a friend. Anyone could know."

"It wouldn't have been Bainbridge who told," said Beefy. "Marvin Gray says she doesn't use the telephone. But it's true that Gray might have passed the word on, without realizing what would happen. And Bainbridge's secretary still lives with her. Her name's Clara Adams. She might have done it."

"Of course," said Jupe. "Beefy, couldn't you arrange an interview with Miss Bainbridge? Then you could ask her whom she wrote about."

"She won't see me," said Beefy. "She doesn't see anyone at all. Marvin Gray took care of the negotiations on the contract."

"Then talk to Gray," urged Jupiter. "He must have read the manuscript."

Beefy groaned. "But I don't *want* to talk to Gray," he said. "He'll ask about the advance, and I don't want to give it to him until I've read the manuscript. And there was only one copy. If he finds out I don't have it, he'll have a stroke!"

"Then don't tell him," advised Jupe. "Tell him there might be some legal problems if you publish the manuscript, and that your lawyer has to look it over before the advance is paid. Ask him if Miss Bainbridge has proof of the stories in the manuscript. Ask him if she's still in touch with any of the people she knew, or if Clara Adams is in contact with anyone."

"I can't do it," said Beefy. "I'd blow it for sure. Gray would guess right away that something was up."

"Take Jupe with you," suggested Pete. "He's an expert at getting information from people, and they don't even know they've told him anything."

Beefy looked at Jupe. "Can you do that?" he asked.

"Usually I can," said Jupe.

"Very well." Beefy took an address book out of his pocket and headed for the telephone.

"You're not calling Marvin Gray?" said his uncle.

"I certainly am calling him," said Beefy, "and Jupe and I are going to see him this afternoon!"

5

The Haunted Grove

"WORTHINGTON TELLS ME you boys operate as a team," said Beefy Tremayne. He and Jupiter were in his car, speeding north on the Coast Highway. "He says Bob is a good researcher, and Pete's the athlete of the group, and that you're a whiz at taking a few clues and figuring out what they mean. He also says that you're a mine of miscellaneous information."

"I enjoy reading," said Jupiter, "and fortunately I remember most of what I read."

"Lucky for you," said Beefy. "You couldn't have a handier talent."

The car slowed and turned off the highway on to a side road just outside the coastal community of Malibu. Beefy was silent as he drove up into the hills above the sea. After five minutes he braked again and left the curving mountain road for a narrow gravel road. He went on for a quarter of a mile, then pulled to a stop in front of a rustic gate. A sign over the gate indicated that they had reached the Half-moon Ranch.

"I don't know what I expected," said Beefy, "but

it wasn't anything like this."

"It does look very ordinary," said Jupe. "You'd expect that a movie star who is also a recluse woud live in a palatial mansion or at least have a ten-foot wall around her estate. There isn't even a lock on that gate."

Jupe got out of the car and held the gate open while Beefy drove through. Then Jupe got in and they headed up the driveway through a grove of lemon trees.

"It's strange that Gray didn't mention the sale of Bainbridge's films to you when he brought the manuscript in yesterday," said Jupiter.

"Very strange," Beefy agreed. "It will make a big difference in sales for the book."

"Was it Gray who chose you to be Bainbridge's publisher?" Jupe asked.

"I'm not sure," said Beefy. "He called me about six weeks ago and said that Bainbridge wanted to publish her memoirs. It's common knowledge that he handles all of her affairs, and he seemed to know what he was doing. I didn't ask him why he chose Amigos Press. I wonder if he's really as sharp as he appears to be. He should have let me know about the sale of the films."

The car emerged from the lemon grove, and a white frame ranch house came into view. It was large and plain, with a verandah that stretched across the front. Marvin Gray stood on the steps, squinting in the sunlight.

"Good afternoon," said Gray as Beefy clambered

out of the car. "I saw your dust as you came through the trees."

Gray frowned slightly at Jupe. "And who might this be?" he asked.

"My cousin, Jupiter Jones," said Beefy His face flushed as he embarked on the cover story that he and Jupe had prepared. It was plain that he was not used to telling even small lies. "You saw him yesterday at Amigos Press," he went on. "He's learning the business. And he's taking a course in the history of motion pictures. I didn't think you'd mind if he came with me to see Madeline Bainbridge's home."

"I guess it's all right," said Gray. "But I'm surprised that you're here today, after the fire. I should think you'd have other things to attend to."

"If I weren't here, I'd be at home brooding about the fact that my office burned down," said Beefy.

Gray nodded. He turned and led the way up the steps. Then, instead of going into the house, he sat down in one of the wicker chairs on the porch. He motioned to his guests to take seats near him.

Beefy sat down. "Mr Gray, I'm afraid there's going to be a delay in issuing the cheque for the advance on Miss Bainbridge's memoirs," he said. "I've looked through the manuscript and found several anecdotes which might cause legal problems. In one place, for example, there's the statement that a Hollywood director was a wizard. I know that the director is dead, but his heirs could sue. So I'm asking my attorney to look at the manuscript. In the meantime, Miss Bainbridge might give us the names of people who could back up her statements. And the addresses, of course."

"We certainly can't give you any addresses," said Marvin Gray. "Miss Bainbridge doesn't keep in touch with any of the old crowd."

"Well, perhaps you'd know how we could get in touch with some of the people," said Beefy. He was looking harassed and uncomfortable. "You've read through the manuscript, I'm sure, so . . ."

"No," said Marvin Gray, "I haven't read it. Miss Bainbridge give it to me only yesterday afternoon. I couldn't help you anyway. I never was friends with any of those people. I was the chauffeur then, remember?"

"How about her secretary?" said Beefy hopefully.

"Clara Adams?" Gray looked surprised. "She hasn't left this property in years."

Beefy looked stumped, so Jupe came to his rescue. He looked around eagerly and asked, "Aren't we going to see Miss Bainbridge?" His voice was naive and somewhat brash.

"Miss Bainbridge doesn't see anyone but myself and Clara," said Marvin Gray. "Even if she was used to having visitors, she wouldn't want to see anyone today. She's upset about the theft of her films. She's upstairs resting, and Clara is with her, and I'd appreciate it if you kept your voice down."

"I'm sorry," said Jupe. He looked around curiously. "Miss Bainbridge is really a recluse, huh?" he said. "Doesn't anyone live here besides you and Clara Adams and Miss Bainbridge? Aren't there any servants?"

"We live very simply," said Gray. "Servants aren't necessary."

"I saw you on television this morning," said Jupe. "Is it true that Miss Bainbridge doesn't watch TV?"

"It's true," said Gray. "I watch, and I tell her about any news I think will interest her."

"It sounds kind of lonely," said Jupe. "Doesn't she see anybody at all? Don't you see anybody? I mean, don't you get tired of just being here all the time? And Clara Adams—doesn't she get tired of it?"

"I don't think so. I enjoy my own company pretty well, and Clara is completely devoted to Miss Bainbridge. I am, too, of course. Extremely devoted."

Jupiter turned to Beefy. "You see?" he said. "You don't have anything to worry about."

Gray looked at Beefy in a questioning way. "You were worried?" he said. "Why?"

"Well, Beefy said on the way up here he was kind of nervous," said Jupe. "He figured if anyone knew where Miss Bainbridge's manuscript was, they might try to swipe it the way they swiped her films, and hold it for ransom. If you told anyone where it is . . ."

"Now who would I tell?" said Gray.

"Sounds like you wouldn't tell anybody," said Jupe, "unless maybe somebody called . . ."

"We have an unlisted number," said Gray. "People don't call. And we only use the telephone when it's absolutely necessary."

"Gosh, the kids at school aren't going to believe this," said Jupe. The stocky boy stood up. "May I wash my hands?" he asked.

"Of course." Gray pointed to the door. "Go straight back through the hall and past the stairs. There's a lavatory next to the kitchen."

"Thanks," said Jupe, and he went into the house.

The hall seemed dim after the sunlight on the porch. The living-room on the left was sparsely furnished with straight-backed wooden chairs. The dining-room on the right had a rude wooden table and backless benches. The wide staircase was uncarpeted. Jupe found the lavatory beyond it. He went in, closed the door, turned on the water, and opened the medicine cabinet above the sink. There was nothing there but a jar which had some dried leaves in it. They smelled like mint. Jupe closed the medicine cabinet, washed his hands, and then dried them on a towel that hung from a hook on the wall. The towel seemed to be home-made.

When Jupe left the lavatory, he looked into the kitchen—and blinked in amazement at the old-fashioned appliances there. The ancient refrigerator had exposed coils on top, and the old gas range did not even have pilot lights. The taps over the sink were worn brass ones. Jupe guessed they had been installed when the house was first built many years before.

A row of glass jars was lined up on a counter near the sink. Jupe crossed to read the labels. He saw tansy and lupine, rose hips, mint leaves, and thyme. One jar puzzled him, for according to the label it contained deadly nightshade.

In a large jar at the very end of the row there were books of matches. Jupe looked at a few of them. They were all from various restaurants. Then he turned towards the window. A movement behind the house had caught his eye.

He found that he was looking out at a large grove of live oaks. The trees were old and gnarled, with twisted trunks that branched out as they stretched above the first floor of the house. The dark green, spiny leaves shut out the sky and made the day seem grey. The oaks had been planted in wide-set rows, and among them two women were walking together. They wore gowns of some dark material, gowns that were caught in tightly at the waist, and which then flowed into wide skirts that brushed the ground. Both women had long hair, which they wore twisted into knots at the back of their heads. A sleek Doberman Pinscher stalked behind them.

As Jupe stood watching, one of the women looked towards the house. Jupe gasped. He had seen pictures of Madeline Bainbridge in books about films, and it was Bainbridge he saw now under the old trees in that grey, dreary wood. Her blonde hair was now closer to white, but her lovely face was still remarkably youthful. After an instant she turned and walked on. Jupe didn't think she had noticed him.

Jupe took a step towards the window and found himself wishing for a glimpse of the sun. He felt chilled. There was an eerie sadness about the trees, and about the women who walked under the boughs dressed in dark, old-fashioned gowns.

A footstep sounded behind Jupe. "Finished washing your hands?" asked Marvin Gray.

Jupe jumped and almost cried out. Then he pointed towards the window. "Those trees make everything look so dark," he said.

"They do, don't they?" Gray agreed. "There's a rancher who used to live up the road who said the grove was haunted. It looks as if it might be, doesn't it? It was a cemetery once—a private one that belonged to the family that lived here. There were graves under the trees. They were moved when Miss Bainbridge bought the house, of course, but the woods still seem gloomy to me.

"I came to find you. Your cousin is ready to start back to town."

Jupe followed Gray back through the house. A few minutes later, he and Beefy were speeding away from Half-moon Ranch.

"Well, that visit was certainly a waste of time," complained Beefy. "We didn't get any leads on who could have stolen Bainbridge's manuscript."

"But we got plenty of food for thought," replied Jupiter.

"Such as?"

"Gray lied to us about one thing. Madeline Bainbridge wasn't upstairs. She was outside with another woman—Clara Adams, I suppose. Gray may tell lots of lies. There are matchbooks from restaurants out in the kitchen. He may get around more than he pretends."

"But why would he lie?" asked Beefy.

"To protect Madeline Bainbridge," said Jupe. "She isn't any ordinary recluse. She's a very odd lady. She and Clara Adams were wearing old-fashioned black gowns—they looked like Pilgrim ladies. And there's a jar in the kitchen that's filled with deadly nightshade."

"You're kidding!" exclaimed Beefy. "Deadly nightshade is a poison!"

"I know," Jupe said. "Madeline Bainbridge may be one of the most fascinating characters I've come across. A lady who has changed very little in thirty years. I recognized her immediately. A lady who keeps poison in her kitchen, who goes around dressed like a Pilgrim, and who owns an oak grove that was once a cemetery. According to Gray, it's supposed to be haunted. At least, that's what some people say. And from the looks of it, it wouldn't surprise me if that were true!"

6

The Magic Circle

"YOU DON'T FIND nightshade in the ordinary kitchen!" said Jupiter Jones. He was sitting behind the desk in The Three Investigators' headquarters, an ancient mobile home trailer that was hidden away behind heaps of artfully arranged junk in a far corner of The Jones Salvage Yard. Pete and Bob had returned from the library, where Jupe had sent them to do some research while he was out with Beefy. Jupe had just finished telling them of his visit to the Bainbridge ranch.

"Nightshade is a name for a whole family of plants," Jupe went on. "Many of them are narcotic poisons, and some of them were once used in magic rituals."

"Madeline Bainbridge must be a real weirdo," said Pete. "Poison in her kitchen and a private cemetery out in the back!"

"It isn't a cemetery now," Jupe pointed out. "It *used* to be one. But there *was* something eerie and unreal about the place. It gave me the creeps."

"A cemetery and strange herbs," said Bob thoughtfully. He took his notebook out of his pocket. "It fits. It fits beautifully!"

49

Bob began to flip through his notes. "I looked up magic and witchcraft because Bainbridge had that story about the director, Alexander de Champley, being a wizard. It must have been important to her, or she wouldn't have taken time to draw the pentacle of Simon Magus in the manuscript.

"Now there are several different kinds of witches. There's the Hallowe'en kind, who is sort of a comic-strip hag with warts on her chin. Then there are the evil ones, the sorcerers and witches who can do dreadful things because they worship the devil. He helps them out, according to the superstitious, and I guess there's no limit to what you can do if Satan is backing you."

Pete scowled. "I don't believe a word of it," he said, "but would you hurry up? I don't like hearing about stuff like that."

"Okay, then you'll like the rest better," said Bob. "There's a form of witchcraft called the Old Religion. People who practise it say that it goes back to very ancient times. It's a sort of fertility cult—it has a lot to do with growing things and harvests. It's kind of nice, really. The witches believe that they have the power to make things happen because they're in tune with the power of the universe. They're organized into groups called covens, and each coven has thirteen people in it. They meet at special places, like a crossroads. An even better place is—guess where?"

"A . . . a cemetery?" said Jupe after a second.

"Right!" said Bob. "When they meet they have regular rites. They eat freshly gathered food and they worship Selena, or Diana, the moon goddess. They perform their rites at night, not because they're wicked, but just so the neighbours won't see them and gossip. The rituals can be performed at any time, but there are four main feasts, called Sabbats, every year. An Old Religion witch always attends the Sabbats. These happen on April thirtieth, August first, October thirty-first—which is our Hallowe'en, of course—and the second eve of February."

Bob closed his notebook. "That's all I got today. There's more, and we can take some of the books out of the library if we need to. I just wonder, if someone wanted the Bainbridge manuscript suppressed, could it be because that person was a witch? It could be someone in the film colony who either was a member of the Old Religion and didn't want it known, or perhaps someone who was a Satanist."

Pete shivered. "If we do have a witch mixed up in this, I hope it's one of the Old Religion witches," he said. "I don't think I want to mess with anybody who worships the devil."

Jupiter nodded. "A Satanist could be a person who is completely without a conscience," he said. "Or he could be a person who is somewhat simple-minded. In either case, he could be dangerous. But what did you do, Pete, while Bob was reading about witches?"

"I was reading about Madeline Bainbridge," said Pete. "I went back into the microfilm files."

The Second Investigator took an untidy sheaf of papers out of his pocket and began to read his pencilled notes.

"She came here from Fort Wayne, Indiana, when she was eighteen. She'd won a beauty contest and the prize was a trip to Hollywood. Alexander de Champley spotted her while she was touring the Film Art Studio. Three weeks later she had a contract with Film Art and was set to play Mary Queen of Scots in Champley's version of the picture. That's some kind of an all-time record for getting discovered and cast in a motion picture."

Pete looked up at his friends. "All the stories said she was very, very beautiful."

"She's still beautiful," said Jupe. "I saw her today. Anything more, Pete?"

"Just general stuff," said Pete. "She seems to have been a pretty quiet person. She didn't get into scandals. She made a lot of very good pictures. Most of her roles were historical, like Cleopatra and Catherine the Great. She had the best leading men, but she never bothered with them much once a picture was finished. She didn't make lots and lots of friends. She was sort of a loner, and there was never any gossip to link her romantically with any actor until the last of her leading men—Ramon Desparto."

"What about him?" asked Bob.

"He died shortly after he finished making the picture *The Salem Story*. That was a very strange picture about the witch trials in Salem and—"

"And there we have witchcraft again," interrupted Jupe.

"Right. But this movie was very hokey. The plot was weird. Bainbridge played a Puritan maiden who is accused of witchcraft, and who saves herself by running away with an Indian brave so that she doesn't get hanged. Ramon Desparto played the Indian brave, and he also got engaged to Madeline Bainbridge just before shooting started on the picture. There was some nasty talk that the engagement was just to help his career. He got engaged a lot to his leading ladies. Not long after *The Salem Story* was finished, he was killed in a car accident. It happened after a party at Bainbridge's ranch, and Bainbridge had some kind of nervous collapse. She never worked again. She bought up all of her pictures and spent the next thirty years keeping out of sight."

"And avoiding her old friends?" said Jupiter.

"There may not have been that many old friends," said Pete. He unfolded a photocopy of a picture that he had tucked in with his notes and handed it across the desk to Jupe. "This picture was taken at the Academy Awards dinner the year *The Salem Story* was made," he said. "That group of people is called 'Madeline Bainbridge's magic circle' because they're the ones she spent her time with. There aren't so many. Marvin

Gray isn't in the picture, though."

"He wasn't a friend then," Jupiter reminded Pete. "He was still just the chauffeur."

Jupe studied the picture and read the caption. Madeline Bainbridge and the darkly handsome Ramon Desparto sat at the head of the table. On the star's other side was Jefferson Long, looking very young and handsome. The caption identified a man named Elliott Farber as Bainbridge's favourite cameraman. An actor named Charles Goodfellow sat next to an actress named Estelle DuBarry. Nicholas Fowler, a scriptwriter, was there, and so was Clara Adams, who sat next to a character actor, Ted Finley. Janet Pierce was identified as costume designer for the Salem picture, and Lurine Hazel and Marie Alexander were actresses. A very plain girl named Gloria Gibbs stared straight ahead, and was referred to as Desparto's secretary.

"How interesting!" said Jupiter Jones. "A magic circle indeed! There are thirteen people here, and thirteen at a table is considered unlucky—unless you are a witch. For a coven, thirteen is the right number!"

Jupe beamed at his fellow investigators. "Bob, your notes indicate that August first is one of the four great Sabbats of the year. This happens to be the first of August. Was Madeline Bainbridge a witch? Is she still a witch? If so, who is in her coven today? There's one way to find out! Who's game for a ride up the coast to the Malibu hills tonight?"

"Hey, that's crazy!" cried Pete. Then he grinned. "What time do we start?"

7

The Creature in the Dark

IT WAS DUSK when The Three Investigators reached the spot where the narrow gravel road to Bainbridge's ranch crossed the paved mountain road that wound up through the Malibu hills. Jupe stopped, resting on the seat of his bike. Pete and Bob drew level with him, and Jupe pointed to the left.

"The Bainbridge place is down that way," he said. "I've gone over a map of this area. There are several places where a coven could meet, if Bainbridge is going to pay attention to the rules. One is this crossroads right here. One is the grove of trees behind her house—the place that was once a cemetery. And one is about half a mile north of her house, where two footpaths meet. I suggest we spread out to make sure we don't miss Bainbridge if she leaves her property."

Jupe dug into a knapsack that was strapped to the handlebars of his bicycle. "There's a dog, so we've got to be careful," he warned. "We can't get too close to the house. I brought the walkie-talkies."

He produced three small radio sets which he himself had rigged up in his workshop at the salvage yard. Each set was a little larger than a regular transistor radio, and consisted of a combined speaker and microphone. There were also three belts with copper wire sewn to them, and each had a lead-in wire which could be plugged into a radio. The belt with the wire acted as an antenna, and the little radios operated like Citizens' Band radios, broadcasting for about half a mile. When the user wanted to speak into the microphone, he pressed a button on the side of the radio set. When he wanted to listen, he released the button.

Jupe handed a radio set to Bob, and one to Pete. "I'll watch from the hill behind that haunted-looking grove," he said. "Bob, you can hide in among the lemon trees between the road and the house. Pete, your post can be on the north side of the house—that's the left side. There's a field there with some tall grass that you can use for cover. If Madeline Bainbridge leaves the house tonight, we'll spot her no matter which way she goes. Keep an eye out for cars, and for other people walking around. They might lead us to a Sabbat."

The other two boys murmured in agreement and took the radios. The three then rode down the gravel road to the front gate of the Bainbridge ranch. There they hid their bikes in the tall grass beside the road, and separated. Bob's slim figure disappeared among the lemon trees. Pete went on

57

down the gravel road towards the north side of the property. Jupe trudged up through the fields, skirting the house and the grove of live oaks. On the hillside behind the grove he found a clump of manzanita. He crouched behind the shrub and held his walkie-talkie to his mouth.

"This is One," he said softly. "Come in, Two."

He released the button on the radio and listened. "This is Two," said Pete's voice. "I'm in the field to the north of the house. I see lights in the house, at the back, and I see people moving around inside, but I can't tell what they're doing. Over."

"Stay put," ordered Jupiter. "How about you, Three?"

"I can see the front of the house from the lemon grove," said Bob. "It's all dark. Over."

"Now we wait," said Jupiter. "Over and out "

He leaned back against the hillside and studied the grove oaks which completely hid the ranch house from view. The trees looked even more sinister by moonlight than they had that afternoon. The moon was climbing into the sky now, casting intense black shadows under the gnarled limbs.

The radio in Jupe's hand crackled.

"This is Two," said Pete. "The lights in the house have just gone out. Now there are some little lights out in the back. Over."

A tiny light flickered in the dark woods below. Then Jupe saw a second light. Then a third.

Jupe pressed the button on his radio. "They're

moving into the live-oak grove," he said softly. "I can see candles."

He waited. The candle lights moved beneath the twisted trees. Then the movement stopped and the candles glowed steadily. And there were more lights.

"I'm going in closer," said Jupe into the walkie-talkie. "You stay just where you are for the moment."

He released the button on the radio and slipped out from behind the manzanita. He half-slid down the hillside until he reached level ground behind the Bainbridge house. Then, like a chubby shadow, he stole from bush to bush until he was at the edge of the stand of oak trees. He paused, looking towards the candle flames that burned inside the grove. There were dozens of lights now, forming a circle, and for a moment Jupe could see only the candles against the darkness that pressed in around them. Then, beyond the candles appeared a woman who stared straight ahead into the night. It was Madeline Bainbridge. Her long, white-blonde hair was loose on her shoulders, and she wore a wreath of flowers on her head. She moved slowly forward into the circle of light.

There was a movement beyond Madeline Bainbridge. A second woman appeared out of the darkness. She carried a tray that was heaped high with fruit. It was the woman Jupe had seen with Madeline Bainbridge that afternoon. Jupe knew she must be Clara Adams. She entered the circle of light and put the tray down on a table draped with a black cloth.

Another face glimmered in the dark wood. It was Marvin Gray. He, too, wore a wreath of flowers on his dark hair. Jupe realized that he could scarcely see Gray's body. The man wore a black robe. So did the two women. They were invisible in the night except for their faces and for the circlets of flowers that crowned their heads.

"I will draw the circle," intoned Marvin Gray. His hands moved, white against his black robe. The blade of a knife glinted in the candlelight.

Jupe backed away from the ghostly woods and the strange trio under the branches. When he felt it was safe to speak, he pressed the button on his walkie-talkie. "Pete? Bob? I'm in the field just behind the grove. I'm pretty sure there's a Sabbat going on here."

"Be right there," said Bob.

"Me, too," Pete said.

Pete appeared in a very few minutes, coming as quietly as a ghost. Then Bob came stealing towards them through the night.

"There are only three people, but they're getting ready for some sort of ceremony," Jupe told his friends. "Marvin Gray has a knife."

"I read about that today," said Bob. "He'll draw a circle on the ground with the knife. Witches believe that the circle increases their power."

"Let's watch," said Jupiter.

Bob and Pete silently followed Jupe in among

the trees, looking nervously ahead. What strange rites were they about to witness? They saw the three white-faced people standing in the ring of candlelight. They saw Madeline Bainbridge lift a cup high and close her eyes as if she were praying. The boys held their breath.

Then, suddenly, Pete uttered a small, wordless cry of terror. For out of the darkness, some silent-footed beast had come to stand beside him. For an instant the creature was still. Pete could feel its hot breath on him. Then it growled, low and ominously.

8

Murder by Magic?

"WHAT'S THAT?" cried Marvin Gray. "Who's there?"

The three boys froze, and the growling went on and on.

Clara Adams put her hands to her mouth and gazed out from the circle of light. Madeline Bainbridge did not move. She was like a carving in ivory and ebony. From somewhere beneath his black robe, Marvin Gray pulled out a flashlight. He charged towards The Three Investigators and the flashlight snapped on. Jupe saw that the animal standing near Pete was a dog—the sleek Doberman he had seen that afternoon. Obviously the animal had been trained to hold intruders motionless, but not to attack unless greatly provoked; it made no more to harm Pete.

"What do you boys think you're doing here?" demanded Gray.

Jupe felt Gray's gaze on him and his heart sank. How could he explain to this man that Beefy Tremayne's young cousin, who had been such a polite visitor that afternoon, had returned after dark to spy on Gray and the two women?

"Who's there, Marvin?" called Madeline Bainbridge.

"Bunch of kids. They probably came up from Malibu," said Gray. "Ought to call the sheriff and have them thrown in the clink!"

Jupe's heart began to beat wildly. Was it possible that Gray didn't recognize him?

"Hey, mister," said Jupe. "Call the dog, huh?"

"All right, Bruno," said Gray. "Here, boy!"

The dog stopped growling and went to Gray.

"Now what are you doing here?" asked Gray again. "Can't you see this is private property?"

"Not in the dark," said Jupe boldly. "We were hiking in the hills. We got off the path and we couldn't find our way back."

"Marvin!" Madeline Bainbridge sounded impatient. "Let the boys go, and come back. You're holding us up!"

Jupiter looked past Gray to Madeline Bainbridge. Then he glanced at Gray. Gray looked hesitant. He obviously couldn't decide what to do.

Jupe started towards Bainbridge. "We're really very sorry," he said. "We didn't mean to disturb you."

"The circle!" gasped Clara Adams. "He's profaning the circle!"

Jupe went on towards the table where the women stood, repeating his apologies. One hand was at his belt, unfastening the antenna of the walkie-talkie. With the other hand he held the little radio set at his side, out of sight of the women. He was quite near the table when the antenna came away from his waist. He stumbled on something in his path and fell, stretched out full length on the ground, his head and shoulders almost under the table.

"Marvin!" cried Madeline Bainbridge.

Jupe's hands disappeared for a moment under the black cloth that draped the table. Then he pulled himself to his hands and knees. "Sorry," he said again. "That was clumsy of me. We didn't mean to upset you, honest. If you could just point us in the direction of the road . . ." Jupe got to his feet.

"Marvin, show these boys how to get to the main road," said Madeline Bainbridge.

"Thank you," said Jupiter.

Gray led The Three Investigators out from under the trees. He pointed across the fields to the place where, as the boys knew, the paved road led down to the Coast Highway. "There!" said Gray. "Keep going until you hit the road. Then turn right and don't come back."

"Thanks a lot, mister," said Pete.

Gray stood watching as The Three Investigators walked away through the tall, moonlit grass.

"He isn't going to take his eyes off us until we're off this property," predicted Bob.

"I don't blame him," said Jupiter. "Would *you* want strangers at secret rites in your backyard? Let's hope that he doesn't look under the table and discover that I put my walkie-talkie there!"

"So that's why you fell!" exclaimed Pete.

"I thought it might be interesting to listen in on any conversation that occurs after we leave," said Jupe. "I wrapped part of the antenna wire around the set so that the button is pressed down. The radio won't receive, but it should send. Let's not go too far or we'll be out of range."

The boys stepped from the meadow on to the paved road. Bob looked back. Marvin Gray had disappeared. "He's probably back in the grove of oak trees," Bob said. He followed Jupe and Pete down the road to the shelter of a clump of bushes.

"Turn on your set, Bob," said Jupiter. "Let's listen in on the coven."

Bob knelt beside the bushes and turned the knob that activated his set.

". . . gone for the time being," they heard Gray say. "They won't try to come back. Not after Bruno pinned them down that way."

"I had hoped that Bruno was locked up someplace," Jupe muttered.

Gray was speaking again. "It was dumb to let them go," he declared.

"What should we have done?" said Madeline Bainbridge.

"Run them off a cliff!" growled Gray.

"Marvin!" cried a woman's voice. It was not Madeline Bainbridge, so the boys assumed that Clara Adams had been shocked at Gray's suggestion.

"Well, I don't like kids snooping around," said Gray. "They'll go home and talk about what they've seen. Next thing we know, there'll be photographers and reporters hiding behind every tree. I can see the headlines now: 'Mystery Rites at Movie Star's Ranch!' Before you know it, the cops are poking around and—"

"We hardly need to worry about the police," said Madeline Bainbridge. "We're doing nothing wrong."

"Not now!" said Gray.

"Not ever!" said the actress.

"Then you *want* the cops up here?" asked Gray. "You should have used your power on those kids, just the way you did on Desparto that night!"

"I never harmed Ramon!" cried the movie star. "Not even when he betrayed me!"

"Of course not!" Gray's voice was mocking. "You wished him long life and happiness."

"Marvin, don't!" Clara Adams pleaded.

"You keep bringing that up!" The actress's voice was rough with anger. "Over and over again. All right, I was furious with Ramon. But I didn't hurt him. I wouldn't use my power to hurt anyone, and you know it. In fact, you're counting on it, aren't you?"

"Madeline! Please!" said Clara Adams.

"Okay, okay!" grumbled Gray. "There's no use going on with the rite now. Let's get into the house." He raised his voice. "Bruno! Here, Bruno!"

"Perhaps we should leave the dog outside," said

Clara Adams, "just in case those boys come back."

"They won't come back," predicted Gray. "And if we leave him out, he'll get restless at three in the morning and set up a howl, and I'll have to get up to let him in. That's what we get for raising a guard dog who thinks he's a member of the family."

There was no more conversation from the walkie-talkie. After a few moments, Jupiter drew a deep breath. "Marvin Gray wanted Madeline Bainbridge to use her power on us, just as she used it on Ramon Desparto," he said. "What, I wonder, did she do to Desparto?"

"Nothing, according to her," answered Bob. "She said she never harmed anybody."

"Desparto died in an auto accident," said Pete. "The brakes on his car failed when he was leaving here one night after a party."

"Was it a party?" said Jupiter. "Or was it like the ritual we saw tonight? One thing we now know for sure: Madeline Bainbridge *is* a witch, or she thinks she's a witch. And she believes she has some kind of power."

"The power to . . . to kill someone?" said Pete. His voice was very low.

"Murder by magic?" Bob shook his head. "Impossible!"

"Perhaps," said Jupiter. "However, it appears that Madeline Bainbridge feels some guilt about Desparto. She wouldn't deny her responsibility so furiously if she didn't believe it was possible for her to have hurt him in some fashion."

"That Marvin Gray," said Pete. "Why'd he get her all stirred up that way? He didn't have to rake up that stuff from the past."

"Perhaps he's manipulating her," said Jupe. "He may be the real power in her household—perhaps the only power."

"I don't like him," said Pete.

"Nor do I," agreed Jupe. "Not after hearing him over the walkie-talkie. The man's a bully. I wonder if he tells lies just to protect Madeline Bainbridge's privacy. He may be even more interested in protecting his own."

"Jupe?" said Bob. "Could Gray have been involved in the theft of her manuscript?"

Jupe shrugged. "I don't see why or how. He couldn't have taken the manuscript himself—he was being interviewed by Jefferson Long when it was stolen. And he has no apparent motive for theft. Quite the opposite. As Bainbridge's business manager, it's to his advantage to have the book published and earning money. But did he talk to someone—anyone—about the book? Or did Bainbridge? After what we've heard tonight, I'm almost sure the answer to the mystery of the missing manuscript is hidden in Bainbridge's past —in that magic circle which existed long ago."

Jupe stood up. "We've done all we can do tonight. I'll go and retrieve my walkie-talkie and meet you where we left our bikes. Tomorrow . . . tomorrow we investigate the former coven."

"If that's what it was," said Bob.

"I think that's just what it was," said Jupiter, and he started across the fields towards the haunted wood.

9

The Crime Fighter

"You're kidding!" said Beefy Tremayne. "Madeline Bainbridge really is a witch?"

Beefy was guiding his sports car along Santa
Monica Boulevard. Jupiter sat beside him, and
Pete and Bob were squeezed into the back seat.

"She's a witch now," declared Jupiter, "and it
seems more than likely that she was a witch back
in the days when she was active in films. We think
that she may have headed a coven, and that sinister
things may have gone on among the people in it.
Someone who was involved may well want to
prevent her memoirs from being published. We
plan to interview her close associates to see if we
can establish some connection with Bainbridge
within the last couple of days. We have to find
someone who knew where the manuscript was on
the night before last."

"But you can't expect anyone to admit he knew
where the manuscript was," objected the young
publisher. "I mean, if that person stole it."

"We don't intend to ask about the manuscript at
all," answered Jupe, "at least in the beginning.

First we have to find out who in the coven is still in touch with Madeline Bainbridge, or is getting news of her. I don't think anyone will be afraid to admit a connection with her."

Beefy turned north on La Brea Avenue towards Hollywood.

"And you're going to talk to Jefferson Long for openers?" he said. "Long, the crime fighter? He's so foursquare and true-blue. I just can't imagine him being mixed up in anything weird like a coven."

"He wasn't always Jefferson Long, the crime fighter," Jupe pointed out. "He used to be an actor, and he was in Bainbridge's last picture. He had to know Ramon Desparto. Also, it's logical to begin our interviews with him, since we know where to find him. The offices of Video Enterprises, which include the studios for Station KLMC, are on Fountain Street just off Hollywood Boulevard. I called there earlier this morning, and he agreed to see me."

"Did you tell him why you wanted to talk with him?" asked Beefy.

"Not exactly. I said I was doing a report for my school paper as a summer project."

"Long must like publicity," said Pete from the back seat. "Even publicity in a school paper."

"Perhaps we all would, if we were in the public eye," said Jupiter. He glanced at Beefy. "It's really nice of you to drive us," he said. "We could have taken the bus."

"If I stayed at home, I'd only stew and worry," declared Beefy. "I'm kind of lost without an office to go to. Besides, you guys fascinate me. I don't think I'd dare just walk in on somebody like Jefferson Long."

Bob laughed. "Jupe doesn't scare easily."

"And how are you going to find the other people in the magic circle?" asked Beefy.

Pete answered, "My father works for a movie studio. He's getting us the addresses of Madeline Bainbridge's friends through the unions."

Beefy had been navigating carefully down Hollywood Boulevard. Now he turned right on to Fountain and pulled to the kerb in front of a building that looked like a huge cube of dark glass. "We'll park here and wait," he said as Jupe got out. "Take your time."

"Right," said Jupe. He turned and went into the building.

The reception room was cool, shielded from the glare outside by polarized glass. The tanned young woman at the desk directed Jupe to the elevator, and he rode up to the fourth floor.

Jefferson Long's office was filled with glass and chrome and furniture upholstered in black leather. The windows faced north, towards the Hollywood Hills. Long sat behind a teakwood desk, his back to the view, and smiled at Jupiter.

"Nice to see you," said the crime reporter. "I'm always glad to do what I can to help young people."

Jupiter had a feeling that Long had made that short speech hundreds of times before.

"Thank you very much," said Jupiter in his most humble voice. He gazed at Long, and he let his round, cheerful face take on a look of almost idiotic innocence. "I saw your telecast the other morning," he said. "The interview you did at Madeline Bainbridge's estate. I was surprised! I didn't know that you were an actor and that you knew Madeline Bainbridge."

Jefferson Long's smile vanished suddenly. "I have done more important things in my life than being an actor and knowing Madeline Bainbridge," he said. He swung around in his chair and gestured towards the shelves that lined one side of his office. "The law enforcement people would be the first to agree."

Jupiter got up and went to the shelves. There he saw plaques and medallions from cities up and down the coast. There were photographs of Long with the police chiefs of various large and small towns in California, Nevada, and Arizona. There was also a framed parchment announcing that Jefferson Long was an honorary member of a sheriff's posse.

"Golly!" said Jupe. He hoped that he sounded properly impressed.

"I have some scrapbooks, too," declared Long. "You can look through them if you're interested."

"Well, I'd sure like to," said Jupiter eagerly. "And a friend told me you're doing a series on drug abuse. That must be pretty exciting."

Jefferson Long's handsome face flushed. "It is. Can you imagine, even some people who are employed in legitimate pharmaceutical firms are involved in the illicit distribution of drugs? But I won't be able to put my series together this year. Some people not very far from here believe that it's more important to spend money on mouldy old movies than on producing a documentary series on a major problem like drug abuse."

"Oh," said Jupiter. "Oh, well. I see. That's too bad, I guess. But the Madeline Bainbridge movies must have been very expensive."

"They will be even more expensive when they have been ransomed," said Long.

"That's tough luck for you, I guess," said Jupiter. "Except maybe it could be a break, couldn't it? I mean, you're in one of the movies!"

"*The Salem Story* was an extremely bad movie," said Jefferson Long. "In fact it was such a flop that after the premiere, I never got another job as an actor. I found a much more satisfying career as a crime reporter."

"But Madeline Bainbridge retired," said Jupe. He was rambling like an artless youngster. "My aunt Mathilda remembers Madeline Bainbridge, and she says there was always some mystery about her. She said people used to say strange things about her friends. They used to talk about her and Madeline Bainbridge's coven."

"Coven?" Jefferson Long's face was suddenly wary, as if he sensed some enemy. He smiled stiffly. "Ridiculous," he said. "A coven is a group of witches."

"Yes," said Jupiter. "You worked with Miss Bainbridge. Was there a coven?"

"Certainly not!" declared Jefferson Long. "That is, so far as I know, there was no coven. Madeline Bainbridge's friends were—they were just the people she worked with, that's all."

"Did you know them?" Jupiter asked.

"Well, certainly. I was one of them."

"Well, maybe some of them knew something you didn't know," said Jupe. He gazed at Long without blinking. "Do you keep in touch with any of the others? Do you know where I could reach them? Or maybe you'd be able to put me in touch with Madeline Bainbridge herself."

"Certainly not!" exclaimed Long. "I don't have anything to do with those people any more. My friends are all in law enforcement. As for Bainbridge, I haven't seen her for thirty years—and I don't care if I don't see her for another thirty! She was a spoiled, temperamental would-be actress. Almost as bad as that Desparto character she was engaged to. Now there was a real ham!"

"He died after a party at her house, didn't he?"

"Yes." Jefferson Long looked old then, and his eyes were bleak. "After a party. Yes."

He straightened up and shook himself, as if shaking off a bad memory. "But that . . . that was a long time ago," he said. "I never think about those days now. No use dwelling in the past. And why are we talking so much about Madeline Bainbridge, anyway? I assume you've come because you're interested in my crime-fighting programmes."

"I came because of Madeline Bainbridge," said Jupe simply. "I'm doing a paper on her for my course in the history of films. If the paper's good enough, it'll get published in the school journal."

Jefferson Long looked intensely annoyed. "I wish you good luck," he said coldly. "Now you'll have to excuse me. I can't give you any more time. I have a luncheon appointment."

"I understand," said Jupe. He thanked Long and left.

"Well?" said Beefy as Jupe got into the car.

"Jefferson Long does not like Madeline Bainbridge, and he doesn't like the idea of her films being shown on television," Jupe reported. "Video Enterprises isn't going to finance a series he wants to do on drug abuse because they spent so much money on the Bainbridge pictures. Long says he hasn't seen Bainbridge for thirty years and he hasn't kept up with any of her friends. Also, he denies that there was a coven. He may be telling the truth about everything else, but I think he was lying about the coven. Actually, I think that there is something odd about Jefferson Long, but I can't quite say what it is."

Pete chuckled in the back seat. "You'll figure it

out. You always do," he said. "Anyway, here's something else to work on. I called my father at the studio while you were gone. He's got an address for us already. Elliott Farber was Bainbridge's favourite cameraman, and he was in the magic circle at that Academy Awards dinner. He isn't a cameramen any longer. He runs a television repair shop on Melrose. Let's go over there!"

10

The Witch's Curse

IT WAS NOT necessary for The Three Investigators to fabricate a story about a school journal in order to see Elliott Farber. The former cameraman was not protected by a receptionist, and the three boys had only to walk into his dusty little shop in order to talk with him. Once they were in the shop—a narrow hole-in-the-wall sandwiched between a barber shop and an upholsterer—Jupe said, quite simply, "Mr Farber, you were Madeline Bainbridge's favourite cameramen, weren't you?"

Elliott Farber was a thin man with a yellowish tint to his skin. He squinted at the boys through the smoke that wafted from the cigarette between his lips. "Don't tell me," he said. "Let me guess. You're old movie buffs."

"Something like that," said Jupe.

Farber smiled and leaned back against a counter. "I worked with Bainbridge on almost every picture she ever made," he said. "She was tremendous. Great actress!"

Farber dropped his cigarette to the floor and ground it out with his foot. "She was beautiful,

78

too. Some of the so-called glamour queens needed every bit of make-up and ever trick of lighting to look good. They had to have every break the cameraman could give them. That's why I quit the business. I got sick of taking the blame if some dame didn't look enough like Cleopatra, Queen of the Nile. But with Bainbridge, there was no sweat. She was purely and simply beautiful. I couldn't make a mistake when I was filming one of her scenes."

"Was she difficult to work with?" asked Jupe.

"Oh, she liked to get her own way, once she got established. That's how we all got involved in that horrible turkey about witches and Puritans."

"*The Salem Story?*" prompted Jupe.

"Right," said Farber. "Ramon Desparto thought that one would be great. Madeline was nuts about him, so anything he wanted, he got. Madeline saw to it. We used to worry about her—that he'd wreck her career."

"That's what he did, didn't he?" asked Pete, who had been listening quietly. "I mean, after he died, she was so heartbroken she didn't work again."

"She blamed herself," said Farber. "She and Desparto had quarrelled just before he had the car accident that killed him. She'd said some pretty nasty things to him. Not that I blame her. He was playing around with another actress, Estelle DuBarry, and Madeline was jealous. If you're organizing some fan club for Madeline, or doing an article for some kid magazine, you could just forget I told you that bit. No sense in stirring up old troubles."

"Do you ever see Madeline Bainbridge these days, Mr Farber? Or talk with her?" asked Jupiter.

"Nope. Nobody sees her. Nobody's in touch with her at all."

Bob showed Mr Farber the copy of the picture he had found at the library. "Wasn't Estelle DuBarry one of the people who were very close to Madeline Bainbridge?" he asked. "She's in this photo that was taken at an awards dinner."

"Oh, that?" Farber took the picture from Bob. "Yes. The magic circle. There they are—all thirteen of them—including yours truly."

"Isn't thirteen an odd number to have at a dinner table?" said Jupe.

Farber smiled. "Not if you're a witch," he said.

"Then there *was* a coven!" cried Bob.

Now Farber laughed out loud. "Sure. Why not? Madeline was a witch—or at least she thought she was. She called it the Old Religion. It didn't have anything to do with riding broomsticks or selling your soul to the devil, but Madeline was convinced that she had some magical powers. We all went along with the act. Madeline was the star, after all, and if she'd decided that we were all going to paint ourselves purple, we'd all have done it. We became members of the coven. Estelle DuBarry and Lurine Hazel and Janet Pierce and even poor, dull Clara Adams—witches one and all."

"And Jefferson Long?" said Jupe.

"Sure," said Farber. "I don't suppose he'd like it known today. He's got kind of a stuffy image on his television show. But he was a witch."

Jupiter smiled. "Do you keep in touch with any of those people?"

"With some of them," said Farber. "Jefferson Long speaks only to policemen these days, so nobody keeps in touch with him. Poor little Estelle, who caused all the trouble between Madeline and Desparto, never made it to the big time. She didn't really have talent and she didn't wear well. She now looks like my grandmother and she runs a little motel in Hollywood. She's not a bad sort."

"Do you think she'd consent to be interviewed?" asked Jupe.

"Sure. She'd enjoy the attention. Hey, what are you kids doing, anyway? The project of the year for a juvenile fan magazine?"

"Well, I'm taking a course on the history of films," said Jupe, "and . . ."

"I see." Farber took the photo from Bob and studied it. "I'll give you Estelle DuBarry's address," he said. "And I've got Ted Finley's telephone number. He's a great old guy. And still working in pictures even though he must be about eighty. Mention my name when you call him."

"How about the others?" asked Bob.

"Well, Ramon Desparto is dead, of course," said Farber. "I don't know how you'd get to talk to Clara Adams. She lives with Madeline and they don't see anyone. Nicholas Fowler, the scriptwriter, is dead, too. He had a heart attack a few years back. Forget about Janet Pierce. She married a count or a duke or somebody like that and went to Europe to live and never came back. Lurine Hazel's gone, too. She married her hometown sweetheart and went to live in Billsville, Montana. And Marie Alexander—well, it's a shame about Marie."

"She's the pretty girl with the long hair, isn't she?" said Pete. "What happened to her?"

"She went swimming off Malibu one day and got caught in a riptide and drowned."

"Good grief!" exclaimed Pete. "That's three people in the coven who are dead!"

"It's been a long time since that picture was taken," said Farber. "We haven't done too badly. Now Gloria Gibbs, the plain one who was Ramon Desparto's secretary, she works for a broker out in Century City. Every once in a while I take her out to dinner."

Jupiter took the photo and looked at it again. He pointed to the man who was identified in the caption as Charles Goodfellow. He was a very thin young fellow with dark hair that was slicked back. "He looks familiar," said Jupe. "Is he still working in films?"

Farber frowned. "Goodfellow? I'd almost forgotten about him. He did bit parts back in the old days—you know, playing taxi drivers and doormen. You've probably seen him if you watch a lot of old movies on TV. I don't know what happened to him. He's the only one I've completely lost track of. He's one of those people who are easy to forget. About the only thing I remember is that he was American, but for some reason his parents lived in Holland when he was a child. He was a strange one. Very fussy. He almost had a fit when he found out that we were all supposed to sip honey and water out of the same cup at the Sabbats. He used to do it, but he always went and gargled afterwards."

The three boys laughed. "You make a witch's coven sound as sinister as a square dance," said Jupiter.

"It was all very innocent," said Farber. "Only, after Desparto died, some of the people began to wonder whether Madeline didn't, in fact, have some power."

"She put a curse on Desparto?" asked Jupiter.

Farber sighed. "Maybe I shouldn't tell you. It was . . . well, the sort of thing people say when they're very angry. She told him to go hang himself. Now that's just an expression. I'm sure she didn't mean it. Only right after she'd said it, Ramon Desparto climbed into his car and drove away—and the brakes failed so that he drove into a tree. There were no seat belts in those days, and he was thrown clear of the car. We found him wedged in the fork of a tree part way down an embankment on the side of the road. He was just hanging there with his head to one side. His neck was broken."

"My gosh!" said Pete.

"So the coven broke up, and Madeline withdrew, and that was the end of that. Now no one talks to Madeline, and I guess not many talk about her."

"How about her manager? He used to be her chauffeur," said Jupe.

"Didn't really know him," said Farber. He took a piece of paper from a pad on the counter and wrote Estelle DuBarry's address on it. Then he added Ted Finley's telephone number and the address where Gloria Gibbs worked in Century City. He gave the paper to the boys, and when they left the shop he stood leaning on his counter, staring straight ahead in an unseeing fashion.

"Nice guy," said Pete, when they were outside, "and he sure likes to talk."

"Yes, even though I guess we stirred up some bad memories for him," said Bob. "He looks as if he's seeing Ramon Desparto again, hanging in the fork of a tree with his neck broken."

II

Friends and Enemies

THE MOTEL THAT Estelle DuBarry managed was on a side street off Hollywood Boulevard. When Bob rang the bell outside the office, an ageing woman with bleached blonde, curly hair and very black eyelashes came to the door.

"Miss DuBarry?" said Bob.

"That's right." She squinted slightly, as if she might need glasses.

"Elliott Farber told us you might be willing to talk with us," said Bob. "We're doing a paper for school. It's a summer project on the history of the motion picture."

"Why, how nice!" said the woman. "I'll be happy to talk with you." She opened the screen door and swung it wide. The boys went into a stuffy little room that was part office and part living-room. They took seats, and the faded actress immediately launched into the tale of her career in films. She had come to Hollywood as a young girl, and had taken a screen test. She told them how she had been given roles in several unimportant pictures and a few important ones. And since Estelle DuBarry's career hadn't been outstanding, she soon ran out of things to say to the boys.

Jupiter mentioned Madeline Bainbridge then, and the atmosphere in the little room changed abruptly.

"That terrible woman!" cried DuBarry. "She hated me. She always hated me! I was pretty, and not so high and mighty as she was. If it hadn't been for her, I wouldn't be running this crummy motel today. If it hadn't been for her, Ramon and I would be married and living in some big house in Bel Air!"

There was shocked silence. DuBarry glared at Jupe and he looked away. "Mr Farber mentioned a coven," he said at last. "Can you tell us anything about the coven?"

The colour left Estelle DuBarry's face, then flooded back in a crimson tide. "We . . . we were just playing games, you know," she said. "We didn't believe in it. Except for Madeline. She believed in it."

"So you didn't believe in witchcraft, and you still don't?"

"Of course not!" cried the former actress.

"You said an interesting thing a few moments ago," said Jupe. "You said that if it weren't for Madeline Bainbridge, you and Ramon Desparto would be living in Bel Air today. How could that be? Ramon Desparto died in an accident."

"That was no accident!" cried the woman. "It was . . . it was . . ."

She didn't finish the sentence.

Bob moved awkwardly in his chair. "It was very nice of you to take the time to see us," he said. "Do you know of anyone else we should see—any friend of Madeline Bainbridge who might still be in touch with her? Or with her secretary for that matter?"

"I do not," said the woman.

"There was a man named Charles Goodfellow," said Jupe. "Do you know what became of him?"

She shrugged. "He just dropped out of sight."

"I see," said Jupe.

The boys left, and walked down the drive to the car, where Beefy waited.

"She doesn't know anything that can help us," said Bob.

"She thinks Bainbridge murdered Desparto," Pete put in. "I think she's really afraid of Bainbridge."

"Elliott Farber suggested as much," said Jupe. "I wonder if Ted Finley will have any information we need."

"I wonder if Ted Finley will even talk to us," said Bob.

"I imagine he will," said Jupiter. "Madeline Bainbridge is big news today, after the theft of those films. Ted Finley won't object to being associated with her."

Jupe proved to be correct. After a quick lunch, he telephoned Ted Finley from Beefy's apartment. He got an answering device, but Ted Finley called back almost immediately. The old character actor was cheerful and co-operative. He quickly admitted that there had been a coven, and that he had been a member. However, although he expressed great admiration for Madeline Bainbridge, he denied that he was ever in touch with her.

"Nobody keeps in touch with Madeline," he said. "That chauffeur of hers—that Gray—he took over completely once Madeline retired. He always answered the telephone, and he always said she didn't want to talk to anyone. For a while after Desparto died, I tried to keep her from being a complete hermit. It didn't do any good, and after a while I gave up. Maybe things will be better, now that her pictures have been sold to television."

"And stolen," Jupe reminded him. "They're being held for ransom."

"And they'll *be* ransomed," predicted Finley. "They're priceless. Now that you young folks will have a chance to see them, I expect I'll be getting a lot of calls about Madeline."

"Just one more thing, Mr Finley," said Jupe. "Do you know what happened to the man named Charles Goodfellow? He's the only one of Madeline Bainbridge's close friends that I haven't been able to locate."

"Goodfellow? No, can't say that I do know. He was kind of a dim young man. Maybe he went back home—wherever that might be—and got a job clerking in a hardware store or something."

Jupe thanked the actor, and Ted Finley hung up.

"Nothing," Jupe said to his friends. "He doesn't know anything and hasn't been in touch with Bainbridge for years."

"We haven't contacted Gloria Gibbs yet," Bob reminded Jupe. "You have the name of the broker she works for."

Jupiter nodded. "I'll call her, but I think we're wasting time."

In a dogged and discouraged way, Jupiter dialled the number of Gloria Gibbs's employer. The woman who answered the telephone turned out to be Gloria Gibbs herself. She was even less helpful than Madeline Bainbridge's other friends had been, and more hostile. "That was all a long time ago," she said, "and I don't feel that I'm any more important because I once knew that blonde witch."

"Yes, she was a witch," said Jupe quickly. "You were a member of her coven, weren't you?"

"Yes, and it was a big bore. I don't like staying up late just to dance around in the moonlight."

Gloria Gibbs then brusquely denied ever being in touch with Madeline Bainbridge, or with the missing coven member, Charles Goodfellow. She announced in sharp tones that Clara Adams was a poor, beaten-down creature in whom nobody would be interested, and she hung up.

"Unpleasant woman," was Jupe's comment. "However, she only confirms what others have told us. There was a coven, but if that's the sinister secret in Madeline Bainbridge's memoirs, it isn't making anyone nervous. We don't know about our missing coven member, Charles Good-fellow, but no one else is worried about witch-craft. So that's not it unless . . ." Jupe stopped and frowned. "Jefferson Long!" he said. "He's the only one who wouldn't admit to being a member of the coven. But he couldn't have stolen the manuscript. He was on camera with Marvin Gray at the time the manuscript was taken."

"He could have hired somebody," Pete sug-gested. "And maybe Gray did mention it to him. He could even have told him it was here, and then forgotten he did it."

"It's a bare possibility," said Jupe, "but not likely. Where would Long find the time to arrange a theft while he was busy setting up an interview? Still, for some reason Long makes me uneasy. I wonder what the law enforcement people really think about him."

"You think he's a phoney?" asked Pete.

"I had the impression he was playing a role," said Jupe. "He seems to know everybody in law enforcement in Southern California. If that's true, he's got to know Chief Reynolds in Rocky Beach. Let's see if the chief can give us some background on him. Somehow I'll believe the chief better than I'll believe a lot of plaques and scrolls."

12

The Man from Arson

"JEFFERSON LONG?" Chief Reynolds leaned back in his swivel chair. Sure, I know Jefferson Long. He shows up at every convention of law enforcement people that's held anywhere in the state."

The Chief of Police of Rocky Beach leaned forward and stared curiously at The Three Investigators. The boys sat on straight chairs across the desk from him. "Why are you interested in Long?" he wanted to know.

"I can't say exactly without betraying a confidence," Jupe told him.

"Hm!" said the chief. "That sort of talk usually means your juvenile detective firm has a client. Okay. Just so you keep out of trouble.

"I've seen Long around at meetings, and every once in a while I watch him on television. He's okay. He gives people some straight scoop on crime and criminals. Of course, he claims to be an investigative reporter. That would mean that he actually does some detective work on his own. He doesn't. In my opinion, he's just a brain-picker—he gets his information from people who have done the hard work of digging out facts. I don't even think he's all that interested in law and order. He just latched on to that as a cause; he wanted to make a name for himself and promote his crime reports on TV."

"So he's a phoney," said Pete. "But how come he gets all those awards from police departments and sheriffs' offices?"

Chief Reynolds shrugged. "He does keep the public informed about things like fraud and burglary and forged money and such things. Law enforcement people want the public to trust them, and Long does encourage people to trust the police—and to call the police if they think there's anything strange going on in their neighbour-hoods. So the man does help us a lot that way."

"But he isn't the hotshot crime-fighter he pretends to be," summarized Jupiter. He nodded with satisfaction. "I had a feeling he was acting a role."

"He does it twenty-four hours a day," said the chief.

The boys thanked the chief, then left the police station and started hiking up the highway.

"Another dead end!" complained Jupiter. "We punctured Long's balloon, but now I'm sure that he had nothing to do with the theft of Madeline Bainbridge's manuscript."

"Why do you say that?" asked Bob.

"Because, from everything we've heard, I think Long really values his good relations with the police. He's built a successful career on that, and I don't think he'd jeopardize his career by stealing a manuscript that would merely embarrass him."

"Then why did he lie to you about the coven?" demanded Pete.

"It's not surprising. Why should a man in his position tell a strange kid about some silly stuff in his past? And that's all it was—silly stuff, not crimes. Anyway, even if Long knew about the manuscript and wanted to steal it, he didn't have any opportunity. The timing's all wrong."

Glumly, the Investigators separated and headed for their homes. Jupiter was moody and absent-minded during dinner with Aunt Mathilda and Uncle Titus. After the dishes were done, he went to his room to lie on his bed and stare at the ceiling. He felt utterly discouraged. It seemed that there was no way to connect any of Madeline Bainbridge's old companions to the theft of the manuscript. But if none of the actress's friends had stolen her memoirs, who had?

Jupe recalled the night of the fire. Again he seemed to hear the roar as the flames licked at the timbers of the old Amigos Adobe. After they had been hauled out of the basement, he and Bob and Pete had stood across the street watching the fire. Mr Grear had been with them, and then Beefy and his uncle had come hurrying up. Mr Thomas had been there, too, and so had Mrs Paulson. They, and only they, had known that the manuscript was in Beefy's apartment. Yet it seemed most unlikely that any of them would have taken it.

After a while, Jupe drifted off to sleep. When he woke, the sun was coming in the window. Still feeling frustrated and lethargic, Jupe got up, showered, and dressed. Then he telephoned Bob and Pete and arranged to meet them after breakfast at the bus stop on the Coast Highway.

It was almost nine when Jupe walked from The Jones Salvage Yard down to the highway. Bob and Pete were already there, waiting for him.

"You have any brainstorms overnight?" asked Pete.

"No," said Jupe. "I can't think of anything to do but go back to Beefy's and keep plodding along, checking on people."

"We're just about out of people we can check," Bob pointed out.

"We're out of people who had an obvious motive," said Jupiter. "We are not out of people who had an opportunity. In fact, we haven't even started on them!"

"The employees at Amigos Press?" asked Pete.

Jupiter nodded.

"I can't quite see any of them swiping that manuscript," said Pete, "but we've tried everybody else."

The three boys rode into West Los Angeles and arrived at the door to Beefy's apartment just as a slender man wearing gaberdine slacks and a seersucker blazer was leaving. He smiled at the boys as he passed them in the hall.

Beefy's usually ruddy face was pale when he let them in. Behind Beefy, William Tremayne paced up and down and shouted.

"It's a conspiracy!" he cried. "They hate me! They've always hated me! Bunch of idiots!"

"Take it easy, Uncle Will," pleaded Beefy.

"What do you mean, take it easy? You haven't been accused of arson!"

"Arson?" cried Jupe. "The fire was arson?"

"'Fraid so," said Beefy. "The man who just left here was from the arson squad. He wanted a list of all the employees at Amigos Press, and he wanted to know who visited the office the day the fire broke out."

"He also wanted to know to whom the insurance money would be paid," said Will Tremayne. "I know what he was *really* saying when he asked that question. He was saying that he thought I set the fire! Well, of course the insurance money will come to me. I handle all of the publishing house's financial affairs. But even if the income from my stocks *is* down . . ."

"Uncle Will, are you in trouble?" asked Beefy.

"Just a bit short of ready cash," said Will Tremayne. "Nothing important. Nothing that won't right itself in time. Now don't *you* start! It was bad enough talking to the arson investigator. I wasn't anywhere near Amigos Press when the fire started. I was here at home with you."

"Whoever started the fire didn't have to be

there," said Beefy. "You heard the man. It was an incendiary device using magnesium and a battery-operated clock. It could have been put into the cupboard under the stairs anytime after six in the morning."

"You think I did it!" shouted Will Tremayne.

"I didn't say that," declared Beefy. "I only think an alibi isn't any good in this case. The arsonist was probably miles away when the fire began."

"Grear!" said Will Tremayne. "He did it! He's always hated me. Dull little mole of a man! He hates anybody who has any style. Or Thomas! What do we know about Thomas? He's only been with the firm for three months!"

"Uncle Will, *you* hired him!"

"Well, he had such good references. But that doesn't really mean anything!"

Will Tremayne went to the coffee table and snatched the lid off the box that usually contained his cigars. "Oh, blast!" he cried. "Empty!"

He glared at Beefy. "It was Grear or Mrs Paulson," he said. "They hate me! They've never forgiven me for taking your father's place! Or it was Thomas. We don't know about Thomas. Now here's what we do. You hired these three boys to find that silly manuscript by that has-been actress. We'll just have them go and watch Grear's apartment, and Mrs Paulson's house, and Thomas's place, too. They'll see what happens after the detective from arson visits them. I'm betting that after they're questioned, the one who did it will give himself away. He'll pack up and run. You'll see!"

Beefy looked helplessly at The Three Investigators.

"Why not?" said Jupiter. "Stranger crimes have been committed for stranger motives. If you'll give us the addresses, we'll go and stake out the three houses. It can't hurt."

"Okay." Beefy went into the small study off the living-room. He was back in a minute with three addresses written on three pieces of paper.

"Now," said Jupiter, "suppose I watch Mrs Paulson's. Bob, you can see what Mr Grear does when he's not working. And Pete can keep an eye on Mr Thomas."

The boys went to the door, with Beefy following them. He came out into the hall, his face grave and concerned.

"You're just doing this to humour Uncle Will, aren't you?" he said.

"Not quite," said Jupiter. "We've checked on all the members of Madeline Bainbridge's magic circle—all that we could find, that is. As far as we can tell, none had any opportunity to take the manuscript, and none of them even knew it was here. Now we had better check the people who *did* know—and who did have the means. Any one of the three could have taken your keys from your desk and had a duplicate set made. All three were at the fire and heard where the manuscript was. Perhaps the visit of the man from the arson squad *will* stir something up. Not that I think the theft of the manuscript is necessarily connected to the fire. But we can't be sure.

"There is one thing you can do for us while we're gone," Jupe added.

"What's that?" asked Beefy.

"Your uncle says he was playing bridge with friends at the time the manuscript was taken. You could talk with his hosts and make sure this is true."

Beefy looked startled. "You suspect Uncle Will?"

"I don't know," said Jupiter. "I'd just like to have his alibi confirmed."

Beefy nodded.

"We'll meet back here after the man from the arson squad has seen our three friends," said Jupiter. The Investigators went off, leaving Beefy standing in the hall, frowning to himself.

13

The Deadly Trunk

HAROLD THOMAS lived in a small apartment house not far from Beefy's building. There was a little park directly across the street, and Pete settled himself on a bench there, tried to ignore the children playing under the trees, and watched.

It was almost an hour before a plain dark sedan parked in front of Thomas's building. The man in the seersucker blazer got out of the car and went into the apartment house.

Pete didn't move, but his heart beat a little faster.

The investigator from the arson squad wasn't in the apartment more than fifteen minutes. Pete saw him come out and get into his sedan and drive away. Still Pete waited.

Half an hour after the detective had left, Harold Thomas came out and glanced up and down the street. He hesitated, looked back at the apartment, then turned south towards Wilshire and strode briskly away.

When Thomas was half a block from the apartment, Pete began to follow him, walking on the opposite side of the street. He tailed Thomas south, across Wilshire, and soon reached a dismal little area where small industrial buildings were clustered together. There were a few apartments, but these were shabby little places with peeling paint and torn screens.

Harold Thomas stopped in front of one of these run-down houses and looked up and down the street. Pete ducked out of sight behind a parked car.

After a moment, Thomas crossed the street and went in through the open gate of a car wrecking yard. He stopped briefly at a shed which stood beside the gate, then went on. Through the fence that enclosed the yard, Pete saw him threading his way past heaps of rusting car bodies and rows of mechanical parts.

Pete frowned, wondering if he should attempt to follow Thomas. Then he decided that if Jupiter had been in his place, he would keep tailing the prim accountant. If there was someone in the shed at the entrance to the yard, Pete would make up a story in grand style—just as Jupiter would. He would say that he was looking for the transmission from a 1947 Studebaker Champion.

But the shed at the gate was empty. Pete went on into the yard, moving carefully and quietly around the stripped-down car bodies and the piles of rusting used parts.

Suddenly Pete stopped still where he was. He had heard a car door open.

The tall boy listened intently. There was a tinny clanking—the sound of pieces of metal hitting together. It came from off to his left. It seemed to be just on the other side of a pile of bumpers.

Pete crept forward and peered around the bumpers. He held his breath. Harold Thomas was not five feet away. He stood next to a grey van that was parked in a clear area in the very centre of the yard. The rear doors of the van were open, and inside the vehicle were piles and piles of film cans. Pete had seen cans of motion picture film many times when he visited his father at the studio where Mr Crenshaw worked. Now Pete stared at the cans, trying to read the labels on their rims. He made out "Cleopatra—Reel I" on one label. Another was marked "Salem Story—III." The wrecking yard seemed suddenly still. There was only the roar of blood in Pete's own ears and the beating of Pete's own heart.

Then Harold Thomas slammed the doors of the van. He walked to the front of the vehicle, climbed behind the wheel, and started the engine. A moment later the van was rolling up the rutted dirt drive that led to the gate.

Pete stayed where he was for a second, stunned by what he had seen. The film cans! It seemed impossible—unbelievable—but it had to be true. Those had to be the films that had been stolen from the laboratory next to Amigos Press. And Harold Thomas had them!

Pete forced himself to move. He ran, not worrying now about caution. At the gate of the salvage yard he was in time to see the van heading north. He tried to read the licence plate, but he couldn't. Whether by accident or not, the plate was too dusty.

Pete ran to the door of the shack near the gate. He saw a desk and a couple of battered chairs—and a telephone. He took Beefy's telephone number out of his wallet with shaking fingers, and dialled.

The telephone at the other end rang once, twice.

Outside the shed, someone was walking on the hard earth that had been packed down by the passage of hundreds of cars and trucks. Pete did not look around. If the owners of the yard objected to his using the telephone, he would simply say that he had to call the police.

Beefy answered at the other end of the telephone.

"Beefy, listen," said Pete quickly. "This is Pete and I'm at a car salvage yard on Thornwall, two blocks south of Wilshire. Tell Jupe and Bob that I just saw . . ."

A shadow fell across the desk, and Pete started to turn towards the door of the shed. But something crashed into the back of his neck. Then the light was gone and the telephone clattered to the floor, and Pete was falling . . . falling . . . falling!

Pete didn't know how long he was unconscious, but when he came to his senses he was in a close, dusty place—a place that smelled of grease and old rubber. It was hot—terribly hot—and it was dark. Pete tried to move, to turn over or stretch out, but he couldn't. There was no room for him to straighten himself. His neck hurt, and there was something hard pressing down on his shoulder. His hands touched metal surfaces that were rough, as if they had been eaten away by rust and time. Pete realized that he was probably still in the wrecking yard. He was locked in the trunk of some old car, and the sun was beating down on it, turning it into an oven.

Pete tried to shout, but his throat had gone dry with heat and fear. He closed his mouth and tried to swallow. There was silence outside in the yard. No one was there. No one would come to help him. He felt a surge of panic. No one would ever come!

14

The Mysterious Second Man

BEEFY'S CAR ROARED DOWN the street, then screeched to a stop at the entrance of the wrecking yard. Bob and Jupe tumbled out and darted into the office.

Bob looked wildly around the empty shack. "Where is he?" he said. "This has got to be the place. It's the only wrecking yard near here."

Beefy stumbled through the doorway. "There's a man coming," he reported. "He looks as if he might work here."

The boys went to the door. A man with thick, curly black hair was striding up the drive, coming from some far corner of the yard. He wore overalls that were stained with grease. "Anything I can do for you folks?" he said cheerfully when he saw Beefy and the boys at the office.

"We're looking for a friend," Jupe told him. "He said he'd meet us here. Have you seen a boy about our age? A tall boy who's muscular and rugged-looking?"

"Sorry," said the man. "Haven't seen anyone like that today."

"But he must have been here!" said Jupiter. "Are you sure you didn't see him?" In spite of himself, Jupe's voice went up. It was rough now with fear and anxiety.

"I haven't seen anybody," insisted the man. "Now look, kid, I'm sorry if you missed your friend, but this is a wrecking yard, not a hangout for kids. And I can't be at this gate non-stop. Hey! Hey, where do you think you're going?"

"Pete's here!" declared Jupe. He had darted past the salvage man and stood in the drive staring at the yard—at mounds of heaped-up car parts, bumpers and doors and engine blocks and rims—and at mountains of balding tyres. "He saw something. It was something important, and he called. And somebody got to him before he could give us the message. He's here. I know it!"

Bob started suddenly and touched Jupe's shoulder. "The trunk of one of these wrecks," he said. "If I had to get rid of somebody quickly, that's where I'd put him!"

The man scowled at the two boys. "You kids are crazy!" he said, but there was an edge of doubt in his voice. "Nobody'd put your friend in one of those cars. Hey, you're kidding me, aren't you?"

"Pete!" Jupe shouted. "Pete! Where are you?"

There was no answer.

"You're not kidding, are you?" said the man, after a second. He stared about at the acres of rusting, ruined cars. "There must be about a hundred cars here that still have their trunk lids," he said. "It could take all day to find the right one."

"No," said Jupiter firmly. "If he's hidden in one of these old cars, we can get to him quickly."

Jupiter began to walk through the jumble of auto bodies. He stepped along purposefully, his eyes darting to one side and then the other. Beefy and Bob trotted after him, and the man in the overalls trailed behind, looking worried. "That kid—your pal—he could be having heat prostration if he's locked up in one of these things."

Jupe didn't answer. He had stopped beside the body of an old blue Buick. He pointed. There was a thick coat of dust over the remains of the car, but on the lid of the trunk there was a place where the dust had been disturbed and the paint showed through, clear and still fairly blue.

"Was that trunk lid open before now?" demanded Jupe.

"It . . . it could have been," said the man.

"Get a crowbar, will you?" said Jupe. "I think someone saw the open trunk lid, shoved Pete inside, then slammed the trunk shut, disturbing that dust!"

The salvage man didn't question Jupe now. He disappeared briefly, then returned with a crowbar. He jammed the tool in under the trunk lid. Then he and Beefy both leaned on the crowbar. Metal groaned as the trunk lid was forced open.

"Pete!" Bob darted forward.

Pete lay curled in the trunk. He didn't stir.

"Good grief!" The salvage man raced off towards the office. He returned in seconds with a towel which was soaked and dripping.

Pete was sitting up by this time, with Jupiter supporting him one one side and Bob on the other.

"Okay," he said. His voice was barely a whisper. "I'm okay. Just hot in there. Not enough air."

"Take it easy, kid," said the man. He dabbed at Pete's face with the towel. "I'm going to call the cops! I could have wound up with a corpse in one of my cars!"

"Pete, what happened?" said Jupiter.

Pete took the towel and held it to his face. "I saw Harold Thomas leave his apartment and come here," he reported. "I tailed him. There was a grey van parked here among the wrecks. He opened the back doors and looked in. It was full of film cans."

For an instant no one spoke. Then Bob said, "Great jumping catfish!"

"The Bainbridge films!" exclaimed Beefy. "Harold Thomas had them?"

"Sure looked like it," said Pete. "I saw a few of the labels. After he checked the films, Thomas got into the van and drove away. That's when I tried to call you and didn't quite make it."

"So Thomas stole the films," said Jupe. "He could have set the fire, too, to draw attention away from the robbery at the film laboratory."

"He must have noticed you as he drove away,"

107

said Bob. "He came back and bopped you while you were trying to make your telephone call."

"No." Pete frowned, remembering the incident. "It wasn't him. The guy who hit me didn't come from the street. He was walking towards the office from someplace inside the wrecking yard."

Bob's eyes went to the man in overalls.

"Oh, no!" cried the man. "It wasn't me! I don't know what all this is about, but it wasn't me. I wouldn't hit anybody. Listen, I've got kids of my own. I find kids poking around here, I just yell at them and chase them over the fence!"

"I believe you," said Jupiter. "But if Pete is sure it wasn't Harold Thomas, there had to be another man."

"Thomas's confederate," declared Bob. "Remember, there were two hold-up men who stole the films."

"Clever of them to hide the van with the films here, where there are hundreds of other vehicles," said Jupe. "But they took a terrible chance." Jupe looked at the owner of the yard. "You could have started stripping it, or . . ."

"The grey van?" said the man. "No. I wouldn't touch that grey van. A guy was paying me to let him park it here."

"Oh?" said Jupiter.

The man looked terrified. "Something stolen in it?" he said. "I didn't know there was any stolen property involved. I run a clean operation. There aren't any hot cars on my lot. Listen, are you guys going to call the police?"

"Do you want us to?" said Jupe.

"They'll never believe me," said the salvage man. "I don't know anything about stolen property, but they'll never believe me. This guy came driving in in that grey van see. He's about so tall, with dark hair slicked back."

"Thomas," said Beefy.

"That wasn't his name," declared the salvage man. "He had a funny name. Puck. Mr Puck, that's what it was. He said he didn't have any place to park his van at home. He said he couldn't park it on the street in front of his house because he's in a two-hour parking zone, and he'd get a ticket. So he wanted to know if he could leave the van here in the yard. I know that sounds kind of screwy now that I hear myself saying it, but it sounded okay then. So I figure, what the heck? It's ten extra bucks a week. Why not?"

"Because he's a crook, that's why not!" said Bob.

"Okay, okay. How was I supposed to know that?"

"Never mind," said Jupiter. "It doesn't matter now. And let's not notify the police. They wouldn't believe any of us. What we have to do now is get evidence."

"The stolen films are evidence," declared Pete. "Good solid evidence!"

"True. But Thomas has had time to hide them someplace by now. Maybe . . . maybe if we can get into his apartment, we can find something else that would be incriminating."

Pete stood up and took a step or two, as if testing his legs.

"You okay?" said Bob anxiously. "Are you going to be well enough to go with us?"

"Yes. I'm okay now."

"Then let's go," said Jupe. "Only let's be careful. Thomas could have been warned by now. He could be waiting for us."

"And there's that second man," said Bob. "We know he exists. We'd better watch out for him."

15

The Vanishing Suspects

"I'M GOING IN WITH YOU," said Beefy Tremayne after he pulled to the kerb in front of Harold Thomas's apartment building.

"Fine," said Jupiter, looking appreciatively at Beefy's broad shoulders. "We may need all the muscle we can get. Anyone who would put Pete into the trunk of that car and leave him there is bound to be dangerous."

The Three Investigators and Beefy went up the path and into the vestibule of the little apartment house. There were only four doors. One of them had a nameplate beside the doorbell that said "Harold Thomas."

Beefy rang the bell firmly. "Thomas?" he called. "Are you there?"

No one answered.

Jupiter put his hand on the doorknob and turned it. "Careful," said Bob in a low voice. "These guys are dangerous. You said it yourself."

Jupe pushed the door wide, and the boys and Beefy looked into a living-room that was quiet and orderly to the point of being bare.

"Mr Thomas?" called Jupe. He walked through the living-room and peered into an immaculate kitchen. The others followed him, and they explored the little square hall between the living-room and the bedroom, then went into the bedroom.

A closet door stood open. Except for a number of empty hangers, the closet was empty.

"Too late!" said Jupe. He went to the dresser and pulled open one drawer after another. They were all empty.

"He's gone!" said Bob.

Jupe looked at his wristwatch. "It's almost two hours since Pete saw him drive away. The second man had plenty of time to warn Thomas. Thomas and his confederate hid the films somewhere. Then Thomas came back here, packed up, and left."

Beefy stood awkwardly and watched while the boys searched the apartment. They found nothing —nothing but immaculate emptiness.

"We knew Harold Thomas was a tidy man," said Jupe at last. "He's also extremely well organized. With almost no warning, he's been able to clear out of here and not leave a trace. Well, that only makes sense. The theft of the Bainbridge films was well organized. It took place on the very day the films were delivered, and at a time when there was no one in the laboratory except one technician. Just by sitting in his office and looking across to the building next door, Thomas could have learned the routine there. But how did he know that the films were going to be sold to Video Enterprises, or that they'd be delivered to that laboratory?"

Jupiter turned to Beefy. "Did Thomas have much contact with Marvin Gray when Gray came into your office?"

"No. None that I know of."

"Hm!" Jupe's eyes were fixed on the floor next to the sofa. He bent and picked up something. "Just about the only thing in this apartment to show that Thomas was ever here," he said, and he held up a matchbook for the others to see. "The table next to the sofa is wobbly. Thomas must have jammed this matchbook under the leg to steady it."

"Just what you need!" said Bob in a mocking tone. "In the Sherlock Holmes stories, the great detective finds a collar button and immediately he can tell all about the suspect, including the fact that he was born in Ireland and that he likes kippers with his tea. You have a matchbook which is doubtless a priceless clue. Tell us about Harold Thomas!"

Jupe turned the matchbook over in his hands, and there was a strange smile on his face. "It's from the Java Isles Restaurant," he said. "From the address, I'd say that's quite near Amigos Press. In fact, Thomas could have been having dinner there the night of the fire. Except that of course he stopped first to rob the film vault."

"So?" said Pete.

"The Java Isles is an Indonesian restaurant," said Jupiter. "And suddenly it all fits together! When Harold Thomas persuaded that man at the car wrecking yard to let him park the van there, he said his name was Mr Puck. There's a character in Shakespeare called Puck. He's a sprite who goes around making trouble, and he has a second name. It's Robin Goodfellow!"

"Goodfellow?" cried Bob. "Charles Good- fellow was one of Madeline Bainbridge's magic circle!"

"Right!" said Jupiter. "The missing member of our coven. We know that Charles Goodfellow was raised in Holland, and many Dutch people are fond of Indonesian food because Indonesia was once a Dutch colony. Harold Thomas was also fond of Indonesian food, since he patronized the Java Isles Restaurant."

"Wow!" said Pete. "Harold Thomas is the same person as Charles Goodfellow! He was a member of the coven and he knew everybody."

"And how did he learn about the sale of the films? Which member of the coven told him? Or did he just happen to know someone at Video Enterprises? Jefferson Long, or someone else entirely? We can speculate on that all day without getting an answer. But we do know he stole the films."

"Maybe he swiped the manuscript, too," said Bob. "He knew where it was and he could have had a set of keys. He could have duplicated a set from the ones Beefy kept in his desk at the office."

"He could have set the fire too," said Pete.

"But why would he take the manuscript?" wondered Beefy. "How could that manuscript hurt him?"

Jupiter shrugged. "Who knows? Madeline Bainbridge may have written something that would expose him, even after all these years."

"I think we'd better call the police," said Beefy. He stood up. "It will be awkward explaining to them how we know all the things we know, but we have to call them. The Bainbridge films are involved, and they're of inestimable value. I think we'd better call them from my apartment. We don't really have any right in here, you know."

During the short drive to his home, Beefy grew more and more excited. "This will be a load off Uncle Will's mind!" said Beefy as he let himself and the three boys into the apartment. "We can definitely tie Thomas in with the theft of the films, and if the police can turn up some solid evidence to tie him in with the fire, Uncle Will is off the hook!"

Beefy went through the apartment, calling to his uncle. There was no answer.

"That's funny," said Beefy. "He left here right after you left this morning. He said he was going to play golf. He ought to be back by now."

Suddenly uneasy, Beefy went into his uncle's bedroom. The boys in the living-room heard a closet door open, and then heard a thumping and a clattering as Beefy knocked several things over.

After several minutes, Beefy appeared again in the living-room. "He's gone," he said. "He must have come back here while we were out and packed a small suitcase. There's one missing. He's . . . he's panicked and he's running. Now we can't call the police. They'll think he *did* set that fire."

"They often do think that, when suspects vanish," said Jupiter, "and are we sure—are we really sure—that he didn't?"

The Sleeping Beauty

"JUST BEFORE WE LEFT here this morning, I asked you to call the people who played bridge with your uncle the night the manuscript was taken," said Jupiter to Beefy.

"I did," Beefy replied. The young publisher looked haggard. "Uncle Will didn't arrive for the bridge game until almost ten-thirty. He said there'd been a minor accident on Beverly Drive and he'd been held up in traffic."

"So he could have set the fire at Amigos Press, and he also could have taken the manuscript from this apartment," said Jupe.

Beefy nodded. "I can't imagine Uncle Will as an arsonist, and yet he did have a motive. He was short of money. But why on earth would he steal the Bainbridge manuscript?"

Jupiter scowled and pulled at his lower lip—a sign that he was thinking furiously. "Could there be something damaging about *him* in that manuscript? Did he know Madeline Bainbridge when he was younger? Maybe that's why he always speaks of her so scornfully!"

Jupiter thought some more, then sighed. "No matter which way we turn, we keep coming back to the mysterious Madeline Bainbridge. Only she knows what's in her manuscript, and only she could tell us who might want it suppressed. We've just *got* to talk to her—and we have to talk to her when Marvin Gray isn't around. For whatever reason, he's too obstructive."

"But how do we reach her?" asked Beefy. "She doesn't answer the telephone. She doesn't go out. Perhaps she doesn't even open her own mail."

"You can call Gray and set up a lunch date," Jupe suggested. "Tell Gray you have something important to discuss with him and it has to be over lunch. Then pick a good restaurant and make sure the lunch lasts a couple of hours. That will give us time to get to Madeline Bainbridge."

"But . . . but what'll I discuss with Gray?" said Beefy.

"Someday you're going to have to tell him about the missing manuscript," said Bob.

"But . . . but you were going to get it back!"

Jupiter shook his head. "It's been gone for three days, and few things are easier to destroy than a manuscript. We are probably not going to get it back, and sooner or later Marvin Gray will have to be told. You can call him now and ask him to meet with you to discuss something very important."

Beefy groaned. "Okay. I'll do the best I can."

Beefy went into the den to make the telephone

call. When he came back into the living-room a few minutes later, he said, "Okay. I'm meeting Gray tomorrow at twelve-thirty at the Coral Cove in Santa Monica."

"Good," said Jupiter.

Peter was scowling. "You're so sure we're going to get in to see Madeline Bainbridge," he said. "Maybe she doesn't answer the door when Gray's not around. Or maybe that Clara Adams will block you. And don't forget there's a dog there— a big Doberman!"

"I haven't forgotten anything," said Jupiter. "I think we can see Madeline Bainbridge—if we're determined enough."

But at noon the next day, even Jupiter had some qualms. He and Pete and Bob had ridden their bicycles up the Coast Highway, and then had taken the paved mountain road to the turn-off a quarter of a mile from Madeline Bainbridge's front gate. There they took shelter with their bikes amid the oleanders that grew raggedly on the edges of Bainbridge's fields.

"We'll see Marvin Gray when he drives down to the highway," said Jupe to his friends. "Let's hope that he doesn't let the dog out on to the grounds before he goes. If he does and we meet the dog, we'll just stand still and call for Madeline Bainbridge to come and rescue us."

He looked out from behind the oleanders. A car was turning on to the road from the Bainbridge ranch.

"Here comes Gray," said Bob.

A dark grey Mercedes swept past the boys, throwing up a cloud of dust. When it had disappeared down the road towards the highway, Jupiter, Pete, and Bob pushed their bikes out on to the gravel road. They pedalled through the gate and up through the lemon grove. The dog did not appear, but when the boys reached the house and got off their bicycles a frantic barking began inside the house.

"Oh, great!' moaned Pete.

They went up the steps to the porch and Jupiter rang the bell. They heard it buzz angrily somewhere in the back of the house. They waited.

When no one came, Jupiter rang the bell again. "Miss Bainbridge!" he shouted. "Miss Adams! Please open the door!"

The dog began to leap at the door. The boys could hear him clawing at the wooden panels.

"Let's go, huh!" said Pete.

"Miss Bainbridge!" called Jupiter.

"Who is it?" cried a voice on the other side of the door. "Quiet, Bruno! Good boy!"

"Miss Adams?" said Jupiter. "Miss Adams, please open the door. My name is Jupiter Jones and I have something important to say to you."

There was a fumbling with the locks. The door opened a few inches, and a pair of faded blue eyes looked out in sleepy wonder. "Go away," said Clara Adams. "Don't you know you're not supposed to ring this doorbell? No one rings this doorbell."

"I have to see Miss Bainbridge," said Jupiter. "I'm from her publisher."

"Publisher?" echoed Clara Adams. "I didn't know that Madeline had a publisher."

Clara Adams stepped back, letting the door open wide. Her hair straggled around her face and her eyes, which looked full at Jupe, did not really seem to see him.

"Miss Adams?" said Jupe. "Are you all right?"

She blinked sleepily, and the dog growled.

"Could I ask you to shut the dog up some-place?" said Jupe. "He's . . . he's making us all nervous."

Clara Adams took the dog's collar and, walking unsteadily, led him back to the kitchen, where she shut him in. Then she came back into the hall. "Madeline?" she called. "Where are you, Madeline? Come here, please. There are some boys here to see you."

Jupe looked around. He saw the living-room, with its austere wooden chairs. He saw the dining-room, and its backless benches. He listened, but he heard no sound except the slow ticking of the clock in the living-room. "This place is like an enchanted castle," he said. "Nothing moves here, does it? No one comes or goes."

"Comes or goes?" said Clara Adams in her drowsy, rusty voice. "Who should come? We don't see anyone any more. Once we were very lively here, but no more. And when Marvin isn't here..." She stopped and seemed to be puzzling something out. "What happens when Marvin isn't here?" she said. "Hard to remember. He's always here. Only where is he now?"

"She acts as if she's been drugged," Pete whispered to Jupiter.

"She certainly does," agreed Jupe. He turned to Clara Adams. "Where is Madeline Bainbridge?" he demanded.

Clara Adams waved vaguely, then sat down on a chair and began to doze off.

"Something's fishy here!" exclaimed Bob.

The three boys searched then, peering into all the rooms on the ground floor. It was Pete who was the first to run up the stairs to the first storey. In a big corner bedroom with windows that looked out towards the sea, he found Madeline Bainbridge. She was lying on a homespun coverlet on a big wooden bed. She wore a long brown gown, and her hands were folded on her bosom. Her face was very quiet. It seemed for an instant that she wasn't even breathing.

Pete touched her on the shoulder. "Miss Bainbridge?" he said softly.

She didn't stir. Pete shook her, and called her name again—and again. Jupe's words went through his mind. An enchanted castle where nothing moved. And here was the sleeping beauty in the castle.

122

But why didn't she wake? Why didn't she answer him?

"Jupe!" shouted Pete. "Bob! Come quick! I found Madeline Bainbridge, but I'm . . . I'm not sure I found her in time!"

17

Conspiracy!

"MAYBE WE'D BETTER phone for an ambulance," said Bob.

"Hold it," said Pete. "She's coming round."

Madeline Bainbridge made a small, protesting sound. Then she opened her eyes, which were glazed and blurry with sleep.

"Miss Bainbridge, I made some coffee," said Bob. "Try to sit up and drink some."

"Madeline, dear!" Clara Adams sat down on the bed, holding her own cup of coffee. "Do wake up. These young men seem so concerned. I don't understand it, but they say Marvin gave us something to make us sleep."

The actress pulled herself up so that she was sitting on the bed. In a dazed fashion she took the cup of coffee that Bob held out to her. She sipped a little, making a wry face as she did so. "Who are you?" she said groggily to the boys. "What are you doing here?"

"Drink your coffee and we'll tell you," said Jupiter. "You need to be awake to hear our story."

When Madeline Bainbridge looked more alert,

Jupiter started explaining. "We work for Beefy Tremayne," he said. "We're trying to help him find your manuscript."

"My manuscript?" said Madeline Bainbridge. "What manuscript? I don't understand."

"Your memoirs, Miss Bainbridge," said Jupe.

"My memoirs? But I haven't finished my memoirs. Why, I know you boys! You're the ones who came down the hill the other night when we were having our . . . our . . ."

"You were celebrating the Sabbat," said Jupiter. "We know all about it, Miss Bainbridge."

Jupe then held out a pill bottle to the actress. "We found this in the bathroom off the back bedroom. It's sleeping medicine of some sort. We think Marvin Gray put it in something you ate or drank to make sure you wouldn't answer the door or the telephone while he was away."

The actress looked at the little vial. "Drank?" she said. "We drank some tea that Marvin made for us."

"Has it happened before, do you think?" asked Bob.

"Several days ago I fell sound asleep in the middle of the afternoon. It was very odd. Clara slept all afternoon, too."

"Probably the afternoon Gray brought the manuscript in to Beefy Tremayne," said Jupe.

"You keep prattling on about a manuscript, and about a person named Beefy Tremayne," said Madeline Bainbridge. Her voice was strong and assured now. "What exactly are you talking about?"

Jupiter told her then, with Bob and Pete chiming in from time to time to add details. The boys told of Gray's delivery of the memoirs to Amigos Press. They told about the fire at the publishing house, and about the theft of the manuscript from the Tremayne apartment.

"Your signature is on the contract for the publication of your memoirs," said Jupiter. "A forgery, I presume."

"Certainly," said Madeline Bainbridge. "I never signed a contract. And my memoirs are still here in this house. I worked on them only last night. Look in that big chest at the foot of the bed."

Pete opened the chest and the boys looked. There was a thick heap of papers, all handwritten.

"Marvin Gray must have copied them by hand," said Bob. "Then he delivered the copy to Beefy Tremayne. And then what? Did he arrange to have it stolen, perhaps by Charles Goodfellow?"

"Goodfellow?" said Madeline Bainbridge. "Don't tell me that little thief is still in town!"

"So you know Goodfellow is a thief," said Jupe.

"I know he was one. I caught him trying to take a diamond necklace out of my dressing-room on the set of *Catherine the Great*. I was going to call the police, but he persuaded me he'd never do anything like that again. Then later I found out he'd been going through the women's purses while we were filming *The Salem Story*."

"A real sneak thief," said Bob. "Did you put anything about that in your memoirs?"

"I may have. I think I did mention it."

"That would have given him a motive. Even though he wasn't using the same name, he might be afraid he'd be found out. And with the theft of the films from the laboratory—"

"What films?" said Madeline Bainbridge.

"Your pictures that were sold to Video Enterprises," said Jupe. "Did you know that the negatives of all your films had been sold to television, or is that something that Marvin Gray engineered while you were asleep, too?"

"Oh, no! I knew all about the sale of the films. Marvin handled the negotiations, and I signed a contract. But you say the films were stolen?"

"They were, from a laboratory next door to Amigos Press, just before the fire started. They're being held for ransom. No doubt they're safe enough, and no doubt the ransom will be paid. Did you know that Jefferson Long came out here the night of the theft to interview you? He does a TV series on law and order."

"No!" exclaimed Madeline Bainbridge. "Is that who was here? Marvin just told me that he had some business clients coming by. I stayed out of the way, as usual. I pay Marvin to deal with the outside world."

"You were keeping out of sight the next afternoon, too, when Beefy and I came here," said Jupe. He shook his head. "Miss Bainbridge, you've put yourself into a dangerous position, having no contact at all with anyone outside this house."

The actress sighed. "I let Marvin handle everything for me. It begins to look as if he handled it too well, doesn't it?"

"He must intend to swindle you out of the advance from Amigos Press for your manuscript," said Jupiter.

"That scoundrel?" said the actress. "I can't believe it!" Then she stopped and thought for a moment. "Yes," she said, "I can believe it. He was always greedy. But to think he's been deliberately withholding information and using drugs on me! Ugh! It's horrible!"

"Wouldn't it be interesting to see how much he's swindled you, and what he plans for the future?" asked Jupe. "Why not play along with him? Pretend to be asleep when he comes home today, then watch him. I'll give you a telephone number where we can be reached—a couple of numbers, in fact."

"Oh, Madeline, let's do it!" said Clara Adams. "I've always wanted to play a joke on Marvin. He's so grumpy and serious all the time."

"It will be a marvellous joke," said Madeline Bainbridge. "I can't think of a single reason why I should trust you boys, and yet I do. I have to see exactly what Marvin is up to."

"It could be almost anything," said Bob. He held up a bright orange matchbook. "I found this in a jar with a lot of other matches when I lit the stove to make coffee. It's from the Java Isles, that restaurant where Harold Thomas ate."

"So Gray and Thomas probably were in touch," said Jupe. "Gray could have been involved in some way with the theft of the films, with the theft of the manuscript, and even with the fire at Amigos Press."

"Isn't this fun?" said Clara Adams. "Like those nice old-fashioned movies where the heroine helps the detectives. We're going to nail him!"

18

The Search

It was almost four when The Three Investigators rode up in the elevator to Beefy's apartment. They found the young publisher pacing and brooding.

"How was your lunch?" Bob inquired brightly.

"As lunches go, it wasn't bad," said Beefy. "But it was a lousy business conference. I bought Marvin Gray the most expensive lunch on the menu, and I also ordered a couple of martinis for him. He ate and drank everything, and when he began to glow like a neon sign I decided he was ready. I told him the bad news about the Bainbridge manuscript.

"Well, it didn't get to him right away. He'd been talking about Jefferson Long, and how tickled he was that Long was the one assigned by the television station to interview Madeline Bainbridge after her films were stolen. Then Bainbridge couldn't see him. Gray really enjoyed that. Gray doesn't like Long a bit. I guess Long was uppity to him in the old days, when Gray was just a chauffeur.

"How interesting," said Jupiter.

"It gets more interesting," said Beefy. "When Gray finally got the message that the Bainbridge memoirs were missing, he sat and blinked like a stuffed owl for a couple of seconds. Then he decided that it was all a terrible shame, but maybe not quite as terrible as I might think. He decided that maybe Madeline Bainbridge wouldn't mind writing her memoirs all over again—provided I paid her double the amount of the advance we'd agreed on when she signed the contract."

Beefy put his head in his hands and shuddered. "What a mess!" he said. "I've got to get going again on Amigos Press. I've got to rent an office and get the staff together and go to work. But it's all going to take money, and I don't have any money without Uncle Will. Maybe I don't have any money even *with* Uncle Will, because if he shows up here he may be charged with arson. And the insurance company sure isn't going to pay him for burning down his own property. And then Gray tells me I should double the advance I pay Madeline Bainbridge!"

Beefy look up at the boys. "I hope that very expensive lunch wasn't a total waste of time," he said. "Did you manage to talk with Madeline Bainbridge?"

"We sure did. Bob wrote up a report while we were coming here on the bus."

Bob grinned and took his notebook out of his pocket. He then summarized briefly the events of the day. As Beefy listened, his woebegone expression gradually disappeared. By the time Bob finished, Beefy was grinning broadly.

"I'm off the hook!" he cried. "I don't owe any advance!"

"You do not," said Jupiter. "Also, we found evidence that Gray—as well as Thomas—dined at the Java Isles restaurant. Gray could have tipped Thomas off about the films. He could have been involved in that crime."

"He could have planted the incendiary device at Amigos Press, too," said Beefy. "He had the opportunity, as did Thomas. What a relief! Of course, we'll have to prove it. Nobody will take our word for it. Is there some way we can tie the fire to Gray, so we can clear Uncle Will? Wouldn't the arsonist have to buy magnesium for his incendiary device, for example?"

"He would certainly have to get it somewhere," said Jupe cheerfully. "Suddenly a number of things have become clear to me. Beefy, may we search your apartment?"

"Search?" Beefy sat up straight. "What for?"

"For the magnesium," said Jupiter.

"Jupe, you've got to be kidding! You can't really believe that Uncle Will set that fire. Look, I know he's not the most lovable guy in the world, but he isn't a criminal. Can you picture him hiding in a corner someplace, putting together a gadget that will go off at six o'clock and destroy my office? It isn't in character."

"I know it isn't," said Jupiter. He stood still, his

head to one side as if he were listening to voices that the others couldn't hear. "There's been something that's been bothering me about this case all along—something I've been missing. I know what it is now. It's something I saw, but I didn't see. Not at the time. As a matter of fact, there were a couple of things that I missed. We can verify them when we need to. The evidence will be there. I know it will."

"Jupe's having one of his brainstorms," said Pete, who was amused by the look on Beefy's face.

"It'll be okay," Bob assured the young publisher. "Jupe has a photographic memory, and if he's just recalling something he heard or saw, you can bet he's recalling it *exactly*!"

"Now I'd like to search the apartment," said Jupe. "I'd like to start with your uncle's room."

"Well . . . well, I guess it's all right," said Beefy. "If it will help."

Beefy led the way to the big bedroom that had windows facing to the south. The boys followed him.

Jupe went directly to the closet, which had sliding doors that took up almost an entire wall of the room. He pulled back the doors. The boys saw dozens of neatly tailored jackets and racks of gleaming shoes.

Jupiter started to go through the pockets of the jackets. He worked quickly. After only a few minutes he said, "Aha!" and pulled a strip of metal from the pocket of a tan flannel jacket.

"Don't tell me that's magnesium!" said Beefy.

"I'm sure that any laboratory test would confirm it," said Jupe. "And now I am quite positive that your uncle didn't set the fire. He just panicked and ran. If he were guilty, he'd have taken the magnesium with him."

The telephone on the table beside the bed began to ring.

"Want to answer that?" said Jupiter to Beefy. Jupe looked almost joyful. "I gave this number to Madeline Bainbridge and asked her to call here or at Headquarters in Rocky Beach if Gray did anything unusual. Perhaps that's her now."

Beefy picked up the telephone and said, "Hello." He listened for a moment, then handed the telephone to Jupe. "It *is* Madeline Bainbridge," he said, "and she wants to talk with you."

19

Setting the Trap

JUPITER STOOD with the telephone to his ear, and as he listened to Madeline Bainbridge, he grinned.

"That's fine, Miss Bainbridge," he said at last. "I was hoping for something like this. Now if Gray offers you something to eat or drink tonight, just pretend to take it. And warn Miss Adams. Both of you want to be alert when Gray has his visitor. Of course, you'll pretend to be asleep.

"I think we'll be able to solve the entire series of crimes, and get proof that will satisfy the police. But there is one other person who should be there —Jefferson Long."

The telephone made muted noises which the others in the room with Jupe couldn't understand. Jupe nodded. "It won't be difficult at all," he said. "You can reach Long through Video Enterprises. He does his television series for them. Tell him that there are some things about him in your memoirs, and that you're having doubts about some of them. Say you want to go over the incidents with him because you'd hate to embarrass him in public. That will surely bring him running.

Tell him to be at the house about nine."

Jupe waited, then nodded and smiled. "Fine.
We'll be there, so see that the dog isn't loose."

He hung up. "Madeline Bainbridge overheard
Gray making a telephone call to someone named
Charlie. He told Charlie to come tonight, and he'd
have the money ready for him."

"Charles Goodfellow!" exclaimed Pete.

"It seems likely," said Jupiter. "And if Madeline
Bainbridge is able to get Jefferson Long to the
house, we should be able to settle everything at
once. I think it will be very interesting to see Long
and Gray and Goodfellow all together. Who wants
to come along?"

"Are you kidding?" cried Pete. "I wouldn't miss
it!"

"I hope I'm invited," said Beefy.

"Certainly," said Jupiter. "I think we should
bring your uncle, too. He's had a bad time, and he
might appreciate seeing the situation straightened
out."

"Great," said Beefy. "How do we find Uncle
Will?"

"Where does he buy his cigars?" said Jupiter.

"Huh?" said Beefy.

"Yesterday morning, just before he left here, he
was out of cigars," Jupe pointed out. "From what
I've seen of Mr William Tremayne, I'd guess that
he smokes something expensive and unusual. Am
I right?"

Beefy nodded. "He smokes special Dutch cigars.

You can't get them everywhere."

"He took his car when he left here, didn't he?"

Again Beefy nodded.

"Well, if he's driving, the cigars may not help us. But I have a feeling he isn't driving anymore than he has to. He was very frightened, and he may think the police are looking for him already. But wherever he is, he's smoking. Smokers always smoke more when they're nervous. Where does your uncle buy his cigars?"

"In a little shop on Burton Way," said Beefy. "They order the brand especially for Uncle Will."

"I'm betting they've seen him in the last twenty-four hours," declared Jupiter.

In a very few minutes, Beefy and The Three Investigators were in Beefy's car, headed towards Burton Way.

"You'd better talk to the shopkeeper," advised Jupe. "He'll think it's odd if any of us start asking questions. Tell him you and your uncle had a quarrel and your uncle walked out. Ask him if he's seen your uncle."

"That sounds like some dumb soap opera," said Beefy.

"Don't worry. The man will believe you," Jupe predicted. "It sounds more likely than the truth, which is that your uncle is hiding from the police."

Beefy laughed, and he pulled in to the kerb in front of a small shop called The Humidor. "You coming in with me?" he asked the boys.

"You go, Jupe," said Bob. "It would look weird

if all three of us went in."

Jupe and Beefy got out of the car and went into the shop, where a white-haired man in a chamois waistcoat was dusting a counter.

"Mr Tremayne, good afternoon," said the man. "Don't tell me your uncle is out of cigars already."

"No. Uh . . . not exactly." Beefy's face was redder than usual. "He bought some cigars yesterday, did he?"

"Why, yes," said the man at the counter.

"Good," said Beefy. "We . . . uh . . . we had a quarrel yesterday, you see, and he walked out and hasn't come back. I'd like to find him and . . . uh . . . apologize. Did he . . . er . . . mention where he might be going when he was here?"

"No, he didn't."

Jupiter murmured something in Beefy's ear.

"Did he have his car with him?" asked Beefy.

"Why, I don't believe he did," said the man. "He seemed to be walking. He turned towards the right when he went out, if that's any help to you."

"That's fine," said Beefy. "Thanks very much."

He fled from the shop, tripping over the doorstep as he went.

"How you guys manage to do this sort of thing all the time, I can't imagine," he declared when they were back in the car. "My mind went blank about four times."

Jupiter was grinning. "The shopkeeper said your uncle was on foot, so there's a chance he's staying somewhere in the neighbourhood. Drive down that way, slowly."

Beefy started the car. They rolled along for a short distance, with Jupe scanning the fronts of the various buildings along the way. Suddenly Bob leaned forward and pointed towards a small motel on the left side of the street.

"Aha!" said Jupiter. "Exactly the sort of place Mr Tremayne would want—ultra-respectable, and the sign in front advertises locked garages. He could get his car out of sight."

"The only garage that's closed right now is the one next to room twenty-three," said Pete.

Beefy pulled into the parking place next to the room, and an instant later he and The Three Investigators were knocking on the door of number 23.

"Uncle Will!" called Beefy. "Open the door."

There was no answer.

"Mr Tremayne, we know you didn't set the fire at Amigos Press," said Jupe. "We're going to trap the real criminals and prove that they did it. If you want to come along and help us set our trap, you'll be welcome."

There was silence for a minute more. Then the door to room 23 swung open. "Very well," said William Tremayne. "You can come in if you want to, and we'll talk about it."

20

The Surprise Party

AT DUSK THAT evening, Beefy drove up from the
Coast Highway to the Bainbridge ranch. The
Three Investigators were with him, and so was his
uncle. For once, William Tremayne did not seem
bored. His eyes were eager, and from time to time
he touched his pocket, where he carried a revolver.

There was a Mercedes parked near the porch of
the Bainbridge house. Behind it was a light-
coloured Ford. "The Ford must belong to Harold
Thomas," said Jupe. "The Mercedes is Gray's.
Let's make sure that neither of them leave here
before we're ready for them to leave."

Pete smiled and tried the doors of the two cars.
Neither vehicle was locked. "Very good," said
Pete. He took a pair of pliers out of his pocket and
went to work. In seconds he had disconnected the
ignition wires, disabling both cars.

"I'll stay here and keep out of sight until Long
arrives," he told the others. "Good luck."

Jupiter, Bob, and the Tremaynes started up the
front steps. There was an outburst of barking. It
sounded muffled and far away.

"Sounds like somebody locked Bruno in the cellar," said Bob.

"Thank goodness," exclaimed Jupe. "I don't want to meet him face to face. Not when he takes his orders from Marvin Gray."

Jupe then strode boldly across the porch and rang the doorbell.

After a moment, there were footsteps in the hall. "Who's there?" called Marvin Gray.

"I have something for Mr Gray," said Jupe loudly.

The front door opened and Marvin Gray looked out.

"Mr Horace Tremayne would like to talk to you," said Jupiter. "So would Mr William Tremayne."

Jupiter stood aside, and Beefy stepped forward and planted his foot squarely on the doorsill. "Sorry to be dropping in so late," he said, "but somehow this seemed like the right moment."

Gray drew back. "Mr Tremayne! What is it? I'd invite you in but . . . but the ladies have retired and I don't want to disturb them."

Beefy shoved the door wide and stepped across the threshold. His uncle and the boys were close behind him.

"You've met Jupiter Jones before," said Beefy. "Jupiter is a very curious young man. Some people might even say he's nosey. We're here tonight to help him satisfy his curiosity—and mine!"

Gray retreated as Beefy and Jupiter advanced.

141

He backed into the living-room, where Harold Thomas was looking around wildly, as if trying to find a place to hide the package he held.

"That's the manuscript, isn't it?" said Jupiter. "You stole it from Beefy Tremayne's apartment the same night you burned down the Amigos Adobe."

Thomas dropped the package, which broke open and spilled loose pages across the floor. He spun around and started towards the windows.

"Stay right where you are, Thomas!" shouted Uncle Will.

Thomas looked over his shoulder and saw that William Tremayne had a gun. He stopped where he was.

Beefy picked up the manuscript from the floor. He flipped through it, stopping a few times to read a paragraph or two. Then he grinned. "This is it," he said.

Jupe went back out into the hall. "Miss Bainbridge?" he called.

"She's asleep," said Marvin Gray. "She's asleep and you'd better not wake her up. I don't know anything about that bunch of papers, or the guy who brought them here, and—"

Gray stopped talking, for Madeline Bainbridge was coming down the stairs. Her white-gold hair was done up in a knot at the nape of her neck, and on her handsome face there was a smile that was both sad and triumphant.

"Marvin," she said, with a scolding note in her

voice. "You hadn't planned to see me awake, but here I am."

Her eyes went to Harold Thomas, who stood gaping. "So, Charles. It *is* you. I wish I could say that it's pleasant to see you again, but it is not."

She seated herself in the living-room. Clara Adams scampered down the stairs, her faded eyes twinkling with enjoyment. She perched on a window-sill behind Madeline Bainbridge.

"What is that?" asked the actress, pointing to the sheaf of papers which Beefy held.

Beefy smiled and handed the manuscript to the woman. "I'm Horace Tremayne, Miss Bainbrdge," he said, "and this is the manuscript that Marvin Gray delivered to my office the day your films were stolen from the laboratory in Santa Monica."

Madeline Bainbridge looked quickly at the first page. "An exact copy of the manuscript that is upstairs in my room," she said. "How tiresome of you, Marvin, to copy my manuscript and sell it. Didn't you know you couldn't possibly get away with it? Sooner or later I'd have found out."

There was a step on the front porch, and the doorbell buzzed.

"That will be Jefferson Long," said Madeline Bainbridge. "Would you let him in, Clara?"

Clara Adams darted out of the living-room. She returned in a few moments with Jefferson Long walking behind her. Long's face was stoney as he looked at the group in the room. He bowed to Madeline Bainbridge.

"I didn't know you were having a party this evening," he said.

"The first one in years," said Madeline Bainbridge. "Do sit down while our young friend here—his name is Jupiter Jones, and I think you've met—tells us why Marvin Gray copied my manuscript and sold it to Mr Tremayne. He then arranged to have it stolen. At least, I imagine that's what happened."

"That's precisely what happened," said Jupiter. "Here's the story. A certain amount of it is speculation, but I think we'll be able to verify it.

"Some time ago, Marvin Gray happened to run into Charles Goodfellow, alias Harold Thomas, in an Indonesian restaurant called the Java Isles. At this meeting, Gray learned that Goodfellow was employed by a book publishing firm. Gray has a nimble brain, and it occurred to him that he could copy the memoirs which Miss Bainbridge was writing, sell the manuscript to Goodfellow's employers, then either bribe or blackmail Goodfellow into stealing the manuscript to prevent its publication. He wanted to prevent publication because Miss Bainbridge was almost ready to find a publisher herself, and it would never do to have two publishers preparing to bring out the memoirs of the same actress.

"Gray thought he could pocket the advance that is usually paid to an author upon delivery of a manuscript. Once the counterfeit manuscript was destroyed, he could stall Beefy Tremayne for a while, and then perhaps sell the true manuscript to Beefy all over again. He was counting on the fact that Beefy would feel terribly guilty about losing the first manuscript.

"Goodfellow agreed to go along with Gray. He didn't want Gray to expose him to his employers as a person who once tried to steal a necklace from Madeline Bainbridge. First Goodfellow set Amigos Press on fire, hoping to destroy the manuscript. When he learned that he had failed, he went to Beefy's apartment and stole the manuscript. I am sure he used keys which he had duplicated from the set in Beefy's desk. I think we'll find that duplicating keys is a habit with Goodfellow, and that he had keys to the pharmaceutical firm where he used to work. That's where he got the magnesium that he used to construct the incendiary device that started the fire. Magnesium is used in pharmaceuticals. It was foolish of him to plant magnesium in William Tremayne's jacket pocket when he took the manuscript. He went too far when he did that."

Madeline Bainbridge looked up. "What about the theft of my films?" she said to Jupiter. "The counterfeit manuscript was nothing compared to that theft. They'll get a quarter of a million dollars for that one!"

"The thieves collected the ransom for the films late this afternoon, Miss Bainbridge," said Jupiter. "It was on the news at six o'clock. Video Enterprises left a package containing two hundred and fifty thousand dollars in small bills in a parking lot near the Hollywood Bowl. They were advised by telephone a short time later to recover the films from a van parked in Bronson Canyon."

Madeline Bainbridge looked surprised. "That's wonderful, but . . . but Marvin was home this afternoon!

"Marvin Gray wasn't involved in the theft of the films," said Jupe. "Charles Goodfellow was— and Jefferson Long was the mastermind."

"What?" shouted Long. "You brat! How dare you?"

"We have a witness," said Jupe. "And we can tie both Goodfellow and Long in with the missing films."

"You're crazy!" cried Long.

Jupiter didn't answer. He went out into the hall and opened the front door." Come on in," he said.

A moment later he appeared in the living-room doorway. Pete was at his side.

"Surprised?" Jupe said to Jefferson Long. "You should be. Because the last time you saw Pete, he was unconscious, and you were locking him in the trunk of a wrecked car!"

21

Crash!

"YOU'RE MAD!" said Jefferson Long. "I don't have to stay here and be insulted!"

"We would all appreciate it if you'd stay," said William Tremayne, and he waved the gun in his hand.

Long sat back and folded his arms. "Very well," he said, "if you're going to use strong-arm tactics."

Beefy grinned. "Okay, Jupe. Go ahead."

"When I was in his office the other day," said Jupiter, "Jefferson Long said that he'd researched a television series on drug abuse, and that he'd found that some people employed in legitimate drug firms were involved in the illicit distribution of drugs. My guess is that in the course of his investigation, Long happened to meet Harold Thomas, who was an employee at one of these firms. Like Marvin Gray, Long recognized Thomas. He knew he had once attempted to steal a necklace from Miss Bainbridge, and that he was once known as Charles Goodfellow. Perhaps he checked up on Goodfellow. Perhaps Goodfellow had a record. He might even be a fugitive. In any case, Long could blackmail him—or at least put considerable pressure on him."

"Is that the way it was, Long?" asked Beefy.

"I have nothing to say," announced Jefferson Long.

"Thomas, was Long blackmailing you?" the young publisher asked his former accountant.

"I'll talk to my lawyer," said Thomas. "No one else."

"All right," said Jupe, undismayed. "Now at about this time, something happened which disturbed Long very much. Video Enterprises decided to purchase Madeline Bainbridge's films, and they told Long that the series on drug abuse would be cancelled because the money originally budgeted for this series would be used for the films.

"No doubt Long was very bitter, especially since he had never liked Madeline Bainbridge. And it must have occurred to him that he could get back at Madeline Bainbridge and could also make a great deal of money if he could steal the films.

"Jefferson Long knew he could find out what day the films would be transferred to the laboratory in Santa Monica. Anyone at Video Enterprises could learn this. It wouldn't be any secret. But before that day came, while the negotiations for the films were still going on, he had Harold Thomas apply for a job at the business firm closest to the laboratory. Doubtless Thomas would have accepted a much humbler position than accountant to get into Amigos Press.

"By the time the films arrived at the laboratory, Thomas knew the routine at the film lab perfectly. He saw most of the employees leave at five that day. Then he left Amigos Press, joined Long, and they forced their way into the lab. They knocked out the technician who was there, loaded the films into a van, and drove off.

"Thomas was, of course, busier than he had planned to be, since that afternoon Marvin Gray had delivered the counterfeit memoirs from Madeline Bainbridge. Thomas had to plant his incendiary device and later, after helping to steal the films, return to Amigos Press to check on the fire. Then he had to burgle Beefy's apartment."

"You haven't a shred of evidence to back up what you're saying," declared Jefferson Long.

"But we do have evidence," said Jupiter. "I overlooked it for a long time, but when I finally remembered, everything else fell into place.

"You interviewed Marvin Gray the night the films were stolen. You said that the hold-up was perpetrated by a couple of men. It was a statement that sounded perfectly correct. But there was no way you could have known that there were two men. There could have been three or four or ten—or perhaps only one. Even the police didn't know, because the technician you knocked out to get those films did not regain consciousness until the next day—hours after the interview with Marvin Gray was taped."

Jefferson Long shrugged. "I assumed that there would be at least two men."

"You might claim that," said Jupiter, "but what are you going to say about the fingerprints?"

"Fingerprints?" said Long. "What fingerprints?"

"You saw Pete follow Harold Thomas from his apartment to that car wrecking yard in Santa Monica. No doubt Thomas was going to move the films because the arson squad was getting too close to him and making him nervous. Seeing Pete made *you* nervous. You tailed Pete, and when you realized that he had seen the van, you decided he had to be put out of the way. You didn't know who he was or what he was up to, but you couldn't take a chance. When he tried to call for help, you hit him on the head and stuffed him into the trunk of that old car. And when you slammed down the trunk lid, you left your fingerprints."

Jefferson Long opened his mouth to protest, and then closed it again.

"How could you!" said Madeline Bainbridge. "How could you do that to a mere boy?"

"And then there's the money," said Jupiter brightly. "The ransom for the films. It was only paid this afternoon. I would not be surprised if at least part of it is still in Thomas's car. And perhaps there's some in Long's car as well. There hasn't been time to put it in a secure hiding place. Shall we look and see what we can find?"

"No!" shouted Thomas. He lurched towards the door.

Beefy tackled him, bringing him crashing to the floor, and sat on him. The material of Thomas's suit ripped, and a wallet spilled out on to the floor, together with three key chains, all loaded with keys.

"Aha!" cried Beefy.

"I'll have the law on you!" shouted Thomas. "You don't have a search warrant!"

Gray had been standing in a corner of the room, quiet and almost forgotten. As Beefy held up the keys, Gray moved. He raced past Beefy, brushed Uncle Will to one side, and was out the front door and thundering down the steps before anyone could move.

"Marvin!" cried Madeline Bainbridge.

"He won't get far," Pete assured her. "I fixed his car so that it won't start. His and Thomas's and Long's, too. We'll just call the police and they can pick Gray up as he's hiking down the hill."

But then, from outside, there came the sound of a car engine starting.

"Oh, blast!" shouted Beefy. "That's my car! He's taking my car! I left the keys in the ignition!"

Peter raced for the kitchen and the telephone, and Madeline Bainbridge went to the window. "He'll be sorry," she said, as the car pulled away from the house. "He'll be very sorry."

Jupiter and Bob saw the car's headlights flash through the lemon grove. The car reached the road and skidded into the turn. It didn't slacken speed one bit.

"Oh my gosh!" yelled Bob.

The watchers in the ranch house heard tyres screech on the road, and Madeline Bainbridge screamed.

An instant later, there was a ripping of metal and a smashing of glass as the car crashed sideways into a tree. And then there was silence—a silence that seemed deadly. Madeline Bainbridge stood with her hands to her face, her blue eyes wide with horror.

"Madeline!" Clara Adams went to her and put her arms around her. "Madeline, it wasn't your fault!" she said.

"It's like the last time. It's like Ramon all over again." And Madeline Bainbridge began to weep.

"It's only a coincidence," said Jupe.

Pete had come back into the room. "The sheriff is coming," he said. "I'll call again, and I'll ask them to send an ambulance."

Jupiter nodded as he, Bob, and Beefy headed outside to see how Gray was. "It's an unfortunate way to end things," he said, "but I think we can say that this case is closed."

22

Mr Hitchcock Declines an Invitation

A WEEK AFTER THE Bainbridge films were recovered by Video Enterprises, The Three Investigators called on Alfred Hitchcock. "I assume that you have been getting your notes in order," said the famous motion-picture director as Jupiter, Pete, and Bob took seats across the desk from him.

Bob smiled and handed a file folder to Mr Hitchcock.

"Excellent," said the director. "The accounts in the press of the recovery of the money paid for the Bainbridge films were interesting enough, but I have looked forward to learning more about the part you lads played in the whole affair."

Mr Hitchcock began to read, and he did not speak again until he had perused the last sheet of paper in the folder. "Fascinating!" he said at last. "A woman victimized by her own guilt—a woman who hid herself away from the world and trusted no one."

"No one but the wrong man," said Pete. "He could have gone on swindling her, too, if we hadn't taken the bull by the horns and gone in that afternoon to find her drugged and asleep. The accountants are going through her affairs now, to see exactly how much Gray took from her. Gray's in the prison ward at the County Hospital. The district attorney will bring charges when he has more complete information."

"He's fortunate to be alive," said Mr Hitchcock. "Ramon Desparto did not survive when his brakes failed on that road. Of course I can't believe that Miss Bainbridge really caused either of those accidents. I admire mystery inordinately, but believing that a witch can cause a car accident is . . . well, a bit much, wouldn't you say?"

Jupiter smiled. "We'll never really know, I guess," he said. "Beefy Tremayne is convinced that Gray hit the tree simply because Gray took Beefy's car, and Beefy and all of his possessions are doomed to malfunction."

"That should be of some comfort to Madeline Bainbridge," said Mr Hitchcock. "She seemed distressed at the thought that she might actually have harmed both Desparto and Gray."

"She's trying to get over the idea that she's to blame," said Bob, "and she's trying to use her magical powers to help Beefy overcome his clumsiness. Actually, he doesn't seem to be tripping over so many things or knocking over so many things as he used to, so maybe the magic works."

"Also, his uncle isn't giving him such a hard time," Pete reported. "Having William Tremayne around would upset anybody and make them drop things."

"Tell me," said Mr Hitchcock, "did the police really find Jefferson Long's fingerprints on that wrecked automobile? The one in which Pete was shut up?"

The boys grinned. "That was Jupe bluffing," said Bob. "He was hoping Long would say something and give himself away. Actually, it was Thomas who cracked and ran—or tried to run. That was just as well. Thomas had all those keys in his pocket, and they included the keys to Beefy's apartment and the keys to that pharmaceutical firm where Thomas used to work. So Jupe was right when he guessed where the magnesium came from."

"Even without that bit of evidence," said Jupe, "the police have plenty on both Long and Thomas. The ransom money for the Bainbridge films was in the trunk of Long's car. He'd been so sure of himself that he hadn't even bothered to move it. He was promptly arrested. Now he's out on bail, and finding that his long friendship with law enforcement people is dead. They know now that he was just using them and they're furious.

"As for Thomas, whose real name actually *is* Goodfellow—he's served time for a number of things, including grand larceny and arson. He tried to go straight and keep an honest job, but he simply couldn't. The pharmaceutical firm where he used to work has had an audit, and there are shortages in the accounts there. Thomas simply couldn't keep from stealing, no matter what."

"How fortunate that he is no longer in circulation," said Mr Hitchcock.

"But Madeline Bainbridge *is* in circulation again," reported Bob. She's decided that it's dangerous to be a hermit, so she's giving a party next Friday evening. She's inviting the local members of her old magic circle."

"Are they coming?" asked Mr Hitchcock. "You state in your report that the ladies seemed to dislike Madeline Bainbridge."

"They do, but they're also curious," said Jupiter. "They want to see what she looks like after all these years, so they're coming. And they'll find her so unchanged that I'm sure they'll believe that she is a witch! A good witch, perhaps, but a witch all the same."

"No doubt the simple life she's led has helped to keep her young," said Mr Hitchcock.

"Wonderfully young," Jupe reported. "She says she owes it all to health foods—she's eaten nothing else for more than thirty years."

"I trust she doesn't consider deadly nightshade a health food," commented Mr Hitchcock dryly.

Jupe laughed. "No, she told us that it was reserved for use in certain Sabbat potions—in very tiny quantities, of course. By the way, you are also invited to her party if you'd like to come. We told her we were seeing you today and she said she'd always admired your work. Would you

156

care to dine on health foods at the ranch above Malibu? Or are you nervous about eating with witches?"

Mr Hitchcock considered this, and then he shook his head. "Please convey my regrets to the lady," he said. "I am not at all nervous about witches—especially charming ones like Miss Bainbridge. However, when it comes to health foods—well, there I draw the line!"

THE MYSTERY OF
THE SCAR-FACED
BEGGAR

The Mystery of the Scar-Faced Beggar
was first published in the USA by Random House Inc in 1981

First published as a single volume
in the UK by Armada in 1984

1

The Blind Man Runs

"IF IT DOESN'T STOP SOON, I'll scream!" said the woman in the raincoat.

A gust of wind whirled up Wilshire Boulevard. It snatched at the woman's umbrella and turned it inside out. Then it rushed on, sending raindrops spattering against the shop windows.

For an instant Bob Andrews, standing at a bus stop, thought the woman really would scream. She glared at her ruined umbrella. Then she looked accusingly at Bob, as if he were to blame. Then, quite suddenly, she laughed.

"Darn!" she said. She tossed the umbrella into the trash basket that stood at the kerb. "Serves me right for coming out in a California rainstorm." She sat down on the bench next to the bus-stop sign.

Bob shivered and hunched his shoulders against the chill and the wet. It had been the rainiest April he could remember. Now, at nearly six o'clock on Easter Monday, it was cold, too, and already dark because of the storm. Bob had come to Santa Monica earlier that afternoon, bound for a fabric store to get a dress pattern for his mother. He hadn't minded giving up some of his spring vacation to do the simple errand, but now the wait for the bus back to Rocky Beach seemed endless. He impatiently wiped his glasses dry for the umpteenth time.

"Oh, here comes the blind man," said the woman on the bench.

Bob looked up the street. Over the sound of rain on the pavement he heard the tap-tap of a cane and the rattle of coins being shaken in a metal cup.

"Poor soul," said the woman. " He's been around this neighbourhood a lot lately. I always try to give him something when I see him."

She fumbled in her purse as the blind man came closer. Bob saw that he was quite thin, and he stooped as he walked. His collar was pulled up around his ears and a cloth cap was pulled down over his brow. Dark glasses covered his eyes, and a neatly lettered sign was pinned to the front of his windbreaker. It was covered with plastic and it read, "God bless you. I am blind."

"Nasty night," said the woman. She stood up and dropped a coin into his cup.

"Argh!" said the blind man. His white stick rapped against the kerb, then banged on the bench. He tapped back and forth along the edge of the bench, then sat down.

Bob and the woman watched the blind man for a moment, then turned away and stared at the lighted windows of the bank across the street.

The cleaning people in the bank had just finished their chores. The counter-tops gleamed and chairs were placed in precise order. There were two cleaners—a man in bib overalls who wore his grey hair long and shaggy, and a short, stout woman. They waited at the door that led from the bank out to the lobby of the office building in which the bank was located.

A uniformed security man with a bunch of keys hurried forward from the back of the bank. He exchanged a word or two with the cleaning people, then unlocked the bank door and let them out.

As the cleaning people crossed the lobby and disappeared into an elevator, Bob glanced down at the blind man again. He could see grey hair at the edges of the man's cloth cap, and a stubble of neglected beard on the man's cheeks. A broad, ugly scar ran from the man's jaw to his cheekbone. The accident that caused the scar must have been a terrible one, thought Bob. He wondered whether that accident was what had cost the man his sight.

The beggar leaned forward, as if to get up from the bench. His foot somehow caught on his cane and he lurched sideways, half-sitting and half-standing.

"Oh!" cried the woman. She seized the beggar's arm to steady him.

The metal cup fell to the ground and bounced away. Coins scattered in all directions.

"My money!" cried the beggar.

"We'll get it!" said the woman. "Don't you move."

She crouched to pick coins off the wet pavement and Bob began to fish in the gutter for the money. The woman retrieved the metal cup, which had rolled against the trash basket, and dropped the coins into it.

"Have you got it all?" said the blind man. "It took me all day to get that much."

Bob dropped a wet quarter and two dimes into the cup. "I don't think we missed any," he said.

The woman handed the cup to the blind man, who dumped the coins out into his palm and fingered them over. He made a wordless, guttural sound, then said, "Yes. It's all right."

"Are you waiting for the bus?" said the woman. "I think I see it coming now."

"No," said the man. "Thank you, lady. I live near here."

Bob glanced across the street. The cleaning man had appeared again in the lobby. He stood rattling the bank door. The security man was coming from the back of the bank with his keys out. He opened the door and there was a brief exchange between himself and the cleaning man. Then the cleaner went into the bank.

The blind man got up and started away, tapping at the pavement with his stick.

"Poor soul," said the woman. "I hope he doesn't have far to go."

Bob watched the blind man's slow progress down Wilshire.

"Oh, he's dropped something," said the woman.

"Hey, mister!" called Bob. "Wait a second!"

The beggar didn't hear him. He tapped on down the street.

"Wait!" called Bob. He trotted forward and scooped a wallet from the pavement.

The blind man reached a side street now. He stepped to the kerb, felt his way with the cane, and stepped out on to the road.

The beggar's thin figure was caught in the glare of oncoming headlights. A car was coming up the side street, a little too fast. As it braked for the stop sign, it skidded on the wet surface. The woman at the bus stop screamed, and Bob shouted. Brakes squealed. The blind man twisted and tried to dodge away from the car that sped down upon him. Then there was a thud, and the beggar was rolling on the road.

The car stopped. The driver leapt out. Bob ran, and so did the woman. All three reached the fallen man at the same time.

The driver went down on his knees beside the blind man and tried to take his arm.

"No!" screamed the beggar. He struck at the man with his fist and the man pulled back.

"My glasses!" The beggar groped wildly.

The woman picked up the dark glasses. They had not broken, and she handed them to the beggar.

The blind man put the glasses on and felt for his cane.

The driver of the car was a young man. Bob saw in the glow of the headlights that his face was white with shock. He picked the cane up and put it into the blind man's hand.

Slowly the blind man got up. He turned his head in a searching way, as if he could see if only he tried hard enough, and he started off down the side street. He was limping now. As he went he gasped with pain.

"Mister, wait a second!" cried the driver.

"We ought to call the police," said the woman. "He must be hurt!"

The blind man went on, striking out with the stick, limping, gasping, yet moving almost at a trot.

Bob ran after him, calling for him to wait.

The man disappeared into an alley behind a row of stores. Bob followed. It was so dark that he stumbled, his hands out in front of him to feel for obstacles. At the end of the alley he came out into a little yard. A light bulb burned over the back door of a building, shining on a garbage bin and a cardboard carton that was slowly disintegrating in the rain. Bob saw a second passageway that led back out towards Wilshire, but he saw no sign of the beggar. The man had vanished!

2

The Lost Wallet

"HE COULDN'T REALLY BE BLIND," said Bob. "How could a blind man get away so fast?"

"Perhaps a blind man can move quite rapidly when he's familiar with a place," said Jupiter Jones. "And, of course, a blind person is used to navigating in the dark." Jupe spoke in the careful, somewhat fussy way that was characteristic of him.

It was the next morning, and Bob was with his friends Jupiter and Pete Crenshaw in Jupe's outdoor workshop at The Jones Salvage Yard. The rain had passed. The morning was clear and fresh, and the boys were reviewing the events of the evening before. The wallet that the beggar had dropped lay on Jupe's workbench.

"Even if he was a phony, why would he run?" said Bob. "He acted as if he were scared of us."

Bob stopped and thought for a moment. "I guess none of us were acting as if we had much sense," he said. "The lady who was waiting with me at the bus stop just disappeared while I was in the alley. I suppose the bus came and she automatically got on it. And the driver of the car that hit the blind man drove off when I told him the man was gone. And I stood there like a dope with the wallet. I should have given the driver the blind man's name, and my name too."

"You were in shock," said Jupe. "In emergencies, people often behave in odd ways."

While listening to Bob, Jupe had been tinkering with an old television set that his Uncle Titus had brought into the salvage yard the week before. Jupe had replaced worn tubes with new ones and had made several adjustments to the inside of the set. Now he put the television upright on the workbench and plugged in the set.

There was a promising hum. "Aha!" said Jupe.

"You've done it again," said Pete, in mock admiration.

"Perhaps," said Jupe. He twisted a dial.

The three boys grinned. Jupiter Jones was something of a genius when it came to repairing things or making things out of salvaged parts. He had put together three walkie-talkie radios which the boys used with great enjoyment. He had repaired the old printing press that now stood in one corner of the workshop. He was also responsible for the periscope that was part of the equipment in Headquarters—an old mobile home trailer which was hidden away near Jupe's workshop, concealed by piles of junk and all but forgotten by Jupe's Uncle Titus and Aunt Mathilda.

Jupiter's aunt and uncle were aware that Jupe, Bob and Pete were interested in crime and detection. They knew that the boys called themselves The Three Investigators. But they did not know how really active the boys were in the field. The mobile home had been fitted with all sorts of equipment to help the Investigators solve the puzzles that came their way. It held a small crime lab, complete with fingerprint equipment and a microscope. The boys did their own film developing in the photographic darkroom. A filing cabinet was filled with notes on their cases, and there was a telephone which they paid for with money they earned helping out around the salvage yard.

It appeared that a television set would now become part of the furnishings in Headquarters. The set on Jupe's workbench squawked to life, and a picture flickered on to the screen and steadied.

". . . coming to you with a mid-morning news-break," said an announcer.

A newscaster appeared on the screen and wished everyone a good morning. He then said that the latest Pacific storm had passed through Los Angeles, and that Southern California could look forward to several days of clear weather.

"There have been mudslides in the hills above Malibu," said the newsman. "And in Big Tujunga Canyon, residents are mopping up after yesterday's flash flood.

"On the local crime front, our remote unit is on the scene of a daring robbery that took place at the Santa Monica Thrift and Savings Company less than two hours ago.

"Thieves entered the bank yesterday evening disguised as the cleaning crew. They imprisoned the security guard in the bank's board room, and were waiting this morning when employees reported to work. When the time lock was released at eight forty-five this morning, Samuel Henderson, executive vice-president of the bank, was forced to open the vault. The holdup men escaped with approximately a quarter of a million dollars in cash and an unknown amount in valuables from the safe-deposit boxes. Stay tuned for additional details when we return at noon."

"There!" said Jupe. He switched the set off.

"Good grief!" exclaimed Bob. "The Santa Monica Thrift and Savings! I was right across the street from that bank last night when the blind man . . . when . . ."

Bob stopped. He looked rather pale. "I must have seen one of the holdup men," he said.

Pete and Jupe waited, watching Bob.

"Yes, sure I did," he said. "From the bus stop I could look across the street right into the bank. I saw the cleaning people leave and go up in the elevator. Then the man came back—the cleaning man—and he knocked at the bank door and the security man opened it."

"He came back?" said Jupe. "The same man?"

"Well, I suppose . . . I suppose . . ." Bob looked puzzled. "I don't know," he said. "The blind man dropped his cup and his money rolled all over the place. So the lady and I picked it up, and after we gave the cup back to the blind man, that's when I saw the cleaning man at the bank door."

"So it could have been a different man?" said Jupe.

Bob nodded.

"What a scheme!" cried Pete. "The cleaning people finish their work and go upstairs. Then somebody who's dressed up to look like a cleaning man comes and knocks at the door. The security guy lets him in and whammo! The security guy winds up stashed in a back room and the crooks are inside the bank and they're home free. No alarms. Just sit and wait for the employees to show up."

170

"Why sure!" said Bob. "It must have been that way."

"Did you see where the cleaning man came from?" asked Jupe. "I mean, whether he came into the lobby from the elevator or the street?"

Bob shook his head. "The guy was already at the bank door in the lobby when I noticed him. I thought he'd come back down in the elevator. But I guess he could have come in from the street, if he wasn't one of the cleaners in the building."

"Which opens up an interesting line of thought," said Jupiter. He picked up the wallet that Bob had left on the workbench. "Say the man came down the street. The blind man dropped his money just as the bogus cleaning man was approaching the bank door. You and the woman at the bus stop bent down to pick up the money. Anyone would do the same. And you were so occupied with the task that you didn't see the robber enter the lobby. Does that suggest anything?"

Bob gulped. "The blind man was a lookout!"

Jupe examined the wallet. "This is very nice," he said. "It's made of ostrich skin and it came from Neiman-Marcus. That's one of the most expensive stores in the city."

"I didn't notice that," said Bob. "I only looked to see if the blind man had a telephone number in it so I could call him. But he doesn't."

Jupe looked through the wallet. "One credit card, twenty dollars in cash, and a temporary driver's licence. Now what would a blind man be doing with a driver's licence?"

Bob nodded. "Right. Of course. He was faking. He's not blind."

171

"Hector Sebastian," said Jupe, reading from the licence. "According to this, he lives at 2287 Cypress Canyon Drive in Malibu."

"Malibu is a nice place," said Pete. "Maybe being a beggar pays better than you'd think."

"It may not be the beggar's address," Jupe pointed out. "Perhaps the man is a pickpocket and he stole the wallet. Or perhaps he just found it somewhere. Have you looked in the telephone directory for Hector Sebastion, Bob?"

"He's not listed," Bob answered.

Jupiter stood up. "We may have something here that would interest the police," he said. "On the other hand, the fact that a blind man dropped this wallet may mean nothing at all. The fact that the blind man ran away may mean nothing. But Cypress Canyon Drive isn't very far from here. Shall we investigate before we decide what action to take?"

"You bet!" said Bob.

The boys all had their bicycles with them. In a few minutes they were on Pacific Coast Highway pedalling north towards Malibu. In less than half an hour they had passed the main shopping area of the famous beach community.

Cypress Canyon Drive was a narrow road that turned and twisted for a couple of hundred metres as it climbed up from the Coast Highway, then ran roughly parallel to the highway but some distance inland from it. As the boys rode along the drive they could hear cars and trucks on the highway, and they could glimpse the ocean between the trees that lined the drive on the left. On the right, the coast range sloped up and away, with the sky clear and blue beyond the tops of the mountains.

172

"I don't think anybody really lives here," said Bob, after they had gone some distance along the rutted, muddy road. "I don't see a single house. Do you suppose the address on that driver's licence is a phony?"

"The plot thickens," said Pete. "Why would a blind man have a driver's licence? And if that *is* the beggar's licence, why would it have a fake address?"

The drive dipped into a hollow where a small stream of water ran across. Then it climbed again. On the far side of the rise the boys stopped. There was a gully in their path which might have been dry in summer, but which was now a torrent of brown water. And beside the road on the left, almost at the edge of the muddy wash, there was a shabby, barnlike old building with dormer windows in the second story. Neon tubing ran along its eaves. A sign across one end proclaimed that it was Charlie's Place.

"A restaurant?" said Bob.

Jupe took the wallet out of his pocket and looked again at the driver's licence. "Number 2287," he said. "That's the number on that new mailbox out in front."

The boys heard a car on the road behind them. They moved aside, and a red sports car came splashing slowly through the little stream they had already forded. A thin man with greying hair and a lined, somewhat sad face passed without seeming to notice the boys. He turned into the muddy yard that was the parking lot of Charlie's Place, stopped his car, got slowly out, and took a cane from the floor of the vehicle. Then he went slowly up sagging steps

173

into the ramshackle building, letting a dilapidated screen door slam behind him as he disappeared.

"He's got a limp!" exclaimed Pete. "Hey, Bob, didn't you say that the beggar limped when he ran off last night?"

"Well, he limped after he got hit by the car. Who wouldn't limp?"

"Could that man be the beggar?" said Jupe. "Is he at all like the beggar?"

Bob shrugged. "He's about the same size, and I guess he's about the same age, but there must be a million guys like that."

"Very well," said Jupe. Suddenly he was brisk and businesslike. "I'm going in there."

"What are you going to do?" asked Pete. "Go in and buy a hamburger?"

"I may," said Jupe. "Or I may simply ask for directions. But one way or another, I'll find out who that man is. Bob, you had better keep out of sight. If that man was outside the bank in Santa Monica last night, he might recognize you—and he might get nasty."

"I'll wait with Bob," said Pete. "I'm allergic to guys who might get nasty."

"Chicken!" Bob taunted.

"I'm only ambitious," said Pete. "My ambition is to live until I am very, very old."

Jupe chuckled. Leaving his friends standing beside the road, he pushed his bicycle into the parking area of Charlie's Place. He leaned the bike against the wall of the building and went up the steps. He crossed the little porch, put his hand on the screen door, and pulled. The door opened.

Jupe stepped out of the sunlight into a place that

174

was dim. He saw polished hardwood floors and dark wood panelling. Straight ahead through a wide doorway was a large, empty room. Its front wall was made entirely of windows, which looked out through the trees to the sparkling ocean beyond. Jupe guessed this room had once been the main dining room of a restaurant. The restaurant was clearly out of business now.

Jupe was standing in a wide passageway that was really a sort of lobby outside the huge room. To the left of the lobby was an area that was a dusty jumble of coffee urns and counters and stools and booths. Jupe realized that this had once been a coffee shop. He looked to the right and saw a wall with several doors in it. There were cartons and crates piled in the coffee shop and more cartons piled up in the lobby. Several crates stood on the hardwood floor of the big room. One crate was open, and packing material overflowed and drifted down its side.

Jupe moved forward slowly. He was about to call out when he heard the sound of a telephone being lifted from its cradle. He stood still and listened. Someone out of sight in the big, bright room ahead of him dialled a number.

There was a pause, and then a man said, "This is Sebastian."

After another pause the man spoke again. "Yes," he said, "I know it will be expensive, but everything has its price. I'm prepared to pay for it."

At that moment something small and hard pressed into Jupe's back just above his belt.

"Please to reach for the sky," said a soft voice. "If you move I make you in two pieces!"

3

A Man of Mystery

JUPITER RAISED HIS HANDS above his head. He could feel his scalp prickle.

"I only wanted . . ." he began.

"Please to be quiet!" said the person behind him.

There were footsteps on the hardwood floor. The grey-haired man who had driven up a few minutes before appeared in the doorway to the big room. He stood leaning on his cane, looking at Jupe with his head slightly to one side, as if he were puzzled.

"What is it, Don?" he said. "Who is this?"

Jupe frowned. There was something familiar about this man. Jupe could not be sure whether it was just the voice, or the tilt of the head. Had they met somewhere? If so, where? And when?

"This person breaks and enters," said the individual who was holding Jupe at gunpoint. "He stands and listens to you talk on the telephone."

"I only wanted to ask directions," said Jupe. "The sign outside says this is Charlie's Place. Isn't it a restaurant? And I didn't do any breaking and entering. The door was open."

"Well, of course," said the grey-haired man. He came towards Jupe, smiling. "It used to be a restaurant, and the door *is* open, isn't it?"

Jupe saw that the man's cheeks were ruddy, and that his high, thin nose had recently been sunburned. It was now peeling. The eyes under the thick, grey-black brows were very blue. "Relax, young friend," said the man. "Don couldn't shoot you even if he wanted to."

Jupe cautiously lowered his arms. He turned to look at the person called Don.

"You think I have gun," said the man with satisfaction. He was an Oriental, not much taller than Jupe, quite slim, with a smooth, pleasant face. He held a wooden mixing spoon with the handle pointed towards Jupe. "You see it is not really gun," he said. "It is trick I see on television."

"Hoang Van Don came from Vietnam recently," said the grey-haired man. "He is presently learning English by watching late-night television. I see now that he is also learning other useful things."

The Vietnamese man bowed. "If imprisoned in upper room, proper course to follow is to braid bedsheets into rope. If bedsheets not available, slide down drainpipe."

The Vietnamese bowed again and disappeared into the shadows of the coffee shop. Jupe stared after him with curiosity.

"You wanted directions?" said the grey-haired man.

"Oh!" Jupe started. "Oh, yes. A river crosses the road just beyond here." Jupe pointed. "Does the road continue on the far side? Is there any place we can cross, or should we go back to the highway again?"

"The road doesn't go on. It dead ends just beyond the river. And don't even try to cross that gully. It's quite deep. You'd be swept off your feet."

177

"Yes, sir," said Jupe, who was not really listening. He was staring curiously at one of the cardboard cartons that stood in a corner of the lobby. Half a dozen books were piled on the carton, and all seemed to be copies of the same title. Jupe saw black dust jackets and brilliant scarlet lettering. The cover illustration on the top copy showed a dagger stuck through a document. *Dark Legacy* was the title of the book.

"Hector Sebastian!" said Jupe suddenly. He walked over and picked up one of the books. Turning it over, he found a photograph on the back—a photograph of the man who now stood facing him in the dim little lobby.

"Why, it *is* you!" said Jupe. For once the poise on which he prided himself completely deserted him. "You are *the* Hector Sebastian! I mean, you're the one who's been on television!"

"Yes, I have," said the man. "A few times."

"I read *Dark Legacy*," said Jupe. His voice sounded strange in his own ears. It was high and excited. He was babbling like a star-struck tourist. "It's a terrific book! And so is *Chill Factors*! Mr. Sebastian, you sure don't need to rob any banks!"

"Did you think I did?" said Hector Sebastian. He smiled. "Well, now, I don't think you just wandered in here looking for directions. What's this all about?"

Jupe's face got red. "I . . . I don't even like to admit what I was thinking," he said. "Mr. Sebastian, are you missing your wallet?"

Sebastian started. He felt in the pocket of his jacket. Then he patted his hip pocket. "Good heavens!" he exclaimed. "It's gone! Do you have it?"

"My friend Bob has it," said Jupe. Very quickly he

178

told Sebastian of Bob's adventure the night before. He described the blind man who had dropped the wallet, and he mentioned the bank robbery and the accident in which the blind man was hit.

"Terrific!" said Mr. Sebastian. "It sounds like the beginning of a Hitchcock movie."

Jupe immediately looked crestfallen.

"What's the matter?" said Mr. Sebastian. "Did I say something wrong?"

"Not really," said Jupe. "It's only that Mr. Hitchcock was a friend of ours. When Bob wrote up our cases, Mr. Hitchcock used to introduce them for us. We felt very bad when he died, and we miss him."

"I'm sure you do," said Mr. Sebastian. "But I don't understand. What sort of cases? And where is your friend Bob, who found my wallet?"

"I'll get him!" said Jupe. "He's right outside."

Jupe barrelled out the door and trotted across the parking lot. "Come on!" he called. "Mr. Sebastian wants to meet you. You know who he is?"

Bob and Pete looked at one another, and Pete shook his head. "Should we know?" he asked.

Jupe grinned. "*I* should have known," he said. "I should have recognized the name right away. My brain must be turning to oatmeal! He's the one who wrote *Dark Legacy* and *The Night Watch* and *Chill Factors*. He's been on all the television talk shows lately. Moorpark Studios just finished making a movie of *Chill Factors*, and Leonard Orsini is going to compose the score for the picture."

Pete suddenly grinned. "Oh yeah! I heard my father talking about *Chill Factors*. You mean this guy Sebastian is the writer?"

"You bet he is!" said Jupe. His face was flushed with excitement. "He used to be a private detective in New York City, but he was hurt when the small plane he was piloting crashed. His leg was crushed. While he was waiting for it to mend, he began to work on a novel inspired by one of his cases. It was called *The Night Watch*, and it became a big-selling paperback. After it came out Mr. Sebastian wrote another book called *Dark Legacy* about a man who pretended to be dead so that his wife could collect his insurance, and that was made into a movie. Remember? And then Mr. Sebastian gave up completely on being a private detective and became a full-time writer. He wrote the screenplay for *Chill Factors* after the book was sold to Moorpark Studios. Come on! Don't you want to meet him? Bob, have you got the wallet?"

"I gave it to you," said Bob. "Don't you remember? Boy, you really are bowled over!"

"Oh," said Jupe. He patted his pockets, then grinned. "Yes. Okay. Come on."

Pete and Bob followed him back to the building, and when they were inside he introduced them to Mr. Sebastian. Sebastian ushered them into the big windowed room and motioned them to the folding chairs that were placed around a low, glass-topped table. It was the sort of table that is usually outdoors on a terrace or beside a pool. The table, the chairs, and a telephone were the only furnishings in the room.

"Eventually we'll have all sorts of luxury here," said Sebastian. "Don and I moved in only last week, and we haven't had time to do much."

"You're going to live here?" said Pete.

"I *am* living here," answered Sebastian. He limped to the lobby and bellowed for Don. Presently the Vietnamese appeared with a tray on which there was a glass coffee server and a cup and saucer.

"Something for the boys," ordered Sebastian. "Do we have any soft drinks in the refrigerator?"

"Lemonade," said Don as he set down the tray. "Nature's Own, for tree-ripe flavour."

Jupe smiled, recognizing the advertising slogan of one of the popular brands of lemonade. No doubt this was a bit of wisdom that Don had learned from his television watching.

"Lemonade okay?" said Mr. Sebastian. He looked to the boys, who quickly nodded. Don went back to the kitchen, which was located in the far corner of the house, beyond the coffee shop.

"I wish Don would watch some cooking programmes, instead of all those old movies with commercials stuck in every five minutes," said Mr. Sebastian after the Vietnamese left. "Some of the meals that we have are unbelievable."

Mr. Sebastian then went on to talk about the old restaurant that he had just moved into, and the plans that he had for making it over into a home. "Eventually the coffee shop will be a formal dining room," he told the boys. "There's a storeroom next to the lobby that can become Don's bedroom, and I'll have a bathroom put in for him over there, under the stairs."

The boys looked towards the staircase that went up along the inner wall near the lobby. At the top of the stairs was a gallery that ran the length of the building, overlooking the huge room where Sebastian sat with the boys. The big room had a vaulted ceiling that was two stories high. The other half of the building—the front half occupied by the lobby, storeroom, coffee shop and kitchen—had rooms on the second floor, with doors opening on to the gallery.

"I know this place is a wreck," said Mr. Sebastian. "But it's structurally sound. I had an architect and a building contractor look at it before I bought it. And do you know what it would cost me to buy a house this size so close to the ocean?"

"A fortune, I'm sure," said Jupe.

Sebastian nodded. "And think what a beautiful place this will be once it's fixed up. This is a great room just the way it is—a fireplace at each end and all these windows facing the ocean! And the roof doesn't leak. That's the sort of thing you may take for granted, but I lived for twenty-three years in a Brooklyn apartment where the roof leaked regularly. I had to keep a collection of buckets and pans to set under the drips when it rained."

Mr. Sebastian grinned. "Who was it who said that he'd been rich and he'd been poor, and rich was better? Whoever it was, he knew what he was talking about."

Don came in then with the lemonade. As he served the boys, Sebastian picked up the handsome wallet that Jupe had put on the glass-topped table.

"Dropped by a blind beggar, eh?" said Mr. Sebastian. He looked into the wallet. "He couldn't have been a beggar in great need. He didn't spend any of the money."

"But he *was* begging," said Bob. "He had a tin cup with coins in it. He kept shaking the cup."

Mr. Sebastian looked thoughtful. "I wonder how he found the wallet?" he said. "If he was blind . . ."

"Exactly," said Jupiter. "Blind people don't see things that are lying on the pavement. Of course he might have stumbled on it and picked it up. Where did you have it last, Mr. Sebastian?"

"You sound very professional," Sebastian told Jupe. "I almost expect you to whip out a pencil and pad and take notes. You mentioned Alfred Hitchcock a while ago. You said he used to introduce your cases? Are you boys learning to be detectives?"

"We *are* detectives," said Jupe proudly. He pulled out his own wallet and took a small card from one of the compartments. He handed the card to Mr. Sebastian. It read:

THE THREE INVESTIGATORS
"We Investigate Anything"
? ? ?

First Investigator	Jupiter Jones
Second Investigator	Peter Crenshaw
Records and Research	Bob Andrews

"I see," said Sebastian. "You call yourselves The Three Investigators, and you volunteer to investigate anything. That's a rather brave statement. Private investigators can be asked to do some very odd things."

"We know," said Jupiter. "We have encountered some highly unusual circumstances—even bizarre ones. That's our speciality. We have often been successful in cases where ordinary law enforcement people have failed."

Mr. Sebastian nodded. "I believe you," he said. "Young people have nimble minds, and they aren't burdened with notions about what can happen and can't."

Bob leaned forward. "We're interested in the blind beggar because we wonder whether he might have something to do with the robbery at the bank," he said. "Were you in Santa Monica yesterday? Did you drop the wallet there? Or could he have picked your pocket?"

"No." Mr. Sebastian leaned back in his chair. "I know I had the wallet yesterday morning. I remember putting it in my pocket when I left the house to go to Denicola's. I never thought of it again until just now. Obviously I must have dropped it at Denicola's, since that's the only place I went yesterday, but it must have been an accident. I certainly didn't get into any crowds where someone could have jostled me and picked my pocket—and I would have noticed a blind man."

"Isn't Denicola's the place up the coast where they have a charter boat for sports fishermen?" said Pete.

Mr. Sebastian nodded. "I keep my speedboat there," he said. "It's closer than any of the marinas. When I want to use the boat, the boy who works for Mrs. Denicola rows me out to the buoy where it's tied up. I had the boat out for a run yesterday. I must have dropped the wallet near the dock, or maybe in the parking lot there."

"And the blind man picked it up," said Pete.

"Then the blind man went to Santa Monica without saying anything to the people at Denicola's about the wallet," said Bob. "And he happened to be across the street from the bank at the exact moment the holdup men got in disguised as cleaning people. Maybe he even created a diversion by dropping his cup of coins so that the people at the bus stop wouldn't guess what was going on."

184

"The cup of coins may have been slippery in the rain," said Mr. Sebastian. "Or the man may have been tired. It could mean nothing at all that he dropped the cup."

"He ran away after he dropped the wallet and Bob went after him to give it back," Jupe pointed out. "He ran again after he was hit by a car."

"Not unusual," said Mr. Sebastian. "He could have been in shock. He could have had a guilty conscience about carrying a wallet that wasn't his. He could have been afraid of the police. The police are often hard on beggars. It doesn't seem likely that he has any connection with a bank robbery, but why don't you go to the police and tell them what you've just told me? Give them my name if you want to. I'll be glad to co-operate in any way I can."

"Of course," said Jupiter, disappointed. "That's the thing to do. And probably you're right and the blind man happened to come along only by coincidence. I guess this case is over before it really began."

"Looks that way," said Mr. Sebastian. "Listen, I really appreciate your coming here with the wallet." He was fumbling in the wallet now, frowning at the bills there.

"It was no trouble," said Pete quickly.

"We were glad to do it," Bob put in. "Please don't even think about giving us anything."

"Well then, can I reward you some other way?" asked Mr. Sebastian. "How about a ride in my speedboat? Want to go with me the next time I take it out?"

"Hey, could we?" cried Pete.

"You sure could. Just give me your telephone numbers so I can give you a call."

"We can be here in half an hour," said Pete happily.

He gave Mr. Sebastian his telephone number, and so did the other boys. When the Three Investigators left, the famous detective-turned-writer trailed them to the door and stood watching as they wheeled their bikes out on to the road.

"Nice guy," said Pete when they were out of earshot.

"Yes, he is," Jupe agreed. "He seemed sorry to see us go. I wonder if he isn't kind of lonely out here in California. He's lived almost all of his life in New York."

"Anytime he wants company on his speedboat," said Bob, "I'll be ready. Wow! That's really—"

Bob stopped. A small, tan sedan had appeared on the road. It passed the three boys at a sedate pace, then slowed at the entrance to Mr. Sebastian's yard and turned in. An elderly man got out. He approached the steps of Charlie's Place and said something to Mr. Sebastian, who still stood in the doorway.

The boys were too far away to hear the conversation, but they stayed on the road and watched. After a moment Mr. Sebastian stepped back. The newcomer went up the steps and disappeared into Charlie's Place.

"Well, how about that!" exclaimed Bob. "This investigation isn't over yet!"

"Why do you say that?" asked Pete.

"The security man," said Bob. "That guy was the security man who let the robbers into the bank in Santa Monica. Now why would he come calling on Mr. Sebastian?"

4

The Investigators Find a Client

"IT DOESN'T MAKE SENSE!" said Jupiter. "Hector Sebastian must have more money than he can ever spend! His books are best sellers!"

"Okay!" said Bob. "But if he didn't have anything to do with that bank robbery, why did the security man from the bank go to see him?"

"I don't know," said Jupe.

It was early afternoon, and the Three Investigators were in their secret Headquarters at The Jones Salvage Yard. The boys had waited in the road outside the old restaurant on Cypress Canyon Drive until the security man from the Santa Monica bank had left Hector Sebastian's home and driven away. They had briefly considered talking to Sebastian again, and asking about the visit of the bank guard, but Jupiter vetoed the idea. He was reluctant to intrude a second time on the famous writer for no better reason than curiosity. So the boys had returned to Headquarters to discuss the events of the morning. They were now sitting around the old oak desk in the trailer. Bob was jotting down items in a notebook as he remembered them.

"The beggar limped last night after the accident, and Mr. Sebastian has a limp," he said.

"Mr. Sebastian broke his leg in a dozen places," Jupe pointed out. "His limp is permanent. Did the beggar limp last night *before* the accident?"

"I'm not sure," said Bob.

"The limp could be a coincidence," said Pete, "but what about the wallet? That's another coincidence. And then the man who actually let the thieves into the bank goes calling on Mr. Sebastian. That's a third coincidence, and three is too many."

"Why don't we go to the police?" said Bob. "It's what Mr. Sebastian said we should do. And why would he say that if he's involved with the robbery?"

"He had to say it," Pete declared. "He'd be afraid not to. It's what grownups always say."

"I think the police would feel that our theories are far-fetched," said Jupiter. "Perhaps they'd be right. It's impossible to believe that Mr. Sebastian helped rob a bank. He has too much to lose. But there must be some connection between him and that event. Perhaps Mr. Bonestell can help us find it."

"Bonestell?" said Bob.

Jupiter unfolded a newspaper which had been lying on the desk. It was the early edition of the *Santa Monica Evening Outlook*. He had purchased it from a rack when the boys stopped for pizza on their way home.

"Walter Bonestell is the name of the security man who let the robbers into the bank," he said. "It's here in the story on page one." He reached for a stack of phone directories and found the one he wanted. "Hmmm . . . the Santa Monica telephone book lists a Walter Bonestell who lives at 1129 Dolphin Court. That's just a few blocks up from the beach."

"Jupiter!" The call came from outside the trailer. "Jupiter Jones, where are you? I want you!"

Jupe sighed. "Aunt Mathilda sounds annoyed. She hasn't seen me since breakfast. By this time she must have a whole list of things for me to do."

"My mother is probably looking for me, too," said Pete.

"I was going to suggest that we visit Mr. Bonestell," said Jupe. "Perhaps we could do that early this evening. Can you get away then? If we could meet in front of the Rocky Beach Market about seven, we could ride down the coast and see the security man on his own ground."

"Sounds okay to me," said Pete.

Bob grinned. "No school tomorrow. Shouldn't be any problem. See you tonight."

The boys left the trailer, and Jupiter spent the afternoon working in the salvage yard. That night, after an early supper with Aunt Mathilda and Uncle Titus, he was waiting with his bicycle in front of the market. Bob and Pete appeared at five minutes to seven, and in the dark the boys set out for Santa Monica.

Dolphin Court turned out to be a short, dead-end street in a neighbourhood of small, single-family homes. Number 1129 was a frame house halfway down the street. The little car that the boys had seen on Cypress Canyon Drive stood in the driveway. The front of the house was dark, but a light showed at a window in the back. The boys drifted down the driveway and looked through the window into the kitchen.

The security man was there, alone. He sat at a table near the window with a heap of newspapers in front of him and a telephone at his elbow. He was not calling anyone at the moment. He was simply staring at the plastic tablecloth in an unseeing way. He looked older than he had that morning, and more frail. His hair seemed thin and sparse and there were purple shadows under his eyes.

The boys did not speak. After a moment Jupe turned to go to the front of the house and ring the doorbell.

Blocking his way in the driveway was a man who held an automatic pistol!

"Exactly what are you up to?" demanded the man.

He did not aim the pistol, and his voice was low and controlled, but Jupe had the nightmare feeling that he and his friends were in deadly peril. There was something cold and determined about the man with the gun. His mouth was a straight, thin line, betraying no hint of humour. Wrap-around sunglasses perched on his head like a second set of cold eyes.

Pete made a startled sound, and the man snapped, "Be still!"

The kitchen window went up and Mr. Bonestell leaned out. "Shelby, what is it? What are you doing?"

The man with the gun gestured towards the boys. "These three were looking in the window at you."

"Oh?" said Mr. Bonestell. He sounded puzzled and curious. But then he said "Oh!" again, and his tone was alarmed.

"Into the house!" ordered the man with the gun. "That way! March!"

190

The boys marched. They went around to the backyard and in through a service porch to the kitchen.

"What is this all about?" said Mr. Bonestell. "When I went to see Mr. Sebastian this morning, he said three boys had just called on him. It was you three, wasn't it? You were on the road when I drove up, weren't you? With your bicycles."

"Yes, Mr. Bonestell," said Jupiter.

"Won't you sit down?" said Mr. Bonestell. He pulled a chair out from the table near the window.

"Walter, what is all this?" demanded the man with the gun. "What's going on?"

"I'm not sure," said Mr. Bonestell. "Shelby, would you put that gun away? Guns make me nervous!"

Shelby hesitated. Then he hitched his trouser leg up over his shin and slipped the gun into a holster that was strapped to his leg just below the knee.

Pete blinked and stared, but said nothing. The boys took seats at the table.

"Mr. Sebastian said you'd seen a suspicious character near the bank," said Mr. Bonestell.

"Will you please tell me what's going on?" cried Shelby.

Mr. Bonestell sighed. "Haven't you heard the news on the radio?" he said. "There was a robbery at the bank this morning."

"A robbery? I didn't hear. I didn't have the car radio on. What happened? And what about these kids? I don't understand."

Mr. Bonestell quickly related the details of the robbery. "And I'm the one who let the thieves in," he said. "I think the police suspect that I'm involved with them."

191

Mr. Bonestell's expression was bleak. "It was careless of me," he admitted. "If I'd really looked at that man at the door, I'd have know it was a stranger. But even if I was careless, that doesn't mean I'm a crook! I never did a dishonest thing in my life! Only, the police don't know me, so I have to find someone to help me prove I'm innocent."

"A lawyer," said Shelby. He nodded smugly, like one who always has the correct answers. "Very wise of you, Walter, but what has that to do with these boys. Why were they looking in the window?"

Mr. Bonestell looked downcast. "I suppose they're suspicious,too." He leaned towards Jupe. "At first I thought maybe Mr. Sebastian might help. He was on the *Harry Travers Show* last week talking about the movie he just finished working on, and he said that sometimes people get into trouble just because they happen to be in the wrong place at the wrong time. I'm one of those people, aren't I? So I thought maybe Mr. Sebastian would be interested in my . . . my case. One of the secretaries at the bank thought maybe he'd help me, and she got his address for me from the Downtown Credit Reporting Service. He's got an unlisted phone—I guess a lot of famous people do—so I went to see him and . . ."

"Walter, stop blithering!" ordered Shelby. "Who is Mr. Sebastian, for heaven's sake?"

Jupe cleared his throat. "He's a novelist and a screenwriter," he said. "He used to be a private investigator. We saw him this morning. You see, someone dropped a wallet belonging to Mr. Sebastian outside the bank, and Bob here—Bob Andrews—picked it up."

"I think I was across the street from the bank when

the robber came to the door," Bob put in. "I saw you let him in, Mr. Bonestell."

"When we saw you come to Mr. Sebastian's house this morning after we returned the wallet," said Pete, "we *were* kind of suspicious. We thought that there might be some connection between you and Mr. Sebastian and . . . and the robbery."

Pete paused, his face growing red. "It sounds silly now that I'm saying it out loud," he confessed.

"I was only going to ask for help, " said Mr. Bonestell, "but Mr. Sebastian is starting work on a new book, and he doesn't have time to help. He gave me the names of some private investigators here in Los Angeles, but he thinks if I see anyone, I should see a lawyer. I made some calls this afternoon. Do you know what lawyers cost? And private detectives? I can't afford either!"

Jupe sat straighter in his chair. "Mr. Bonestell, perhaps we were suspicious when we first came here, but I'm not suspicious any longer. I think we can help you. You see, Mr. Bonestell, we are private detectives."

Jupe took out a Three Investigators business card and handed it to Mr. Bonestell.

"How quaint!" said Shelby, reading over Mr. Bonestell's shoulder. His tone was sarcastic.

"We are hardly quaint," said Jupe. He kept his voice even. "We have a record of success that many conventional agencies might envy. We are not hampered by many prejudices, as older people often are. We believe that almost anything is possible, and we believe in following our best instincts. Mr. Bonestell, I don't believe that you

193

could have had a part in a bank robbery. I think my friends feel the same way."

Jupe looked at Bob and Pete, who nodded.

"Mr. Bonestell," said Jupe, "if you will accept us, The Three Investigators would like to have you as a client."

Walter Bonestell seemed stunned. "You're so young!" he said.

"Is that really such a handicap?" asked Jupe.

Bonestell twisted his hands nervously. "I should get a real firm only . . . only . . ."

"Walter, what would that cost you?" said Shelby.

The younger man pulled a chair up to the table. He looked past Mr. Bonestell and the boys to the night-black window, frowning at his own reflection. He brushed back his straight fair hair with his hand, took off his sunglasses, and put them into the pocket of his corduroy jacket.

"I don't know why you're so worried," he finally said. "According to your system of justice, you're innocent until you're proven guilty."

"I don't feel so innocent," said Mr. Bonestell. "I did let the robbers in, you know."

"They can't send you to jail for that," said Shelby. "But if you're going to get into such a stew, why not hire these boys? I don't know how they can prove you didn't do it, but maybe they can."

"We'll sure try," promised Pete.

"You do seem eager to help," said Mr. Bonestell. "I can't tell you how nice it is. So few people today have been that nice. I think . . . if you really may be able to help . . . well, I'll be your client. It's high time I had someone on my side!"

194

5

Mr. Bonestell's Story

"IT'S BEEN A NIGHTMARE!" said Mr. Bonestell. He
fingered the design in the plastic tablecloth, and
looked anxiously from Jupiter to Bob and from Bob
to Pete. "They asked me not to come to work again
until the robbery is cleared up. They didn't say I'm a
robber, but I could tell. How could they think a thing
like that? Do I look like a man who'd help rob a bank?
Does this look like a place where crooks hang out?"

The boys looked at Mr. Bonestell, and then at his
orderly kitchen. Jupe wanted to smile. He could not
imagine Mr. Bonestell plotting a crime, and he could
not believe thieves had ever conspired in this place.
The house was so neat that it managed to have no
character at all.

"Oh, gosh!" said Shelby. "My groceries!"

He disappeared into the service porch, and the boys
heard the back door slam as he went outside.

"Why not begin at the beginning, Mr. Bonestell?
said Jupiter. "If you'll tell us everything you
remember about the robbery, perhaps you'll recall
some detail that you may have overlooked earlier."

Bonestell did not look hopeful. "Sebastian said it's
harder to prove that a man is innocent—if he has no
alibi, that is—than to prove that he's guilty."

195

"Well, are you sure you have no alibi?" said Jupe. "Stop and think about it. If you were one of the robbers, some of your time in the last few days would have been taken up with planning the robbery. And you would have to know the other robbers. Can you give an account of your activities for, well, for the last two weeks?"

Mr. Bonestell shook his head sadly.

"What about your friend Shelby? I take it he lives here. Can he tell much about what you've been doing for the past few days?"

Again Mr. Bonestell shook his head. "Shelby rooms here, but he isn't home much. He's a field representative for Systems TX-4. That's a computer company. He travels around advising companies that are putting in computer systems. He was gone all last week and over the weekend. A firm in Fresno is buying the TX billing system and he was working with them. He got home just a while ago. Even when he's home, he doesn't pay much attention. When I was with TX-4, he seemed much friendlier than he does now."

"You worked for Systems TX-4?" said Jupe.

"That's right, after they took over Jones-Templeton Office Machines." For the first time, a hint of pride showed in Mr. Bonestell's face. "I was with Jones-Templeton for over thirty years," he said. "I started there right after World War Two. I was in the mail room at first, and then I went into purchasing and worked my way up. At one time we had twelve people in the department, and I was second in command. That was while the kids were growing up. It was a good place to be, and my kids had a good life. Stable, you know. Not all that moving around that some men get into."

Mr. Bonestell got up and went to the living room. He returned after a moment with a framed photograph. It was a picture of himself—a younger self with dark, thick hair. He was posed with a round-faced, fair-haired woman and two children.

"My wife, Eleanor," said Mr. Bonestell, indicating the woman. "We were married the year after the war ended. She died four years ago of congestive heart failure. She was very young to go that way."

He stopped and cleared his throat.

"I'm sorry," said Jupiter.

"Yes. Well, these things happen. But it was lonely here with the children gone. My son is a production co-ordinator at Elliott Electronics in Sunnydale, and Debra is married now. Her husband is an insurance adjuster. They live in Bakersfield and they have two children.

"So that's a lot to be grateful for—to raise two kids and have them turn out well. But I wish they lived closer. They don't, though. They won't live at home again, so while I was still at TX-4 I started looking for someone to help with expenses. Shelby—Shelby Tuckerman—needed a place to live, so we got together. . . ."

The back door opened and Shelby came in carrying a brown paper bag. He went to the refrigerator and began to store away packages of frozen foods.

"About what happened last night," said Jupe after a moment. "Would you mind going over it for us?"

"If you think it will help," said Mr. Bonestell. "There wasn't anything unusual at first. I've had the job almost a year. I go in at noon and take care of some odds and ends—nothing important. I only took

the job because time hung heavy after I was . . . uh
. . . retired from Systems TX-4. I was replaced by a
computer.

"So now I'm sort of a uniformed odd-job man at
the bank. After the bank closes I supervise the
cleaning people. They don't take long. They're
usually finished by six. After I let them out and lock
up after them, I check the place one last time to
make sure everything is in order. Then I leave.
There's no night security man at the bank. With a
time lock on the vault, they don't need one. No one
could open the vault without setting off an alarm that
would bring every cop in the city."

"That's why the crooks kept you prisoner all
night," said Bob. "They couldn't move while the
time lock was in operation."

"That's right," said Mr. Bonestell. "There were
three men, and of course they knew the system.
They must have been watching and waiting
someplace until the cleaning people left and went up
in the elevator. Then one of them came to the door
and rapped. There isn't too much light in the lobby,
and when I looked out through the door I saw a man
in bib overalls with a lot of shaggy grey hair and a cap
pulled down over his eyes. I thought it was Rolf
coming back for something. I opened the door and
he came in, and then I saw it wasn't Rolf. He had a
gun, so it was too late to do anything.

"Two other people came right away. They had
wigs and fake beards and fake moustaches. They
made me go back to the board room where I couldn't
be seen from the street. They kept me covered all
night, and they didn't even go near the vault. When
the staff started to arrive in the morning, they herded

198

them into the board room. And when Mr. Henderson came in—he's the one who has the combination and opens the vault—they knew who he was. They made him open the vault as soon as the time lock went off."

Shelby Tuckerman sat down next to Pete. "I think someone in the neighbourhood's been spying on you," he told Mr. Bonestell. "Either that or one of those old codgers at the senior citizens' centre decided that the bank would be a pushover."

Mr. Bonestell looked annoyed. "Shelby, I would recognize a neighbour or a friend. I did not know those men last night. They were strangers."

Shelby got up and put a kettle on the stove. "They were disguised, weren't they?" he said. "I don't think it would hurt if the boys kept an eye on the neighbours. They aren't really a superior lot."

"Are they supposed to be superior?" demanded Mr. Bonestell.

Jupe leaned forward. "Of course you don't want to be suspicious of your neighbours," he said, "but it does seem that someone is thoroughly familiar with the routine at the bank. Are you sure no one has been watching you in recent days? Has anyone been asking questions about your job?"

"No." Mr. Bonestell looked completely miserable.

The kettle began to boil, and Shelby spooned instant coffee into a cup and poured hot water over it. He came back to the table and sat sipping the black liquid, looking from Jupe to Mr. Bonestell and then back again.

"Perhaps we will have to prove that someone else is guilty before we can prove that you're innocent," said Jupe. "We may have a clue."

"A clue?" said Mr. Bonestell eagerly. "What is it?"

"At this point we can't be sure that it is a clue," said Jupe. "It's probably best if we don't discuss it with you. We'll investigate, and we'll call you in a day or two. Meanwhile, if you notice any unusual behaviour or any extreme curiosity among your acquaintances, let us know. You have our number on the back of our card."

"Yes, of course."

The boys left the house. When the door had closed behind them, Bob said, "A clue? You mean that wallet? Is that the clue?"

"A very slim clue," said Jupe, "but it's all we have. I think we have already concluded that neither Mr. Sebastian nor Mr. Bonestell is a criminal. But if the blind man had any connection with the robbery, Mr. Sebastian may well have come into contact with a crook. His wallet is the link, so it's worth following up."

"If you say so," said Pete. "Just try to keep us out of places where people pull guns on us, okay?"

6

The Frightened Dreamer

BOB ANDREWS LEFT Rocky Beach before nine the next morning. He rode his bike south along the Coast Highway, bound for Santa Monica. He was to ask in stores near the Thrift and Savings Company if the blind man had returned to the neighbourhood since the robbery. Then he had to return to Rocky Beach to put in some hours at the library, where he had a part-time job shelving books.

Jupiter and Pete watched Bob go. Then they started north, and before nine-thirty they had passed Malibu. They pedalled up a steep rise beyond the town, then sped down the other side towards the pier that was owned by the Denicola Sport Fishing Company.

The boys stopped on the shoulder of the road across from the Denicola pier. They had both seen the place thousands of times as they went up and down the highway, but neither had paid much attention until now. Before this morning, Denicola's had been simply another wide spot on the road where fishermen gathered. Some campers and vans were parked beside the highway now, and men and women were fishing off the beach to the south of the pier. Even in the chill spring wind, a few hardy people in wetsuits rode surfboards out where the breakers began to crest.

"Good surf today," said Pete, envy in his voice. Pete was an excellent surfer, and he would have loved to be out on his board.

But Jupe wasn't interested in the surf. He was studying the pier and the fishing boat that was tied up beside it. The boat was the *Maria III*. She was a sturdy, well-kept craft about fifteen metres long, with a wheelhouse for the pilot and open decks for the fishermen who chartered her. A hatch in the deck was open, and a young man in a blue windbreaker was peering down at the engine of the boat.

Tied to the north side of the pier, opposite the boat, was a raft with a gangway leading down to it. A rowboat was tied to the raft. In the deep water beyond the pier, the boys saw a sleek white motorboat moored to a buoy. The cockpit of the motorboat was covered with a tarpaulin.

"That must be Mr. Sebastian's speedboat," said Jupe.

"Um," said Pete. His eyes were fixed on the surfers.

"Want to stay there and keep an eye on the bikes?"

Again Pete said, "Um."

Jupe smiled, left his bike, and crossed the road.

A driveway led from the highway straight down to the pier. To the left of it was a small parking lot, empty at the moment. To the right, a spur of the driveway went to a house with faded grey shingles and white wooden trim. A station wagon stood in the carport next to the house. Between the house and the pier there was a tiny office cabin which had large windows on three sides and a door in the side nearest the dock. Through the office windows Jupe saw that a grey-haired woman in a black dress sat at a desk examining a ledger, while a younger woman with a mass of very curly red hair talked on a telephone.

Jupe went to the office, smiled through the glass at the red-haired woman, then opened the door and went in.

The office smelled of sea water and rubber boots and seaweed and mildew. There was a wooden bench against one wall, and a table with brochures about sport fishing and charter trips to the Channel Islands off the coast.

The red-haired woman covered the mouthpiece of the telephone with her hand. "Be with you in a minute," she said.

"No hurry," said Jupe.

The older woman looked up, and suddenly Jupe felt pierced by her gaze. A thrill of fright went through him. The woman's dark eyes were strangely knowing, as if she were aware of Jupe's thoughts. Yet her smile was absent-minded. She seemed unaware of the effect she was having on Jupe. After a glance at him, she went back to her ledger.

Uncomfortably, Jupe turned away and looked out at the dock. The young man in the windbreaker had finished checking the engine of the *Maria III*. He closed the hatch, jumped from the boat to the pier, then came whistling towards the office.

"Okay," said the red-haired woman. "We'll expect forty-three on Saturday. If there are any more, let me know, huh?"

She hung up as the man in the windbreaker came in. "Can I help you?" she said to Jupe.

"I was wondering if you've seen a wallet?" said Jupe. "Has anyone turned one in? Mr. Sebastian lost his wallet a day or two ago."

"Mr. Sebastian? Was he here recently? I didn't see him. Ernie, did you row him out to his boat? Want to check the rowboat? See if there's a wallet in there."

"There isn't," said the man in the windbreaker. "Mr. Sebastian was here two days ago. I bailed out the rowboat after I brought him back to the dock. I'd have found a wallet if he'd dropped it in the boat."

He looked at Jupe in a puzzled way. "How come Mr. Sebastian didn't come himself? Or telephone?"

"He's busy," said Jupe. "He was at a couple of places in the last two days, and he doesn't remember where he had the wallet last. I said I'd check for him. You get better results that way. If you just call, people don't always take time to look for lost things."

Jupe was about to go on to say that Mr. Sebastian had seen a man with grey hair and dark glasses and a scar on his face, but before he could describe the blind beggar, the older woman looked up at him.

"You ask about a wallet," she said. "That is strange. Last night I dreamed of a wallet."

The younger woman smiled. "My mother-in-law is a terrifying person," she told Jupiter. "She dreams dreams that sometimes come true."

"It is not I who am terrifying," said the older woman. There was a trace of accent in her speech, and it grew stonger now. "Sometimes the dreams make me afraid. Last night I dreamed that a man came who is a stranger. He picked up a wallet from the ground and put it in his pocket, fast.

204

"He was a strange man, that one. He had grey hair like my Vincenzo's hair before he died, but he was not small and old like Vincenzo. He was younger, and he had black glasses. On his face was a scar, like someone cut him once with a knife. He tapped his way with a stick like a blind man, but he knew that I was watching him. He was a danger to me, I knew. It was a bad dream, and very real."

She looked around to the younger woman. "It makes me uneasy, Eileen."

Next to Jupe there was a sound that was almost a gasp.

Jupe turned. Ernie had gone pale, and it seemed to Jupe that he shook slightly.

"What's the matter, Ernie?" said the younger woman. "Does that description fit anyone you know?"

"Oh, no!" Ernie spoke quickly and too loudly. "It's just scary when Mrs. Denicola does that."

"I know what you mean," said the younger woman.

No one spoke for a moment. Then Jupe thanked the two women and backed out of the office. He hurried across the highway to Pete, who was still watching the surfers in a dreamy way.

"We have just hit the jackpot!" said Jupe. "The old lady in the office there is Mrs. Denicola, and the younger woman is her daughter-in-law, and she says the old lady dreams true dreams."

"You mean she dreams about things that are going to happen?" said Pete.

"Maybe," said Jupe, "but she also dreams about things that have happened. She just dreamed of a man who found a wallet and put it in his pocket. He was a man who tapped his way with a stick—a blind man. And he was a danger to her!"

Pete stared. "You made that up!" he accused.

"I didn't. I'm repeating exactly what she said. She's afraid, and so is that guy who was out on the boat when we first got here. Hearing about that dream scared him stiff. He knows something about the blind man, and he doesn't want anyone to know that he knows! He has something to do with our puzzle. I intend to find out what it is!"

7

Pete Gatecrashes a Meeting

IT WAS PETE who decided that he would stay near
the Denicola pier and watch the man named Ernie.

"If he's up to something, we'd better find out what
it is," said Pete, "and he's seen you. He'll think it's
funny if you hang around. He hasn't seen me, so I
can stick close. He'll never notice."

"Be careful," warned Jupe.

"You know I'll be careful—which is more than I
can say for you!"

Jupe went off then, skimming down the highway,
and Pete crossed the road to the beach. He wheeled
his bicycle in under the pier, which near the water's
edge was tall enough to stand up under, and locked it
to one of the pilings. He was careful not to show any
interest in Denicola's. Anyone watching him would
think he was just another kid looking for a safe place
to park his bike.

Pete moved down the beach a short distance, past
some fishermen. Then he sat on the sand and looked
out across the water towards the *Maria III*. Ernie
was aboard the boat again. He was polishing the
brass fittings.

The morning passsed pleasantly enough. A group
of children came to play in the sand near the pier.

Pete found out they lived nearby and started questioning them. They told Pete that Ernie lived in the little house just up the highway, and that he had two friends who lived with him. They were men who spoke to each other in a foreign language. Pete was pleased with the information. He thought that Jupe couldn't have done any better.

Pete lunched on a sandwich which he bought in a small market down the highway from Denicola's. Then he returned to the beach and watched Ernie through the afternoon. Shortly after five, Ernie left the pier and started up the highway, walking on the shoulder of the road. Pete followed at a distance.

Ernie made straight for a dilapidated little house that stood with its face to the highway and its back extending out over the sand, supported by pilings. When he disappeared into the seedy, sagging cottage, Pete stood and wondered what to do next. How could he find out more about this man who might know the beggar?

A shabby old truck came rumbling up the highway. It pulled to the side of the road across from Ernie's cottage, and a young man got out of the cab. He waved and called out thanks to the driver, then crossed the road and went into the house. The truck went on its way.

A few minutes later a third young man appeared on the scene. This one was driving an ancient Buick. He parked it in a weed-choked patch of level ground next to the house, then went into the house and slammed the door.

There were few fishermen left on the beach now. The sun was dipping towards the west. Pete decided that he would watch for ten more minutes, and then he would get his bike and go home.

No sooner had he made the decision than the door of Ernie's cottage opened. Ernie and the other two men came out and headed down the highway. Pete trailed after them. The men passed Denicola's, then crossed the road and began trudging up a winding driveway. It led to a building that stood atop the cliffs and overlooked the sea. A sign on the hillside announced that this was the Oceanview Motel.

Ernie had his friends had reached the top of the hill when a car turned into the motel driveway and climbed the grade. A second car arrived and followed the first one up the hill, and a third car stopped beside the road. A man and a woman got out of that car and started up the drive on foot, just as two young men on motorcycles roared up the incline.

Pete watched and wondered. When a van loaded with young people pulled to the side of the road, he decided to act. He crossed the highway as a small sedan parked. A middle-aged couple got out, accompanied by a pair of teenage boys. The man and woman started up the driveway and the boys trailed after them. Pete fell into step a few yards behind the boys.

He followed the family to the top of the hill and around behind the motel to the parking lot and pool area. The doors of the motel rooms all opened on to the back. Above them, lights already beamed out from under the eaves. Rows of folding chairs had been set out on the decking around the pool and in part of the black-topped parking area. Beyond the pool was a clear area where Ernie and his two friends were putting up huge easels and mounting great photographic blow-ups on them. One black and white portrait photograph showed a white-haired man who wore an elaborate uniform which was heavy with braid. A colour picture showed a city that was golden with sunlight. The third picture made Pete gasp. It was a photograph of a man who had shaggy grey hair, a scar that ran from his cheekbone to his chin, and eyes covered by dark glasses. He looked just like the blind beggar Bob had described.

Pete began to feel nervous. He had no right to be here. He felt a strong urge to flee, but he knew Jupe would never forgive him. Some kind of meeting was going to take place, and it might tell him who the scar-faced man was. The meeting seemed to be free; no one was taking tickets. And no one was paying any attention to Pete. He guessed that he could safely stay if he kept quiet and pretended to belong.

He sat down on one of the folding chairs, and managed a friendly smile when a stout man, who was breathing heavily after the climb up the hill, sat down next to him.

More and more people came. When the chairs were filled, people sat on the steps outside the motel office and on the wall at one side of the swimming-pool area. No lights showed inside the motel, and Pete wondered if the place was open only in the summertime.

It was nearly dark when Ernie stood up at a small lectern which had been placed in front of the row of photographs. One of Ernie's friends came marching from behind the motel office with a flag made of blue satin edged with gold. There was a cluster of golden oak leaves in the centre of the banner.

A woman in the audience began to sing. Another woman joined her, then a man. Soon everyone was standing and singing. The music swelled and grew majestic. Pete stood up and pretended to sing. He'd never heard the tune before, but it sounded like a battle hymn or an anthem. When the music ended, the singers sat down with much coughing and scraping of chairs, and Ernie stepped back away from the lectern.

An older man came to the lectern and began to speak in Spanish. Pete groaned silently. He didn't understand Spanish! If only Jupe were here!

At first the speaker's voice was subdued. Soon it became stronger. The man waved a raised fist as if he were angry with the crowd, or with someone who was just beyond the circle of light there at the top of the hill.

There were cheers when the man finished speaking and stepped back from the lectern. Then a young woman with long, straight blonde hair came out of the audience. She stood before the crowd and shouted something that sounded like a slogan. People clapped and whistled, and some stamped their feet.

The woman held up her hands and the audience grew quiet. She began to speak. She was fiery, almost dancing in the glare of the floodlights, gesturing to the photographs behind her. Every time she pointed to the picture of the man with the scar, there was a new roar from the crowd.

There were more cheers and whistles when she finished. Ernie came back to the lectern, and gradually the crowd became quiet. Then, to Pete's horror, Ernie began to single out people in the audience, pointing, urging them to get up and speak. One by one they did, always speaking in Spanish. First there was a man in the first row, then a woman halfway back in the crowd, then a boy who sat on the motel steps. As each one got up, Ernie shouted encouragement, applauding and laughing.

Then Ernie was pointing to Pete, and the men and women around Pete were looking at him.

Pete shook his head, but the man who sat on his right tugged at Pete's elbow and gestured to him to stand.

Slowly, as if he were caught in a nightmare, Pete got to his feet. He knew he had to think fast, but his brain was frozen.

Ernie said something, and there was laughter in the crowd. Then there was silence. Pete saw faces, all of them turned towards him, waiting.

Pete wanted to run. He wanted to get away, out of the crowd and down the drive, before these people found out that he was a spy.

The man next to Pete said something softly. Was it just a question? Or was it a threat?

Suddenly Pete put his hand to his throat. He opened his mouth and pointed and made a sound that was half-gasp and half-gurgle. Then he shook his head.

"Aha!" said the man next to him. "Laryngitis!"

Pete nodded, forcing a smile. There was laughter and Pete sat, weak with relief. His neighbour patted him sympathetically. The crowd turned away. Ernie made some remark and pointed to another person in the audience, and that person stood and spoke. At last Ernie and one of his friends began to pass a basket down the rows of chairs. The young woman

212

with the blonde hair spoke again, evidently urging the audience to be generous.

The basket was heaped with paper money when it reached Pete. He put a dollar on top of the pile and passed it along. And then someone called out from the top of the driveway, and the basket was whisked out of sight.

There was a shuffle and a rush, and Ernie and two other men were suddenly seated in front of the audience with guitars and an accordion. Ernie struck a chord on his guitar. The accordionist began to play and the blonde young woman sang softly.

The audience joined in a melody that was sweet and simple, like a country song sung by children.

Pete heard the roar of a motorcycle. He turned as a uniformed highway patrolman sped up the drive.

The singers wavered and the song died.

The highway patrolman left his motorcycle and went to clear the area near the lectern. "Sorry to interrupt you folks," he said. "Who's in charge here?"

"I am." Ernie stood up. "What's the matter? We have permission from Mr. Sanderson to rehearse here."

"Sanderson?" The highway patrolman looked towards the motel office. "He the guy who owns this place?"

"That's right. We rented the community room from him. Want to see the receipt?

"No. I believe you. But this isn't the community room, and didn't Sanderson—or somebody—tell you the motel is unsafe? Why do you suppose it's closed? The ground is unstable after all the rain, and the hill can slide any minute. What are you doing here, anyway? Who are all these people?"

Ernie's smile was beautifully innocent. "We're the Sunset Hills Music Federation," he said. "We're practising for the Country Music Jamboree at the Coliseum on the twenty-seventh."

The officer stared at the audience. "All of you?" he said. "You're all rehearsing for this . . . this jamboree?"

"The Country Music Jamboree is for large amateur groups," said Ernie patiently, "and yes, Mr. Sanderson did say the hill was unstable. But it was too late to cancel the rehearsal, and some people here come from as far away as Laguna, so we decided to practise out here in the open. It's safer. Even if the motel goes, nobody will get hurt, huh?"

"Don't count on it," said the highway patrolman. He raised his voice. "Sorry, folks, but I've got to ask you all to leave just as quickly as you can. Don't panic, but there is some risk, so don't delay. Come on now. Move out, please. Never mind about the chairs. Just leave them and go."

The crowd began to stream out, quietly and in good order. As Pete started down the hill, he heard Ernie saying to the officer, "Well, okay, but give me a chance to pack my guitar, will you?"

Pete shook his head in amazement. He could only think, wait till Jupe hears about this!

8

New Leads

"I DON'T KNOW WHAT they were up to," said Pete, "but I'll bet my entire allowance for April that it had nothing to do with folk singing."

It was the next morning, and Pete sat on the floor of Headquarters. He scowled fiercely at nothing in particular.

"I won't take your bet," said Jupe. He had the entertainment section of the *Los Angeles Times* open on the desk in front of him. "There's a livestock show at the Coliseum on the twenty-seventh."

Bob sat on a stool near the curtain that separated the office in the trailer from Jupe's crime laboratory. He had been discouraged when he returned from Santa Monica the day before, for he had been able to learn nothing more about the blind man. Now, having heard Pete's story, his spirits were high. He held a world atlas on his lap, and was slowly turning the pages.

"The flag they used at that rehearsal or rally or whatever it was—it isn't the Mexican flag," he reported. "The flag of Mexico is red and white and green. And it isn't the Spanish flag, and it doesn't belong to any of the Central American countries."

215

"Maybe it isn't the flag of a country at all," said Jupe. "Maybe it's the banner of some organization."

But then Bob said "Aha!" loudly, and Jupe sat up straight.

Bob studied a page in the atlas for a moment, and then looked up. "Mesa d'Oro," he said. "It's a small South American country. There are two flags shown next to the map. One is green with a state seal in the centre and one is blue with a cluster of gold oak leaves. The green one is the official flag of the country; the blue one is the flag of something the atlas calls the Old Republic. There's a note that the blue flag is still used in some remote provinces and by some conservative groups on special holidays."

Bob looked down at the atlas again. "Mesa d'Oro has seaports on the Pacific," he told his friends. "It exports coffee and wool. Barley is grown in the uplands south of the capital, which is a port named Cabo de Razon. Population is three and a half million."

"That's it?" said Pete.

"An atlas doesn't give a lot of information," said Bob. "Just maps and population and stuff like that."

"Very curious!" said Jupiter. "A rally of some sort at which money is collected—possibly money for a small South American country. The leaders of the meeting are furtive; they lie to the highway patrolman when he appears. A huge photograph of the blind beggar is displayed, and the man who is leading the meeting is the same one who reacted with alarm—or at least with strong emotion—when

216

Mrs. Denicola told of a dream in which a blind man appeared and picked up a wallet.

"What were those people really doing last night? Did they have anything to do with the robbery or do we have a separate puzzle here? Certainly they didn't want the police to know the purpose of their gathering."

"They couldn't have been planning any crime," said Bob. "That would be ridiculous. Not with so many people, and not without any security. Pete just walked in and sat down and was accepted."

Jupe frowned and pulled at his lip—a sure sign that he was trying hard to find the answer to a question.

"Maybe the man whose picture I saw last night isn't the same man Bob saw outside the bank," said Pete. "Maybe it's a different blind man."

"That would be too much of a coincidence," said Jupe quickly. "There is the scar, and there is the fact that Mr. Sebastian must have dropped his wallet near Denicola's pier, and the fact that Ernie recognized the description of the blind man when Mrs. Denicola told about her dream. It must be the same man. But what does he have to do with a country called Mesa d'Oro? And does he have anything at all to do with a bank robbery in Santa Monica?"

"Maybe Ernie is a foreign agent and the blind man is his contact," Pete said. "If Ernie is really a spy, he wouldn't want the highway patrol to know, so he'd pretend to be something else—like a folk singer."

"You watch television too much," said Bob. "In real life, people don't act like that."

"I think that in real life people behave in ways that are even more fantastic," said Jupe. "But we don't know enough yet about Ernie—or anyone— to

217

understand what's going on in this case. Fortunately, Pete's adventure last night gives us some new leads to investigate. Mesa d'Oro, for one. We've got to keep digging until we find something that will clear Mr. Bonestall."

Bob said, "I'm due at my job at the library at ten. I'll look up Mesa d'Oro there and see what I can find out."

"Jupiter!" It was Aunt Mathilda calling from somewhere in the salvage yard. "Jupiter Jones, where are you?"

Pete grinned. "Aunt Mathilda sounds as if she really means it," he said. "She wants you—on the double!"

Bob opened a trapdoor in the floor of the trailer, and a moment later the boys had lowered themselves through it. Beneath the old mobile home was the end of a large corrugated iron pipe which was padded inside with pieces of discarded carpeting. This was Tunnel Two. It ran through heaps of neglected lumber and other junk to Jupe's outdoor workshop. It was only one of several hidden passageways that the boys had rigged up so that they could go in and out of Headquarters without being seen by Aunt Mathilda or Uncle Titus.

It took the Three Investigators only moments to crawl the length of Tunnel Two, push aside an iron grating that covered the exit from the pipe into the workshop, and emerge into the open.

"Jupiter Jones!" Aunt Mathilda was very close now.

Jupe hastily pulled the grating over the pipe.

"There you are!" said Aunt Mathilda. She had appeared at the entrance to the workshop. "Why didn't you answer when I called? Hans needs you. He has to make a delivery. You go along, too, Pete, as long as you're here. There's some furniture—you know those tables and benches that your Uncle Titus painted blue and red and green and yellow? What gets into that man sometimes I can't imagine. But a woman was in yesterday and bought the lot of them. She's opening a nursery school in Santa Monica, on Dalton Avenue. Thank heaven for nursery schools, or we'd have that furniture forever. Bob, where are you going?"

"My job," said Bob quickly. "I'm due at my job in the library in ten minutes."

"Then don't dilly-dally," ordered Aunt Mathilda.

She bustled away, and Jupe and Pete went to look for Hans, one of the two Bavarian brothers who worked in the salvage yard. In a very short time they had helped Hans load the nursery furniture on to a salvage-yard truck and were headed south, with Hans at the wheel.

The Children's World Day Nursery was on a side street near the ocean front in Santa Monica. When Hans pulled to the curb in front of the place, the boys saw that the Ocean Front Senior Citizens' Centre was just beyond. It was a one-storey brick building surrounded by lawns and benches. Four elderly men were playing shuffleboard in front. One of the men stood leaning on his stick, watching the other players. He looked weary and discouraged, and Jupe sighed when he saw him.

It was Walter Bonestell.

Pete pointed. "He doesn't look as if he's slept a lot, does he?"

Jupe shook his head.

219

"Is it my imagination," said Pete, "or are those other guys ignoring him?"

"Perhaps they are," said Jupe. "That's the trouble with being under suspicion. People don't really know how to behave with you."

"You know that man?" asked Hans, curious.

"He's a client," said Jupe. "I should go and talk with him, but I really have nothing to tell him. We are trying to help him."

"Then he will be all right," Hans declared.

Hans climbed out of the truck and marched up to the door of the nursery school. While he waited for someone to answer the bell, Pete looked ahead, beyond the senior citizens' centre, and suddenly gasped.

"What's the matter?" asked Jupe.

"That girl!" Pete pointed, then slid down in the cab of the truck so that he could not be seen from the outside.

Jupe saw a remarkably pretty young woman come striding along the sidewalk. Her long blonde hair bobbed with each step she took. She wore slacks and a huge, shapeless sweater, and a Saint Bernard dog trotted beside her with his mouth open and his tongue lolling out.

"Who is it?" said Jupiter. "Do you know her?"

"The girl at the meeting," said Pete. "You know, the one who got up and made that speech? Everybody cheered for her?"

"Hm!" Jupe sat up straighter, taking in every detail of the young woman's dress and her walk. "She looks very . . . very friendly," he said. "In fact, she's giving Mr. Bonestell a hug."

"What?" Pete straightened up and stared.

The blonde girl let go of the dog's leash. She stood with her arm around Walter Bonestell's shoulders and smiled warmly at him. Then she kissed Mr. Bonestell on the cheek.

Mr. Bonestell flushed and looked pleased.

"That's it!" crowed Pete. "There's the link between Mr. Bonestell and the bank robbery and that bunch of people at Denicola's pier and . . . and Mr. Sebastian's wallet and the blind man!"

"That girl is the link between all of those things?" said Jupe.

"Sure," Pete declared. "It's simple. The girl is a member of the gang, see, and she gets to know Mr. Bonestell and she pumps him about the bank—the routine there and the cleaning people and all. The blind man is the boss of the gang, and he acts as the lookout before the others rob the bank. The girl could be one of the robbers, couldn't she? She could be wearing a disguise when she went into the bank so Mr. Bonestell wouldn't recognize her. Or she could just be an informer."

"You mean informant," said Jupe absently. He was busily examining Pete's theory. "It's possible," he said. "But what about all the other people who attended that meeting last night?"

"Why they're . . . they're . . ." Pete stopped, at a loss. "They're innocent dupes?" he ventured. "The crooks are using them to . . . to . . ."

Again Pete fell silent.

"The crooks took up a collection last night because people who have just stolen a quarter of a million dollars from a bank need more money," suggested Jupe.

"Well, I know it sounds dumb," said Pete.

221

"Actually, it doesn't sound that dumb," said Jupe. "It is yet another remarkable coincidence that the girl who had such a prominent role in last night's performance seems to know Walter Bonestell rather well. When he is alone, we must ask Mr. Bonestell how much information he has given her about the bank."

The blonde girl was laughing now. Her dog had tangled his leash in a hibiscus bush, and she went to rescue him.

"You stay here and help Hans," said Jupe softly. "I'm going to follow that girl and see where she lives and who her friends are. Psst, get down! Here she comes."

Pete slid down below the dashboard so the girl couldn't see him. "Come on, boy!" Pete heard the girl say, and she walked past the truck, her heels clicking on the sidewalk.

Jupe waited for a moment, then slipped out of the truck and took off after the girl.

9

The Makeup Artist

JUPE LAGGED half a block behind the blonde girl, but when she reached the end of the street and turned to the right, he stepped along a bit faster. He reached the corner in time to see her go into the courtyard of an older apartment building partway down the block.

Jupe walked slowly down the street. The building the girl had entered was built around three sides of a swimming pool. A white-painted iron fence protected the fourth side of the pool from the street. Jupe did not see the girl, but an apartment door on the first floor of the building stood open. As Jupe hesitated outside the fence, the Saint Bernard came bounding out of the door.

"Brandy, you come back here!"

The girl dashed out and the dog retreated to the far side of the pool, where he sat down in a flower bed.

"Monster!" she cried. "Want to get me thrown out of here?"

Jupe quietly opened the gate in the fence and stepped into the courtyard. He stood gazing thoughtfully at the bank of mailboxes beside the gate.

"You looking for someone?" asked the girl.

"N–not exactly," said Jupe. "I was wondering

. . ." He paused as if he were afraid to ask a question.

"What?" said the girl.

"I was wondering if . . . if you'd like to subscribe to the *Santa Monica Evening Outlook*?"

"Sorry," said the girl. "I don't have time for a daily paper. Thanks anyway."

Jupe produced a small pad and a stub of pencil from his pocket. "How about the Sunday edition?" he said.

"Thanks, but no thanks," said the girl.

"Oh." Jupe looked downcast. "Hardly anyone wants to take a newspaper anymore," he said.

"Times are tough." The girl smiled at him. The dog, unwilling to be ignored, came out of the flower bed and sat down on her feet. She rubbed his ears. "Are you working your way through school?" she asked Jupiter. "Or will you win a ten-speed bike if you get a hundred subscriptions?"

"Neither," said Jupe. "I'm just trying to get a paper route and earn some money. Do you suppose there's anybody else here who might like the paper?"

"Nobody else is home right now," said the girl. "Not on a Thursday. Everyone works."

"Oh." Jupe let the corners of his mouth droop, and he sat down gingerly on the edge of one of the chairs that faced the pool. "Delivering papers is easy," he said sadly. "Selling them is the hard part. Would you . . . that is, could you . . . could you . . ."

"Could I what?" said the girl. "What's the matter? Are you okay?"

"Oh, yes. I'm just thirsty. Do you suppose you could let me have a glass of water?"

She laughed. "No problem. Just sit right there. I'll be back in a second."

She disappeared into the open apartment, and the big dog followed her. She was back in a few moments with water in a tall tumbler. As she came out she shut the door, closing the dog inside.

"I should always ignore him," she said. "He only gets out of hand when I try to make him behave."

Jupe thanked the girl and sipped the water. The girl sat down in a chair near him and leaned back to catch the sun on her face.

"You should do your selling at night when people are home," she said.

"Guess so," said Jupiter. He gazed at the girl as if he weren't too bright. "Still, you'd think a few people would be around. Like you. You're home."

"Not often," said the girl.

"Oh," said Jupe. "You work, too?"

"Sure. But not right now."

"Oh?" Jupe looked distressed. "Did you lose your job?"

"No. Not at all. I work in the motion-picture industry, and that's an on-again, off-again sort of thing. I do makeup, and when a picture is in production, I work. When it isn't, I don't."

Jupe nodded. "I have a friend whose dad works for the movies. He does special effects."

"What's his name?" said the girl. "Maybe I know him."

"Crenshaw," said Jupe.

She shook her head. "Doesn't ring a bell. Guess we haven't been on any of the same pictures. Those special effects people are really something. Sometimes I think I should forget about makeup and try to get into effects. On the other hand, I do okay with makeup, and I still have time for my courses."

"You're going to school?" said Jupe.

"Not exactly. I take lessons—acting lessons—with Vladimir Dubronski. In case . . . you know . . . I get a chance for a part."

Jupe nodded. He tried to look sleepy, but his brain was racing.

"I guess everybody wants to act," he said. "But makeup can be terrific. I saw a picture last week about this guy who stole an idol out of a temple, so he had a curse put on him.

"Oh," said the girl. "One of those. I suppose he turned into a turnip when the moon was full, or something."

Jupe laughed. "He turned into a snake, only he still looked like a man."

"Oh, yes," said the girl. "*The Invasion of the Cobra Men*, wasn't it? They made that picture for about thirty-seven cents, but it wasn't too bad. I know the guy who did the makeup for the snakeman. Arnold Heckaby. He's really into that sort of thing. One of these days he'll get a big budget picture and then he'll probably be up for an Academy Award."

"Did you ever do any of that special makeup?" Jupe asked. "I mean, making somebody look like a bat or a werewolf or anything like that?"

"I've made a few people look older than they really are," said the girl. "That takes more time than regular makeup, but it isn't really hard. I've never done a monster or a werewolf."

"Is it hard to do monsters?" said Jupe. "What about scars? Remember the story about the wax museum where the villain was all scarred?"

226

The girl shrugged. "It takes time," she said. "Given enough time, you can do almost anything. Except you can't make old people look young. You can age a young person, but once an actor gets really old, well, they're old. You can help a little bit, and of course lots of them get face lifts or have tucks taken in their chins, and they dye their hair and the cameraman shoots them with a soft focus, but eventually they're just too old to play young romantic leads anymore."

Jupiter's glass was almost empty. He'd asked for water so he'd have an excuse to sit around talking, and he now decided he'd learned enough. Finishing the water in a gulp, he set the glass down on the small table beside his chair.

"Thanks very much," he said. "That was good."

"Okay," she said. "Want some more?"

"No thanks. I'm going to tell Mr. Crenshaw I met you. Maybe you'll meet him sometime when you're working on a picture."

"Your friend's dad?" she said. "The one who does special effects? That would be nice."

"What should I say your name is?" Jupe asked.

"Graciela Montoya," said the girl, "but everyone calls me Gracie."

"Okay," said Jupe. "Thanks again for the water."

He went out through the gate and headed back to the nursery school, pleased with the results of his dumb-kid act. But when he rounded the corner on to Dalton Avenue, he stopped and groaned.

Hans and Pete and the truck were gone! Jupe would have to get back to Rocky Beach as best he could.

"Blast!" he said out loud. Then he set out for Wilshire, where he could get the bus. As he went his head buzzed with a new idea.

10

The Terrorists

JUPITER SAT BEHIND THE DESK in Headquarters and looked at his two friends. It was after lunch, and he had just finished relating his talk with Graciela Montoya.

"Just suppose," said Jupe, "that the blind beggar is a woman."

Bob thought about this for an instant, then shook his head. "No. I don't think so."

"But isn't it a possibility?" said Jupe. "She's a makeup artist and she seems to be very friendly with Mr. Bonestell. Pete, perhaps you're right. Perhaps Gracie Montoya *is* the link between the beggar and the robbers and the crew at Denicola's."

"She isn't the beggar," insisted Bob. "The blind man had whiskers. I was standing right behind him at the bus stop, looking down at his face. He hadn't shaved for a couple of days. Would a makeup artist bother with whiskers?"

"Hm!" said Jupe. He looked disappointed. "Still, the girl might have pumped Mr. Bonestell for information and then passed it along to the robbers—one of whom might have been the blind man. The scar—"

"The scar is a fake," said Bob.

"Oh?" Jupe grinned. "You found something at the library."

"I sure did," said Bob. He had been holding a Manila envelope on his lap. Now he took copies of several news magazines out of it.

"Mesa d'Oro is an interesting little country," he said. "Only fifteen thousand square miles and less than four million people, but it's had its share of trouble."

Bob opened one of the magazines to a place he had marked with a slip of paper. "Here's a recap of its history in *World Affairs*, from three years ago," he said. "As you'd suppose, the country was once a Spanish colony. Then in about 1815 the landowners threw out the Spanish governor and declared the country's independence. They elected a president and formed a legislature."

"That's nice," said Pete. "And what does that have to do with blind men and bank robbers?"

"Maybe nothing," said Bob. "It's background. Now, in 1872 there was a revolution. People got killed, and they're still getting killed today!"

Pete and Jupe both sat up straight.

"A revolution that started in 1872 is still going on?" cried Pete. "You've got to be kidding!"

"Well, yes and no," said Bob. "The revolution of 1872 was something like the French Revolution or the revolution in Russia in 1917. The landowners in Mesa d'Oro—the ones who had thrown out the Spanish governor—they'd become corrupt. They got rich on the labour of the poor people and didn't give anything in return. Most of the poor people were descended from the Indians who had owned the country in the first place, but the landowners didn't think they were important.

229

"Finally an Indian named Juan Corso began to get his own people organized. He went around the country giving speeches about rights for everyone. The landowners didn't like this at all, so they tossed Corso in jail."

"You said something about a revolution," reminded Jupe.

"Jailing Corso was the start of it," explained Bob. "Corso was very popular with the common people. They got mad and stormed the capital. They freed Corso from prison, and then hanged the president, a guy named Arturo Rodriguez from a tree. The president's son, Anastasio Rodriguez, fought back. There was a lot of bloodshed, and the government changed hands several times, but finally Corso was made president and Rodriguez fled to Mexico City.

"Now that should have been the end of that," continued Bob, "but it wasn't. Rodriguez sat in Mexico City and began acting like an exiled king. Meanwhile the landowners left in Mesa d'Oro weren't a bit happy because the labourers now had the vote and made the rich people pay heavy taxes."

"Must have been frustrating," said Pete.

"You bet it was," said Bob. "Anyhow, the landowners started talking about the good old days when Arturo Rodriguez was president, and how nice it would be to bring Rodriguez' son back. They called themselves Soldiers of the Republic. They used the blue flag with the golden oak leaves as their banner. That was the flag of the Old Republic—the government that existed under Rodriguez. The new government that began with

230

Juan Corso used a green flag with a seal in the middle."

Jupiter frowned. "All of this took place more than a hundred years ago," he pointed out. "What could it possibly have to do with our client? Don't tell me the landowners are still agitating for a return of the old president's son. He must be dead by now!"

"Well of course he is," said Bob, "but today his great-grandson, Felipe Rodriguez, lives in Mexico City. This Felipe is waiting for a chance to return to Mesa d'Oro and be the head of the state. He has spies who report to him on conditions in his homeland—which he's never seen!"

"Oh, come on!" cried Pete.

"I know it sounds fantastic," said Bob, "but it's all true. *World Affairs* says that the conflict in Mesa d'Oro is called a traditional cause. The side a citizen is on depends on his family. Descendents of the old landowners become Soldiers of the Republic. That isn't an outlaw party. It's recognized, and the members are called Republicans—not that they're much like our Republicans. On Sundays they have rallies and they make speeches about how great it used to be. They manage to elect a representative to the legislature every now and then.

"Now if that's all there was to it, nobody would care. But some people in Mesa d'Oro aren't satisfied just to be Soldiers of the Republic. There's an extremist group of Republicans that wants to throw out the present government by force. They call themselves the Freedom Brigade, and they *are* outlaws. They stir up riots and kidnap people and blow things up. And when the police get too close, they flee the country—and some of them come here!"

231

Pete gulped. "Do you mean to tell me that those people I was with last night are a bunch of terrorists?"

"Perhaps," said Bob. "Perhaps not. There are a lot of expatriates from Mesa d'Oro who live in the United States. Some of them support the Soldiers of the Republic—the legal, nonviolent party. They contribute money to help Rodriguez in Mexico City, for instance, and to try to elect Republicans in Mesa d'Oro. But some of them do support the outlaw Freedom Brigade."

"Oh, great!" exclaimed Pete.

"Okay. So much for ancient history," said Bob. "What's really interesting is that I saw a blind man outside the bank and he ran when the police were mentioned. Then that guy named Ernie got scared when old Mrs. Denicola mentioned a dream about the blind man and the wallet. And then last night Pete saw a photograph of a man with a scar and dark glasses. He was definitely a hero to the people at that rally or meeting or whatever it was."

Bob turned back the pages of one of the magazines he had brought from the library. He held up the magazine, and Jupe and Pete stared at a picture of a man with dark glasses and a scar. The man stood at a microphone, his arm upraised. He looked as if he were shouting.

"Pete, was this the photograph you saw?" said Bob.

"It's . . . it's not the same picture," said Pete, "but it's the same man. Yes. I'm sure it is!"

"And it's the man I saw outside the bank," said Bob. "And yet I couldn't possibly have seen this man. This is a picture of Luis Pascal Dominguez de

232

Altranto. At one time he was an aide to the Felipe Rodriguez who is in Mexico City right now. He was a terrorist. He masterminded a bombing in Mesa d'Oro that killed fourteen schoolchildren. He claimed that justice was on his side, and that the blood of the innocent children was on the heads of the government which takes away property from his countrymen."

"A fanatic," said Jupe. "A real fanatic. But why can't he be the same person you saw outside the bank?"

"Because Altranto is dead!" said Bob. "He's been dead for several years."

No one spoke for a moment or two. Then Pete sighed. "But if Altranto is dead . . ." He didn't finish the sentence.

"The beggar looked exactly like a dead man—even to the scar? And the blindness? Was Altranto blind?" asked Jupe.

"Yes. He was blinded in a fire he set himself in a warehouse in Mesa d'Oro. The handicap didn't stop him. In fact, it helped make him sort of a hero."

"So the beggar was disguised to look like Altranto," said Jupe. "All it took was makeup and a pair of dark glasses. I wonder if Gracie Montoya was the artist behind the disguise? But . . . but why *was* there a disguise? What was gained by it? There was no one—"

Jupe stopped in mid-sentence. The telephone on the desk was ringing. He glared at it, annoyed by the interruption. Then he picked it up.

"Hello," he said. "Oh. Oh, yes, Mr. Bonestell."

Jupe listened for a minute, then said, "Well, it may not mean a thing, but it could be disturbing. I can come over if you want me to. I'd like to talk to you about . . . about a new element that has been introduced into the case."

Jupe listened for another minute, then said, "Yes. It will take me about half an hour."

He put the receiver back in its cradle.

"Mr. Bonestell has been questioned again about the robbery," he said. "He's very upset. I doubt that the police are really as suspicious as he thinks, but I'll go see him and try to make him feel better. I'll also ask him about Gracie Montoya. We need to learn how well he knows her."

Jupe looked eagerly at Bob and Pete. "We also need to keep her under surveillance. I wonder if she's in close contact with the group at Denicola's—Ernie and his friends."

"Don't look at me," said Pete. "My mother is going to do something really desperate if I don't mow the lawn this afternoon. Our grass grew about six inches in all that rain we had last week. Anyway, that girl might recognize me."

"Bob?" said Jupe.

"I can watch the girl's house," Bob said. "They don't need me at the library this afternoon."

"Better watch out," warned Pete. "If these people think it's okay to go around bombing and killing . . . you don't want to mess with them."

11

Attack!

WHEN JUPITER RAPPED at Mr. Bonestell's door half an hour later, Shelby Tuckerman let him in. He was wearing a black turtleneck shirt and his wrap-around sunglasses.

"Ah, good!" said Shelby. "Our super-sleuth! Maybe you can think of something encouraging to say to Walter."

Jupe felt a twinge of anger, but he said nothing. He followed Shelby through the dustless and orderly living room to the kitchen. Walter Bonestell was there, sitting at the table near the window and stirring a cup of coffee. Jupe sat down across from him. Shelby offered Jupe some coffee, which Jupe politely refused. "I don't drink coffee," he said.

"Of course," said Tuckerman. "I forget. Kids don't, do they, in this country."

"We have some grape soda," said Mr. Bonestell.

"I don't need anything, thank you, Mr. Bonestell," said Jupe. "I had lunch just a little while ago."

"Aren't kids always supposed to be stuffing themselves on junk food?" said Shelby. "Don't tell me you're an exception. You don't look like one!"

Jupe gritted his teeth. He was overweight, and he was sensitive about it. But he wasn't about to show his annoyance to Shelby.

"I suppose you do diet . . . now and then," said Shelby.

Jupe held his tongue, and Shelby turned to the stove, where the kettle was beginning to sing. He made a cup of instant coffee for himself, then sat down between Mr. Bonestell and Jupe. There was a sugar bowl with a lid in the centre of the table. Shelby reached for the bowl and spooned a bit of sugar into his coffee.

"I hope you have some progress to report to Mr. Bonestell," he said.

"Not really," said Jupe. "We have a lead, but it may not pan out."

"And if it does?" said Shelby.

"Who knows? Perhaps we'll share it with the police."

"The right thing to do, of course," said Shelby. He drank his coffee down then, and got up to rinse his cup out at the sink. He went out and Jupe heard a car start in the driveway. Then Shelby drove past the kitchen window in a late-model sports car.

Mr. Bonestell sat brooding.

"When the police were here earlier, they weren't accusing, were they?" asked Jupe.

Mr. Bonestell shook his head. "Not really. But they made me tell what happened three times. Three times, right from the beginning!"

He looked up at Jupe. "Do you suppose they were waiting for me to make a mistake? I . . . I don't think I made any mistakes."

"If you told your story just as it happened, how could you make mistakes?" asked Jupe reasonably. "Mr. Bonestell, are you sure you're not getting upset about nothing? It was unfortunate that you were alone at the bank when the thieves came, but that's only an unhappy accident. I'm sure the police understand that. They know that the robbery would have taken place no matter who was there. At least the robbers weren't violent."

"No, they weren't," said Mr. Bonestell. "Actuallly, they were quiet and polite. At least the one who did all the talking was polite."

Jupe pricked up his ears. "One of them did all the talking?"

"Yes. The one who was gotten up to look like Rolf, the regular cleaning man."

"Don't you really mean that he did *most* of the talking?" asked Jupe. "He gave the orders, and the others didn't say anything important. Isn't that it?"

Mr. Bonestell shook his head. "No. He did *all* the talking. The others didn't say anything at all."

"You spent an entire night with three people, and two of them didn't talk at all?"

"That's right."

"Not one word?"

"Not one word," said Mr. Bonestell. "Now that I think of it, it does seem strange, but at the time it didn't strike me as odd. What was there to talk about? It was just a matter of waiting until morning, when the rest of the bank staff came in."

"Hm!" said Jupe. "Could one of the robbers have been a woman? Is that possible?"

"A woman?" Mr. Bonestell looked startled. "I suppose it's possible. They were all about the same

237

size—about five foot seven or so. They all had on baggy overalls and loose shirts. And gloves. They wore gloves. And they had so much stuff on their faces, you couldn't tell what they really looked like. One of the silent ones had those sunglasses that reflect everything, so you can never see the person's eyes behind them. That one also had a beard that I think was fake. The other one had a red wig and a big moustache, and big, bushy fake eyebrows that hung over his eyes."

"What about the man who did the talking?" said Jupe. "Did he have an accent? Was he young? Old? What could you tell about him?"

"His voice didn't sound like an older man's voice. I think he was young. In his twenties or thirties. With no accent."

Jupe said, "Hm!" again, and sat thinking for some time. Then he said, "Mr. Bonestell, do you know the Denicola Sport Fishing Company? They run a charter fishing boat out of the dock up the coast past Malibu."

"Yes, I know the Denicolas," said Mr. Bonestell. "I used to go fishing with my son before he was married. I remember the old woman there—old Mrs. Denicola. She was a handsome lady. And her daughter-in-law, Eileen. Irish. Pretty. Eileen's husband died young, and she got her own master's licence. Did you know that? She's the pilot when the boat goes out."

"There's a young man named Ernie who works for the Denicolas," said Jupe.

"Is that so? When my son and I went fishing, there was a young man named Tom or Hal or something like that. They probably change pretty often. It's the kind of job boys have when they're still in school."

"You haven't been to Denicola's recently?" said Jupe.

"No."

"So you don't know Ernie. What about the blind man?"

Mr. Bonestell looked blank. "A blind man?" he said. "What blind man?"

"You haven't seen anyone near the bank—or anywhere else—who is blind? A man with a scar on his face? He taps his way with a cane and wears dark glasses."

Mr. Bonestell shook his head.

"There's a pretty girl who talked with you this morning when you were playing shuffleboard," said Jupe. "What about her?"

"Gracie? Gracie Montoya? What about her? And how did you know that I talked with her this morning.?"

"We just happened to see you," said Jupe, "and we saw Miss Montoya."

Mr. Bonestell looked at Jupe in a defiant way. "What about it?" he demanded. "A pretty girl comes along and I talk to her. I may be old, but I'm not dead yet!"

"I didn't think you were, Mr. Bonestell, but we have to check everything out. Do you know her well?"

"I've talked to her quite a lot," said Mr. Bonestell. His tone was still defiant. "She walks her dog around the block all the time. I think she does some kind of work for the movies. She's a nice girl—always willing to stop and spend a few minutes."

"Does she know that you work at the bank?" Jupe asked.

"I'm not sure. I may have mentioned it. But she's never made a point of finding out anything, if that's what you're getting at. She's just friendly."

"I see," said Jupe. "And what about your other friends, Mr. Bonestell? Have you talked with them about your job?"

"I suppose I have. But I can't recall anybody being especially interested in what I do."

"What about Mr. Tuckerman?" said Jupe.

"Shelby? Shelby is interested only in Shelby," said Mr. Bonestell. "He's out of town most of the time, and when he's here he keeps himself to himself. He eats out usually, and when he's here in the house he's usually locked in his room. And I'm not kidding about that—I can show you the locks."

"That won't be necessary." Jupiter stood up. "Don't be discouraged, Mr. Bonestell. The police have to keep going over the story with you. They may not have any other leads, and perhaps they hope you will come up with some detail you forgot earlier."

Walter Bonestell did not answer. He did not look at all cheered up. Jupe left him sitting at the table, staring straight ahead.

It was four-thirty when Jupe reached The Jones Salvage Yard again. Instead of going in through the main gate, he stopped his bike at a front corner of the yard, outside the wooden fence. The fence had been colourfully decorated by the artists of Rocky Beach. This corner showed a sailing ship about to be overwhelmed by gigantic green waves. A fish reared up in the foreground to watch the ship. When Jupe put his hand on the painted eye of the fish and pushed, two boards in the fence swung up, making the opening that the boys called Green Gate One. It was one of the secret entrances that allowed them to move in and out of the salvage yard without attracting the attention of Aunt Mathilda and Uncle Titus.

Jupe opened the gate now and pushed his bike through into his outdoor workshop. Pete's bike was there, leaning against the printing press. Jupe smiled and let the boards in the fence drop closed.

And then he heard a small sound in that corner of the workshop. It was no more than a rustle of clothing and a drawn breath.

Jupe turned his head.

The blind beggar was there! His scarred face was turned towards Jupe, his head lifted slightly. There was no stubble on his cheeks now, and he wasn't carrying a cane. Jupe saw with a shiver that the scar pulled one corner of his mouth into a sinister sneer.

For a heartbeat Jupe did not move. The beggar was still. Then Jupe took a breath and the beggar moved, his head still lifted in an attitude of surprise, his mouth still twisted disdainfully. There was something in his hand. His fingers were closed tightly. He started to dodge past Jupe, and suddenly Jupe wanted to know—had to know—what he was holding. Flinging his bike to one side, Jupe threw himself at the man and caught at the closed fist with both hands.

The man shouted and pulled back, but Jupe held fast to the fist, prying at the fingers. They opened slightly and something fell to the ground.

The beggar jerked away. Then he attacked! He struck, and the blow landed high on Jupe's cheekbone. Lights flashed in Jupe's head. There was

241

a stab of pain under his eye. Waves of blue and red and yellow filled his vision, and he went limp.

For a bare instant he lost consciousness. Then he was aware of himself again, and of the beggar stepping over him. The boards in the fence swung open and banged shut, and Jupe was alone.

12

The Bug

JUPE SAT ON THE GROUND, feeling slightly dizzy. As
his vision cleared, his eyes fell on the thing the
beggar had dropped. It had bounced under the
workbench. Jupe saw a little plastic box with some
perforations in one side.

"How interesting," he said.

He said it aloud, and as if in response to the
remark, the iron grillwork to the side of the printing
press swung open. Pete put his head out of Tunnel
Two.

"What's the matter?" said Pete. "Did you yell?"

"We had a visitor," said Jupe. He got to his knees
and crawled to the workbench to retrieve the little
box. He held it up for inspection. "Unless I'm
mistaken, this is a listening device," he said. "It's a
tiny microphone, usually called a bug. I've seen
pictures of them. The blind beggar was here, and he
sure didn't act blind. I think he was trying to wire the
workshop for sound."

"The beggar?" Pete took the tiny device from Jupe
and peered at it. "W-why would he want to bug us?
And how did he find us?" Pete looked around as if
the scar-faced man might be standing right behind
him. "Creepy!" he said.

243

Jupe sat down in the chair near the workbench. He took the listening device from Pete and prised it open with a penknife. "It's really a miniature broadcasting unit," he said. "It picks up sounds and sends them a short distance—up to a quarter mile or so. Usually a bug broadcasts to a voice-activated tape recorder that's hidden somewhere nearby. With a bug and a recorder, the beggar could eavesdrop on the conversations taking place here in the workshop."

"Are you sure the bug isn't working right now?" Pete said. "It could be broadcasting every word you're saying!"

With the tip of his knife, Jupe removed several tiny components from the unit. Then he snapped the plastic box shut.

"There!" he said.

He sat thinking for almost a minute, then looked up at Pete. "How long ago did you enter the salvage yard?"

"Oh, maybe twenty minutes ago."

"Did you come in through Green Gate One?"

"Yep."

Jupe looked grim. "I think the beggar must have followed you in here."

"Not a chance!" cried Pete. "No way!"

Ignoring Pete's protest, Jupe went on. "Maybe he spotted you at that rally and followed you back to Rocky Beach. Or maybe he spotted the two of us at Denicola's yesterday, or maybe all three of us at Mr. Bonestell's the night before. Sometime in the last three days we crossed his path, and he followed us here. And just now I think he followed you inside. I wonder if he had a chance to plant another bug before I came in."

Again Pete looked around as if the blind man lurked at his elbow. Then he and Jupe began to search the workshop. There was no trace of a second bug, and no sign that anything had been disturbed. The barriers of junk that surrounded the workshop were just as usual.

Pete looked very troubled. "I came here from home," he said. "If he followed me here, you . . . you don't suppose he was watching my house, do you?"

"Not necessarily," said Jupe. "He could have been waiting here at the yard."

Jupe got nails and a hammer and was preparing to nail up the gate in the fence when Bob appeared. After Bob helped close the secret gate, the three boys withdrew through Tunnel Two to Headquarters. Jupe took his accustomed place behind the desk and prepared to listen to Bob's report on Gracie Montoya.

"It got interesting for a while," said Bob, "because somebody named Ernie showed up to see Gracie. He looked like the guy you told me about. He rang the doorbell and Gracie didn't invite him in. She came out of her apartment and stood by the swimming pool and they yelled at one another in Spanish."

"No kidding!" Pete looked amused.

Bob nodded. "Actually, she did most of the yelling. He sounded as if he was trying to explain something to her, and she wouldn't listen. Finally he got mad and he yelled, too. A lady who lived in the next building came out and stood on the sidewalk and listened, and then she threatened to call the police.

"Then the guy left, and Gracie Montoya went

back in and got her handbag. I saw her drive away a few minutes later. I waited for half an hour or so but she didn't come back, so I left."

"Hm!" said Jupe. "I wonder what that was all about. Now, let's see where we are."

Jupe leaned forward, intent. "We can place the beggar at the scene of the crime," he said. "And through the wallet, we can also connect him with Ernie and his friends up near the pier. Gracie Montoya is involved with that group and also with Mr. Bonestell, and it is most interesting that she is a makeup artist. Could she have been the one to disguise someone as the dead terrorist from Mesa d'Oro—Altranto? And could she have disguised herself as a man and taken part in the robbery? She's tall enough to be one of the thieves, according to Mr. Bonestell's description. And he told me this afternoon that only the thief who impersonated the cleaning man spoke during that robbery. The other two people never said a word."

"If one of them was Gracie Montoya, she wouldn't have said anything," Pete said. "Her voice would have given her away."

"So one of the other robbers may have been a woman," said Jupe, "or perhaps the other robbers didn't speak English and didn't want to reveal that fact. Perhaps they're from Mesa d'Oro."

"They could be the two guys who share the house with Ernie," said Pete. "I mean, I don't know where those guys come from, but they speak Spanish like natives. Maybe they don't know any English."

"And Ernie is fluent in both languages," said Jupe. Suddenly he was brisk. "I think it's time we learned more about Ernie and his friends. Bob,

246

you're the only one who isn't known to the people at Denicola's. You could simply hang around the pier. Someone is always hanging around watching whenever a person works on a boat. Ernie has already seen both me and Pete, so we can't do it."

"Sure," said Bob.

"Then I'll go to Gracie Montoya's and see what's to be seen there," said Jupe. "And Pete, can you stay here in Headquarters? The blind man made a move today. I have a feeling we'll see him again, and if we do, we may need to contact one another. You can be our liaison person."

"You mean I can mind the phone," said Pete. "Okay. Glad to do it. But if the blind man shows up here, you can bet I'll use the phone to call the cops."

"You do that!" said Jupe cheerfully. "Of course," he added, "I think we should all be careful. The beggar knows where we are, and he may know—or suspect—what we're doing. He ran earlier, but he may not always run. He could be a threat—anytime!"

13

The Warning

"THAT LOOKS FUN," said Bob Andrews.

Bob stood on the edge of the Denicola pier. It was Friday morning. The tide was out, and Bob looked down on the deck of the *Maria III*. Ernie was there, painting the outside of the wheelhouse.

Bob waited for a moment. Ernie did not respond to the remark. He did not even look up.

"We had our house painted last year," said Bob. "The painters let me help. I did the window boxes."

Ernie paused and looked up at Bob. He looked down at the brush in his hand. Then he stepped back away from the wheelhouse and held the brush out to Bob.

Bob jumped from the dock to the deck of the boat. He grinned, took the brush, and began to paint, being careful and neat. Ernie watched with amusement.

After a few minutes of silent work, Bob started talking.

"Gee, it must be really neat to work on a boat!" he said.

Ernie merely grunted.

"I went on a boat ride once," confided Bob. "My friend's uncle took us. It was terrific—until the waves got rough." Bob then made up a long gruesome story about being seasick. Ernie finally laughed.

"Yeah, it hits some people like that," said the young man. He spoke without a trace of accent. "Me, I never get seasick."

With a little prompting, Ernie told Bob about the worst storm he'd ever been in. Bob questioned him like an admiring little kid, and Ernie got more friendly. But before Bob could learn anything useful, two men about Ernie's age came strolling down the pier. They addressed Ernie in Spanish, and when he answered them he looked sideways at Bob. An instant later Ernie had climbed on to the dock, and he and his two friends walked away from the *Maria III*.

When they were out of earshot, the three men plunged into a discussion. Bob tried to watch them without seeming to. The men gestured towards the shore, and one pointed as if to indicate that something was approaching down the coast from the north. Ernie shrugged and one friend clenched his fists and waved his hands in the air. The other pointed to his wristwatch and made some extremely emphatic statement to Ernie.

Ernie turned away from his two friends at last. They wandered off the pier and back up along the beach to the shabby little house that stood with its face to the highway and its back to the sea. Bob concluded that they were Ernie's room-mates.

Ernie came back on to the boat and examined Bob's work with appreciation.

"Very good," he said warmly.

"You sure talk Spanish like a whiz!" Bob exclaimed. "Your friends, too."

"It's my second language," bragged Ernie. "My friends are from South America. They aren't so good with English, so we speak Spanish."

Bob saw old Mrs. Denicola come out of the house near the parking lot. She was carrying a tray with what looked like a Thermos jug and some cups. Halfway between the house and the little office where Eileen Denicola sat, the old lady looked out to the *Maria III*. She saw Ernie and Bob there, with Bob holding the paintbrush, and she paused for an instant. Though he was at least thirty metres away from the old woman, Bob saw that there was tension in her figure.

After a few seconds the old woman went on into the office. A moment later Eileen came out along the pier.

The younger woman wore a rough blue work shirt, open at the neck, with a blue and white bandanna knotted around her throat. She had on faded jeans and worn blue sneakers. She looked confident and also somewhat angry.

"You're the one who's supposed to be painting the wheelhouse," she said to Ernie. She did not raise her voice, but she sounded stern.

Ernie shrugged. "The kid wants to help. He likes painting."

"That's right, ma'am," said Bob. "I do. Really."

"Okay, but Ernie will do the rest," she said. "My mother-in-law wants to see you."

"Me?" said Bob.

"She's in there." Eileen gestured towards the office. "I don't know what it's about, but she sent me to get you. Give Ernie the brush and come along."

Bob surrendered the brush and followed Eileen Denicola towards the office. She turned back to tell Ernie to be ready to take the boat out right after lunch. "Don't be late," she warned. "We've got to go to Kelleher's and get gas. There will be forty-three people here at seven tomorrow morning and we won't have time then."

"Yes, Mrs. Denicola," said Ernie, and he began to paint faster.

Bob smiled. Obviously Eileen Denicola was used to being obeyed. She marched in front of him now with her red hair bouncing at every step. Old Mrs. Denicola came out of the office to meet them.

"We will go to the house," said the older woman. She gestured to Bob. "You, young man, you come with me."

Bob followed her to the house, wondering what was going on. She led him into a living room that had a stiff, rather foreign air, with great high-backed armchairs and a long, very ugly sofa.

"Sit down." Mrs. Denicola pointed to a chair that stood at right angles to the sofa. They both sat. The old woman folded her hands in the lap of her black dress. Then she looked at Bob with eyes that were so keen that Bob had to look away.

"I have seen you before," she said.

"I . . . I don't think so," said Bob.

"You would not know of it, but I have seen you," said Mrs. Denicola. "It was in a dream that I saw you, and then I saw you again out there." She waved towards the window. "I think you should not be here."

She seemed to expect some reply. Bob opened his mouth to speak, but his voice had deserted him.

What came out was something between a choke and a cough. He closed his mouth and took a deep breath, then cleared his throat.

"I was just . . . just helping with the painting," he said. "I was never here before, and . . ."

He stopped, suddenly feeling awkward and anxious. He did not want to offend this old woman, or to displease her, but he felt scared of the power he sensed in her. She reminded him of the oracles in the old myths—those wise women of ancient times who lived hidden away in caves, and who foretold the future and warned men when doom would come upon them.

It was stuffy in the little house, and yet Bob felt cold.

Mrs. Denicola bent towards him, her hands still folded against her black dress. Her face was an arrangement of crags and shadowy hollows. She looked gaunt and weary.

"You should not be here," she said again. "You came for some purpose, I think. Why did you come?"

"W-why?" whispered Bob. He was surprised to find himself whispering, yet he could not speak more loudly. "No reason. I was only . . . only killing time."

Then he looked away, sure that the old woman could see into his mind and know that he lied.

"You are in danger," she said. "You must go away. Go now and do not come back. If you stay, there will be a great trouble. A terrible thing will happen. In my dream you were in a place that twisted and shook. There was a loud noise and you were falling and the place was falling, too, and all around the earth was tearing apart."

252

Bob stared at her, frightened. He realized his hands were clenched into fists. He forced them to relax.

Eileen Denicola had told Jupiter that the old woman sometimes dreamed true dreams. And the old woman had told Jupe she had dreamed of a blind man who picked up a wallet from the ground. Now she had dreamed of the earth tearing apart and Bob falling. What did it mean?

An earthquake! She had dreamed of an earthquake! But what good did it do to tell Bob about it? He could not escape an earthquake by leaving the pier.

She sighed. "You think I am a crazy old woman," she said sadly. "Perhaps I should not tell you of my dream. You will go and bring other boys and they will laugh and call me an old witch—a crazy old Italian witch! But it is true that I saw you in this place that was breaking to pieces and I . . . I was there, too!"

The front door of the house opened and a gust of fresh air blew into the house. Eileen Denicola appeared in the hall and looked in on them. Her face was amused, but there was concern, too.

"What's going on?" she said. There was a note of forced heartiness in her voice. "Not another dream, I hope."

"And so? If there is?" said the old woman. She leaned forward and touched Bob's knee. "I sense this boy is a good, hard-working boy," she said. "I am telling him he should do well and go far—so long as he listens to the advice of those who wish him well."

She stood up. "I think I must hurry now," she told Eileen. "Our guest will come before the afternoon is half over, and there is much to do."

She went out without speaking to Bob again.

"Everything all right?" said Eileen Denicola.

"Yes," said Bob weakly. "Thank you."

He got up and went out past the younger woman in a rush. This place gave him the creeps. He couldn't wait to get away!

14

Ernie Makes a Deal

THE TWO YOUNG MEN who roomed with Ernie were coming back down the beach towards the pier. Ernie was still painting away at the wheelhouse. Everything was as it had been twenty minutes earlier, and yet it was all changed.

Danger! Mrs. Denicola had spoken of danger.

About a hundred metres down the highway there was a tiny shopping plaza. Bob saw a little market, a launderette, and a real-estate office. And he saw a telephone in front of the market. He went down to it and dialled the Headquarters of The Three Investigators.

Pete answered immediately. When he heard Bob on the telephone he said, "You okay?"

"Yes, I'm fine. I guess I am. But the old lady—old Mrs. Denicola—she told me she had a dream about me. You remember that her daughter-in-law said she dreamed true dreams? Well, in this dream she had about me, I was in danger. I was in a place where everything was twisting and falling. Like in an earthquake. She told me I shouldn't be here. Creepy, huh?"

There was silence for a second. Then Pete said, "Hey! Hey, Bob, if that old lady really does dream

255

true dreams, maybe you should get away from there. You want me to come and take over for you?"

"It was only a dream," said Bob. He said it more to convince himself than to persuade Pete.

"Well, listen, be careful, huh?" said Pete.

"I will," Bob promised. "I don't want to leave right now. There's something up. You know those two guys who are Ernie's room-mates? They're churning around the dock today, talking Spanish with Ernie. They're really excited about something."

A pickup truck was coming slowly down the highway. It turned in at Denicola's drive and stopped in the parking area. A tall, rangy man in khaki work clothes got out and started towards the pier.

"Stay by the phone," said Bob. "I'll keep in touch with you."

Bob hung up and stepped out of the phone booth. There were campers and vans and cars parked along the highway, and Bob kept these between himself and the pier as he walked back towards Denicola's.

The newcomer from the pickup truck had joined Ernie and his friends on the dock beside the *Maria III*. Bob paused and watched Ernie talk to the man. Ernie's expression was angry, and he gestured with great animation.

Bob edged around a parked van and stepped down from the shoulder of the road to the beach. The men did not notice as he crossed the sand, and in a few minutes he was under the pier. Ignoring his bicycle, which was padlocked to a piling, he headed down to the waterline.

When Bob reached the edge of the water, he stopped and listened. He could hear the voices of the four men, but he could not make out what they were

256

saying. They were still too far away, and the noise of the breaking surf was too near.

Bob frowned. Probably he could make no sense of the conversation even if he could hear it. They were probably speaking in Spanish.

But then there were footsteps on the pier. The men were coming closer. They walked, then stopped to talk for a moment, arguing about something, and then walked again. They came nearer, and nearer, and then they were directly over Bob's head and he was moving with them, looking up, listening, his feet noiseless on the sand.

"Okay, Strauss." That was Ernie speaking. He stopped walking, and so did the others. "I can understand that you don't want to move until you see some money, but we need to see the merchandise. It had better be good, too!"

"It's good," said a second voice. It had to be Strauss, since he spoke without an accent. His tone was brisk and businesslike. "But you guys don't look as if you're good for it. Why am I talking to you at all? I want to see Alejandro. He's the one who set up the deal."

"I speak for Alejandro," said Ernie. "If you insist, we can arrange for an advance."

"I insist," said Strauss.

"One quarter of the total," said Ernie. "The balance we hold ready, so you get it after we take delivery—if the things are as promised."

"One half in advance," said Strauss. His voice was flat now. He sounded almost indifferent. "The second half on delivery. But nothing moves without the advance—not a thing. I don't need you, you know. I have plenty of places I can peddle the stuff."

There was silence for a few moments, then Ernie said, "All right, one half in advance. But we get the merchandise before you see the other half. You go back to Pacific States and wait there. I'll call you when I have the money."

"Why don't I wait here?" said Strauss. "I don't like all this running around."

"Because it will take time and that lady who's my boss is sitting in her office right now getting very irritated because she thinks I'm loafing on the job. So you go back up the coast and wait for my call."

There was silence, and Bob assumed that the man turned towards the glass-enclosed office. No doubt Eileen Denicola was there, and no doubt she was watching.

"Yeah," said Strauss at last. "Okay. Maybe I shouldn't have come here in the first place. Okay. I'll wait for your call at Pacific States. But don't try to stall. Remember, you need me more than I need you."

Strauss walked away from Ernie and his friends, and Ernie said something in Spanish. It did not sound like a compliment, and the young men with Ernie murmured in angry agreement.

There were light footsteps on the dock then, and Bob heard a voice that was tight with annoyance.

"Who was that?" demanded Eileen Denicola.

"Somebody who belongs to some kind of fishing club," said Ernie. "He said he saw the *Maria III* from the highway. He wanted to know if she's available.

"The next time someone wants to know if the boat's available, you send them to me," said Eileen.

"Yes, Mrs. Denicola," said Ernie.

"Now go and get your lunch," Eileen ordered. "I want you back here at one o'clock sharp so we can go and get gas. And leave you pals at home, you hear me?"

"Yes, Mrs. Denicola," said Ernie meekly.

The young men moved off, and Eileen walked away. Bob waited in the shadows under the pier. When he saw Ernie and his friends strolling across the sand towards their ramshackle little house, Bob turned and went in the opposite direction. He wanted to find out where Pacific States was. It sounded like a town, but Bob had never heard of it before. He jogged back to the market and the telephone booth.

The telephone directory in the booth did not list a town of Pacific States, but under the P's Bob found a Pacific States Moving and Storage Company on West Albert Road in Oxnard. He called the number listed and asked to speak to Mr. Strauss.

"He isn't in right now," said the man who answered the telephone. "Can I have him return your call?"

"No," said Bob. "I'll call back."

He hung up. He was about to dial Headquarters again when he spied a familiar-looking man coming out of the market. As the man headed for his parked car, Bob stepped out of the telephone booth and casually walked in his direction.

"Hey, Bob!" said the man. "What you doin' here?"

"Hi, Mr. Soames!" It was a neighbour—a man who lived just across the street from Bob in Rocky Beach. "I was just . . . just checking out the fishing here," said Bob. "My dad and I might go fishing this weekend."

The man looked around. "You come on your bike?"

Bob shook his head. "I got a lift with a friend," he said, lying almost as expertly as Jupe could when the need arose. "Say, you wouldn't be headed north, would you?"

"Well, yeah," said Mr. Soames. "I'm going to Carpinteria to see my sister."

"I thought that's where you might be going. Could I ride with you as far as Oxnard?"

"Sure, but . . . but I won't be coming back today. How are you going to get home from Oxnard?"

"I'll catch the Greyhound," said Bob easily. "Gee, thanks, Mr. Soames. I sure appreciate this."

Bob slid into the passenger seat of Mr. Soames's little sedan, smiling to himself. Jupe couldn't have done it better. He was saved a long trip on the highway by bike, and perhaps, before the day was over, he would know what sort of merchandise Ernie and his friends had bargained for—and how much they planned to pay for it!

15

Trouble for Bob

JUPITER SAT on the curb across the street from Gracie Montoya's apartment. He felt frustrated and bored. He had rung Gracie's doorbell at nine that morning, and had tried once more to interest her in subscribing to the *Santa Monica Evening Outlook*. She had refused to take the paper, and this time she had not been inclined to stop and chat.

Jupe had retreated to the apartment house across the street and watched Gracie's apartment all morning. He watched her carry laundry into a room at the back of her building, and later return with piles of neatly folded clothes. She was now sitting beside the pool fixing her nails. Jupe wanted very much to talk to her again. He decided that he would pretend to be searching for a lost order book.

Jupe got up from the curb and crossed the street. But when he reached the gate of Gracie's house, he stopped. The girl had a telephone now, on a long cord, and she was talking with someone named Marilyn.

"The acting isn't any good," she said, "but I hear the effects are great. When they blow up the spaceship, you can feel the seats shake. I called, and the first show's at two. Want to have a sandwich before we go in?"

Jupe turned away. Grace Montoya was about to leave for a movie. Even if he could follow her, he decided he would learn little sitting in a theatre all afternoon.

Jupe wondered whether Bob was having a more rewarding time at the Denicola pier. He wondered, too, whether he and his friends were really doing anything to help Mr. Bonestell. Could Ernie and his friends be the bank robbers? And if they were, how could The Three Investigators prove it?

Suddenly Jupe remembered something he had seen in movies and on television shows. He got his bike and sped back to the salvage yard.

Pete was in Headquarters, leafing through a sports magazine and looking bored.

"Glad to see you," said Pete. "It's been dull here. But Bob called once."

"Oh?" said Jupe. "What did he say?"

"He thinks there's something up at Denicola's. Ernie's two room-mates are hanging around talking with Ernie. Bob says they're excited about something. And old Mrs. Denicola had a dream about Bob. She said he was in danger, and told him he shouldn't be there at the dock!"

Jupe felt a flicker of excitement. He wasn't sure he believed in Mrs. Denicola's dreams, but Ernie was another matter. "How long ago did Bob call?" he asked.

"Maybe half an hour, maybe a little longer. I said I'd go to Denicola's to take over for him, but he wanted to stay."

Jupe nodded. "Okay. Listen, I'm going up there. I'm going to try to photograph those three guys. If I make prints of the photos and touch them up with a felt pen—draw on moustaches and wigs—I can show them to Mr. Bonestell. He might recognize them."

Jupe ducked into the darkroom and brought out a camera equipped with a telephoto lens. "You stay with the phone," he ordered. "I'll call you after I've seen Bob."

Half an hour later Jupe was across the road from the Denicola pier. The *Maria III* was not there, and the little glass-enclosed office near the dock was empty. Ernie and Eileen were nowhere about.

Shrugging, Jupe wheeled his bicycle across the highway. He bumped down over the rocks to the beach and found Bob's bike locked to a piling under the pier. Jupe locked his own bike next to it, then looked up and down the beach. He saw surf fishermen, and children playing with a dog, but no Bob. Carrying his camera, he climbed back up to the Denicola parking lot. There was no one around. Then he spotted the station wagon in the carport of the grey-shingled house near the pier. Someone was home at the Denicolas'.

Jupe crossed over to the house. He did not have to ring the bell. The door opened and old Mrs. Denicola stood there. She looked at him piercingly.

"Mrs. Denicola, have you seen my friend?" said Jupiter.

"Your friend?"

"He was here this morning and you talked to him then," Jupe told her. "You had a dream about him."

"Ah!" said Mrs. Denicola. "So that boy—the small one with glasses—he is a friend of yours. I think somehow that I knew this."

She frowned at Jupiter in a severe manner, but Jupe guessed that she was not really angry.

"Have you seen my friend since this morning?" asked Jupe. "His bicycle is under the pier, but he isn't here. Could he have gone out in the boat? Would your daughter-in-law have taken him for a boat ride?"

Old Mrs. Denicola shook her head. "Ernie went with Eileen on the *Maria*," she said. "I saw them go. There is no one with them."

"I wonder where Bob could have gone," Jupe said, almost to himself.

"I do not know," said Mrs. Denicola. She stepped back and opened the door wide. "But I think something bad is going to happen. I dreamed it, and I am afraid. I think you must tell me about you and your friend. Please come in."

The old lady sounded like the voice of doom. For the first time Jupe wondered if Bob could be in danger.

Miles away in Oxnard, Bob approached the Pacific States Moving and Storage Company. It was on a barren lot on Albert Road. Bob saw a high chain-link fence, a windowless cement-block building, and a few grime-spattered white moving vans. The driveway that led away from the gate was rutted and pocked with puddles, and the gate was padlocked shut.

There was no one in sight. Bob started to circle the property. He saw weeds and broken crates and crumpled papers around the blank-walled building. At the back, parked vans prevented him from seeing the rear of the building, but he could hear voices from somewhere inside the yard.

Bob stood still and listened. The conversation continued, but Bob couldn't make out the words. He noticed that one of the vans was parked alongside the fence here. He looked left and right, then took a deep breath. Putting his toe into a link in the fence, he climbed to the top and scrambled on to the roof of the moving van.

Bob lay still for a second and caught his breath. He was not as athletic as Pete, but he had done it! He was safely inside the yard. He got to his hands and knees and crept forward.

"It ain't gonna dry in time," said a voice that was quite near now.

"Who cares?" said a second voice. "We can take it dry or not."

Another van was backed up close to the one Bob was on. He stood up. His sneakered feet made no sound as he stepped across the small space to the second van. He crouched again, and again crept forward. Then he was looking down into a clear area where two men with their backs to him were staring at a gleaming white truck. Bob immediately flattened himself on the van's roof and raised his head to watch.

"It's okay, Harry," said one of the men. It was Strauss. He stood with his hands on his hips and his head cocked to one side. "You do nice work."

The man named Harry made a wordless sound. He had a can of paint in one hand and a small brush in the other. The odour of paint was strong in the air. The truck that the men were admiring had freshly painted lettering on the side, replacing the name of the moving and storage company. The new lettering said: McCutcheon's Maritime Supplies.

Bob grinned to himself. The men had disguised one of the moving vans.

"A lot of trouble to go to," said Harry, gesturing with his brush.

"There's a lot at stake," said Strauss. "We can't take a chance. Anybody sees a moving van parked outside Denicola's, there might be questions."

Strauss turned away and vanished into the open doorway of the huge, windowless building. After a moment his companion followed him, and for a time Bob heard nothing except the sound of wood scraping on concrete. At last Strauss appeared again. He was wheeling a dolly that held three wooden crates. Strauss trundled them to the newly painted truck.

Harry came bumping out of the building with a second load of crates. Before he had gone two metres, however, he ran his dolly into a rut. One of his crates slid to the ground and broke open, spilling dozens of small boxes into the dirt.

"Hey, watch it!" yelled Strauss.

"Okay, okay!" said Harry. "Take it easy, huh?"

He knelt down and gathered up the smaller boxes, crammed them back into the broken crate, then hefted the crate on to the dolly again.

From his perch on top of the idle truck, Bob saw that one of the small boxes had split. Several objects had escaped from it, and they now lay on the ground. Bob held his breath and waited. Neither Strauss nor Harry noticed the fallen objects. They went on loading crates into the back of the refurbished truck, then returning to the building to bring out more crates.

The two worked for nearly half an hour. They loaded crates of all sizes and shapes. Some were made of wood and some of corrugated cardboard. Some were so heavy that it took both men to lift them. At last, the men closed the doors at the back of the truck and secured them with a padlock.

"We could've used some help on that one," said Harry. He mopped his forehead with his handkerchief.

"We don't need more witnesses," said Strauss.

The men moved off into the cement-block building, and Bob lay still, waiting. Five minutes went by, and then ten. Strauss did not appear again, and there was no sign of Harry. Bob judged that the two were not going to return to the loaded van.

Bob crawled to the front of the truck that had been his hiding place. He slid down to the top of the cab, then to the hood, and then to the ground. He went swiftly to the spray of small objects that had fallen from the broken box and knelt to pick one up.

It was heavy. Bob felt cold with fright when he saw what it was. A bullet!

Then he looked up, and his fright became utter terror. He tried to swallow, but his throat was dry. He was frozen—too paralysed even to tremble.

A dog was watching him! A Doberman! It stood at stiff attention not three metres away. Its black eyes were fixed on Bob, and its ears were erect. It made no sound. It watched, pinning Bob with its gaze.

"Hey!" said Bob. It was a whisper—a breathless, rattling little whisper. "Hey, fella! Hey there, boy!"

Bob stood up slowly, and took one step back from the dog.

The black lips lifted from white teeth, and a low, threatening growl sounded.

"Hey!" said Bob.

The growl was louder. The dog moved forward, then stopped.

Bob did not move again. The dog was a guard dog, and Bob knew it. It would hold Bob there all day if it had to. Bob was caught!

16

Hot Water for Jupe

THE DENICOLA HOUSE was warm with the smell of cheese and herbs and rich tomato sauce. But for once Jupe was unaware of the smells of good food. He sat in the living room across from old Mrs. Denicola, listening to her tell about her dream.

"In my dream I saw your friend in a room," said the old lady. "There was a terrible noise, and the walls twisted and came apart. I did not know the room where he was, and I did not know the boy. Then this morning I saw the boy painting for Ernesto, and I knew he was the boy from the dream and that he must leave here. The danger is here. I feel it very strongly. And the danger is not just for him. It is for me, too. So I tell him to go, and he must have listened. He is not here."

Jupe frowned. "Mrs. Denicola, do your dreams always come true?" he asked.

"No. Most of my dreams are like the dreams of everyone. They are nonsense. They are made of the pieces of old memories. But some dreams are different. Sometimes in dreams I meet strangers. Then, when I am awake, I meet these same people and I know that it was a true dream. I do not know everything, of course. In my dream I have only a glimpse of something. It is like a light that flashes—a beacon. If it is a bad dream you know to beware, for the beacon marks the place where there is danger."

"Are your dreams always about danger?" Jupe asked.

"Oh, no!" She smiled suddenly. "I dreamed of a young lady with red hair before my son Alfredo met Eileen. That was a good dream . . ."

Jupe saw that she was about to embark on family history, and hastily changed the subject. "The man you call Ernesto—is he a relative?"

"No that one!" She looked scornful. "He is what we call the beach bum, eh? He does not amount to much. But perhaps he has a good heart. Those two who live with him in the little house on the beach, they are from South America. Always Ernesto has one or two from South America. They live with him until they have jobs. They learn a little English. Then they move on. I think Ernesto's father was from South America, and once he needed such help, and now Ernesto gives help out of respect for his father. And so no one is completely without worth."

Mrs. Denicola frowned now. "And you?" she said to Jupe. "You did not really come to find a wallet, did you? And your friend who pretends to be a schoolboy idler—I think he was spying, was he not? Who does he spy on? On Ernesto? Something is happening that we do not know. Something that is hidden from Eileen and me."

"I think something *is* happening," said Jupiter. "But I don't know exactly what. Mrs. Denicola, you dreamed of a blind man who found a wallet. Have you seen that man since your dream? When you were awake?"

269

"No. I have not seen him."

"But my friend Bob has seen him, and so have I," said Jupe.

Jupe took a Three Investigators card out of his wallet, wrote a number on it, and gave it to her. "If you see the blind man, would you call this number?" he said. "If I'm not there, someone will take the message. And if anything unusual happens—perhaps something Ernie does or says—would you let us know? I'm worried about my friend."

"Yes," she said. "You are wise to worry."

"In fact," said Jupe, "I'd like to use your telephone, if I may. Maybe there's been some word from Bob."

Mrs. Denicola gestured towards the hall, and Jupe went to the telephone there. He dialled the number of Headquarters. Pete answered after half a ring.

"Hey, Bob called," said Pete. "Just after you left. He was somewhere in Oxnard. He said there's a new person in our puzzle—a guy named Strauss. He's going to see if he can find out what he's up to, and he'll check in later this afternoon."

"Good!" said Jupe. "He left his bike here, and I was afraid something had happened to him."

"No. He's okay. Where are you?"

"I'm with Mrs. Denicola. I'll be back later."

Jupe hung up. Mrs. Denicola had come to stand beside him. "So your friend is all right?" she said.

Jupe smiled. "Yes. He called from Oxnard. He had an . . . an errand to do there."

"Very good," she said. "So for now the mind is relieved and I go to get dinner for my guest, who comes soon. And you, you will be about your business, I think. But go carefully, eh?"

Jupe promised he would. He then headed up the

highway to the house where Ernie lived with the two young men from South America.

Jupe found a good place to sit on a bank of ice plant across the road. He held his camera and he waited. It was more than an hour before a dusty old truck rolled down the highway and deposited one of Ernie's room-mates beside the road.

Jupe aimed the camera. The shutter clicked and clicked again. Before Ernie's friend disappeared into the little house, Jupe had photographed him six times with the telephoto lens.

Jupe relaxed and prepared to wait some more. When the *Maria III* came into view, he smiled. The fishing boat ran past him and docked at the pier. Two figures left the boat. Ernie and Eileen. Sooner or later, thought Jupe, Ernie would return to the house across the road. In the meantime, Jupe would wait for the second room-mate.

The minutes ticked by, and Jupe watched the gulls dip and soar over the beach. When he looked to the left he could see Denicola's driveway. Now and then a car turned in there, and now and then one pulled out again. The Denicola house blocked Jupe's view of the office, but he guessed Eileen Denicola was inside it. Possibly Ernie was helping her.

Jupe looked away and surveyed the beach to the right. Surf fishermen were there, busy with their lines, and a man was slowly making his way along the beach with a metal detector. Surfers waited for waves far out in the water. Clouds were building up on the horizon, and the wind was colder. The day had started clear and beautiful, but it would end in rain.

Ernie's room-mate came out of the house across the road and started down towards the pier.

Jupe glanced at his watch. It was almost three now. Bob had told Pete that both of Ernie's room-mates were on hand this morning. Where was the third man now?

Jupe looked towards the Denicola house. Earlier he had seen a station wagon parked in the carport beside the house. Now he suddenly noticed that it was gone. When had it been moved? He had not seen anyone drive it away. He had been hypnotized—lulled by the wind and the gulls and the sound of the surf.

Jupe got up and started to walk down the highway. When he was opposite Denicola's driveway, Jupe saw that Eileen Denicola was not in the office near the pier. Ernie was there, sitting in Mrs. Denicola's chair with his feet up on her desk. He was smoking, leaning back and laughing easily. His room-mate sat cross-legged on the desk, and he seemed to be telling a story to Ernie. His face was animated and he talked steadily, his hands making motions in the air.

Where was Eileen Denicola? Was she in the house with her mother-in-law? What would she say if she loked out and saw Ernie and his friend lounging in her office, sitting on her desk? Jupe felt quite certain that she would be furious.

But then Jupe noticed that the house had a vacant air. The windows were closed and the drapes had been drawn. As Jupe wondered, a car pulled into the drive and stopped by the house. A white-haired woman got out, carrying a little package wrapped in pink paper. Jupe guessed that she must be Mrs. Denicola's dinner guest. He watched her ring the doorbell of the Denicola house. No one came, and after a minute she rang again. Still there was no answer. She walked across to the office.

272

Ernie had been watching her, and he got slowly to his feet. His friend still sat cross-legged on the desk.

Ernie and the woman exchanged a few words. Then she wrote something on a paper, folded it, and handed it to Ernie. When she returned to her car, her face was set in angry lines.

Ernie sat down after she drove away. He put his feet back on the desk, and flipped the note the woman had given him into the wastebasket.

Ernie's friend laughed.

Now Jupe was thoroughly alarmed. He turned away and walked up the highway until the Denicola house was between himself and the men in the office. Then he crossed the road to the house.

There was an unlocked window in the rear of the place, next to the kitchen door. When Jupe got the window open, he reached through and turned the lock on the inside of the door. He went into the kitchen and closed the door behind him, but did not lock it again. He might have to leave in a hurry.

The kitchen was warm, and the air was heavy with the smell of food. But the sauce for pasta was congealing in a kettle on the stove, and a roast was cooling in the oven while greens for salad grew warm in a colander. Old Mrs. Denicola must have left in a hurry.

Jupe moved silently into the dining room, where the table had been set for three. The room was gloomy with the drapes drawn, and so was the living room where he had sat with Mrs. Denicola only an hour or two earlier. In the living room there was now an unpleasant tang in the air that almost overcame the odour of food from the kitchen. Jupe saw that someone had dropped a cigarette on Mrs. Denicola's hearth, and had stepped on it to put it out.

Jupe went to the foot of the stairs and called softly, although he really did not expect to be answered.

"Mrs. Denicola! Are you there? It's me! Jupiter Jones!"

There was silence in the house. After a moment Jupe went up the stairs.

The blinds had not been drawn in the bedrooms, and the light streamed in. One room was filled with massive, dark wood furniture, including a bureau crowded with photographs. Across the hall was a room with white furniture and coloured prints on the walls. Jupe had just peeked into this room when a telephone rang loudly.

Jupe jumped. Then he saw that there was a telephone on the table next to the bed. He glanced out the window towards the office.

Ernie was staring at the telephone on Eileen's office desk. He looked doubtful.

The phone on the bedside table rang again.

Ernie picked up the telephone on the office desk. The telephone in the bedroom abruptly stopped ringing. Jupe smiled. This phone was an extension of the one in the office. Quickly, Jupe lifted the receiver and put it to his ear.

"Si," said Ernie.

The caller at the other end of the line plunged into a torrent of Spanish. Jupe held his breath and listened, concentrating, struggling to make out as much of the conversation as he could.

The caller identified himself as Alejandro. He said that he was leaving now to see Strauss. There was something said about money. Jupe heard the name

274

Denicola mentioned, and then his own name! Alejandro reminded Ernie that Jupiter Jones had spoken to old man Bonestell about the Denicolas and about the blind man. Alejandro cautioned Ernie to be careful. Ernie said that he would, and that he and Rafi had everything under control. Jupe gathered that Rafi was the room-mate in the office with Ernie. After a few more words, Ernie hung up.

Jupe put the telephone down and looked out. Ernie was in front of the office now, scanning the beach. He was frowning, and when his friend joined him he gestured up the beach towards his little house.

Rafi shrugged and started towards the place.

Ernie's eyes lighted on the Denicola house. He suddenly looked curious, and he started forward.

Jupe backed away from the window. Darn! he thought. Ernie must have noticed the click when Jupe picked up the telephone.

Jupe heard a step on the porch downstairs, and a key being put into a lock. Ernie was down there. In a second he would be inside. Jupe had no time to get down the stairs. He could be caught and . . .

And what?

A bathroom adjoined the bedroom. Jupe heard a tap in there dripping slightly.

The front door opened with a creak.

In three steps Jupe had crossed the room. He entered the bathroom and turned on the shower. Then he returned to the bedroom, hid his camera under the bed, and stood behind the door.

Ernie pounded up the stairs, lurched to the doorway of the bedroom, and stood there for an instant, staring into the bathroom. Steam was

275

coming from the shower now. It billowed out through the bathroom door.

Ernie strode through the bedroom into the bathroom, and yanked the shower curtain aside. As he did so, Jupe slipped out from behind the door, ran into the hall, and sped down the stairs. He could hear Ernie shouting as Jupe got the back door open, but he didn't pause. He raced out of the house.

But now where could he go! He was out in the open, and Ernie would spot him any second!

17

The Final Clue

JUPITER RACED across the Denicolas' yard towards the highway. He was too heavy to run fast for very long. He needed a place to hide from Ernie. But where?

Jupe saw that a camper was parked nearby on the shoulder of the road. The door in the back was open, and the man who owned the vehicle had turned away for a moment. He stood looking up at the cliffs across the road while wiping his hands on some paper towelling.

Jupe didn't hesitate. He got swiftly and noiselessly into the camper, curled up on the floor next to some buckets of clams, and pulled a stained tarpaulin over his head. An instant later the door of the camper slammed shut. Then the owner got into the cab and started the engine.

The camper pulled away from the shoulder of the road. It drifted south about a hundred metres, then made a U-turn and picked up speed as it headed north. Jupe pushed off the tarpaulin, sat up, and looked out the window. He saw Ernie as the camper passed Denicola's. The young man was looking up and down the highway. His fists were clenched, and on his face there was a look of total bewilderment.

Jupiter laughed out loud.

Halfway through the city of Oxnard, the camper stopped for a traffic signal for the first time since it had left Denicola's. Jupe was ready and waiting. The moment the camper stopped moving, he was out the rear door and heading for the curb.

Jupe walked briskly down the street, turned the corner, and hurried on his way. Ten minutes later he was in the Greyhound Bus Terminal. When the bus pulled out for Santa Monica, Jupe was aboard.

Jupe felt a certain jubilation as the bus sped south. There was now not the slightest doubt that the young men at Denicola's were spying on Mr. Bonestell. They knew of the conversation Jupe had had with him yesterday in which the blind man was mentioned.

But how could they know?

Jupe frowned. Mr. Bonestell must have talked with someone. Was it Gracie Montoya? Was she the connection? Jupe felt a surge of irritation. How foolish of Mr. Bonestell to talk!

The bus sped past the Denicola pier. There were no cars in the parking lot there, and the little office was empty.

Where was Ernie? Where were his friends? And where were the Denicola women? Ernie was up to some villainy, Jupe was certain of that. There was a conspiracy of some sort going on at the pier. Were Eileen Denicola and her mother-in-law victims of that conspiracy? Were they innocent bystanders who had been spirited away somewhere? Or were they part of the plot?

Suddenly Jupe was frightened. Was Mr. Bonestell safe? Eileen and old Mrs. Denicola had vanished. Would Mr. Bonestell be next?

Jupe was the first one out of the door when the bus stopped in Santa Monica. He had money in his pocket and there were cabs at the kerb. He took one to Dolphin Court.

It was four-forty when the taxi set Jupe down in front of Mr. Bonestell's house. Jupe rang the doorbell. He felt real relief when Mr. Bonestell came to answer the ring.

"I didn't even send for you!" exclaimed Mr. Bonestell. He looked hopeful, yet apprehensive. "I was wishing you'd call. Do you have any news?"

"I think so," said Jupe. He followed Mr. Bonestell to the kitchen and sat down at the table.

"Mr. Bonestell," he said, "who have you talked with since I left here yesterday?"

Mr. Bonestell looked startled. "Talked with? Why nobody. I haven't been out of the house."

"Then someone called," said Jupe, "or someone came to see you."

"No," said Mr. Bonestell. "Nobody called. I . . . I don't have lots of really close friends. Why do you ask?"

"Because it's important. Think, Mr. Bonestell. Yesterday afternoon we talked about the Denicolas, and about a blind beggar. Now you must have mentioned this conversation to someone, or how did a person named Alejandro know about it?"

Mr. Bonestell looked upset. "I didn't talk to anyone," he insisted. "There wasn't anyone here—nobody but Shelby, and I didn't say anything to him. I didn't! Nothing at all! Shelby isn't—well, he isn't easy to talk with. He acts as if what I have to say isn't very interesting, and I

279

guess maybe it isn't. Anyway, when he came in last night he went right upstairs and locked himself in his room."

"And you didn't talk to him then? Or this morning?"

"No. No more than to say hello. I'm sure of it!"

Jupe sighed. He pulled at his lower lip and gazed blankly at the sugar bowl. Then into his mind came the picture of Shelby Tuckerman—Shelby with his wrap-around sunglasses and his turtleneck shirt. "According to your system of justice," Shelby had said, "you're innocent until you're proven guilty."

"Odd that I didn't notice that," said Jupe out loud.

"What?" said Mr. Bonestell.

"Shelby doesn't care for your neighbours, does he?"

"I suppose not," said Mr. Bonestell. "He thinks they're common."

"Is he so uncommon?" said Jupe.

Mr. Bonestell shrugged, and Jupe continued to stare at the sugar bowl. "When did Shelby start taking sugar in his coffee?" Jupe suddenly said. "He didn't always do it, did he? The first night we were here he made a cup of coffee for himself, and he drank it black."

"Why . . . why yes, I suppose he did," said Mr. Bonestell. "He only started to use the sugar a day or two ago. He said it gave him a quick lift to have a spoonful of sugar."

Eyes gleaming, Jupe reached for the sugar bowl. He poked a finger deep into it and quickly lifted out a small, flat plastic box with perforations in one side.

Mr. Bonestell looked at the thing. "What is it?" he asked.

"A listening device, Mr. Bonestell," said Jupe. "A bug. You didn't have to talk to Shelby. Once that sugar bowl was put on the table, he was able to eavesdrop on everything that was said here."

Jupe went to the kitchen telephone. "Shelby works at Systems TX-4," he said. "Do you know their number offhand?"

Mr. Bonestell told him the number, and Jupe dialled. It was just 4:59 when his call went through. He asked to speak to Shelby Tuckerman, and was told that no one by that name worked at Systems TX-4.

"Mr. Tuckerman used to work there," said Jupe. "When did he leave?"

"I can't give you that information," said the operator. "If you call back Monday morning, perhaps someone in Personnel can help you."

Jupe thanked the operator and hung up.

"He doesn't work there?" said Mr. Bonestell. "I don't understand. He has to work there. He was in Fresno on a job for TX-4 just the other day."

"I doubt that very much," said Jupe. He went to the refrigerator and opened the freezer compartment. The frozen food that Shelby had put in several days ago was gone. It had been a huge cache of TV dinners and frozen pizzas. But nothing remained except for a single carton of ice cream back in the corner.

Jupiter closed the freezer. "That must be where it was the whole time," he said.

"What?" said Mr. Bonestell.

"Nothing," said Jupe. "That is, I'm not sure. And we may be too late. Mr. Bonestell, did you say that Shelby Tuckerman kept his door locked?"

"That's right. Shelby's a very private person."

"An understatement if ever there was one," said Jupiter. "Mr. Bonestell, I have to get into his room—and I have to do it right away!"

18

The Prisoners

JUPE AND MR. BONESTELL GOT an extension ladder from the garage and put it up on Shelby Tuckerman's window. The window was unlock:d and Jupe got in that way.

There was a recording system set up on the dresser. Jupe rewound the tape on the machine and played it back. He heard the conversation he had just had with Mr. Bonestell. He heard himself dial the telephone and talk with the operator at Systems TX-4. He heard the refrigerator door open and close, and he heard his remark that it might be too late.

Jupe smiled grimly and erased the tape. Then he set the machine to record again, and he turned away and began a quick investigation of Shelby's room.

It was a strangely barren place. No letters or postcards lay on the desk; no books rested on the bedside table. There were no pictures and no plants. There was not so much as a stray safety pin to show that anyone lived there.

Jupe looked into the closet and saw jackets and shirts and slacks. The pockets were empty. He opened the dresser drawers and saw underwear and socks and turtlenecks.

But then, in the bottom drawer, covered over with folded sweaters, he saw the knife.

It was a very sharp knife, in a fine leather sheath. It was not the kind of knife used for sharpening pencils or for cutting bits of fishing line. It was the kind of knife one might use for throwing.

Jupe left it where it was. He climbed out of the window, and told Mr. Bonestell what he'd found while they put the ladder away.

"I wonder if he wears the knife strapped to his ankle, the way he wears the gun," said Jupe.

Mr. Bonestell shook his head in a dazed way. "He says he needs the gun because he's out on the road so much, and you never know what might happen if you break down. But a knife? Why does he need a knife? He doesn't go camping or anything like that. He doesn't do anything interesting. Just watches TV and takes a lot of naps."

Jupe nodded. "He doesn't act very dashing, but he's a man with secrets. He bugged your kitchen. And he kept something very valuable in your freezer."

"What? All he had in there was his frozen food."

"I don't think those packages held food. I think they held money. It may have been the loot from the bank robbery."

"No," said Mr. Bonestell. "That's not it. Shelby's been keeping heaps of frozen food for a long time. It wasn't that he ate at home. It just seemed to make him feel secure to have food on hand. He knew I hardly ever used the freezer, so he kept it filled with his food."

"Hm!" said Jupe. He pulled at his lower lip and frowned. "If he didn't eat at home, what eventually happened to the things in the freezer? Did he ever take anything away?"

"Why, come to think of it, I . . . I don't know what happened to all the food. Once in a while he cooked. And he did bring in a lot, but . . . but it couldn't have been money from a robbery unless Shelby's been a bank robber for a long time. Somehow, I don't think Shelby is like that."

"Aha!" said Jupe. "Then it could be drugs. That would explain his connection with the crew at Denicola's. The *Maria III* might be used to rendezvous with another boat out at sea. Or perhaps to go to Baja California to get drugs.

"Or perhaps Shelby and Ernie are bringing in illegal immigrants and the blind man—"

Jupe pulled himself up short. "No," he said. "That wouldn't have anything to do with the freezer unless . . . well, we can't be sure. We don't have enough to go on. Not yet."

"Are we going to call the police?" said Mr. Bonestell.

"I don't think we can. How could we prove that Shelby didn't take his frozen food and give it to the poor? Or that the bug in the sugar bowl isn't a practical joke? Is Shelby involved with the bank robbery, or is he concerned with something else entirely? What about the Denicolas? Where are they? I have a strong feeling that Shelby knows."

For the first time, Mr. Bonestell looked determined and angry. "I want to help," he said. "What can I do?"

"A lot," said Jupe, and he told his plan to Mr. Bonestell. Bonestell agreed eagerly, and he and Jupe went to the house next door and asked to use the telephone. Mr. Bonestell explained to the woman who came to the door that his own telephone was out of order.

Jupiter called Pete at Headquarters, and Pete agreed to meet Jupe and Mr. Bonestell at the corner of Dolphin Court and Second Street.

"I should be there in twenty minutes," said Pete.

"In case we're not there," said Jupe, "go back to Headquarters and I'll call you when I can."

After Jupe finished talking with Pete, he and Mr. Bonestell went to Mr. Bonestell's backyard and rehearsed. Then they went into the kitchen and put on a brief performance for the benefit of the bug, which Jupe had replaced in the sugar bowl.

"Mr. Bonestell," said Jupe, being careful to speak clearly, "I know you must be getting impatient, but we may have news for you soon. Eileen Denicola may be about to give us the break we need. Pete was in to see Chief Reynolds in Rocky Beach just a little while ago, and Eileen Denicola called while he was there. Pete only got one end of the conversation, of course, but he gathered Mrs. Denicola was hysterical. Chief Reynolds kept trying to calm her down. Finally he said he'd be right there, and he got up and ran out of the office."

"But I don't even know Mrs. Denicola," said Mr. Bonestell carefully. "What could she have to do with the bank robbery?"

"There's some connection," said Jupe. "We're sure of that. Pete wants us to come to the Rocky Beach Police Station. He thinks Chief Reynolds will bring Mrs. Denicola there."

"I'll get my jacket," said Mr. Bonestell.

Jupe snapped off the overhead light in the kitchen, and he and Mr. Bonestell went out and got into Mr. Bonestell's little car. Mr. Bonestell backed out of the drive and went to the corner, where he parked in the shadows beneath a huge willow tree that overhung the sidewalk. They waited.

Soon Pete appeared on his bicycle. Mr. Bonestell flicked his headlights on and off to let him know they were there, and Pete stowed his bike under some shrubs that grew nearby. He climbed into the back seat of the car.

"What's up?" he said eagerly.

"Shelby has been bugging Mr. Bonestell's kitchen with a device in the sugar bowl," said Jupe. "He has a voice-activated tape recorder in his bedroom. Does that remind you of anyone?"

"The blind man!" cried Pete. "He tried to plant a bug in the salvage yard. Do you mean that Shelby . . .?"

"Possibly," said Jupe. "We'll see."

Jupe than told Pete of the message he and Mr. Bonestell had recorded. "The Denicolas have disappeared, and I'm really concerned about them," said Jupe. "I hope that after Shelby plays back that recording, he'll lead us to them."

It was very dark now. The rain that had been threatening half the afternoon had begun to fall. There was little traffic on Second Street, and none on Dolphin Court—not until well after six. Then Shelby's car turned the corner. Mr. Bonestell and the boys watched Shelby turn into Bonestell's drive and park. Shelby got out of the car. A moment later the lights went on in the back of the house, and then in the front rooms.

"He's looking for me," said Mr. Bonestell. "I'm always home at this time unless I'm working."

Soon there were lights upstairs, in the bedroom where Shelby lived.

"It won't be long now," said Mr. Bonestell. He fairly cackled with glee. Jupe realized then how much Mr. Bonestell disliked Shelby Tuckerman.

The lights continued to blaze all over Mr. Bonestell's house, but the front door opened and Shelby came out. He sprinted across the patch of lawn to the drive and got into his car. The engine roared and Shelby shot out into the street. A split second later he passed Mr. Bonestell's car and sped around the corner on to Second Street.

Mr. Bonestell already had his engine running. He followed Shelby up Second and then out across Ocean Avenue and down to the Coast Highway.

"He's going to Denicola's," Jupe decided.

Mr. Bonestell dropped back and let another car get between himself and Shelby, but he kept Shelby's car in view. They went steadily north in heavy rain. Shelby drove exactly at the speed limit. He slowed going through Malibu, then picked up the pace again.

"He has to be going to Denicola's," said Jupe. "I wonder if . . . if . . . Mr. Bonestell, do you know anyone named Alejandro?"

"No. Shelby's middle initial is A, but I doubt it stands for Alejandro. That's Spanish for Alexander, isn't it? Shelby isn't Spanish."

Mr. Bonestell slowed the car. They were approaching Denicola's. There was very little traffic, and they could see Shelby's car ahead of them, the tail-lights reflected in the rain-slick surface of the road. They could also dimly see a white truck backed up to the Denicola pier. But before Jupe could wonder about it, Shelby braked abruptly and turned right, away from the ocean. He roared up the driveway of the Oceanview Motel.

"The motel!" exclaimed Pete as Mr. Bonestell quickly pulled off on to the shoulder. "That could be where Mrs. Denicola is—her and the old lady!"

"I should have thought of it," said Jupe. "Okay. Now we know. Mr. Bonestell, will you wait here for us? If we're not back in fifteen minutes, get to a phone and call the police."

"You bet!" said Mr. Bonestell. "Be careful now."

Jupe and Pete got out and looked up. The motel was no more than a dark shape above the road. There was not a light anywhere. The boys went up the drive without speaking, their shoulders hunched against the driving rain. When they had reached the top and the pavement broadened into the parking area, Pete tugged at Jupe's sleeve.

"There's Shelby's car," he whispered. "I don't see Shelby anywhere."

"Probably inside the motel," said Jupe.

They stole forward into the pool area behind the motel. As soon as they had the motel building between themselves and the ocean, they had some shelter from the wind. The night was not so intensely black, either, for the slanting raindrops now reflected a hint of light.

Jupe pointed. One window in the motel showed a faint glow around the edges. A lamp was lit behind a heavy curtain.

The boys crept towards the window and leaned forward to listen.

And suddenly Jupe heard something behind him that was not just a part of the wind and the rain. Someone was behind him.

Jupe turned his head.

"Be still!" said Shelby Tuckerman. He was holding his gun. "Don't make a move."

Then Shelby shouted.

The door of the motel room opened. Light streamed out. In the doorway stood one of Ernie's room-mates—the one who had been missing all afternoon. He also had a gun.

"In there, you two!" ordered Shelby.

Jupe and Pete went into a room that was rank with cigarette smoke. Eileen Denicola sat there on a small straight chair, her wrists tied to its arms. She looked furious. Her mother-in-law was tied to an armchair near the bed.

Shelby came dripping into the room, and Ernie's room-mate shut the door.

"Hi!" said a very familiar voice.

There in the corner behind the door, also tied to a chair, was Bob Andrews!

19

The Nightmare Comes True!

"THAT CONVERSATION YOU HAD with Walter about the police," said Shelby Tuckerman. "It was a trick, wasn't it? You staged it."

"And you led us here," said Jupiter.

He and Pete were seated now. Ernie's room-mate, who was called Luis, had put away his gun and brought two more chairs from another motel room. He was tying Jupe and Pete to them with strips torn from sheets, while Shelby covered them with his pistol.

"Much good may it do you," said Shelby. "Where is Walter? Waiting for you down on the highway?"

Jupe didn't answer. Shelby smiled angrily. "We'll see that he doesn't wait too long," he said. "I wouldn't want him to get nervous."

Luis finished tying the boys. Shelby put away his gun, too, then he spoke to Luis in rapid Spanish. As he spoke there were two quick raps at the door, then two raps again. Ernie opened the door and came in. He stopped in surprise when he saw Pete and Jupe.

"What are these other kids doing here?" he demanded angrily of Shelby. "One was bad enough. Oh, never mind. You take care of them. I came to

291

get Luis. The boat is almost loaded. Strauss is pulling out now, and Rafi is finishing up."

Bob muttered to Jupe, who sat next to him, "Strauss is a guy who runs a moving company in Oxnard. I watched him load up a truck this afternoon. One of the crates broke open. There were bullets in it."

"Ammunition!" exclaimed Jupe. "And guns, I bet." He looked at Shelby Tuckerman. "I thought it might be drugs," he said. "I thought Ernie and his friends were using the *Maria III* in some sort of drug-smuggling operation."

"Over my dead body!" cried Eileen Denicola. "If you think Ernie ever took that boat six inches from the dock without me aboard, you're sadly mistaken!"

Ernie grinned. "We're going to take it now, Mrs. Denicola," he said, "and you won't be aboard."

"There will be guns aboard," said Jupe. "And that, of course, is why you robbed the bank. You needed the money for guns. What could be more natural for a bunch of revolutionaries? You'll ship the guns to Mesa d'Oro, where they'll be used to shoot innocent people."

Ernie drew himself up to his full height and looked righteous. "They'll be used in the battle for justice," he said.

"According to some published reports," said Jupe, "the battle for justice can include sniping at unarmed civilians."

"If you mean the Civil Guard of Mesa d'Oro, they represent the spoilers who have stolen our land," said Ernie. His cheeks burned with colour.

"Don't listen to him, Ernesto," said Shelby. "It doesn't matter what the boy thinks."

"You were the scar-faced beggar," said Jupe to Shelby. "You used the disguise to watch the bank without being recognized by Mr. Bonestell. You knew about the vault with the time lock, and you knew Mr. Bonestell would be alone in the bank after the cleaning people left. If only you hadn't been so greedy. You found Mr. Sebastian's wallet at Denicola's the day before the robbery. It was a beautiful wallet, and instead of turning it in or dropping it into a mailbox, you put it into your pocket and kept it. But you dropped it at the scene of the robbery, and it led us right back here to the dock."

"I . . . I was going to drop it in a mailbox," said Shelby quickly.

Luis looked from Ernie to Shelby, then back again. He said something in Spanish, and Ernie motioned to him to be quiet.

"So the blind man did pick up the wallet," said Ernie. His face was stern and accusing. "For a wallet, you endangered our cause? Is this true?"

"Certainly not!" snapped Shelby. "I said I was going to drop it in the mail. Let's not stand here and argue. That old man's down on the highway and—"

"Why didn't you give the wallet to me?" cried Ernie. "I would have called Mr. Sebastian and there would have been an end to it. There wouldn't have been anything to bring these kids down on us!"

"I tell you it doesn't matter!" insisted Shelby. "You'll be out of the country soon. I'll take care of the kids!"

"You're not leaving, Mr. Tuckerman?" said Jupe. "I can guess why. You're going to stay here and enjoy some of the loot from the robbery, aren't you? You aren't going to give it to the Republicans."

Ernie stared at Shelby, and Shelby's colour rose, then drained away again until his face was a ghastly white. It was clear that Jupe had hit on the truth.

"What is this?" said Ernie. There was a note of menace in his voice.

"The money has gone to pay for the guns!" snapped Shelby. "You know that, Ernesto!"

"I know only about two hundred thousand dollars," said Ernie. "This afternoon you gave Strauss half. And tonight I gave him the other half. But what about the rest of the bank money? You said you sent it to Rodriguez, but your face says you didn't! Don't worry about a thing, you said. Always you were such an organizer. You took care of the wigs and the funny clothes and the getaway car and the money. And we trusted you. You'd been the courier for such a long time. You carried the money we collected for Rodriguez, and you said it didn't mean anything to you. You said it was like carrying so many cabbages or pieces of paper. It was only a shipment to you. Did some of that money stick to your hands, too?"

"How dare you!" cried Shelby. "You'll answer for that!"

"No. You're the one who's going to answer," said Ernie. "You're coming with us tonight, and you'll speak to Rodriguez' people in Mexico City. And maybe you'll come all the way—to Mesa d'Oro, and—"

"You're being ridiculous!" cried Shelby. "I can't leave tonight! I have important work to do here. My mission isn't finished!"

"There is at least fifty thousand dollars in Mr. Bonestell's house," said Jupiter.

"You lie!" shouted Shelby. He turned suddenly on old Mrs. Denicola. "You old crone!" he shouted. "You dreamed about that, too, didn't you? And you told that kid and . . ."

"Mrs. Denicola told me nothing," said Jupiter. "However, I can tell your friend Ernesto where the money is. It's in the freezer of Mr. Bonestell's refrigerator, hidden in an ice-cream carton."

Shelby took two quick steps across the room and slapped Jupe hard.

Ernie shook his head. "That was very foolish, my friend," he said. "Now you must come, and we won't talk any more about it, eh?"

Shelby's hand went to his coat. A second later there was a gleam of dark steel, and Shelby's gun was in his hand.

"So it's like that, eh?" said Ernie.

Luis had been watching quietly, unnoticed and forgotten. He moved now. So quickly that Shelby could not react, Luis stepped behind him. His hands went to Shelby's neck. Shelby cried out once, dropped his gun, and crumpled to the floor.

Ernie stepped forward, picked up the gun, and pointed it at Shelby.

Shelby groaned and sat up, and Luis yanked him to his feet. A moment later the men were gone. They were out and down the hill, and the rain was drumming on the roof and Eileen Denicola was struggling with her bonds.

"I stalled them as long as I could," said Jupe. "I hope Mr Bonestell got away in time, that he'll get the police and they'll be nabbed before they can leave the pier."

"I think it will not be that way," said old Mrs.

Denicola. "I think there is something that has yet to happen before the police can come—before we can leave this room."

"What?" said Eileen. Then she caught her breath. There was a new sound—a sound that came not from the storm, but from the earth itself. It was a groaning sound. Somewhere close by a window shattered.

"Holy Saint Patrick!" gasped Eileen Denicola.

"My dream!" whispered the old lady. "The danger! The room that twists around the boy and me!" She closed her eyes and began to pray rapidly in Italian.

Timbers groaned again, and more glass smashed. But it wasn't an earthquake, as Bob had thought. Inch by inch the sodden, rain-soaked hillside was sliding out from under the motel!

20

A Fiery End

THE ROOM LURCHED!

Lamps smashed to the floor, and there were showers of sparks as the wiring began to tear apart.

"Don't let it burn!" prayed Eileen Denicola. "Dear heaven, please don't let it burn!"

More sparks flew, blue-white and dying as they fell. Then there was darkness—a darkness filled with the shrieking of timbers and the screech of nails being pulled out of wood.

There was another lurch, and old Mrs. Denicola cried out.

"Help!" yelled Pete. "Hey, somebody! Help!"

No one shouted back. No help came.

"This whole hillside is going to go any minute!" said Eileen Denicola.

She had no sooner spoken than the motel slid another couple of metres, sickeningly, sending chairs tumbling in the dark. Pete crashed into the bed and Jupe's chair went over on its side.

"Mrs. Denicola?" called Jupe. "Are you all right?"

"If it's me you speak to, I have been better," said the old lady. "Eileen, where are you?"

"On the floor," said Eileen.

"The police have got to come!" said Jupe. "Mr. Bonestell must have reached them by now. Bob, are you okay? Pete?"

"Okay," gasped Bob.

"I'm here," said Pete.

They waited, listening again. Jupe heard water running—a sound nearer than the rain that drummed on the roof. He lay on his side, his arms aching where they were tied to the chair. He felt wetness and smelled a muddy, chemical sort of smell. He puzzled about it for a moment, then closed his eyes in terror and despair.

The swimming pool was beginning to break up! It was the water from the pool that was running down through the room. If the pool really went, tons of water—thousands and thousands of gallons of water—would come sweeping down on them.

"Hey, where's all the water coming from?" Pete demanded in the darkness.

Eileen Denicola had realized the truth too. She began to shout for help.

Suddenly there was an answering shout from the treacherous, slippery hill outside.

"Over here!" yelled someone. "They're over here!"

Someone tried to open the door, but it was jammed.

There was another horrid lurch, and the window that faced the pool shattered and fell into the room. Then there was some light. Two men were on the hillside with torches. There was more shouting, and more water pouring through the room.

"Mrs. Denicola!" Jupe yelled. "Get Mrs. Denicola!"

A highway patrolman came through the window, followed by a fireman. When the fireman saw the boys and the women tied to chairs, he said, "What the . . ."

That was all that was said. The two men had old Mrs. Denicola out in a twinkling, still bound to her chair and praying loudly as she went. More men arrived and Eileen was carried out, and then the boys. In seconds they were free of their bonds and stumbling quickly down the hill, falling and being picked up and helped along, and then falling again.

On the highway, traffic was stopped. The night throbbed with the sound of engines, and searchlights swept the hillside. There were flares and barriers. The rescuers hustled the boys and the Denicolas across the road to safety.

"I told them you were up there!" It was Mr. Bonestell. He had fought his way past the barriers, and he almost danced as he grabbed Jupe's hand and shook it. "I told them you were up there! You're safe! Thank God!"

"The boat!" cried old Mrs. Denicola. She pointed.

The Denicola house was dark, and so was the office. There was no sign of the white truck at the end of the pier. But a hundred metres or so beyond the pier were the running lights of the *Maria III*.

"Those . . . those pirates!" yelled Eileen Denicola. She glared after the *Maria III*. "If they think they're going to get away . . .!"

She started towards the pier.

"Come on!" yelled Pete. He grabbed Bob's arm and started after her.

"Mr. Bonestell, tell the police to get the Coast Guard," said Jupe. "The men on that boat are gunrunners!"

"I will tell them all about it," announced old Mrs. Denicola. Jupe nodded, and ran after the others.

Eileen dodged into the office and snatched a key that was hidden away in a desk drawer. She ordered Pete to get a pair of oars from the locker behind the office.

There was a shout from the highway, and a roar of engines as the firemen backed their trucks away. The hill slid at last, bringing the motel crashing and splintering down with it. The wreckage covered half the road. The swimming pool collapsed completely, and a muddy flood rushed down the hill and across the highway.

Eileen and the boys looked at the wreckage for just a moment. Then she turned and ran out on to the rain-swept dock. The boys went after her.

"We'll take Sebastian's speedboat," called Eileen. "She'll overtake the *Maria* easily!"

They got into the rowboat that was waiting there. Pete began to row hard towards the buoy where the speedboat was moored.

"I can't see the *Maria*'s lights anymore," said Eileen Denicola.

"She's heading down the coast," Jupe told her.

"That Ernie is one rotten pilot," said Eileen. "He'll run her on the rocks."

They reached the speedboat and scrambled to uncover the cockpit. Mrs. Denicola got into the boat and the boys tumbled in after her, and Jupe fastened the rowboat to the buoy. The engine choked and ground and then took hold. Then they were skipping and bounding over the water in the rain-dark night. The prow of the speedboat slapped the waves with a report that was a loud as gunfire. Eileen Denicola gripped the wheel with both hands, and the boys hung on to the sides and braced themselves.

The lights onshore were distant and misty when Bob spotted lights ahead of them.

"There she is!" he cried.

"Right!" Eileen Denicola gunned the speedboat to a still wilder rate.

There was a glare of light which blinded them for an instant. They heard a helicopter clatter overhead. Then there was darkness again as the searchlight from the helicopter swept away across the black water.

"The Coast Guard!" said Mrs. Denicola.

The lights on the *Maria III* were doused, and the fishing boat became just a black shape in the night. But the speedboat was close now, and Eileen and the boys could see the wake the fishing boat threw up.

"Blast!" shouted Eileen. "She's heading for the open sea! Those creeps! They'll get away!"

She yanked at the wheel. The speedboat swerved. The engine strained and the small boat flashed through the wake of the *Maria*. Then the hull of the fishing boat was beside the speedboat and someone fired a shot from the deck of the *Maria*.

"Cowards!" yelled Mrs. Denicola.

The speedboat spurted ahead of the larger craft and streaked across the Maria's bow.

The fishing boat veered and lost speed.

Now the searchlight from the *Maria III* stabbed at the speedboat. There was another shot from the *Maria*. It missed and plunked harmlessly into the water. And then the helicopter was there again, and its powerful blue-white beam found the *Maria III*.

"They've got her now!" said Jupe as the helicopter held the *Maria* in a circle of light.

Jupe looked towards shore. The lights there were much closer now.

"Darn!" cried Eileen Denicola. "Where *is* that coast-guard cutter?"

The *Maria* had picked up speed again. She turned and swerved for a few moments, as if she could shake off the hovering helicopter. Then she set her prow towards the open sea again and raced for freedom.

Eileen Denicola laughed roughly and sent the speedboat careering after the fishing boat. Once more the speedboat raced in front of the *Maria*, and once more the man at the helm reacted, swerving to avoid a collision.

Jupe saw foaming surf on his left, and he heard breakers rumble and surge.

"Watch out!" yelled Pete.

Mrs. Denicola pulled hard at the wheel and the small boat stood on its side and almost skidded on the waves. Then they were out in the blackness again, free and safe.

But the *Maria III* struck the rocky seabed with a scraping, grinding crash that tore half her bottom out.

The fishing boat was lifted partway out of the water, and she tilted over on one side. The men on her deck shouted and scrambled. The speedboat passengers saw a flick of orange-red flame.

"She's burning," said Eileen Denicola.

The shouting and the rage were gone. The speedboat drifted in neutral, bobbing on the waves, and Eileen Denicola cried. Tears ran down her cheeks and caught the light from the stricken fishing boat. "A fuel line must have ruptured," she said.

A man dived from the deck of the *Maria*, then a second man, and then two more.

"Get the boat hook," ordered Mrs. Denicola. "Keep it handy. If anyone tries to climb in here, give them a swat."

"Yes, ma'am," said Pete.

A swimmer came splashing through the water. "There are life jackets under the seats," said Mrs. Denicola.

Jupe tossed a life jacket to each shipwrecked man as he approached the speedboat. Ernie tried to swim in close, and Pete brandished the boat hook. All four men got the message and kept their distance.

Bob found a length of rope which the men in the water could hold. They drifted, bobbing in the waves and watching the *Maria*.

The fishing boat blazed with a fierce fire that lit the night. Then there was an explosion. Part of the hull blew out, and the boat slid off the rocks and sank like a stone.

When the coast-guard ship arrived, the speedboat was still there. Four young men clutching at life jackets floated nearby.

There was nothing left of the *Maria III* and its deadly cargo but some bits of wreckage bobbing on the waves.

21

Mr. Sebastian Gets Curious

A WEEK AFTER THE SINKING of the *Maria III*, the Three Investigators rode north again through Malibu, and turned off the highway on to Cypress Canyon Drive. Hector Sebastian was waiting for them outside the old restaurant called Charlie's Place. Inside, in the huge room that looked out towards the ocean, the smiling Vietnamese named Don was setting out a feast on the glass-topped table.

"All-American favourites for all-American champs!" announced Don. "Mr. Goober peanut-butter-marshmallow-fluff sandwich. Super-Juicy frankfurters for taste of yesterday with all-meat goodness. Burger on Sunshine Bran bun and Picky Pickle Taste-Treat relish."

Don grinned broadly and backed out of the room, bowing as he went.

Mr. Sebastian sighed. "I think if Don were turned loose in a market that had no advertised brands, he would be completely paralysed. He wouldn't be able to buy a thing."

"Everything looks very good," said Bob politely.

Mr. Sebastian scowled. "Do you mean that you could eat a peanut butter and marshmallow fluff sandwich?" he demanded.

"Well," said Bob, "I'm not sure about the sandwich, but I like frankfurters."

"And hamburgers," said Pete. "And we get Picky Pickle relish all the time at home."

"Then help yourselves," said Mr. Sebastian.

The frankfurters and hamburgers quickly disappeared, but the plate with the peanut butter and marshmallow fluff sandwiches was left untouched. Pete looked at them in a doubtful way.

"Maybe we should eat some of those," he said. "Don seems so . . . so proud of them."

"Sooner or later, Don has to face reality," said Mr. Sebastian. "It won't hurt him to know that Americans aren't nourished entirely by peanut butter, carbonated drinks, and Hostess Twinkies.

"Now about the scar-faced man and the wallet—I'm curious. I've talked with Mrs. Denicola several times, but she has a temper to match that red hair. When she thinks about Ernie Villalobos and his friends, she gets too mad to talk. She splutters. I think she feels personally deprived."

"Because the fishing boat sank?" asked Pete.

"No. Because the police won't let her get her hands on Ernie and do something drastic to him."

Jupe chuckled. "She's a strong-minded lady. She doesn't like being duped."

"Who does?" said Mr. Sebastian. "However, since she does have this tendency to choke up with rage, and since she's very busy arguing with the insurance agent for the *Maria III* and negotiating for the purchase of the *Maria IV*, I thought you boys might fill me in on the case. After being an investigator for so many years, I have an itch to know more than the newspapers tell."

305

"Would you like to read my notes on the case?" said Bob. He picked up a Manila envelope that had been under his chair and took a file folder out of it.

"Mr. Hitchcock used to review our cases with us," said Pete.

Mr. Sebastian bowed. "I'm honoured," he said, and began to read Bob's notes on the mysterious beggar and the patriots of Mesa d'Oro.

For a while there was no sound in the room except the hum of traffic on the Coast Highway. Mr. Sebastian was completely absorbed in the notes. When he finished reading, he looked away, out at the trees and at the ocean beyond.

"There are times," he said, "when we must be grateful for the small vices of men. If Shelby Tuckerman hadn't been a petty, greedy man, he wouldn't have kept my wallet and you wouldn't have stumbled on the gun-running plot. How many people would have died if that shipment had gone through? We'll never know."

Jupe nodded. "People like Ernie will probably go right on bombing and sniping in Mesa d'Oro, but at least we did stop one shipment of guns."

"I assume that Mr. Bonestell isn't under suspicion anymore," said Mr. Sebastian. "He wasn't mentioned in the newspaper stories."

"He never really was a suspect," said Jupe, "and Ernie and his two friends have cleared him of any suspicion. They're really angry at Shelby, so they're talking. They feel that Shelby is a cheat, that he was just playing at being a spy and courier. There were lots of groups like Ernie's contributing to the cause of the Republicans of Mesa d'Oro. Shelby would collect the money from the leaders, bring it home to

306

Mr. Bonestell's, in frozen-food packages, and hide it in the freezer. Then, once a month or so, he flew to Mexico City to turn it over to Rodriguez' people there. Ernie and his pals think Shelby was siphoning some of the funds into his own bank account—and that certainly seems more than likely."

"Shelby was Alejandro, wasn't he?" said Mr. Sebastian.

"Alejandro is his middle name," said Jupe. "His mother was from Mesa d'Oro. She was a terrorist who had to flee the country, and she married an American named Tuckerman. Shelby is named after his father, and after Alejandro, his mother's father.

"Although Shelby is an American, his mother raised him to believe that he is an aristocrat of Mesa d'Oro, and that the cause there is all-important. Shelby's mother was very active. She spoke at fund-raising events and made a lot of money for Mesa d'Oro. After she died a few years ago, Shelby tried to take over and do the same thing. He didn't have the magic, however. He couldn't persuade people to give till it hurt, so he became a courier instead."

"How did you know he had kept back some of the robbery loot?" asked Mr. Sebastian.

"I didn't, but it seemed a reasonable guess. I had to say *something* to delay Ernie and Shelby so Mr. Bonestell would have time to get the police. Also, I was afraid of what Shelby might do if Ernie departed on the *Maria* and left Shelby behind. We and the Denicolas could accuse him, couldn't we? But if Shelby got his hands on Mr. Bonestell and then silenced all of us . . ."

Jupe stopped. He looked grim.

307

"Yes," said Mr. Sebastian. "Your position was delicate. You're probably lucky that Ernie took Shelby when he got aboard the *Maria III*."

"I *know* we're lucky," said Bob. "You see, it was Shelby who brought me to the motel. He discovered me at Strauss's place when he arrived with the first half of the gun money. Boy, was he mad! I heard him arguing with Ernie about what to do with me. Ernie didn't care because he was leaving the country. But Shelby was on the spot. He tried to convince Ernie to take me on the boat and drop me overboard at sea!"

Mr. Sebastian grimaced. "You boys could certainly make things hot for him, but was there any actual proof that he was part of the bank robbery?"

Pete chuckled. "Right there in the ice-cream carton, like Jupe guessed. Shelby was suposed to fence some jewellery that Ernie took from safe-deposit boxes during the robbery. But Shelby hung on to the prime pieces, and they were there in the freezer for the police to find. They were identified by the owners.

"And the police found the makeup and the wigs in the trunk of Shelby's car. Shelby thought it was daring and dramatic of him to be the lookout for the robbers while he was disguised as the terrorist Altranto."

Mr. Sebastian laughed. "I guess I'm glad this was your case, not mine," he said. "Shelby is so busy playacting it's hard to believe he's for real."

"He's for real, all right," said Jupe. "So are Ernie and his friends. They're doing their own kind of playacting right now. If you're a terrorist in Mesa d'Oro and you get caught, it's stylish to boast about how really black your crimes have been. It seems to make you a hero, instead of just an unbalanced person who likes explosives and firearms."

"Better a revolutionary than a beach bum, eh?" said Mr. Sebastian.

"Nobler," said Jupiter. "Of course, I should have suspected Shelby right away. He was in the perfect position to know about the routine at the bank, and he said to Mr. Bonestell, 'According to *your* system of justice, you're innocent until you're proven guilty.' A person who thought of himself as an American would have said, 'According to *our* system of justice . . .'"

"True," said Mr. Sebastian, "but don't be so hard on yourself. You did all right."

Bob grinned. "Thanks for not saying, 'You did all right for a bunch of kids.'"

"You did all right, period," said Mr. Sebastian. "You did better than a lot of investigators might have done. I imagine Shelby was anxious for Mr. Bonestell to hire you because he thought you *wouldn't* do all right. Then, later, he must have had second thoughts about it and tried to wire your workshop for sound."

"And he wired the sugar bowl on the table," said Jupe. "Once I found the bug in the sugar bowl, I knew he was the scar-faced man and the link to the robbers. But I didn't guess that gun-running was involved. I thought it might be drugs or aliens."

"Speaking of gun-running, what about that moving company in Oxnard?" asked Mr. Sebastian.

"Strauss and his cronies are hijackers," said Bob. "The shipment of guns and ammunition was hijacked from a truck back east. Divers recovered some of the guns and they've been identified. Strauss and his men have disappeared. They left everything and ran. We heard that the trucks and equipment they left behind were no great loss. Pacific States Moving and Storage Company was about to declare bankruptcy."

"It must be hard to run an efficient moving business when you're so busy with stolen goods," said Mr. Sebastian. "Well, what about the makeup woman who made the speech at the rally that night?"

"Gracie Montoya wasn't part of the plot," said Pete. "Her family's from Mesa d'Oro and she was brought up to believe in the Republican cause, that's all."

"It's a tradition," said Jupiter. "It's handed down from parent to child. I think Gracie is having second thoughts about that tradition now. She didn't mind collecting money for an exile in Mexico, but collecting money for guns to kill people—that's something else."

"The police asked her about the fight she had with Ernie," Bob put in. "He wanted a date with her, and she didn't want to go out with him. That's all that was about."

"Good for her," said Mr. Sebastian.

He handed the file back to Bob. "These are good notes," he said.

"I'm glad you like them," said Bob, "because, if you're not too busy, maybe you'd do something for us."

Mr Sebastian looked inquiringly at the boys. It was Jupe who put the request to him at last.

"Mr. Hitchcock used to introduce our cases for us," he said. "I know you're busy with your own writing, but the introduction needn't be long."

Mr. Sebastian grinned. "I'll do my best. And when

I'm finished, perhaps you'll take me up on my original offer of a speedboat ride. Of course, I'm not so dashing with a boat as Eileen Denicola, and we probably won't sink any fishing boats. On the other hand, you never really know."

Mr. Sebastian paused and grinned. "That's what makes life interesting, isn't it? You never really know!"

THE MYSTERY OF
THE BLAZING CLIFFS

The Mystery of the Blazing Cliffs was first published
in the USA by Random House Inc in 1981
First published as a single volume in the UK
by Armada in 1984

1

The Angry Man

"PUT ONE FINGER ON THAT CAR and I'll horsewhip
you!" shouted Charles Barron.

Jupiter Jones stood in the driveway of The
Jones Salvage Yard and stared. He wondered if
Barron was joking.

But Barron was not joking. His lean body was
tense with rage. The face beneath the iron-grey
hair was red. He clenched his fists and glared at
Hans, one of the two Bavarian brothers who
helped out at the yard.

Hans's face was pale with shock. He had just
offered to move Mr Barron's Mercedes, which
was blocking the drive in front of the salvage-yard
office. "A truck comes in soon with a load of
timbers," Hans tried to explain again. "There is
no room for it to pass the car. If I move the car—"

"You will not move the car!" roared Barron. "I
am sick of incompetents making free with my
property! I parked my car in a perfectly good
place! Don't you people have any idea how to do
business?"

Jupiter's uncle, Titus Jones, appeared suddenly
from behind a stack of salvage. "Mr Barron," he
said sternly, „

you have no call to abuse my helpers. Now, if you don't want Hans to move your car, you'd better move it yourself. And you'd better hurry because no matter what you decide to do, my truck is coming in!"

Barron opened his mouth as if to shout again, but before he could utter a sound, a slender middle-aged woman with brown hair hurried from the back of the yard. She took hold of his arm and looked at him in a pleading way. "Charles, do move the car," she said. "I'd hate to see anything happen to it."

"I don't intend to have anything happen to it," snapped Barron. He got into the Mercedes and started the engine. An instant later he was manoeuvering the car into the empty space next to the office, and the larger of the two salvage-yard trucks was rolling through the gate with a load of scrap lumber.

The brown-haired woman smiled at Hans. "My husband really doesn't mean to be unkind," she said. "He's . . . he's got an impatient nature and . . ."

"I can drive a car," said Hans. "For years I am driving for Mr Jones and I do not have accidents."

Hans then turned on his heel and walked away.

"Oh, dear!" said Mrs Barron. She looked helplessly from Uncle Titus to Jupiter and from Jupiter to Aunt Mathilda, who had just come out of the office.

316

"What's the matter with Hans?" said Aunt Mathilda. "He looks like a walking thunderstorm."

"I'm afraid my husband was rude to him, Mrs Jones," said Mrs Barron. "Charles is in a testy mood today. The waitress at breakfast spilled the coffee, and Charles gets so upset when people don't do their jobs well. Nowadays they often don't, you know. Sometimes I wish that the time for deliverance was really here."

"Deliverance?" said Uncle Titus.

"Yes. When the rescuers come from Omega," said Mrs Barron.

Uncle Titus looked blank. But Jupiter nodded with understanding.

"There's a book called *They Walk Among Us* that tells about the rescuers," Jupiter explained to his uncle. "It's by a man named Contreras. It describes a race of people from the planet Omega. They are keeping watch over us, and eventually, after a catastrophe overwhelms our planet, they'll rescue some of us so that our civilization won't be lost forever."

"Oh, you know about the deliverance!" cried Mrs Barron. "How nice!"

"Ridicu—" Uncle Titus started to say when Aunt Mathilda spoke up in a brisk, no-nonsense tone. "Jupiter knows about a great many things," she said. "Sometimes I think he knows too much."

Aunt Mathilda then took Mrs Barron's arm and led her away. She was talking rapidly about the virtues of several used kitchen chairs when Jupe's closest friends, Pete Crenshaw and Bob Andrews, ambled into the salvage yard.

"Morning, Pete," said Uncle Titus. "How are you, Bob? You're just in time. Mrs Jones has a big job lined up for you boys. She'll tell you about it as soon as we finish with these customers."

Without waiting for an answer, Uncle Titus went off with Mr Barron, who had locked his car and who now seemed to be angry with the world in general rather than with Hans in particular.

"You missed the excitement," said Jupiter to his friends, "but there may be more."

"What happened?" demanded Bob.

Jupiter grinned. "We've got a bad-tempered customer. But when he isn't yelling at Hans, he's picking out very unusual items to buy." Jupe gestured toward the back of the yard.

Jupiter's uncle and aunt were showing Mr and Mrs Barron an old-fashioned treadle sewing machine which was still in working order. As the boys watched, Uncle Titus lifted the machine and carried it towards the other things that Charles Barron had purchased that day. These included two wood-burning stoves, a churn with a broken handle, an ancient hand loom, and a hand-cranked phonograph.

"What a pile of junk!" said Pete. "What are those people going to do with a broken churn? Turn it into a plantpot?"

"Maybe they collect antiques," guessed Bob.

318

"I don't think so," said Jupe, "though some of those things *are* old enough to be antiques. But the Barrons seem to want to use everything. Mr Barron has been questioning Uncle Titus to make sure they can. Some of the things are broken, like the churn, but all of them can be fixed again. The stoves are already in good shape. Mr Barron took the lids off and looked at the grates to make sure they were intact, and he's buying all the stovepipe we have on hand."

"I'll bet Aunt Mathilda is happy," said Pete. "Now she can unload some of that junk she thought she'd never get rid of. Maybe she'll get lucky and those people will turn into steady customers."

"She'd like that, but Uncle Titus wouldn't," said Jupe. "He can't stand Mr Barron. The man is rude and unreasonable, and he's been in a rage since he arrived at eight this morning and found the gate still locked. He said it didn't do much good for him to get up before dawn if everyone else in the world slept until noon."

"He said that at eight in the morning?" asked Bob.

Jupe nodded. "Yes, he did. Mrs Barron seems nice enough, but Mr Barron is sure that either everyone is trying to cheat him or no one knows his own business."

Bob looked thoughtful. "His name's Barron, huh? There was an article about a man named Barron in the *Los Angeles Times* a few weeks ago. If it's the same man, he's a millionaire who bought

319

a ranch up north somewhere. He's going to grow his own food and be self-sufficient."

"So that's what the churn is all about," said Pete. "He's going to churn his own butter and . . . and . . . Hey Jupe, he's headed right for Headquarters!"

It was true! At the far side of the yard, Charles Barron had pushed aside a splintery plank so that he could examine a rusted lawn chair. Jupe saw that he was very close to the barrier of carefully arranged salvage that concealed an old mobile-home trailer—a trailer that was the Headquarters of the boys' detective agency, The Three Investigators.

"I'll get him away from there," said Jupe, who did not want to remind Aunt Mathilda that the trailer existed. True, Aunt Mathilda and Uncle Titus had given the mobile home to Jupe and his friends to use for a clubhouse, but they did not know that there was now a telephone in the trailer, a small but efficient laboratory, and a photographic darkroom. They knew that the boys called themselves investigators and had helped solve some mysteries, but they were not really aware of how seriously the boys took the detective business—and how often they found themselves in real danger. Aunt Mathilda would not have approved. She believed in keeping boys busy at safe, practical pursuits such as repairing old items that might be resold in the salvage yard.

Jupiter left his friends standing in the drive and hurried to the side of the yard. Mr Barron looked around and scowled as he approached, but Jupe pretended not to notice.

"You really appreciate old things," he said to Barron. "We have an old claw-legged bathtub over near the workshop, and a buckboard that looks old, but isn't. It was made for a western movie and it's in perfect condition."

"We don't need a bathtub," said Barron, "but I might have a look at that wagon."

"I'd forgotten about it," said Uncle Titus. "Jupe, thank you for mentioning it."

He and Aunt Mathilda led Barron and his wife away from the Headquarters area, and Jupe returned to his friends.

Jupiter, Pete, and Bob were still loitering near the office when Barron and his wife came back, having decided against the buckboard. They stood in the driveway with Uncle Titus and began to discuss arrangements for having their purchases delivered.

"We're about ten miles north of San Luis Obispo and four miles off the main highway," said Barron. "I can send a man down here with a truck to pick the things up, but I'd prefer not to. My people are busy right now. If you can deliver the stoves and the other things, I'll pay you what it's worth."

He paused and looked suspiciously at Uncle Titus. "I will not pay *more* than it's worth," he added.

"And I wouldn't charge more than it's worth, Mr Barron," said Uncle Titus. "Just the same,

321

we're not really set up to handle deliveries so far away. . . ."

Mr Barron began to look angry.

"Just a second, Uncle Titus," interrupted Jupe. His round face was earnest under his shock of dark hair. "You were thinking of going north anyway, remember? To check out that block of old apartment buildings in San Jose, the ones that are scheduled for demolition and that might have some usable salvage. You could drop off Mr Barron's things on the way, and the delivery wouldn't cost too much."

"Good heavens!" exclaimed Barron. "A young person who can think ahead. Will wonders never cease?"

"Young people are often very intelligent," said Uncle Titus coldly. "All right. That's a good idea. Someone should see that demolition job in San Jose. But that's a two-day trip. I couldn't go for at least a week."

"We could go," said Jupe quickly. "You promised that we'd have a chance to try buying salvage one day soon." Jupe turned to include Pete and Bob in the conversation. "What about it?" he said to them. "Want to go up north?"

"Well, okay," said Pete. "If my folks don't mind."

Bob nodded in agreement.

"Then it's settled!" said Jupiter quickly. "Hans or Konrad can drive the truck for us. We'll stop at Mr Barron's ranch on the way to San Jose."

Jupe walked away quickly before Charles Barron or Uncle Titus could think of a better plan.

"What's the big idea?" said Pete when the boys were in Jupe's outdoor workshop, safely out of earshot. "We're probably going to have to unload that truck at Barron's place, and that will be one huge job. Since when are you so eager for extra work?"

Jupe leaned against his workbench and grinned. "First of all, Uncle Titus has been promising us a buying trip for a long time, and something has always gotten in the way."

"Yeah, like a sinister scarecrow," said Bob, remembering a buying trip that had recently been cancelled by a fiendish apparition in a corn patch. That had been one of the scariest mysteries The Three Investigators had ever solved.

"And second of all," continued Jupe, "it would be a good idea for us to get out of town right now."

Pete gaped. "Why?"

"Because of the really huge job Aunt Mathilda has for us. She wants us to scrape the rust off some old playground equipment and then paint everything. But it's not worth the effort. The metal is too badly rusted. I told her that, but she doesn't believe me. She thinks I'm just trying to get out of work."

"Which you are," said Bob.

"Well, yes," admitted Jupe. "But maybe while we're gone, Hans or Konrad will start the job and Aunt Mathilda will see it isn't worth the time and will sell the playground things for scrap metal.

"And there's a third reason for going north," added Jupe. "The Barrons are a very odd couple, and I'd like to see their place. Do they really have a ranch that's entirely self-sufficient? Do they have only old things, or do they use modern technology, too? And is Mr Barron always so angry? And Mrs Barron— does she really believe in the rescuers?"

"Rescuers?" said Pete. "Who are they?"

"A race of superbeings who will rescue us when a great disaster overtakes our planet," said Jupe.

"You're kidding!" said Bob.

"Nope," said Jupe, and his eyes sparkled with glee. "Who knows? Maybe the disaster will hit when we're at the ranch, and we'll get rescued! It could be a very interesting trip!"

2

The Fortress

IT WAS AFTER NOON the next day when Hans's brother, Konrad, set out with the larger of the two salvage-yard trucks. Mr Barron's purchases had been loaded in the back, and Jupiter, Pete, and Bob had wedged themselves in among the old stoves and the other items from Uncle Titus's stock.

"Did you find the newspaper article about Barron?" Jupiter asked Bob as the truck sped north along the Coast Highway.

Bob nodded and took several folded sheets of paper out of his pocket. "It was in the financial section of the *Times* four weeks ago," he reported. "I made a copy of it on the duplicating machine at the library."

He unfolded the papers. "His full name is Charles Emerson Barron," Bob said. "He's a really rich guy. He's always been rich. His father owned Barron International, the company that makes tractors and farm machinery. The Barrons owned Barronsgate, too—the town near Milwaukee where Charles Barron was born. It was an old-time company town, and everybody who lived there worked in the tractor factory and did what the Barrons told them to.

"Mr Barron inherited Barron International when he was twenty-three, and for a while everything was okay. But then the workers at Barron International went on strike for shorter hours and more money. Eventually Mr Barron had to give them what they wanted. That made him mad, so he sold the tractor factory and bought a company that made tyres. But before long the government fined his tyre factory for polluting the air. He sold that and bought a company that had some patents on photographic processes, and he got sued for discriminatory hiring practices. At different times Barron has owned newspapers and a chain of radio stations and some banks, and he has always gotten tangled up in government regulations or labour troubles or lawsuits. So finally he sold everything and moved to a ranch in a valley north of San Luis Obispo, where he lives in the house he was born in—"

"I thought he was born near Milwaukee," said Pete.

"He was. He had the house moved to California. You can do that sort of thing when you've got heaps of money, and Mr Barron sure does have heaps. He always made a profit when he sold things. They called him the Robber Barron."

"Of course," said Jupe. "He's just as high-handed as the robber-barron industrialists of the last century. What else could they call him?"

"I suppose they could call him the world's champion grump," said Bob. "According to Barron, savages are taking over the world and nobody takes pride in his work any more and soon our money won't be worth anything. The only things worth having will be gold and land, and that's why he bought Rancho Valverde. He says he's going to spend the rest of his life on Valverde and raise his own food and experiment with new crops."

Bob put the newspaper article back in his pocket and the boys rode on in silence. The truck sped past small towns and then through open country where the hills were beginning to turn brown under the summer sun.

It was almost three when Konrad turned off the Coast Highway on to State Highway 16SJ, a two-lane road that ran towards the east. In a few moments the truck climbed a short, steep hill. Then the road dipped suddenly into a narrow valley. There were no houses and no other cars.

"This gets to be wild country awfully fast," observed Pete.

"It's going to get wilder still," Jupe told him. "I looked at the map before we left Rocky Beach. There isn't a town between here and the San Joaquin Valley."

The truck rumbled up over more hills, then slowed as it started down a series of hairpin curves. The boys saw that they were headed down into a vast natural bowl, flat at the bottom and bounded with sheer cliffs. The road twisted and doubled back on itself, the engine groaned and complained, and at last they were at the bottom and driving along on flat land. The dark growth of scrub plants crowded the road on the right, and a high chain-link fence edged it on the left. Beyond the fence there was a hedge of oleanders. Occasional breaks in the hedge showed fields where new crops grew in feathery green rows.

"Rancho Valverde," Bob decided.

Konrad drove for more than a mile before he slowed and turned left. The truck passed through an open gate on to a gravelled drive that ran north between cultivated fields and citrus groves.

Jupe stood up and looked over the cab of the truck. He saw a large grove of eucalyptus trees ahead, with buildings sheltered under them. To the right of the drive was a sprawling, two-storey ranch house which faced south towards the road. To the left and also facing south was an old-fashioned, high-roofed house which was almost a mansion. It was ornate with wooden gingerbread trim and had towers jutting above the broad, breezy veranda that ran across the front and around the sides.

"I'll bet that's the house Barron moved here from Milwaukee," Bob said.

Jupe nodded. In a moment they had passed between the big house and the simpler ranch house and were driving past a dozen or more small frame cottages, where dark-haired, dark-eyed children played. The children stopped their games to wave at the truck as it went by. There was no sign of an adult until they reached a huge open area at the end of the gravel lane. It was a place where trucks and tractors were parked near large

328

sheds and barns. As Konrad applied the brakes, a red-haired, red-faced man appeared in the doorway of one of the sheds. He had a clipboard in his hands, and he squinted up at Konrad.

"You from The Jones Salvage Yard?" he asked.

Jupe jumped down from the back of the truck. "I am Jupiter Jones," he said importantly. He gestured toward Konrad. "This is Konrad Schmid, and these are my friends, Pete Crenshaw and Bob Andrews."

The red-haired man smiled. "I'm Hank Detweiler," he said. "I'm Mr Barron's foreman."

"Okay," said Konrad. "Where do you want that we should unload the truck?"

"I don't want," Detweiler said. "Our own people will take care of it."

As if at a signal, three men came out of the shed and began taking things out of the truck. Like the children outside the cottages, these men were dark. They spoke softly in Spanish as they worked, and Hank Detweiler checked off items on a list that was attached to his clipboard. The foreman had blunt, thick hands with the fingernails cut short and square. His face was almost crimson, as if he had a permanent case of windburn, and there were fine lines at the corners of his eyes and around his mouth.

"Well?" he said suddenly, when he glanced up and saw that Jupe was watching him. "Something you wanted to know?"

Jupe smiled. "Well, you could confirm a deduction of mine. Deducing things about people

329

is sort of my hobby," he explained. He looked around at the towering cliffs that enclosed the ranch on three sides, making it a landlocked oasis that was very still and peaceful in the sunny afternoon. "From the way your skin is weathered, I deduce that you haven't been here in this sheltered valley too long," said Jupe. "I think you must be used to wide open spaces and lots of wind."

For an instant there was a sadness in Detweiler's eyes. "Very good," he said. "You're right. I was foreman at the Armstrong Ranch near Austin, Texas, until Mr Barron came to visit there last year and hired me away. He made me a good offer, but sometimes this place does seem kind of hedged in."

Detweiler put his clipboard down on the hood of a pickup truck that stood near the shed. "You boys come all the way from Rocky Beach to help unload this stuff?" he said. "That's pretty generous of you. Don't know as I'd have done the same when I was your age. But then maybe you're curious about the ranch?"

Jupiter nodded eagerly, and Detweiler grinned.

"Okay," said Detweiler. "If you've got time, I'll show you around. It's an interesting place—not your usual run-of-the-mill truck farm."

The foreman led the way into the shed where the purchases from the salvage yard were being stored. Konrad and the boys saw a warehouse that was crammed to the rafters with all sorts of objects, from machine parts to leather hides to bolts of cloth.

Next door to the warehouse was a smaller building that housed a machine shop. There the visitors were introduced to John Aleman, a snub-nosed young man who was the mechanic for the ranch.

"John keeps our vehicles running and all our machinery in order," said Detweiler. "Course, he shouldn't be here. He should be out designing big power plants and irrigation systems."

"Kind of hard to get a job designing a power plant when you quit school after the tenth grade," said Aleman, but he didn't seem unhappy.

Next to the machine shop were sheds used for food storage, and beyond these was a dairy barn which was empty at this hour.

"We have Guernseys here on the ranch," said Detweiler. "Right now the herd is grazing in the pasture up at the north end, under the dam. We have beef cattle, too, and sheep and pigs and chickens. And of course we've got horses."

Detweiler went on to the stable, where a sandy-haired young woman named Mary Sedlack was crouched in a stall next to a handsome palomino stallion. She had the horse's left rear hoof in her hands, and she was frowning at something she saw in the frog of the horse's foot.

"Mary tends to our animals when they get sick," said Detweiler. "Other times she just plain babies them."

"Better stand back," the girl warned. "Asphodel gets nervous if he thinks somebody's crowding him."

"Asphodel is one temperamental horse," said Hank Detweiler. "Mary's the only one who can get anywhere near him."

Detweiler and the visitors retreated to the parking area, where they got into a small sedan. Detweiler drove slowly out along a dirt track that ran north through the fields, away from the storage buildings.

"Forty-seven people work here on the ranch," said the foreman. "That's not counting the children, of course, or the people Mr Barron considers his own personal staff—specialists like Mary and John—and the supervisors. I'm the chief supervisor, and I'm responsible for everything that comes in here or goes out. Then there's Rafael Banales."

Detweiler waved to a thin, not very tall man who stood at the edge of a field where labourers were planting some sort of crop. "Rafe is in charge of the field workers. He is one very progressive farmer. He's a graduate of the University of California at Davis."

They went on, and Detweiler showed them the small building where John Aleman was experimenting with solar energy. He pointed to the slopes under the cliffs to the east, several miles away, where beef cattle grazed. He came at last to a lush green pasture beyond the fields of carrots and lettuce and peppers and marrows. The dairy herd was there, and beyond the pasture was a cement dam.

"We have our own water supply for emergencies," Detweiler told Konrad and the boys. "The reservoir beyond that dam is fed by the stream you see falling down the face of that cliff. We haven't had to use that water yet, but it's there if we need it. Right now we use artesian wells. In an emergency we can generate our own power for the pumps, and for all our other electrical needs. Aleman built the generators and they use diesel fuel. If that runs out, we can convert and burn coal or wood."

Detweiler turned the car around and started back towards the cluster of buildings under the eucalyptus trees.

"We keep bees here so we have a source of sugar," he said. "We also have a smokehouse for curing hams and bacon. We have underground storage tanks for our reserve gasoline supply and root cellars for keeping potatoes and turnips. We have miles of shelves to hold the canned things that Elsie and the other woman put up when the crops are ripe."

"Elsie?" said Jupiter.

Detweiler grinned. "Elsie is not the least of our specialists," he said. "She cooks for John and Rafael and Mary and me, and for the Barrons, too. If you've got time to stop at the ranch house before you leave, she's sure to spring for some soda pop all around."

Detweiler parked the car near the storage sheds

and led Konrad and the boys down the lane towards the ranch house.

Elsie Spratt turned out to be a hearty woman somewhere in her thirties. She had short blonde hair and a broad, easy smile, and she presided over a kitchen that was bright with sunlight and warm with the smell of cooking food. When Hank Detweiler introduced the visitors, she hurried to pour cups of coffee for the men, and she took bottles of soda pop from the refrigerator for the boys.

"Enjoy it while you may," she said cheerily. "Comes the revolution, there won't be any soda pop."

Konrad sat down at the long table beside Detweiler. "Revolution?" he said. "We do not have revolutions in America. If we do not like the President, soon we elect a new one."

"Aha!" said Elsie. "But suppose the system breaks down. What do we do then?"

Konrad looked puzzled, and Jupe glanced around the kitchen. His eyes rested on the wood-burning stove that stood beside the big gas range.

"The system breaks down?" said Jupe. "That's what you're getting ready for here, isn't it? This place is like a fortress—stocked with supplies so that it can go through a siege. It's like one of the castles in the Middle Ages."

"Exactly right," said Detweiler. "What we're doing here is getting ready for the end of the world—or at least for the end of our way of life."

Elsie poured a cup of coffee for herself. As she sat down and took a spoonful of sugar, Jupe noticed that there was a slight deformity on her right hand—a jutting bit of bone and flesh on her smallest finger.

"I don't think we're getting ready for the kind of revolution where we drag the President out and shoot him," she said. "I think what Mr Barron has in mind is a time when everything sort of falls apart and we have famine and looting and confusion and bloodshed. You know. He thinks the world is *really* going to the dogs, and we have to be prepared if we're going to survive."

"Mr Barron believes that gold and land are the only safe investments, doesn't he?" said Jupiter. "Obviously he expects a collapse of the prevailing monetary system."

Elsie Spratt stared at him. "Do you always talk that way?" she asked.

Pete chuckled. "Jupe doesn't believe in using short words if long ones will do as well."

Jupe ignored this jibe. "Do *you* think our world is coming to an end?" he asked Elsie and Detweiler.

Elsie shrugged. "No, I suppose not."

"I think Mr Barron's the only one who really believes it," said Detweiler. "He claims the government is poking its nose into places where it doesn't belong, and people nowadays don't have to work if they don't want to, and so most people don't. He says that sooner or later our money won't be worth anything—"

"Shhh!" said Elsie.

She put a hand on Detweiler's arm and looked past him to the door. Mrs Barron stood there on the other side of the screen. "May I come in?" she said.

"Of course." Elsie got up. "We were just having coffee. Would you like a cup?"

"No, thank you." Mrs Barron stepped into the kitchen and smiled at Jupiter, Pete, and Bob. "I saw you boys come in," she said. "I wonder if you could stay a bit longer and have dinner with Mr Barron and myself?"

Konrad scowled. "Jupe, it is after five," he said. "We should go now."

Mrs Barron turned to Elsie. "We could eat early, couldn't we?" she said.

Elsie looked startled. "I guess so."

"There now!" Mrs Barron smiled again, and Jupe looked questioningly at Bob and then at Pete.

"That would be swell," said Pete.

"Don't worry," said Bob to Konrad. "We'll get to San Jose sooner or later."

"Then it's settled," said Mrs Barron. "We'll sit down at five-thirty."

She went out and down the back steps of the ranch house.

"I do not like this," said Konrad. "I think we should go."

"In a little while, Konrad," said Jupe. "Another hour or so won't make any difference."

Jupiter's deductions and predictions were usually right. But this time he couldn't have been more wrong.

336

3

No Exit

"Mrs Barron likes boys," said Hank Detweiler. "She has two adopted sons and she misses them. One went off to be a drummer with a rock group, and the other lives in Big Sur now and makes wooden clogs that he sells to tourists. He writes poetry, too."

"Gee," said Pete. "How does Mr Barron feel about that?"

"Not a bit happy," said Elsie Spratt. "You boys go along and have your dinner and be nice to Mrs Barron, but watch out for him. When he's in a bad mood, he's cosy as a rattlesnake in a rainstorm."

Konrad looked upset. "I think I will not go," he announced. "I will stay here and wait." He glanced at Elsie. "It is okay if I stay here?" he asked.

"Why, sure," said Elsie. "You can have your dinner here while the boys are living it up over in the big house."

And so Jupiter, Pete, and Bob left the ranch house at five-thirty and walked across the drive to the Barron house. Mrs Barron opened the door for them and then led them into a parlour that was stiffly formal, with settees and chairs upholstered in velvet. Mr Barron was there, complaining loudly that there was something wrong with the television set. "Nothing but noise and snow!" he said. He shook hands with the boys in an absent-minded way. "You young fellows are in school, I suppose," he said. "Learning anything? Or are you just putting in your time?"

Before the boys could answer, a Mexican woman came to the doorway to announce that dinner was served. Mr Barron offered his arm to Mrs Barron, and the boys followed them to the dining room.

The Mexican woman had brought the dinner across from Elsie's kitchen, and it was delicious. Jupe ate slowly and listened to Mr Barron's lecture on the evils of plastic in almost any form. He learned that Mr Barron did not approve of vinyl that masqueraded as leather, or of polyester that pretended to be wool. Mr Barron also took time to condemn termite inspectors who did not understand termites and auto mechanics who could not fix cars properly.

Mrs Barron waited until her husband had finished his list of grievances. Then she began to talk quietly about her son in Big Sur who wrote poetry.

"Trash!" snapped Mr Barron. "The stuff doesn't even rhyme! That's the trouble with the world today. Poetry doesn't rhyme and people don't have to work to earn a living and children don't have to respect their parents and—"

"Charles, dear, I think you have a crumb on your chin," said Mrs Barron.

338

Mr Barron dabbed at himself with a napkin, and Mrs Barron told the boys about her other son who played drums for a musical group.

"He's going to be here in August," said Mrs Barron, "for the convention."

Mr Barron made a choking sound, and his face grew very red. "Mob of zanies!" he grumbled.

"Convention?" said Pete timidly.

"The annual meeting of the Blue Light Mission will take place here in August," said Mrs Barron. She smiled at Jupiter. "You know about that—you've read the book. So many members of our society have talked with the rescuers who come from the planet Omega. They'll share their experiences with the rest of us, and if we're lucky we'll have Vladimir Contreras for our speaker this year."

"Oh, yes," said Jupe. "The man who wrote *They Walk Among Us*."

Mr Barron leaned back in his chair. "Last year the convention of the Blue Light Mission was held in a cornfield in Iowa and a man came who believed that the earth is hollow and that a race of superbeings live inside it," he said. "There was also a woman who told fortunes with magnetized needles that floated on water, and a pimply youth who kept saying 'Om! Om!' until I wanted to hit him."

"*You* went to the convention?" said Pete to Barron.

"I had to!" snapped Barron. "My wife is a remarkable woman, but if I left her to herself, she

339

would surely be victimized by those loonies. Even when I am with her, she becomes over-enthusiastic. I was unable to keep her from inviting that weird group here this summer."

"We should have a large turnout," said Mrs Barron happily. "Many people are keenly interested. They know that the rescuers are out there watching us."

"The only ones who are out there watching us are anarchists and criminals who want to take over," said Mr Barron. "Well, I'm ready for them!"

Pete looked pleadingly at Jupe, who stood up.

"It was very kind of you to invite us," said Jupe, "but we must go. Konrad is anxious to get to San Jose."

"Of course," said Mrs Barron. "We mustn't make you late."

She walked to the door with the boys, and she stood and watched them go down the front steps.

"You have a good time?" asked Elsie Spratt when they came into the ranch-house kitchen.

"Interesting," said Bob, "but not cosy. You said it."

Elsie laughed. "A rattlesnake in a rainstorm."

Konrad had just finished his dinner. He carried his dishes to the sink, and then the four visitors went out to the truck. Detweiler stood on the porch of the ranch house as they drove out, waving goodbye to them.

"Nice people," said Bob.

"Except for Mr Barron," said Pete. "What a grump!"

340

The truck rumbled down the lane, and when it neared the gate a mile away it slowed. Then it stopped and the boys heard Konrad open the door of the cab.

"Jupe?" Konrad called.

Jupe jumped down from the back of the truck, followed by his friends. They saw a man standing in the road, blocking the way. The man wore an army uniform, and there were cartridges in the belt at his waist. A helmet was buckled under his chin. He held a rifle at the ready across his chest.

"Sorry," he said. "The road is closed."

"What's the trouble?" said Jupiter.

"I don't know," said the soldier. His voice shook as if he were afraid. "I've got orders that no one gets past. The road is closed."

He shifted the rifle slightly, as if to draw attention to it. It slipped in his grasp and began to fall.

"Watch it!" yelled Pete.

The soldier grabbed clumsily at the gun, and with a stunning roar it went off!

4

Invasion!

THE SOUND OF THE EXPLOSION echoed through the valley. The young soldier stared at his gun, shocked, his eyes enormous in his pale face.

"That thing is loaded!" said Konrad, outraged.

"It sure is," said the soldier shakily. "We were issued live ammunition today."

He gripped the rifle more firmly, fearful that it might slip and go off again. The boys heard the sound of a car on the road. An instant later a jeep came speeding into sight. It stopped just feet from the armed man.

"Stanford, what do you think you're doing?" demanded the officer who sat in the jeep next to the driver. He glared at the soldier, then at the boys and Konrad.

"Sorry, sir," said the soldier. "The gun slipped."

"Stanford, if you can't hold on to a rifle, you don't belong out here," said the officer.

"No, sir," said the soldier.

The officer got out of the jeep and stalked towards Konrad. The boys saw that he was young—as young as the frightened soldier. His olive-drab field jacket was new. So was his helmet. So were the expensive-looking combat boots on his feet.

"I'm Lieutenant John Ferrante," he said. One gloved hand swung up as if to salute, but then it dropped again. Jupe saw that he was trying to be very military, like an actor portraying an officer in a war film.

"Why is the road closed?" said Konrad. "We are supposed to go to San Jose tonight. We do not have time for the war games that you play."

"Sorry, but it isn't a game." Lieutenant Ferrante's voice was tight. "My men and I were dispatched from Camp Roberts this afternoon and told to keep all traffic off this road. This is an emergency route from the San Joaquin Valley to the coast, and it has to be clear for military vehicles."

"We don't plan to block it," Jupe pointed out. "We're going back to 101, and then north to San Jose."

"Highway 101 is closed, too," said the lieutenant. "Look, why don't you just turn around and go back up that drive and let us do our job?"

The lieutenant put a hand on the pistol he wore at his belt. The boys stiffened.

"I have orders that no one is to use this road," the lieutenant continued. "It's for your own protection."

"Protection?" echoed Konrad. "You protect us with a gun?"

"I'm sorry," said the lieutenant. "Look, I just can't let you through. And I can't tell you any

343

more than I have because I don't know much more. Now be good guys and go back up the drive, huh?"

"Mr Barron won't believe this," said Jupiter. "That's Charles Emerson Barron, the industrialist. He may be quite angry when he learns that his guests are being detained. He might even call Washington. He's a powerful man, you know!"

"I can't help that," said the lieutenant. "I can't let you through!"

Several more uniformed figures appeared on the road. They stood quietly near the soldier who had first stopped the truck. Each carried a rifle, and the boys could see that each was alert.

"Okay, okay!" said Konrad quickly. "Jupe, I do not like this. We go back to the ranch. We tell Mr Barron what happens."

"Good!" said the lieutenant. "You do that. And listen—I'll follow you in the jeep. I'll help you explain to this Barron, whoever he is. I mean, it's just one of those things. We're only following orders."

The lieutenant got into his jeep and the boys climbed up into the truck.

"Crazy!" said Pete as Konrad turned on the gravel drive.

"Yes, it is," said Jupiter.

The truck began to roll towards the Barron house, followed by the jeep.

"There was absolutely nothing wrong when we left Rocky Beach at noon," said Jupe. "What could have happened since then?"

"Beats me," said Pete, "but that lieutenant sure looked scared. Something's up."

Konrad stopped the truck in the drive beyond the ranch house. The jeep pulled in behind, and the lieutenant got out and looked around.

"Who's in charge here?" he demanded. His voice was loud, as if he were blustering to keep up his courage.

Hank Detweiler came down the back steps of the ranch house. Elsie Spratt and Mary Sedlack were with him, and Rafael Banales stood behind them in the kitchen doorway and watched.

"I'm Mr Barron's foreman," said Detweiler. "Can I help you?"

The back door of the Barron house opened and Charles Barron and his wife came out on to the back porch.

"What is it?" asked Barron.

"The road is closed," said Jupiter. "We can't leave."

Jupe turned expextantly toward the lieutenant, and Barron glared at the officer. "My road? Closed?"

Jupe saw with amusement that the lieutenant had begun to sweat in spite of the chill on the evening breeze. Jupe suspected that Charles Emerson Barron often had this effect on people.

"I beg your pardon, sir," said the lieutenant. "It's not y-y-your road!"

Jupe grinned to himself. Mr Barron could do more than make people sweat. He could also make them stutter.

"Well, it certainly isn't *your* road!" cried Barron. "What do you mean, it's closed? It can't be closed! It's a public highway."

"Y-y-yes, sir!" said the lieutenant. "The highway to the San Joaquin, sir, b-b-but—"

"For heaven's sake, speak up!" roared Barron. "Don't stand there blithering!"

"We h-h-have orders, sir," the lieutenant managed to get out. "This afernoon. From Washington. Something h-h-happened in T-t—"

"Lieutenant!" shouted Barron.

"In Texas!" cried the lieutenant. "S-something happened in Texas." Having gotten a grip on his speech, he took off his helmet and ran one gloved hand over his dark hair. "I don't know what it was, but all roads in the state have been closed—all main arteries, sir. No traffic is moving."

"This is preposterous!" shouted Barron.

"Yes, sir," said the lieutenant.

"I'm going to call Washington," said Barron.

"Yes, sir," said the lieutenant.

"The President," Barron announced. "I'll call the President."

Barron stamped into his house. The windows of the big house were open, and the group gathered on the drive could hear Charles Barron dialling the telephone. There was silence for a second, then Barron jiggled the instrument.

"Blast!" he said.

He slammed out on to the back porch and down the steps. "Dratted phone's dead!" he exclaimed. "Must be a line down!"

346

"No, sir," said Lieutenant Ferrante. "I don't think so, sir."

"What do you mean?" Barron demanded. "What do you know about this?"

"Nothing, sir," said the lieutenant, "except that telephones aren't working anywhere in the area. Or radios. No radios, sir. Our orders came by wire from Washington."

"No telephones?" demanded Barron. "No radios?"

Men and women began to drift down the lane from the cottages. They were the people who worked for Barron. They seemed frightened as they gathered in the fading light.

"It is true what he says," said one man. "The radio, it does not work."

"We do not have television tonight," said another. "There was nothing on the television but a strange noise. Now there is not even that. The electricity is gone."

"No television?" said Barron. There was an expression that was half fear and half exultation on his face. "No electricity?"

Elsie Spratt made an impatient noise. "This is a scene out of a bad movie," she said. Her voice was loud and determinedly cheerful. "Why would the roads be closed? That doesn't make sense! Exactly what did it say in that wire from Washington? What happened in Texas?"

"I don't know, ma'am," said the lieutenant. "I wasn't told. I just have—"

"I know, I know!" said Elsie. "You have your orders!"

She turned and went noisily up the steps of the ranch house into the big kitchen. Through the open windows the boys saw her twist the knobs on the battery-operated radio that stood on the counter. Almost immediately the sound of music floated out to the people in the drive.

"Hah!" said Elsie. "No radio, huh?"

"One second!" said Jupe. "That music! It's—"

"'Hail to the Chief'!" said Barron. "It's the piece the Marine Band plays when the President appears!"

The music ended, and there was a moment of silence. Then came the sound of someone clearing his throat.

"Ladies and gentlemen," said an announcer, "the President of the United States!"

Mrs Barron moved close to her husband. He put his arm around her.

"My friends," said a familiar voice, "I was informed shortly after noon today that unidentified aircraft have been sighted in parts of Texas and New Mexico and along the California coast. At this hour we have word—unconfirmed word— of landings by these craft in Fort Worth, Dallas, Taos, and San Francisco. I repeat, these reports are not confirmed.

"Let me assure you that there is no cause for alarm. Although communications in parts of the West seem to be momentarily disrupted, we have been in touch with the Kremlin and with other

348

capitals in Europe and South America. Our relations with governments to the east and to the south have never been closer, and there is no cause for alarm. . . ."

"You already said that, you dolt!" snapped Barron.

"Various military units have been called out," the voice went on, "and we ask that all citizens co-operate with these units by remaining in their homes so that strategic surface routes will not be obstructed. Please keep tuned to your local civil defence—"

There was a mighty blast of static, and Elsie Spratt's radio went dead.

"Idiot!" said Charles Barron. "Infernal idiot! How he ever got elected! On the radio for ten minutes and he told us nothing! Absolutely nothing!"

"Mr Barron, he as good as told us we're being invaded," said Hank Detweiler. The foreman looked stunned. "An invasion! By someone who has cut our communication lines! We're . . . we're alone here! We can't reach anybody to find out what's going on outside!"

5

"Get Off My Land!"

"COMMUNISTS!" shouted Charles Barron. "Anarchists! Riffraff! I don't believe there were any aircraft! They've grabbed the radio stations; that's what they've done! They're trying to frighten us into surrender! Or they've taken the President prisoner, or . . . or . . ."

Barron paused. A look of steely determination came over his face. "I'm going to drive into town," he announced. "Better yet, I'll go to Camp Roberts. I'm going to talk to someone who knows what's going on, and no one had better try to stop me!"

"I have orders, sir," said the lieutenant. "N-n-no v-vehicles on the road."

The lieutenant straightened himself, took a deep breath, and spoke slowly and carefully. "I'd appreciate it, Mr Barron, if you'd remain at the ranch for the time being. My orders, sir, are to keep the road open to the San Joaquin Valley, and to see to the safety of personnel, equipment, and installations at Rancho Valverde."

"Safety?" It was Elsie Spratt who spoke now. She had come out of the kitchen. "Our safety? Why? Who's threatening *us?* What's going on out there, Lieutenant?"

Elsie gestured toward the cliffs—and the world beyond. "What does it have to do with us?" she wanted to know.

"I . . . I don't know, ma'am," said Ferrante.

"Exactly what did your superiors tell you, Lieutenant?" demanded Charles Barron.

The lieutenant did not answer.

"Come, come!" snapped Barron. "What did your commanding officer say to you today?"

Again the lieutenant did not reply.

"It isn't the road they're so worried about, is it?" said Barron. "There are dozens of other roads much more important. It's Rancho Valverde that the people at Camp Roberts want to guard, isn't it? Why? What are we? Some kind of natural resource?"

"Maybe that's just what we are, Mr Barron," said Elsie Spratt. "I mean, how many places are there in this country that are as . . . as self-sufficient as we are? We can live here for years without going outside!"

"Aha!" cried Barron. "So that's it!"

"What, Charles?" asked Mrs Barron.

"It's happening," said Barron. "I said it would! All this falderal about unidentified aircraft is a bunch of nonsense to throw us off guard. They want to make everyone stay at home until the top dogs are safe—safe here in my valley!"

"Mr Barron, I don't understand what—" began Hank Detweiler.

"Understand?" said Barron. "Of course you understand. Either we're being attacked by some

351

foreign power—and you can take your pick which one it might be—or there's been an uprising in the country and it's spreading. Probably started right there in Washington. I read that there was going to be a rally there by some group of people calling themselves Workers United. What are they united *for*, I'd like to know! Sounded like they were up to no good. All they need is a few members in major cities—just a small number of militants—and they can pull down the government in a day!"

"They would have had to do it in less time than that," said Jupiter mildly. "Everything was normal when we left Rocky Beach this afternoon."

"Things are not normal now," said Barron. "Something disastrous is going on and that mediocrity who calls himself a President hasn't the faintest idea how to deal with it, so he'll run away! He'll run to a place where he can be safe and he'll dig in and—"

"Mr Barron," cried Elsie, "I can't manage if he's coming here. I was hired to cook for you and Mrs Barron and Hank and the others, but the kitchen isn't big enough for too many more and—"

"Elsie, you will not be asked to cook for any of that gang from the East," declared Charles Barron. "I prepared this retreat so that I would have a place to live while our civilization is . . . is adjusting itself. I have a right to enjoy this property without the presence of government officials of any stripe!"

Barron glared at Lieutenant Ferrante. "You get

off my land," he said. "I have guns and I'm going to post guards along the perimeter of the ranch. Trespassers will be shot, do you understand?"

"Yes, sir," said the lieutenant. He climbed into the jeep. "Move it!" he said to the driver. "Come on! Let's go!"

A moment later the jeep was speeding off down the lane.

"Hank," said Mr Barron, "pick ten of the most trustworthy men—men who can shoot—and send them in to see me. We'll have the fence patrolled all along the road."

"But Charles, will that help?" said Mrs Barron. "If the President does come here, won't he come by helicopter? If the guards are on the road—"

"Be still, Ernestine!" snapped Barron. "You don't understand about these things."

Barron started up the steps to his house, then paused and looked back at the Three Investigators. "You boys," he said. "You can stay here. You're innocent victims, and I won't put you out on the road where idiots like that lieutenant might—well, God knows what he might do. Elsie, would you mind feeding four more?"

"No, Mr Barron," said the cook.

"Good enough," said Barron, and he went into the house.

Jupiter, Pete, and Bob stood near the truck with Konrad. They watched Hank Detweiler call the names of ten of the ranch workers. The men went one by one up the steps into the Barron house.

By the time the men came out again, it was

getting dark, but the boys could see that each man carried a rifle and wore an ammunition belt. They went off down the lane towards the fence and the gate.

Other residents of the ranch drifted away, and when Hank Detweiler emerged from the Barron house, only Konrad and the boys remained in the driveway.

"I don't know what this is all about," said Detweiler, "but I'm sure it will blow over before long. You'll probably be on your way again tomorrow."

He went into the ranch house, which was now lighted by the soft glow of kerosene lamps. After a moment Konrad announced that he would go in, too.

"Well?" said Bob to Jupiter, after Konrad had gone.

"I don't know what to think," said Jupe. "When we left Rocky Beach at noon, everything was fine. Now, only a few hours later, we have no electricity, the radios don't work, and the telephone is dead. The President has made a speech about strange aircraft landing in several parts of the country, and there are soldiers patrolling the road so that we can't drive away."

"Maybe we can't drive away, but we can walk away," said Pete. "If we can get to someplace that's outside—"

He stopped short. "Hey," he said. "I'm beginning to sound like I really believe this place is a fortress—like the rest of the world is outside. We're inside, where it's safe."

"We aren't even sure it's safe," said Jupe. "But you're right. We should walk out to the nearest town. We won't learn anything by staying here. Maybe there really is some sort of invasion going on and we can get more news about it outside."

"But Mr Barron has guards watching the fence," said Bob. "Will they let us pass?"

"They won't know we're going," said Jupe. "We've gotten past guards before. We can do it again."

"What about the soldiers?" asked Pete.

"We can keep out of their way easily enough," Jupe declared. "They'll probably be watching the gate anyway."

"Okay," said Bob. "Anything's better than just sitting here waiting for the sky to fall."

"Then let's go," said Jupe. "Something strange is going on. I want to know what it is!"

6

The Blazing Cliffs

THE THREE INVESTIGATORS slipped quietly down
the lane in the darkness.

"I can't see a thing," Pete complained. "It's
black as pitch."

"It won't be for long," Jupe predicted.

Even as he spoke, the moon crept up from
behind the eastern cliffs. A faint silvery light
touched the valley, and the gravel lane suddenly
appeared grey-white. In the citrus groves to one
side there were shadows under the trees—deep
black shadows, sharply etched on the ground.

"Everyone off the drive!" ordered Jupe.
"Someone could see us out here." He led the way
to the shadows under the orange trees. The three
boys went on silently towards the southern
boundary of the ranch, where the fence enclosed
the property.

Fifteen minutes later they saw the fence,
grey-white in the moonlight beyond the dark
hedge of oleanders. The boys crept up to the
hedge, and standing in the shadows of the
bushes, they cautiously looked over them. Now
they could see the road beyond the hedge, and
the dark undergrowth of the wilderness on the

other side of the road. They watched, and they waited.

For a minute or two nothing moved on the road. But then there were headlights. A jeep came along slowly. A searchlight was mounted on the jeep, and the boys had to duck to avoid the beam that swept across the hedge and then swung to the south to probe the wilderness there.

As the jeep passed, a beam of light flashed from the cliffs far to the west of the gate. It danced along the edge of Barron's property.

"Someone's up there watching the fence," said Bob.

Jupiter sighed. "Probably one of Barron's men."

"He might spot us if we try to go over the fence," Pete observed, "and there's a guard near the gate. I can see him from here."

The jeep turned and came back past the gate. It stopped in the road near the spot where the boys waited. Again the watcher on the hillside sent his light stabbing through the night. It rested on the men in the jeep. There were three of them. One looked up towards the cliff, then took his rifle from his shoulder and checked it, as if to be sure it was loaded. After a moment the jeep rolled on. It topped a small rise and then dipped out of sight in the hollow beyond it.

"Why would Barron's men stop us if we go over the fence?" Bob asked reasonably. "Why would they bother? Doesn't Mr Barron just want to keep people from coming in?"

"Probably," said Jupiter, "but if Barron's guards see us, they might make some noise that would attract the attention of the soldiers."

"Well, would *they* care?" said Bob. "We're just pedestrians. We wouldn't get in the way of any military vehicles on the road."

"But suppose it isn't really military vehicles the lieutenant is concerned about," Jupe countered. "Suppose what he really wants is to keep the staff of Rancho Valverde bottled up?"

"You sound like Mr Barron," said Pete, "and I think he's *nuts*!"

"Perhaps he is, but I feel he's right about one thing," said Jupe. "The lieutenant's main interest is the ranch, not the road. He'd probably keep us from leaving. But if we can get across the road into that wilderness area, we could get away."

"Hold it!" cried Pete. "We're only a few miles from the main highway, but if it's a few miles of scrub brush, you can count me out! We'd be cut to ribbons in the dark!"

"You're probably right," said Jupe. "Okay. When I looked at the map before we left Rocky Beach, I saw another road. It's to the north of the ranch. If we could climb the cliffs, we could get to it easily."

Pete turned and stared at the nearest line of cliffs, to the west. The moon was high now, and the cliffs looked bleak as they loomed up in the ghostly light. There were black shadows in the places where gullies and ravines broke the surface.

"Okay," said Pete. "We can go out over the cliffs. But not at night, Jupe. Not without a flashlight. It's too steep and the light's too tricky. One mistake there could be our last."

"True," said Jupiter. "All right. Let's go back to the ranch, get some rest, then start out at first light."

The boys began to walk back through the citrus groves towards the ranch house. It was easier going now, with the moonlight and the lamps in the houses ahead to show them their path. When they were a hundred yards or so from the Barron house they got back on to the lane.

"Jupe?" Konrad came around the corner of the ranch house. "Jupe, are you there?" he called. "Pete? Bob?"

"We're here, Konrad," said Jupe.

"Why did you not come into the house?" asked Konrad. "Where did you go? I have been looking for you."

The back door of the Barron house opened and Charles Barron came out. "Who's wandering around out here?" he called.

"It's only us, Mr Barron," said Pete.

And then he saw a sudden, dazzling blue-white flare of light behind Konrad.

"Jupe!" cried Pete. "Look!"

The cliffs to the north of the ranch were enveloped in strange blue flames! The eerie fire leaped skyward like sheets of cold brilliance.

"What on earth?" cried Charles Barron.

For an instant the fire almost hid the bare granite surface of the cliffs. Then dense billows of white smoke gushed from the land beyond the reservoir.

Doors slammed. Feet pounded on the road. There were cries of wonder and of fear. Then, from out of the billowing, gleaming cloud on the land, an oval-shaped object rose. It hovered in the air, silver in the light from the blazing cliffs. Then it lifted upward. In seconds it was above the cliffs, vanishing into the night sky.

The blaze on the cliffs dwindled and died. There was silence at the ranch—a frozen moment when no one dared to move. Then, "Holy cow!" said Pete. "A flying saucer!"

7

An Innocent Victim

"PREPOSTEROUS!" said Charles Barron.

No one answered him.

Mrs Barron came out of the house and down the steps. "Charles!" she said excitedly. "Did you see it?"

"I'm not blind," said Barron. "Whatever it was, I saw it. Hank! Rafael! John!"

Barron pointed towards the northern cliffs. "We're going to see what in tarnation is going on!" he announced.

Jupe heard the roar of a car engine on the road. He turned to see the soldiers' jeep spurting up the lane. It stopped with a lurch just short of the ranch house.

"Mr Barron?" Lieutenant Ferrante leaped from the vehicle and started towards the ranch owner. "Are you all right?" he said. "What happened? We saw the fire!"

"I will keep you informed of all developments that concern you," snapped Barron. "In the meantime, take yourself and your jeep off my property."

"Charles!" exclaimed Mrs Barron. "Really! You needn't be so rude!"

"I'll be as rude as I choose, Ernestine," said Barron. "Lieutenant, I'm waiting."

Ferrante climbed back into the jeep. The driver threw the engine into reverse and the jeep backed away from the people who had gathered on the drive. It made a tight turn and sped down the lane.

"Pablito!" said Barron. He beckoned to a thin boy who had been watching the scene.

"Yes, Mr Barron?" said the boy. He appeared to be eight or nine years old.

"Go down to the fence and find your father and tell him that the guards are to shoot the tyres of that jeep if the soldiers try to bring it through the gate again.

Immediately one of the women spoke up. "Pablito will not go with such a message," she said. "If there must be such a message, I will go."

"Charles, all of this hardly seems necessary," said Mrs Barron. "That poor young man with the jeep is only trying to do his job."

"He's trespassing and I will not put up with trespassers, whatever their age, status, or government affiliation," announced Charles Barron. "We had better get that clear immediately or we'll be up to our hips in refugees and parasites."

Barron turned again to Detweiler. "Hank, you and Rafael and John and I will go to the upper meadow and see what in the name of fury has been going on there."

"Yes, Mr Barron," said Detweiler. The foreman looked puzzled and curious, but not at all frightened.

"I think we should be armed," said Barron. He took a key ring from his pocket and handed it to Banales, who had come out of the ranch house. "You know where the guns are," he said. "Get a rifle for each of us, and make sure they're loaded."

"Charles, you won't shoot anyone, will you?" said Mrs Barron.

"Not unless I have to," her husband answered.

Unseen by any of the adults, Jupe tugged at Pete's sleeve and beckoned to Bob. The three boys slipped back through the crowd on the lane and took shelter in the darkness between two of the cottages.

"If we want to know what really happened up there, we'd better beat Barron and the others up to the reservoir," Jupe told his friends. "Barron might just decide to keep the facts to himself."

Pete gulped. "Jupe, those guys have rifles."

"Barron just promised not to shoot anyone," said Jupe, stretching the truth. He trotted off in the direction of the parking area near the sheds.

"But Jupe," pleaded Pete, running after him, "we just saw a flying saucer! There might be aliens up by the dam!"

"All the more reason for us to get there first!" said Jupe.

Pete groaned but followed along with Bob.

It was dark in the shadows near the sheds, but once the boys started across the fields to the north of the parking area, they moved swiftly. In the moonlight they could see the dam, and when they came to the edge of the pasture between the cultivated fields and the dam, they saw sheep grazing. Several bleated in protest as the boys passed. Pete jumped in fright at the sound, but he kept going. Soon the boys were scrambling over the rocks at one side of the dam.

That afternoon Hank Detweiler had mentioned there was a meadow beyond the dam, although he had not actually showed it to them. He believed that the valley containing Rancho Valverde had once been a lake bed. In some long ago age a great earthquake had torn the lake bed in two and lifted the northernmost section above the level of the rest of the valley. Part of this upper level was now covered by the reservoir, and the rest was a meadow that sloped up away from the reservoir to the base of the cliffs.

When the boys reached the top of the dam, they followed a path around the reservoir to the grassy land on the far side of the water. Pete looked fearfully around. Were the aliens up here? He could see no one but his friends. And there was no trace of the fire that had blazed on the cliffs. In the moonlight the boys saw only naked rocks and the grass that made a dark silver carpet between the reservoir and the cliffs.

"We should have brought a light," said Bob. He started through the knee-high grass, but before he had gone many feet he stumbled and almost fell.

"Careful!" warned Jupe.

Bob took a step backward. "Jupe!" he said. "Pete! Hey! There's something . . . something here!"

Jupe and Pete hurried to his side and knelt in the grass.

"Oh, no!" exclaimed Pete. "A body! Is he . . . is he alive?"

Jupe leaned close to the still body of a man. "Yes. He's still breathing."

There was the sound of voices near the dam, and the clatter of dislodged stones rolling down an incline. Charles Barron and his men were coming.

Jupe gave a mighty heave and the man on the meadow rolled over on to his back. His face showed white in the moonlight. The eyes were closed and the mouth was partly open. His breath came in quick gasps.

There was a faint odour now. It was the smell of singed hair.

"All right!" Charles Barron shouted. "Hold it right there! One move and I'll blow your head off!"

The boys blinked in the glare of flashlights.

"Why, it's the boys from the salvage yard," said Barron.

"Mr Barron, this man is hurt," Jupiter called.

Barron and Hank Detweiler hurried forward.

"De Luca!" exclaimed Barron. "Simon de Luca!"

Detweiler knelt and held his flashlight close to the man's face. He touched de Luca cautiously.

365

"He's got a lump right behind the ear," said Detweiler, "and . . . and some of his hair's burned off!"

The unconscious man stirred.

"Okay, Simon," said Detweiler. "We're with you."

The man opened his eyes and stared up at Detweiler.

"What happened?" asked Detweiler.

De Luca moved his head, then winced. "Did I fall?" he asked. He looked around slowly. "The sheep! Where are the sheep?"

"In the lower field, the other side of the dam," said Detweiler.

De Luca sat up carefully. "I don't understand," he said. "I came out to check on the sheep. I came almost to the dam. Everything was okay."

He looked anxiously at Detweiler. "I was in the lower meadow," he said. "That's the last thing I remember. How did I get here? Did you bring me?"

"No, we didn't, Simon," said Detweiler. "These boys found you here. Do you remember seeing anything? Flames? Smoke? Anything at all?"

"Nothing," said de Luca. He put his head in his hands, and for the first time he touched his hair. "What's happened?" he cried. "My hair! What is the matter with my hair?"

"Simon, you got kind of singed," said Detweiler.

Banales knelt beside the injured man and began to talk softly in Spanish. The others spread out to search the meadow. The light of their torches showed them charred places on the ground, as if flames had burned fiercely and briefly in the green grass. There were sooty streaks on the cliffs where the blue fires had blazed. That was all, except for an object that Detweiler found near the base of the cliffs—a thing no bigger than a man's hand. It was made of lustrous silver-grey metal and it was hinged in the middle. At either end was a series of prongs.

"Some kind of clamp," said Detweiler. "John, do you know what it is?"

John Aleman took the object from Detweiler and turned it this way and that in his hands. "Beats me," he said. "Looks like it's off some sort of machine."

"Or an aircraft?" asked Detweiler.

"Maybe," said Aleman. "The metal—it's some kind of alloy. I don't know just what. It doesn't look like steel. It's more like pewter. And there's no residue of oil on it. Look. You close it like this and the prongs lock. It could be some sort of switch, but it's not like any switches that I've ever seen."

Barron glared around the meadow and then looked up at the cliffs. "Not like any you've seen?" he said.

They were silent then, thinking of the blazing cliffs and the clouds of smoke, and of the strange craft that had lifted from the meadow. De Luca felt his singed hair. His face was bewildered.

"Someone was here," said Aleman quietly. His square, blunt-featured face was grim.

"Somebody came and . . . and did something to Simon and went away again. But where did they come from? And where did they go? Who were they?"

No one answered. From the hills above them came the lonely cry of a coyote. Pete shivered at the wailing sound, and at the memory of the flying saucer. He wondered if aliens had walked in the meadow—if aliens were hiding there right now.

8

Attack!

SIMON DE LUCA was brought back from the meadow by truck. After he was carried into one of the cottages on the lane, Mary Sedlack and Mrs Barron examined him. They tested his reflexes, peered into his eyes with a small flashlight, and decided that he had suffered a mild concussion.

"Mrs Barron acts as if she had medical training," said Bob to Elsie Spratt. The Three Investigators were in the ranch-house kitchen with the cook, who sat nervously rubbing her deformed finger.

"Mrs Barron was in nurse's training when she was a girl," said Elsie. "She does volunteer work one day a week at the hospital in town. Pity she married that old grouch. She'd have made a great nurse."

The boys heard a car in the drive. Jupe got up and went to the open door. A few minutes before, Charles Barron had driven to the gate to demand that Lieutenant Ferrante notify his superiors at Camp Roberts that a herder had been attacked. Barron was back now, and Mrs Barron stood in the lane talking with him.

"Well?" she said. "What happened?"

Barron snorted. "That snivelling excuse for an officer has a field telephone, but it's like everything else around here. It isn't working."

"Of course not," said Mrs Barron happily. "When the rescuers are in our atmosphere, they're able to disrupt our electrical field."

"Ernestine, you don't even know what an electrical field *is*!" cried Charles Barron.

"No, actually, I don't," she said. "But it's terribly important, isn't it? When extraterrestrial visitors cause the field to stop functioning, everything stops—the radio, telephones, cars, everything!"

"Our car still works," Barron pointed out.

"Perhaps the interference isn't complete," said Mrs Barron. "When the visitors return, it will be complete."

"And when will that be?" Barron asked, exasperated.

"They will let us know," she replied. She went up the steps into the big house.

Barron said several things under his breath, then followed his wife.

"Good for her!" said Elsie Spratt, who had come to the ranch-house door to stand beside Jupe. "She got the last word for a change!"

Elsie went back to the table and sat down. "That old goat she's married to is enough to drive a saint mad," she said. "If Mrs Barron says a thing is black, he decides it's white just to spite her. But tonight she's got it all her own way. She's been predicting flying saucers and visitors from outer space all along, and he's insisted that we'll be taken over by Communists or bureaucrats or labour unions, and she turns out to be right!"

"Do you really think she is?" said Jupe. "Do you really think we have visitors from outer space?"

Elsie looked away from him. "What else could it be?" she said. She stood up, suddenly brisk, and got a candle and a tin candlestick from one of the cupboards.

"You can take this with you when you go to bed," she said, handing the candlestick to the boys. Then she went up the stairs carrying a lamp. Mary Sedlack came in and went up, too.

Banales, Detweiler, and Aleman also had rooms in the ranch house, and they came in soon after. Banales showed Konrad and the boys where they were to sleep in a big bunkroom at the front of the house. Konrad declared that he didn't dare shut his eyes, but he stretched out on a cot and was soon breathing deeply and evenly.

The boys lay in the darkness for a long while after the candle was put out. They listened to the noises made by the old house, and by the people in it. Somewhere nearby someone tossed restlessly in bed. Someone else paced in the darkness.

Jupe awoke in the early hours of the morning and couldn't get back to sleep. His mind kept turning over the events of the previous day. After a time he got up and went to the window. The moon had set, and the ranch was dark and quiet. No one stirred outside. Jupe couldn't guess the hour, but he thought that dawn must be fairly close.

Impulsively, he put on his clothes and moved softly to the cots where his fellow Investigators slept. A light touch brought each of them awake. A few minutes later, all three boys were creeping down the stairs and out of the house. By the faint light of the stars, Jupe led the others past the workers' cottages to the parking area near the sheds. There the boys huddled under a tree.

"What gives?" asked Pete.

Jupe frowned and pulled at his lip, as he always did when he was thinking furiously. "Would it be very difficult for someone to imitate the President's voice?" he finally asked. "And would it be hard to get a recording of the Marine Band playing 'Hail to the Chief'?"

"You think this is a hoax?" asked Bob.

"I don't know. But it makes me think of a famous radio broadcast that I once read about," said Jupe. "It was done by Orson Welles, and if it didn't start out to be a hoax, it sure wound up as one."

Jupe leaned against the trunk of a tree and cleared his throat, as if he were about to give a lecture.

"Way back in the 1930s," he said, "before there was any television, Welles went on radio one Hallowe'en night with a dramatization of a science fiction story by H. G. Wells, the English novelist. The story was called *War of the Worlds*. It was about monsters from Mars who came to invade the earth. At the very beginning of the programme, an announcer came on to say that it was only a radio play, but the rest of the programme sounded just like a series of emergency news broadcasts. Anyone who tuned in late heard bulletins about the strange objects from outer space that had fallen to earth near a little town in New Jersey. They heard that the strange objects were spaceships, and that terrible creatures with tentacles were emerging from them. Parts of the programme were supposed to be coming from mobile units at the scene, and the radio audience heard sirens and crowd noises. There were reports of poisonous gases coming from the New Jersey marshes. And there were bulletins on traffic conditions on the major highways as people supposedly fled from the invaders.

"What the broadcasting company didn't know until the programme was over was that people really *were* fleeing from the Martians. Thousands of them thought the reports on the radio were real, and they panicked.

"Now suppose that the broadcast we heard today didn't really come from Washington? Suppose the voice we heard wasn't really the voice of the President? Suppose we were listening to a broadcast that came from around here." Jupe gestured towards the cliffs that surrounded them.

"Okay," said Bob. "There could be a transmitter out there. Maybe it could jam the regular wavelengths by broadcasting noise. Maybe it could broadcast a fake speech. But the soldiers on the road . . ."

"Suppose they're imposters," said Jupe. "That lieutenant is so military—so full of spit and polish. He could be acting a part."

"Maybe he just got his commission," said Bob. "He *is* kind of overdressed. He even wears his gloves nonstop. But I hear that new officers are like that."

"If it's a hoax, somebody's gone to an awful lot of trouble," said Pete. "Why would anyone do that? The fire on the cliffs was—well, it was pretty weird. It can't be easy to make bare rock cliffs look like they're burning. And we did see a spaceship take off. And that sheep herder—his hair was burned! And what about that gadget that Hank Detweiler found on the meadow—that clamp or switch or whatever it was?"

"All very convincing," said Jupe, "But stop and think about it, Pete. Your father works in movie studios. Did anything happen today that couldn't be duplicated by a good special effects man?"

"N-no," said Pete after a second. "I guess not."

"There's only one way to find out for sure," said Jupe. "We have to do what we planned in the first place. We have to hike out to the nearest town and see what's happening there."

"That means we go up those cliffs, doesn't it?" said Bob. "Okay. Let's do it."

"Oh, no!' groaned Pete. "Do we have to go back to that meadow? What if someone—or something—is up there?"

"That's what you said last night," Jupe pointed out, "and we didn't find anyone there besides the herder. Quit worrying. We won't go until it starts getting light."

The boys waited impatiently until a faint, flat light began to replace the blackness in the valley. Then they got up and started swiftly towards the meadow. When they had passed the cultivated fields and reached the edge of the pasture, they saw fog. It rose from the reservoir and flowed down over the dam in a fluffy stream. They hiked towards it, taking care to avoid the sheep on the lower meadow, but at the foot of the dam they paused. Each of them felt a thrill of dread. Into the mind of each came the picture of Simon de Luca lying on the ground, his hair singed as if by rocket fire.

The boys groped around the rocks and bushes at the edge of the dam. When they had climbed to the top of the dam, they started to skirt the reservoir. Pete was in the lead, wading through fog.

Suddenly he cried out.

Someone stood in the path—a tall, thin person who seemed to have a head too large for his body. It took a moment for the boys to realize that this person was wearing a suit of glossy white material—a suit that shone even in the dim light—and that the head was covered with a huge helmet. It was a helmet that might have been used by a diver or an astronaut, or perhaps by an alien who could not breathe Earth's air.

Pete shouted again. Jupe saw the creature lift an arm and strike out. At that same instant, something behind Jupe clutched him around the throat. He was lifted up so that he saw the grey sky above and the pale morning stars. Then came an explosion of pain in the back of his neck. He felt himself falling into darkness and then he saw no more.

9

An Invitation to Snoop

JUPE OPENED HIS EYES and saw that the sky
overhead was blue. The fog was gone and
Konrad was kneeling beside him.

"Jupe, are you all right?" Konrad asked
anxiously.

Jupe groaned. A pain ran from his right
shoulder to his ear. Shaking, he managed to sit
up.

Nearby, Rafael Banales was helping Pete get
to his feet, and John Aleman talked softly to
Bob, who sat on the ground with his knees drawn
up to his chin.

"Konrad," said Jupe, "how did you find us?"

Konrad grinned. "It is not hard. I wake up and
you are gone. I think if I am Jupiter Jones, I go
where there has been excitement. So I wake Mr
Aleman and Mr Banales and we get Mr
Detweiler and come here."

Jupe looked around. Hank Detweiler was
standing behind him, scowling. "What
happened?" said Detweiler.

"Someone was waiting here," said Jupe. "I saw
a person in a spacesuit. He hit Pete."

"You're kidding!" said Detweiler.

"No, he's not kidding." Pete touched his head and winced. "That guy walloped me a good one."

Jupe touched his neck, remembering how it was. "A second person came up behind me," he said. "He used a sort of choke hold on me and I blacked out."

"There must have been three of them," said Bob. "The one who got me smelled like horses."

"What?" Charles Barron had appeared suddenly on the meadow. "Who smelled like horses? Hank, what's going on here?"

"The boys left the ranch house sometime during the night," Detweiler explained. "They came up here and they were attacked. Pete says it was a guy in a spacesuit. Bob says it was somebody who smelled of horses."

"Nonsense!" said Barron. "Spacemen do not smell like horses. Hank, I came up in one of the trucks. Let's get these boys down to the lower meadow. I'll take them back to the ranch house and Mrs Barron can see to them there."

Ten minutes later, Jupiter, Pete and Bob were climbing into their beds in the bunkroom, under orders from Mary Sedlack and Elsie.

"We're having a run of good luck," said Mary dryly. "Simon de Luca could have been killed on that meadow last night, and you might have bought it this morning, but you didn't. Don't push it. Stay away from the meadow. It's not a healthy place right now."

She and Elsie went out and down the stairs.

"She didn't smell of horses just now," said Jupiter, "but she did yesterday afternoon."

"You think she might have been the one who attacked us?" said Bob.

Jupiter shrugged. "Who knows? She's probably strong enough. I think that at least one of our attackers was an earthling. I refuse to believe that an alien from another planet was riding horseback."

Bob stared at the ceiling. "A person who rides horseback? That wouldn't narrow it down much. There's Hank Detweiler. I bet he rides. Barron does, I suppose. Mary spends a lot of time with the horses. Probably Banales and Aleman ride. Then there are the ranch hands who live in the cottages. We know almost nothing about them."

"You know almost nothing about whom?" said Mrs Barron. She had come quietly up the stairs, and now she stood in the doorway smiling at the boys.

"My husband is very upset about you," she said. "He told me you were attacked by . . . well, by the rescuers."

"We were attacked by three people, Mrs Barron," said Jupe. "At least one of them was wearing a spacesuit."

Mrs Barron sat down on the edge of Jupiter's bed. She had a tiny flashlight and she used it to look into Jupe's eyes. "You're all right," she said softly. "You've been fortunate."

She went on to examine Pete. "What were you doing up on the meadow anyway?" she wanted to know.

"We were trying to get off the ranch and get to the nearest town," said Jupe. "Mrs Barron, you seem so sure that we're being visited by people from another planet. Is your interest in the deliverance well known to the people here at Rancho Valverde?"

"I suppose so." Her face was troubled. "I imagine everyone on the ranch knows about it. But . . . but I'm not absolutely sure, you know, that the rescuers were here last night."

"You're not?" said Jupiter.

She shook her head and went to Bob's side. "That craft on the meadow last night looked exactly like spaceships that have been reported in other parts of the country. Earthlings have spoken to the rescuers. But Simon was *hurt*—and you boys were hurt. The visitors have never hurt anyone before. They're so highly developed intellectually that they're telepathic. I can't believe that they'd resort to striking people. That isn't why they come. They come to help us!"

"Yes, of course," said Jupiter. "Mrs Barron, the planet Omega is reported to be in the galaxy nearest to Earth, in the constellation of Andromeda. Do you know how far away that is?"

"Oh, about two million light years," she said. "I know. One can't imagine a journey of two million light years. But the rescuers have a more advanced technology than we have on Earth. Distance doesn't matter much to them. They've explored a lot of deep space. It's all explained in Korsakov's book *Parallels*. Korsakov actually

380

visited Omega and he was returned to Earth so that he could prepare the way for the rescuers. In *Parallels* he tells how our wars have been worrisome for the people of Omega, and since we have the atomic bomb—well, there is increased tension in all of the cosmos."

"Um, yes," said Jupiter.

"The rescuers will eventually remove us from the dangers on Earth," said Mrs Barron. "They won't take all of us, of course, but they will rescue the people who can make the greatest contribution to rebuilding our civilization when the time of chaos is over.

"My husband has always refused to believe that this will happen. But last night after he saw the spaceship, he didn't go to bed. Instead he sat up and read Korsakov's book and the one by Contreras. This morning he is willing to believe that we were visited by rescuers."

"That should please you," said Jupe.

"Not if the rescuers turn out to be ruffians who go about knocking people on the head," she said. "I wish I could be sure they're not."

"You know," said Jupe, "those attackers might not have been aliens at all."

"I know." She smiled sadly. "Somebody could be staging a very elaborate hoax. I mentioned the possibility to my husband this morning and he flew into a rage. I should have known better. He has decided that there are aliens here and he doesn't wish to be contradicted. He believes that they have come to take him away to safety."

"I guess he would like that idea," said Jupe. "Mrs Barron, tell me about the staff here."

She looked surprised. "The staff? You *are* an inquisitive boy, aren't you? I feel as if I'm making a report down at police headquarters."

Jupe's wallet lay on a table next to his bed. Without a word he reached for it, took a card out of one of the pockets, and handed the card to Mrs Barron. It read:

THE THREE INVESTIGATORS
"We Investigate Anything"
?　　?　　?

First Investigator	....	Jupiter Jones
Second Investigator	....	Peter Crenshaw
Records and Research	....	Bob Andrews

"Investigators!" said Mrs Barron.

"Solving puzzles is our special interest," said Jupe, "and we are quite good at it. We are not prejudiced, you see, as many adult investigators are. We are willing to concede that the most absurd events can actually take place, and frequently we are proved correct."

"I see," said Mrs Barron. "Well, perhaps the events that have taken place here are rather absurd, and perhaps we do need some detectives. I think I do, especially. Will you accept me as a client?"

"Certainly," said Jupiter. "You have just retained The Three Investigators. Now tell us about the staff."

"All right." She sat in a small armchair at the foot of Jupe's bed. "We met Hank Detweiler when we visited the Armstrong Ranch in Texas. Charles was impressed with the job he was doing there, and he had the credit bureau in Austin run a check on him. Charles is a great believer in credit ratings. He says if people are careless about money, they'll be slipshod about other things, too. Hank wasn't careless about money, so Charles hired him.

"We found Rafael through the post-graduate office of the University of California at Davis. He graduated six years ago and went to work for West Coast Citrus, and he had a good record. John Aleman owned his own garage in Indio. He worked on our car when we were passing through and did an excellent job."

"His credit record was satisfactory?" said Jupe.

"It was. Elsie's wasn't so good. She paid her bills late, and several times there wasn't enough money in her bank account to cover her cheques. She'd been helping a younger brother, however, so it was understandable that she ran short on cash now and then. She was working as a cook in a small restaurant in Saugus, and with the salary she made there she set her brother up in a little radio shop. She's a very good cook, so Charles decided to take a chance on her."

"What about Mary Sedlack?" said Jupe.

"She used to work in a livery stable in a place called Sunland," said Mrs Barron. "She heard about Rancho Valverde from a friend who lives in

Santa Maria and she applied for a job. She wants to go to school and become a vet, so it's to her advantage to live here and put her salary in the bank. She's never had any credit—never had a charge account or a car loan or anything like that—so there wasn't any credit rating for her, but Mr Barron checked on her father. He's all right. He works for a savings and loan company."

"And what about the people who live in the cottages on the lane?" asked Jupe.

Mrs Barron smiled. "They were all employed by Rancho Valverde before my husband bought the property. Some of them were born right here on the ranch. This is their home."

She stood up. "It doesn't seem possible that any of the people who work here could be involved in a hoax," she said. "Look what they could lose. And what would they gain?"

"Mr Barron is a wealthy man," said Jupe. "Perhaps there's a plan afoot to rob him."

"Rob him of what?" she demanded. "There's nothing of any great value here. We don't collect expensive things. There isn't even a large amount of cash here. My husband keeps his money in a bank, like everyone else. There's a current account in the Pacific Coast National Bank in Santa Barbara. There's a safe deposit box there too. My jewellery is in the box, and I suppose Mr Barron has other valuables there, too."

"Could there be something else?" said Jupiter. "It might be something you've overlooked—something you wouldn't even think was important, but which someone else could want desperately. Or someone might want to trick your husband out of spite."

"I suppose that's possible," said Mrs Barron.

"If the appearance of the spaceship is a hoax," said Jupe, "then there is a reason for the hoax, no matter how far-fetched the reason may be."

Mrs Barron sat thinking for a moment, then said, "I can't imagine what it would be. There simply isn't anything here. You can see for yourself—"

She stopped short, stared at Jupe, then said, "Why, of course. You *can* see for yourself!"

"What, Mrs Barron?" asked Jupe.

"Well, you could see our house," she said. "Everything we have—everything that's personal, that is—is in the house. Except for my jewellery, of course. Now suppose that after lunch, when Maria, who serves our meals, goes to her own house up the lane to have her siesta, and when my husband goes out to ride about the ranch—he does it every day—suppose you come over and we'll go through the house together. Something might occur to you. You might see something that I wouldn't notice."

"A good idea," said Jupe.

"My husband would not approve, of course," said Mrs Barron.

"I'm sure he wouldn't," said Jupe.

"So we won't say anything about it."

Jupe grinned. "You can trust us, Mrs Barron," he said.

"Yes. I believe I can."

She went out and Jupe leaned back against his pillow. He began pulling at his lower lip, a sure sign that he was deep in thought. His face was grave.

Pete grinned. "The great Sherlock Jones is thinking so hard that I can smell the wood burning," he said. "Have you reached any conclusions, Sherlock?"

"No," said Jupe. "I'm only considering a number of bewildering possibilities."

"Which are?" said Bob.

"That someone is trying to isolate Charles Barron completely for some criminal purpose. He is being cut off from all contact with the outside world so that he can be blackmailed or cheated or held for ransom. Then there is the possibility that someone here on the ranch has a grudge against him and simply wants to torment him and hold him up to ridicule. And then there is the third possibility."

"What's that?" asked Pete.

"That our puzzle is intergalactic and we are truly being invaded by people from another world!"

10

Trapped!

THE THREE INVESTIGATORS had their lunch at the long table in the ranch-house kitchen, together with Elsie Spratt, Hank Detweiler, and the rest of Charles Barron's staff. It was a silent meal, with each one absorbed in his own thoughts. When the refrigerator suddenly started just as Elsie was serving the soup, Bob jumped as if someone had shot him.

"The electricity on again?" said Pete.

"I've got the generators going," said John Aleman.

"Oh, yeah," said Pete. "I forgot."

Hank Detweiler looked searchingly at Pete. "Don't forget that Mr Barron's given orders about you boys," he said. "You're to stay off the meadow. We've posted a couple of guards up there to see that you do."

"What does that mean?" said Elsie. "Is Mr Barron really that worried about the boys, or is he expecting another visit by the people from outer space?"

"Probably a little of both," said Detweiler. "He figures the flying saucer's got to come back because they left some of their people here somewhere."

"The ones who attacked us?" said Jupiter.

Detweiler scowled. "Not sure I believe one thing that's happened," he announced. "I'd give a sight to know where that guy in the spacesuit could be—him and his friends."

"Maybe they went out over the cliffs," Jupe suggested.

"Could have," said Detweiler, and he let the subject drop.

The meal continued without further conversation. When they had finished, the Three Investigators excused themselves and went out to sit on the back steps. They were there when Charles Barron slammed out of his house and started up the drive towards the stable.

Barron stopped when he saw the boys. "Don't you wander off again," he warned. "If I hear that you've been up to the meadow—or anywhere near it—I'll see that you're locked up."

"Yes, sir," said Jupe.

Barron went on his way, and soon the woman named Maria came out of the big house. She smiled at the boys and walked past them to one of the cottages up the lane.

When Maria was out of sight, Jupe stood and led the way to the front of the big house.

Mrs Barron was waiting on the veranda. There were a number of cast-iron chairs and tables there, white-painted and formal, looking prickly and uncomfortable with their patterns of twisting vines and leaves. Mrs Barron had seated herself on one of the chairs. Her hands were folded primly in her lap, but her eyes sparkled with excitement. Jupe guessed that she regarded the inspection of her own house as an adventure.

The boys had decided that morning that only Jupiter would go through the Barron house with Mrs Barron, and that while Jupe was in the house, Pete and Bob would try to discover what was happening among the soldiers who kept watch on the road.

"I'll see you later," said Jupe to his friends, "and you watch it when you get down near that fence."

"You bet," said Pete.

Jupe went up the front steps of the Barron house. Mrs Barron rose and went ahead of him into the hall. When Jupe closed the door, the two of them stood for a moment, listening to the grandfather clock that ticked on the stair landing.

"Where do we begin?" said Mrs Barron.

"This is as good a place as any," said Jupe. He glanced into the formal parlour with its Turkish carpets and velvet chairs and settees. He saw nothing there that any thief could want. He turned away and went into the music room, where there was a baby grand piano, a few little gilt chairs, and some cabinets that held heaps of sheet music and a few children's drawings.

"My boys did those when they were in primary school," said Mrs Barron. "I thought they were rather good."

"Very nice," said Jupe, privately thinking they were awful. He put the drawings back into the cabinet where he had found them and went on to the dining room. The sideboards there held some sterling silver.

"Silver is valuable," said Jupe, "but I don't think your things are worth the trouble of constructing an elaborate hoax. If a thief took your crockery, or your silver coffee service, and then had to fence the things—he wouldn't get all that much."

"I suppose not," said Mrs Barron.

In the kitchen there were cupboards crammed with supplies—preserves and jellies that had been produced at the ranch. The labels were dated and none was more than a year old.

When Jupe finished his inspection of the kitchen, he opened the door that led to the basement. Mrs Barron switched on the light below, and the two went down into a shadowy, dusty place where there was a woodpile and a bin heaped with coal.

"It was just like this in Wisconsin," said Mrs Barron. She gestured towards the huge old furnace near the coal bin. "Charles wanted it to be the way he remembered it—furnace and all."

Jupe looked around at boxes and crates and trunks that stood on the cement floor. Through an opening in the back wall he saw another flight of stairs leading out of the cellar, directly to the outside. It was the old-fashioned kind of cellar entrance, with a hinged sheet of plywood over the stairwell serving as both a roof and a door.

Then Jupe's eye was caught by an enclosure in one corner of the basement, reaching from floor to ceiling. It was made of heavy metal mesh, and it had a sturdy metal door secured with a padlock.

Curious, Jupe crossed the room, peered through the mesh, and saw the stocks of rifles standing on a rack against the wall. There were boxes of ammunition on the floor, and there were explosives, too. A second gun rack on the far wall held shotguns and handguns.

"Quite an arsenal," said Jupe. "Was that in the basement in Wisconsin, too?"

Mrs Barron shook her head, and her face was sad. "It's new," she said. "Charles had it put in about six months ago. He . . . he felt that the time would come when we would have to protect ourselves."

"I see," said Jupe.

He turned away from the guns and began to open the trunks that stood around. They were all empty, and so were the boxes and the crates.

"Nothing," he said at last.

"No," said Mrs Barron. "We don't really use the basement much."

The two went up the stairs to the kitchen, and then Mrs Barron led the way up the back stairs to the second floor.

There were servants' rooms near the stairway, but they were unused and empty. In the other rooms were huge antique beds with rich brocade spreads. Jupe saw bureaus topped with marble and mirrors that reached to the ceiling. Mrs Barron went into her room and opened closet doors and bureau drawers.

"There's nothing, really—not even trinkets. I don't wear much jewellery here at the ranch," she said. "I just keep a string of pearls and my engagement ring, and everything else is in the safe deposit box."

"Is there an attic?" said Jupe. "And what about pictures? Are any of the pictures here in the house valuable? And what about papers? Does Mr Barron have any documents that could be the bait for some swindler?"

Mrs Barron smiled. "Our pictures are family portraits, but they're not valuable. Except to Charles, of course. About papers, I wouldn't really know. I don't understand much about finance and business. Charles keeps everything in his office."

Mrs Barron went out past the front stairs and Jupe followed her. A small room in the southeast corner of the house was even stiffer and more old-fashioned than the ones Jupe had already seen. It was furnished as an office, with a roll-top desk, a leather-covered armchair, an oak swivel chair, and several oak filing cabinets. There was a fireplace in this room, and over the mantle there was a steel engraving of a factory building.

"That's a picture of Barron International," said Mrs Barron, gesturing towards the engraving. "The factory that made the first Barron fortune. I don't come in here often, but . . ."

Mrs Barron stopped. From the driveway outside someone was calling her name. She went to the side window and threw up the sash.

"Mrs Barron!" cried a woman who stood in the driveway below. "Please, can you come quick! Nilda Ramirez fell from a tree and her arm is bleeding."

"Be right there!" called Mrs Barron.

She closed the window again. "You get on with the search," she told Jupe. "I'm sure you don't need me hovering at your elbow. I'll get the first-aid kit and go to see about the little Ramirez girl. Don't be too long. Charles will be back from his ride soon."

"I'll hurry," Jupe promised.

Mrs Barron went out, and Jupe heard her rummaging in the big bathroom that opened off the front hall. Then she went downstairs and out. Jupe stood at the side window while she went up the lane with the woman who had come to get her. He then looked out the front window, across the lawn to the citrus groves and the other end of the lane. No one was in sight.

Jupe turned away from the window and crossed to the fireplace. He lifted the engraving of Barron International away from the wall, and he smiled.

"Finally!" he said aloud.

There was a safe under the picture. It was an old-fashioned safe and it did not have a combination lock. Instead it could be opened with a key.

Jupe guessed that Mrs Barron was not aware that the safe was there. He wondered if Barron had found it in some antique store and had had it installed in the house after the place was moved to

California. He tugged at the handle. The safe was securely locked, as he had expected. The roll top of the desk was locked, too, and so were the filing cabinets.

Jupe sat down in the armchair and imagined that he was Charles Barron. What would he lock in a safe? And would he carry the key to the safe with him when he went riding? Or would he leave it in the house? Or would he have a second key?

Jupe brightened when this idea occurred to him. Charles Barron was thorough. Surely there was a second key hidden in the house.

Jupe took heart and began to search. He knelt and felt the undersides of the chairs and the desk. He groped along the tops of the two windows and the door. He peered behind the files. At last he lifted the edge of the rug and saw a floorboard that was shorter than the others, and a different colour. He pulled at the edge of this board with his fingernails, and the board lifted up. Underneath was a compartment with the keys.

"Not really so clever, Mr Barron," Jupe murmured. He took the keys—three of them on a ring—and opened the safe.

There were velvet boxes in the safe—jewel boxes. Jupe opened them one after another and gazed in awe at emeralds and diamonds and rubies. There were necklaces and rings and watches and stick pins and bracelets. Most of the pieces were old-fashioned in design. Jupe guessed that they had originally belonged to Mr Barron's mother.

So Mrs Barron's jewels were not in a safe deposit box as she believed. Did anyone else—besides Charles Barron—know that? The jewels were certainly worth stealing. But were they worth an elaborate hoax? Jupe thought not. He wondered why the jewels had been moved to the house. Then he realized that this was only one more sign of Barron's distrust of his own world. A safe deposit box could only be as safe as the bank it was in, and Charles Barron did not believe in banks. He believed in land and gold.

Jupe locked the safe and turned to the roll-top desk.

The second key on the ring opened the desk. The first object Jupe saw when he rolled the top of the desk back was the metal clamp that had been found on the meadow that morning. Jupe turned it over in his hands, then put it aside. He sat down in the swivel chair and began to go through the chequebooks that were heaped in the desk.

There were chequebooks from a number of banks in several cities—the Prairie Bank of Milwaukee, the Desert Trust Company of Salt Lake City, the Riverside Trust Company of New York, and the Central Illinois National Bank of Springfield. Jupe flipped through the stubs in each of the books and saw that the last cheque written on each account was for the entire balance. Barron had closed out all but one of his accounts. The one that remained open was with the Santa Barbara Merchants Trust. The last entry in the cheque register for this account showed that

395

Charles Barron had more than ten thousand dollars on deposit.

Jupe leaned back in his chair and began to read through the list of cheques, and he almost whistled aloud in astonishment. Millions of dollars had been deposited in the Santa Barbara institution in the past two years, and huge cheques had been written on the account. Some of the money had gone to pay for equipment for the ranch. There were cheques to a feed company and cheques to several oil companies and cheques to auto dealers for trucks and to garages for repairs. There were cheques to engineering companies for irrigation equipment and to cement companies for sand and gravel and cement. Barron had spent enormous amounts to equip his ranch.

But in addition, huge sums had gone to firms with names that Jupiter did not know. A company called Peterson, Benson, and Hopwith had received money from Barron on more than ten occasions, and the amounts varied from fifty thousand dollars to more than two hundred thousand. Numbers of cheques had been written to the Pacific Stamp Exchange, for sums that were stunning.

Jupe put aside the chequebook, frowning. He had seen nothing to indicate that Barron was interested in stamps. And Mrs Barron had said that she and her husband weren't collectors of any sort.

In addition to the chequebooks, there were papers in the desk—statements from a brokerage firm that had an office on Wilshire Boulevard in

Los Angeles. They had sold several million dollars' worth of securities for Barron over a period of eight months. Among the statements there was not a single notification that Barron had purchased any new securities. He had sold and sold and the brokers had forwarded cheques to him following each sale.

Jupe put the brokers' statements back where he had found them and began to leaf through another stack of papers. These were invoices and notes, and again they had to do with purchases that Barron had made for the ranch. Jupe was impressed again with the enormous amounts Barron had spent on his fortress. The bill for lawn furniture alone was enough to furnish most homes from attic to cellar.

Jupe smiled at that particular invoice. It was for forty-three cast-iron chairs, Swedish ivy design, ten tables, same design, all to be made to Mr Barron's specifications as discussed, and to be delivered to Rancho Valverde within ninety days.

It was typical of the millionaire, Jupe supposed, that he had had lawn furniture made to order when he could have purchased it at almost any patio shop. But Charles Barron was used to having things exactly as he wanted them. Perhaps he hadn't liked the designs or the craftsmanship of the furniture in patio shops.

Jupiter put the invoices back in place, closed the roll top, and locked the desk. He sat for a moment, bothered by a small, nagging feeling that he had seen something important. While he was trying to think what it could be that pricked at the edge of his consciousness, he heard a sound below.

Someone had opened the kitchen door and come into the house. Someone was walking across the kitchen. The tread was heavy. It was not Mrs Barron coming back.

Jupe came to his feet, took one soundless step, and knelt to put the keys into the compartment in the floor. He closed the loose floorboard over the hidden place and pulled the rug over the board.

The footsteps below sounded in the dining room and then in the hall.

Jupe looked around frantically. The footsteps were coming up the front stairs. There was no time for Jupe to get through the hall to the back stairs without being seen. Jupe was trapped!

11

Bob Takes a Chance

AFTER JUPE LEFT THEM, Bob and Pete hiked down through the citrus groves to the fence that ran along the southern edge of Barron's property. The boys crouched behind the thick hedge of oleanders that grew near the fence and looked out at the road.

A tent had been put up in the wilderness area across the road from the gate of the ranch. Two men in uniform lounged on the ground in front of the tent and sipped something from tin cups. They resolutely ignored the ranch hand who was guarding the gate. He in turn ignored them. He was leaning against a gatepost and holding a rifle. His back was to the boys, who were hiding to the west of the gate.

Pete nudged Bob and pointed to a bulky piece of equipment that hung on a tree near the soldiers' tent.

"What is it?" whispered Bob.

"I'm not sure, but I think it's a field telephone," said Pete.

As if to confirm this opinion, there was a tinny, jangling sound. One of the men got up and went to the tree. He took a receiver from a hook and spoke, saying something the boys could not hear.

"How about that!" murmured Bob. "And they told Mr Barron their telephone wasn't working."

Bob strained to hear the conversation that was going on, but the campsite was too far away. He could catch only an occasional word or two. After a few minutes the soldier hung the receiver back in its place and said something to his companion. They both laughed, then grew silent as they watched one of Barron's men come along from the east, walking between the oleander hedge and the fence.

The man patrolling the fence glanced across the road at the encampment there. He paused to exchange a few words with the man who watched the gate, then he turned and started back the way he had come.

"Hey, we'd better get away from this hedge," said Pete softly. "I bet another man will come along from the west any second now."

The boys retreated to a nearby stand of eucalyptus trees. Sure enough, a second sentry on patrol appeared, approaching the gate from the opposite direction. After he left, a jeep drove slowly past the gate. It was headed west and it did not stop at the camp. The two men in the vehicle ignored Barron's guard, and the guard did not even glance at them.

"The two sides sure aren't talking to one another," said Pete.

"I'd give a lot to know what they're saying to each other over in that camp," said Bob. He looked at the fence in a calculating way, then stared up and down the road.

"I'm going over the fence," he said suddenly.

"Huh?" Pete gaped at his friend in surprise.

"I said I'm going over the fence." Bob pointed. "Look down there. There's a bend in the road so that the guard at the gate won't be able to see me and neither will the soldiers. The sentry on this side should be out of sight by now. And the trees grow close to the fence there, so even if one of Mr Barron's men is up on the cliffs watching, he won't spot me."

Pete looked doubtful. Bob was the smallest of the Three Investigators, and he was better at research than he was at feats involving physical effort. Pete was the strong, agile one, but he hated taking unnecessary risks.

"If I can cross the road and get into the woods without being seen," Bob said, "I can work my way behind the camp. Then I can come in close enough to hear what those guys are saying."

"Hey, Bob, suppose they catch you spying on them?" said Pete. "They could get rough."

"I'll yell if they do," promised Bob, "and then you get the guard at the gate to come across the road with his rifle and rescue me. I'll get into trouble with Mr Barron, but I don't suppose he will murder me."

"I'm not so sure about that," said Pete.

"Jupe would spy on the camp if he were here," said Bob. He then darted forward to the oleander hedge and, keeping low so as not to be seen from the gate, ran along behind the bushes.

When he reached the place where several eucalyptus trees crowded close to the fence, Bob stood straight and peered out over the bushes. He could not see the gate or the camp when he looked to the left. When he looked to the right, he saw only the empty road. There were no sentries in sight.

Bob slipped through the oleanders and began to scale the fence. Once he started to climb, he did not look around. He got over the fence as quickly as he could and jumped to the ground on the far side.

The road was still empty when he trotted across to take cover in the wilderness area. A little way into the scrub growth, he found a dry gully that ran almost parallel to the road. He let himself down into this and began to move silently along on the sandy earth.

After a few minutes he paused and listened. He could hear men talking and he judged that he was almost directly behind the soldiers' camp. He climbed cautiously out of the gully and found himself atop a small, brush-covered hill that rose behind the tent. Lying face down for a moment, he listened.

The voices of the men were still indistinct murmurs. Bob could not make out the words. He lifted himself to his hands and knees and peeked over the tops of manzanita bushes. There was plenty of cover on the hillside, and Bob decided that he could get closer if he was careful not to make a sound.

He felt himself tremble as he started down the hill, but he forced himself to move slowly. Inch by inch he went, creeping, watching where he put his hands and how he moved his legs, careful not to disturb a pebble or cause a twig to snap.

"Old geezers!" said one of the men. The words were clear now, and Bob stopped his painful descent of the hill.

"I get a kick out of it," said the second man. "The bigger they are, the harder they fall."

Bob stretched out behind a clump of sage and tried not to breathe too loudly. He raised his head and looked.

"Gimme that," said one of the men. His voice was suddenly loud.

Bob saw the smaller of the two men reach out and take a flat bottle from the other. He poured something into his tin cup.

"You don't need all of it, Bones," said the larger man. He grabbed the bottle and poured a drink into his own canteen cup. Then he set the bottle on the ground.

The tent flap was pushed back and Lieutenant Ferrante came out into the sunlight. He scowled at the two men.

"Okay, Al," he said. "I thought you weren't going to drink while we're here. You either, Bones."

"What's the harm?" said Al. "There's nothing doing."

"We don't need any boozed-up guys," said

Ferrante. He seized the bottle and hurled it off into the bushes.

"Hey, you didn't need to do that!" cried Bones.

"Yes, I did," said Ferrante. "Suppose the guy on the gate goes back and tells old man Barron you're drinking? How would it look? You're supposed to be soldiers in the United States Army, remember? You're answering the call of duty when your country is in danger."

"Just what I've always wanted to do," said Bones. His voice was heavy with sarcasm. "Save my country!"

"I know it's hard for you—" began Ferrante.

"But it's easy for you," said Bones, "because you've got so much class! Only if you're so smart, why do you need this end-of-the-world caper?"

"I need it for the same reason you need it," said Ferrante, "and we're going to do it my way or not at all. Now shape up or else beat it back to Saugus and stay there. This is a tricky operation. Don't louse it up."

"Why are we going to all this trouble?" demanded Bones. "We've got the muscle. Why don't we just go in there and make old man Barron talk?"

"We've got muscle?" echoed Ferrante. "You think we've got enough muscle to take on fifty of Barron's ranch hands? And he's got an arsenal in his basement, remember? We wouldn't just be dealing with a bunch of scared lettuce pickers."

"Give them a small cut and they'll change sides so fast it'll make your head spin," said Bones.

"No way," said Ferrante. "I've talked to some of them. Met them in town, accidentally of course, in the Sundown Cafe or the penny arcade. The way they have it figured, so long as Barron keeps this ranch, they've got it made. They don't want anybody to rock their canoe."

"You think they'd fight for him?" Bones demanded.

"If you threaten what they've got, they'll fight," Ferrante declared. "My way's the only way we'll ever get the stuff. The old guy is beginning to buy it, so let's keep cool. He's no dimwit, you know, and he's touchy as a rattlesnake in a rainstorm."

The field telephone jangled again. Ferrante answered it.

"Anything up?" he said. His voice was flat and tense.

He listened, then said, "Okay. Let me know if there's any change."

He replaced the receiver and started towards the tent. "Barron's on his regular afternoon tour of the ranch," he told his companions. "The hands are working the fields. They're trying to keep everything normal. It's going the way we figured it would."

"Sounds to me like it isn't going at all," said Al.

"Did you expect Barron to act like Chicken Little?" said Ferrante. "He's not the type."

He went into the tent and let the flap fall shut behind him.

"The guy thinks he's Napoleon," said Bones. He leaned back against a rock and closed his eyes. Al didn't answer him, and after a minute or two Bob retreated up the hillside, going even more slowly and carefully than he had when he came down.

A few minutes later Bob was back over the fence in the comparative safety of Barron's land. He found Pete under the trees, looking anxious.

"Did you find out anything?" Pete wanted to know.

"Plenty!" crowed Bob. "They're crooks and they're just about ready to fight one another and let's go find Jupe!"

The two hurried back towards the ranch buildings. When they came out of the citrus groves on to Barron's front lawn, they stopped dead and stared up at the big house.

Jupiter was standing on the roof of the front veranda. He was pressing himself close to the wall of the house and was scowling at a corner window only inches from his elbow. It was an open window; Bob and Pete could see the curtains blowing ouward on the breeze. They could also see Jupe's face. It was red with embarrassment—or perhaps with desperation.

"I think we'd better do something," said Pete, "and we'd better do it quick!"

12

Jupe Has a Brainstorm

WITH A WAVE TO JUPE, Pete began to jog across the lawn to the drive. Bob followed, wondering what Pete had in mind. The taller boy kept moving until the drive took them between the Barron house and the humbler ranch house to a point where Jupe was no longer in sight.

Pete stopped suddenly and turned.

"Do that again and I'll knock your block off!" he shouted at Bob.

Bob froze, his face startled. "Hey!" he said.

"Cut it out!" roared Pete. "You know what you did!"

Pete leaped at Bob and struck him lightly on the arm. "Come on!" he yelled. "Put 'em up!"

"Oh!" said Bob. "Oh yeah!" He darted at Pete, his fists flailing.

"Boys, you stop that!" called Elsie Spratt from the side window of the kitchen. "That's enough! Stop it, you hear me!"

She clattered down the steps of the ranch house and waded into the battle, grabbing Bob by the arm and yanking him away from Pete.

"What's this?" demanded a gruff voice from above.

The boys looked up. Charles Barron was scowling down at them from a side window in the second storey of the big house.

"It's nothing, Mr Barron," said Elsie. "Boys do this sort of thing all the time."

Jupiter walked around the corner of the big house just then. He looked rumpled and soiled, but he was smiling. "Trouble?" he said.

"Not really," said Elsie, and she went back to her kitchen. Barron drew in his head and slammed his window shut. Grinning at one another, the boys walked off behind the big house.

"Thanks for creating a diversion so I could climb down off that roof," said Jupe. He sat down under a eucalyptus tree in the Barrons' backyard and the other boys crouched beside him.

"I was alone in Mr Barron's office when he came back to the house," Jupe reported. "He started upstairs and there was no place to go except out the window on to the roof. Once I was on the roof I didn't dare climb down. I didn't know exactly where he was, and he might have seen me."

"Did you find out anything?" asked Pete.

"I'm not sure. I have to think about it. What about you? Were you able to learn anything about the soldiers on the road?"

"You bet!" said Pete. "For openers, they lied. The field telephone they have is not out of order. We saw them use it twice. Then Bob went over the fence and got close to the tent. Bob, tell Jupe about that."

"Okay," said Bob. "I heard the second call that came in on the field telephone. That lieutenant asked someone what was new, and they told him that Mr Barron had just gone on an inspection tour."

"Oho!" said Jupe. "So there *is* a conspiracy against Barron. And someone who works here is in on it!"

"Right," said Bob. "Those guys in the jeep aren't soldiers—none of them. The two who were sitting outside the tent were drinking whiskey, and when the lieutenant called them on it they gave a lot of backtalk. Soldiers don't talk back to officers, do they?"

Jupe shook his head.

"The lieutenant said if they made any more trouble they could beat it back to Saugus, and one of them said he didn't see why they were going to so much trouble when they had enough muscle to just walk in and force Mr Barron to talk."

"That sounds ugly," said Jupe.

"Sure does," Bob agreed. "The lieutenant said Barron has an arsenal here and his ranch hands would be armed and they'd fight for him. Does Barron have an arsenal?"

"Yes, in his basement," said Jupe. "I wonder why the lieutenant thinks the ranch hands would side with Barron."

"Ferrante said he's been feeling some of them out," Bob reported. "Some of them go into town and Ferrante managed to talk with them. He says they like things here just the way they are, and he believes they'd fight to keep them that way."

"Good!" said Jupe. "We can eliminate the ranch hands as suspects. They are what they seem to be—agricultural workers who are permanently settled at Rancho Valverde. They don't want to be disturbed. But there must be a spy here if Ferrante knows about the guns in Barron's cellar. And he knew Barron went out to ride this afternoon. Did Ferrante mention anyone on the staff? Detweiler? Aleman? Banales?"

"What about Elsie Spratt and Mary Sedlack?" said Pete. "It doesn't have to be a man, does it?"

"Ferrante didn't mention any names," said Bob. "I've already told you most of what he said, except that Mr Barron is beginning to buy it. I guess he meant that Mr Barron is beginning to believe in the spaceship. He said he didn't want the other guys to louse things up, and he said Mr Barron was smart, but touchy as a rattlesnake."

"He knew that Charles Barron is beginning to change his attitude towards the supposed aliens from another planet?" said Jupe. "Hmm! The spy is someone close to Barron. And Ferrante and his men are after—they're after—after gold! That's it! I should have known all along!"

"Gold?" Bob looked startled. "What gold?"

"The gold that Charles Barron has hidden here on the ranch," said Jupe smugly.

"You found gold?" said Pete.

"No, I didn't, but I'm sure there's gold here someplace. I found papers showing that Barron has sold millions and millions of dollars' worth of securities. He's closed out his bank accounts in several cities. So far as I can tell, he now has only one account, and huge amounts have gone in and out of it.

"I think if we could call some of the companies that received cheques from Barron, we'd find that they deal in gold coins or gold bullion. One of the places is a stamp exchange, and places that sell stamps often sell coins as well. Barron has said that only land and gold are safe investments."

"Why sure!" cried Bob. "It figures! He's sold everything he owned and he's bought gold!"

"Exactly!" said Jupiter. "He's keeping the gold here on the ranch because he doesn't trust banks. He doesn't even keep a safe deposit box in the Santa Barbara bank any longer. Mrs Barron thought her jewellery was there, but it isn't. It's in a wall safe in Barron's office.

"Now if *we* could figure out that Barron must have gold, so could other people here on the ranch. I'll bet the conspirators are looking for the gold, and they've staged the landing of the flying saucer to somehow make Barron reveal the hiding place."

"Crazy!" said Pete.

"Totally mad," Jupe said, "but it's the only explanation that fits the facts."

"We're going to tell Barron what we know?" Bob asked.

411

"We'll certainly tell Mrs Barron," said Jupe. "She is our client. And she's used to dealing with Barron. He might not believe us."

"What next?" asked Bob. "Do we search for the other field telephone? If we can find it, we can find out who's using it."

"Lots of luck," said Pete. "This place is huge. We'd be searching for a needle in a haystack."

Jupe pulled on his lower lip. "We wouldn't have to search the whole ranch," he said. "The spy has to be able to use the field telephone where he or she can't be seen. That means it's almost certainly in a building."

"Yeah, but there are an awful lot of buildings here," Pete objected. "And people are in and out of them all the time."

A door banged, and the boys looked up to see Elsie Spratt coming down her kitchen steps. She was carrying a blue garment over her arm. She smiled when she saw the boys and gestured toward one of the small cottages up the road. "I'm off to see Mrs Miranda," she said. "She's going to help me shorten my skirt—and we can all hope that the world doesn't end before I have a chance to wear it. There's milk in the refrigerator and there are cookies in the big jar near the stove if you want a snack."

The boys thanked her. After she disappeared into the Miranda house, Pete looked at his pals and grinned. "I'll bet there's no one in the ranch house right now," he said. "Elsie's getting her skirt fixed and the others are off doing their jobs. What say we take a look around?"

"Okay, but I don't think the ranch house is a safe place to hide a field telephone," said Bob.

"But the house holds clues to the people who live in it," said Jupe, "and one of those people is our spy! Come on, let's go!"

13

A Message from Outer Space

THE BOYS WORKED QUICKLY, keeping alert for the sound of someone returning to the ranch house. In minutes they had examined Hank Detweiler's room. They saw that Hank possessed a number of trophies, which he had won in calf-roping contests, and also clear title to a Ford pickup truck. There was no evidence that he wrote letters or that he ever received any.

"A loner," Jupe decided, "with little interest in material things and mementos. He's hardly got any personal possessions."

"So he wouldn't even care about gold, right?" said Pete.

Jupe shrugged. "We can't tell for sure. Maybe he hoards his money. Or maybe he just likes to live simply."

The boys went on to John Aleman's room and found a bookcase crammed with books on hydraulic power, on electricity, on engineering, even on aero-dynamics. And under the bed Pete discovered a pile of paperbacks on science and space. Some of the titles were intriguing.

"Here's one called *The Ancient Future*," said Pete, holding up a book. "It's by Korsakov.

Didn't he write that other book that Mrs Barron talks about?

"*Parallels*," said Jupiter. "Yes, he did."

"Here's more," said Bob, who had opened Aleman's closet and found a carton of paperbacks. He picked them up one by one and read the titles aloud. "*The Crowded Cosmos. The Second Universe*. And *Black Holes and Vanishing Worlds*. And lots more."

"I didn't know it was so busy in outer space," said Pete.

"I didn't know so many people had been there," Bob remarked. "Is it important that Aleman reads this stuff? Do you suppose he's studying, trying to figure out how the Barrons will react to things?

"But that's what really doesn't make sense," Bob went on. "I mean, if the soldiers want to hoodwink Mr Barron, aren't they going at it the wrong way? Mrs Barron is the outer-space nut. So why would crooks work so hard to make *him* believe in visitors from another planet?"

"They may know that Barron isn't a man who doubts his own eyes," said Jupe. "They did stage a very convincing takeoff of a flying saucer, and Barron saw it himself."

"Jupe, maybe he's right to believe," said Pete. His voice was suddenly nervous. "Suppose we're the ones who are wrong? Suppose there really is a spaceship?"

"No," said Jupiter. "If there is really a spaceship, why are those imposters camped down on the road?"

"I don't know," said Pete miserably. "I just don't understand. What will anyone get out of faking a spaceship? Mr Barron's gold? How will a flying saucer help anyone get that?"

"If you were going to leave the Earth and travel to another planet," said Jupe, "what would you take with you?"

"Oh," said Pete. "Yeah. I see. I'd take the thing that was worth most to me. But so far nobody's asked Mr Barron to pack up his gold and fly away."

"Maybe they're just softening him up," said Bob. He piled the paperback books into the carton again, and decided that the book collection might mean nothing more than that Aleman liked science fiction adventures.

"Just the same," he said, "I'm going to keep an eye on Aleman."

The boys went down the hall to the room occupied by Elsie Spratt.

"Not very neat," said Pete when he opened the door.

"It sure isn't," said Jupiter. He gazed at the wilderness of tubes and bottles and vials, half-read magazines, paperback romances, and slippers left lying on their sides. There was perfume and makeup and hand lotion on the dresser, all jumbled together with hairpins and a few pink plastic curlers. The dresser drawers were equally messy.

Pete got down on his knees and peered under the bed.

416

"Does she read science fiction, too?" asked Bob.

"No," said Pete. "Nothing here but dust and a pair of shoes."

Jupe turned to the small table next to the bed. He opened the drawer there and saw more hand lotion and more curlers and a few snapshots.

Carefully, disturbing the other things as little as possible, Jupe picked up the photographs.

There was a Polaroid picture of Elsie at the beach. There was another of Elsie sitting on the front steps of a frame house. She was smiling and holding a small ragmop of a dog on her lap. There was a larger photograph of Elsie in a satin blouse and a paper hat. She was seated at a table with a bull-necked, dark-haired man. Behind her were balloons and bunting, and a girl with long, sandy hair danced with a slender, bearded young man.

"Looks like a New Year's Eve party," said Bob.

Jupe nodded, replaced the pictures in the drawer, looked into Elsie's crowded closet, then went on to Mary Sedlack's room.

The quarters occupied by the girl who served as veterinarian on the ranch were prim and austere. There were few cosmetics. Clothes were hung precisely in the closet or folded neatly in drawers. The top of the bureau was bare except for the china figure of a galloping horse. There were several books on the care of animals in a bookcase under the window and there was a box of tissues on the bedside table.

"She's crazy about animals, and that's all," Pete declared.

417

"At least it's all that she allows to show," said Jupiter.

They went on to Banales' room, where they found lists and schedules for planting and several books on cultivating and harvesting.

"I don't think we're finding out much we didn't already know," said Pete. He and Bob followed Jupe downstairs to the huge living room of the ranch house. This contained shabby sofas and chairs and a collection of dog-eared magazines. The pantry was filled with food. When they went outside and looked under the house, they saw cobwebs and bare earth and beetles and spiders.

"Sometimes searches reveal nothing," said Jupiter. "Very well. So much for that. Now we had better find Mrs Barron. At least we can tell her that the soldiers are imposters."

The boys went across the drive and up the back steps of the mansion. Jupe rapped at the door. When no one answered, he turned the handle and pulled the door open. "Hello!" he called. "Mrs Barron?"

He heard the scratchy, raspy noise of static coming from the dining room. An instant after he called, it ceased.

"Who's there?" said a woman's voice.

"Jupiter Jones," said Jupe. "And Pete and Bob."

The Three Investigators went through the kitchen and into the dining room. Mary Sedlack sat there with a portable radio and a tape recorder on the table in front of her. "You want to see Mrs

Barron?" she asked. "She's upstairs. Go through the hall and yell up the stairway. That'll get her."

Jupe nodded at the radio set. "Are you getting anything?" he asked.

"Just static," said Mary. "Mr Barron asked me to listen in and if anything comes through that makes sense, to put it on tape."

She turned the volume up slightly, and the static blared again. Then suddenly it faded away, to be replaced by a low humming noise.

"Whoops!" said Mary. "Now what?"

She touched the record switch on the tape machine and the spools of tape began slowly to turn.

"Charles Barron," said a voice—a deep voice that was strangely musical. "Charles Emerson Barron. This is Astro-Voyager Z-12 attempting contact with Charles and Ernestine Barron. Repeat! We are attempting contact with Charles Barron! Please attend, Mr Barron!"

"Hey!" cried Mary Sedlack. "Hey, it's a message! Hey, you guys, get Mr Barron! Quick!"

14

Doomsday!

"REPEAT," said the voice on the radio. "This is Astro-Voyager Z-12 calling Charles Emerson Barron and Ernestine Hornaday Barron. We are at present in orbit three hundred miles beyond your atmosphere."

Charles Barron and his wife came into the dining room. Barron was frowning, puzzled and also hopeful. He stared at the radio, and after a moment the voice went on.

"Infra-red scanners aboard our patrols have detected tremendous inner stresses in your planet. Before many days there will be an earthquake, with volcanic activity more violent than any we have witnessed before. The Earth will tilt on its axis so that the area now covered by the polar icecaps will move. The Antarctic continent will shift to the equator. The eternal ice will melt so that the seas will rise, and those cities that have not already been levelled by the Earth's upheaval will be inundated by water."

"He's kidding!" cried Mary Sedlack. "Hey, Mrs Barron, he *is* kidding, isn't he?"

Mrs Barron didn't answer, and Mary looked at

her in sudden fright. "Hey, come on!" she said pleadingly. "Tell me it's some kind of joke."

"The Supreme Council of Omega has chosen to remove certain individuals from the Earth before this devastation occurs," said the voice on the radio. "After the time of chaos has passed, these people can return to be the leaders of a new civilization. Charles and Ernestine Barron are among those to be taken. We attempted a rendezvous last night, but we failed. Tonight we will try again to complete our mission. We will land at 2200 hours to take aboard our own people who are on your planet at this moment. If they have the courage, Charles Barron and his wife should be at the edge of the lake on the Barron land at 2200 hours. They should have with them any belongings they wish to save from destruction. That is all."

The voice stopped and there was silence for a second. Then the blare of static came again from the radio.

Barron reached past Mary Sedlack and snapped off the radio. Then he pushed the stop switch on the tape recorder. He picked up the recorder and went out of the room, and the boys heard him on the stairs.

"Mrs Baron, can I talk with you for a second?" said Jupe.

She shook her head. Her face was white. "Not right now," she said. "In a little while." She went out and up the stairs.

Mary Sedlack sat staring at the radio. "Did you hear what he said?" she whispered. "He . . . he sounded so real!"

She pushed back her chair abruptly and bolted away from the table and out through the kitchen. The boys could hear her calling to Elsie Spratt.

Pete looked searchingly at Jupe. "Well!" he said.

"We aren't going to die," said Jupe. "At least not right now."

"You're sure?" said Pete.

"Positive," said Jupe.

"I hope you're right," said Pete, and he and the other two went out into the late afternoon sunshine.

There was no sign of Mary or Elsie on the drive, but a group of men and women were coming up the lane towards the big house. They carried tools and they talked softly to one another as they walked. One young man who looked especially serious and solemn nodded to the boys as he came abreast of them.

"Say, just a minute," said Jupe. He touched the man's sleeve.

"What is it?" said the man.

"I was wondering," said Jupe. "There must be some talk among the people here. What are they saying?"

The man looked after his companions. Several had gone on into their homes, but a few stood in the lane and looked back as if they were waiting for him.

"Some say that the world will end," answered the man nervously. "Some say it will not be the world. It will only be California that will disappear into the ocean and be lost forever."

"What do the people here think of the soldiers on the road—the ones who are camped near the gate?"

"The soldiers are afraid," the man said. "They drink and their officer—he does not make them stop. They do not care about their officer." The man's voice was scornful, but fearful, too. The strange behaviour of the soldiers seemed to confirm his belief that something terrible was happening in the world.

"And what about getting out?" asked Jupe. "Does anyone want to walk out of here and get to the nearest town?"

"No. Mr Barron has spoken with us about this. He says if we wish to go we should try, but he fears there is much trouble in the towns. He thinks that perhaps the trucks do not move so there is not enough food, and when that happens people will fight with one another. What he says is true. If we stay here, at least we have food to eat."

"I see," said Jupiter.

The man moved away and joined his companions. As they went on towards their homes they passed Konrad, who was coming down the lane from the parking area.

"Hey, Jupe!" Konrad called. His broad face was solemn. "I have been in the fields. Hey, that Mr Barron, he scares everyone really bad."

"I heard," said Jupe.

"I think maybe we should take the truck and go home," said Konrad. "I do not like it here. Here we do not really know what is true and what is not. If we are where there are many people, then we know better."

"Konrad, please don't worry," said Jupe.

The big Bavarian looked hopeful. "You know something?" he said. "Maybe it is all a trick, what happens here?"

"It *is* a trick," said Jupe. "If I hadn't guessed it before, I would now, after hearing that message from the intergalactic traveller."

"The message?" said Pete. "What about the message? It sounded pretty real to me—if you believe in flying saucers in the first place."

"Lacking in originality, though," said Jupe. "Did you see *The Saturn Syndrome* when it was on television last week? There was an end-of-the-world sequence in it, and when the spaceship came to rescue the scientist and his daughter, it radioed a message."

"Oh, no!" cried Bob. "The same message we just heard?"

"Almost word for word," said Jupe, "including the idea that the world will tilt on its axis and the polar icecaps will melt."

Bob sighed. "Too bad," he said. "And I thought we had something very unusual going on."

"You're crazy!" said Pete with a little shudder. "I sure don't want to be around for the end of the world!"

15

Getting Ready for the End

PETE AND BOB SAT ON THEIR BEDS in the ranch-house bunkroom and waited. Jupiter had gone back to the Barron house, and Konrad lingered in the kitchen below. He had been warned not to tell the staff that Jupe suspected trickery.

After fifteen minutes Jupe came back to the ranch house. He climbed the stairs slowly, and his face was downcast when he came into the bunkroom.

"Mr Barron didn't believe you," said Bob.

Jupe sighed. "He says I couldn't possibly remember the dialogue from a movie word for word."

"You told him you have a mind like a tape recorder?" asked Pete.

"I did," said Jupe. "He told me not to be impudent."

"That's the trouble with being kids," Pete declared. "When grownups don't want to listen, they say you're impudent."

Bob said impatiently, "What about the fact that the soldiers are imposters? And your theory about the gold? Did you tell Mr Barron about that?"

Jupe looked shamefaced. "I didn't get a chance. You know what Mr Barron is like when he doesn't want to be bothered with something. You can't get a word in."

"Well, what about telling Mrs Barron?"

"She couldn't get away from Mr Barron long enough to talk. But at least she believed me about the movie dialogue. She said to come back after supper and tell her the whole story."

"Oh, great," said Bob. "Here we've practically got the mystery solved and we can't even get our client to listen!"

Jupe flushed. He prided himself on making adults pay attention, but this time he'd failed.

"Why can't we go ahead and tell some others about the hoax?" asked Pete. "Everybody on this ranch is a nervous wreck. We could save them a lot of grief."

"But we'd tip off the spy," Jupe pointed out. "And we might put the Barrons in real danger. What if those soldiers decided to come in here and take the gold by force?"

Bob shuddered. "I can see it now. We'd get caught in a shoot-out."

Jupe nodded. "No, we have to wait and convince the Barrons that we know what's going on. It won't be hard to persuade Mrs Barron. She seems to have a lot of faith in boys. But Mr Barron might disagree just because she does believe us. As Elsie said, he's contrary."

"Touchy as a rattlesnake in a rainstorm," said Bob. "Elsie has a way with words."

Jupe stared at Bob in silence for an instant. Then he said, "Oh!"

"What's the matter?" asked Bob.

"You said something just now," Jupe answered.

"Yes. I said Elsie has a way with words. She said Mr Barron is as touchy as a rattlesnake in a rainstorm."

Jupe grinned. "No. What she really said was he's *cosy* as a rattlesnake in a rainstorm! But that's close enough!"

"Boys!" called Elsie. She stood at the foot of the stairs. "Supper! Come on down!"

"Jupe, you're on to something!" said Pete.

"I'll tell you about it later," promised Jupe.

When the boys came into the kitchen, Elsie was serving the soup while Mary Sedlack passed plates of hot biscuits.

"You were there," said Mary to the boys. "Tell them about the message on the radio. They think I've been eating magic mushrooms or something."

Jupe sat down next to Hank Detweiler. John Aleman and Rafael Banales were already seated. Konrad was opposite Detweiler, carefully not looking at him.

"The message was for Mr and Mrs Barron," said Jupe. "It was from a spaceship that is now orbiting the Earth."

Pete and Bob sat down, and Elsie put plates of soup in front of them. "If I were you, I wouldn't tell that to any of the ranch hands," she said. "Most of them are scared enough already."

"They aren't children, Elsie," said Hank Detweiler. "They've got a right to know what's going on."

The foreman picked up his spoon, scowled at it, then put it down again. "Mr Barron made me take the guards off the meadow," he said. "He doesn't want anyone up there."

When no one commented on this, Detweiler went on. "Crazy!" he said. "I just talked to him about taking a bunch of men up over the cliffs into the hills behind the ranch, and he wouldn't hear of it. He doesn't want anyone up there. Now Mary says that's because the world is going to end and the aliens are coming to take the Barrons away. Well, if we have to go through the end of the world, I think we all deserve a little notice."

"Hank, everybody would panic if they knew about the message on the radio," said Elsie.

"They're in a panic now," said Detweiler. "The only thing that's keeping them from trampling each other is the fact that nobody's running. And nobody's running because there's no place to run to. Why should the people here run when they're already in the last safe place there is?"

Detweiler looked searchingly at Jupe. "Mary says Mr and Mrs Barron are supposed to go to the meadow tonight and the spaceship will take them away."

Jupiter nodded. "They're to rendezvous with the rescue ship at 2200 hours tonight. That's at ten o'clock. The spaceship is returning for them and also some people from the planet Omega. I guess those would be the ones who attacked us this morning. Perhaps they're here to keep the people of Rancho Valverde from leaving and carrying the word to the outside world."

Jupe took a spoonful of his soup. "They wouldn't want to be met by a mob when they landed, would they?" he said.

"Just want the Barrons, huh?" said Detweiler.

"No one else was mentioned," said Jupe.

Detweiler snorted. "That's a laugh! Why should they want Barron? He's no genius. He's rich, that's all. Do the rich go first class even on doomsday?"

"It's some kind of gag," said John Aleman. "Somebody's playing a joke on us. The radios—it isn't such a trick to put radios out of commission, or to broadcast special messages. Elsie, I'll bet if your brother was here he could tell us exactly how it's being done."

Elsie didn't respond to this, but the hand with the deformity went to her throat.

"I'll bet I could do it myself if I had the right equipment," said Aleman.

"Probably you could," said Mary Sedlack, "but if someone's playing a joke, why are they doing it? They've gone to tons of trouble for that joke!"

"Is it possible that Mr Barron has enemies?" said Rafael Banales. His voice was low and quiet. "He is a rich man and the rich are not always liked. But is

429

it also not possible that a ship has come here from some faraway planet? Could it not happen? The disasters you speak of could happen, too. The climate of Earth has changed in the past. We know that. It could change again. The ice age could come again, or there could be the melting of the polar icecaps. Why not? But even if these things are going to happen, what can we do? Get aboard a spaceship? Even if I could, I don't think I would do it. I don't want to go to some place where the sun is not the same and the sky is not blue and perhaps the grass is not green. I will stay here and take my chances."

"And if nothing happens?" said Detweiler. "If there is no spaceship?"

Banales shrugged. "Then it is indeed a joke—a joke which I do not understand."

The meal went on in silence. The boys ate heartily, but the men only picked at their food. Elsie and Mary ate nothing at all.

After supper the Three Investigators went out and looked up at the Barron house. Immediately a window in the big house went up and Mrs Barron put her head out.

"Go around to the front of the house," she said softly.

The boys did as she asked. They found Charles Barron sitting on one of the cast-iron chairs on the veranda.

"Good evening, Mr Barron," said Jupiter.

Barron scowled.

Jupiter went up the steps, followed by his friend. "Mr Barron, I have a theory about today's events," he said.

"Young man," said Barron, "I thought I made it clear this afternoon that I'm not interested in your theories."

Barron got up and went into the house.

Mrs Barron came out a moment later and took a chair on the veranda. "I'm sorry," she said. "I guess my husband simply doesn't want to hear the truth. He's planning to leave with the spaceship. He says I must come with him." She looked down at her green sweater and skirt. "He says I'm to go in and change soon. I'm not supposed to wear a skirt to travel to a new planet. Charles believes that slacks would be more appropriate."

Jupiter grinned and sat down. "What about your other preparations? Has Mr Barron started to gather the things he wants to take with him? What does he want to save when the Earth is destroyed?"

"He says he'll pack his things after dark," said Mrs Barron.

"I see." Jupiter leaned to one side on his seat and put his arm along the back of the chair. His fingers found a flaw in the metal work. It was a small opening like a slot. He touched it, then turned and looked curiously at it.

"Irritating, isn't it?" said Mrs Barron when she saw him examining the chair. "All the furniture has holes like that. It's something the ironworkers did when they cast the things."

431

Jupe nodded. "I see. Mrs Barron, does your husband realize that what he's doing may be dangerous? He's allowing himself to be manipulated. He's seeing events that conspirators want him to see, and he's hearing what they want him to hear. He's doing exactly what the plotters want him to do."

"Jupe, are you so sure there is a plot?" she said.

"I'm positive," said Jupiter. "Actually, Mrs Barron, we're prisoners here. We wouldn't be allowed to leave if we tried." Bob and Pete nodded in agreement.

"But why?" she cried. "Who are these conspirators? What do they want?"

"They're the men on the road, and some others," said Jupe, "and they want Mr Barron's gold."

The front door opened and Charles Barron came out on to the veranda. Mrs Barron jumped slightly, and he smiled at her.

"Ernestine, my dear, surely you guessed that I would listen," he said. He sat down near his wife. "You spoke of gold," he said to Jupiter. "Very well. I am now interested in hearing what you have to say."

"Yes, sir," said Jupe. "Mr Barron, it's common knowledge that you've liquidated all of your assets, that you distrust the financial institutions of this country, and that you believe gold and land are the only good investments. From these facts I deduce that you have put all of your money into gold, and that the gold is concealed here on this ranch. Nothing else would make sense."

"Why, Charles!" said Ernestine Barron. "You have gold here? You never told me."

"There was no need for you to know, my dear," he said.

"The conspirators who want to get the gold have reached the same conclusion I have," said Jupe. "They know the gold is here, but they don't know exactly where it is. They staged the fire on the cliffs and the takeoff of a flying saucer, and of course the radio message from the spaceship, believing that you'll take the gold with you when you go to meet the rescuers. Then they'll have it!"

Charles Barron took a deep breath. "Yes," he said. "I planned to do that. Perfectly ridiculous. I can't think why I've been so credulous. But only a coward is afraid to admit when he's made a mistake, and I'm not a coward—or a fool." He glowered at the three boys, as if daring them to disagree.

"No sir," said Pete.

Barron shook himself. "Well now, I'll be blasted if I'll let a bunch of green striplings in fake uniforms manipulate me! That young man with the jeep is scarcely old enough to shave. Shouldn't be too much of a problem to deal with him. I have dozens of stout young men of my own, and I have plenty of rifles and ammunition. If we need to, we can drive out of here with guns blazing."

"Yes, you can, sir," said Jupe, "provided all of your people are trustworthy."

"Trustworthy?" said the millionaire. "You don't think they are?"

433

"Someone on the ranch has been getting information to the men on the road," said Jupe. "Bob can tell you about what he heard this afternoon."

"I climbed the fence when no one was looking," said Bob quickly. "I got near the tent where the men are camped and I heard them talking. They knew you were beginning to believe in visitors from another planet, and the lieutenant spoke to someone on the field telephone and whoever it was said you were out on your regular tour of the ranch."

"The field telephone?" Charles Barron snorted. "They said it wasn't working. Why wasn't I informed of all this sooner?"

"You haven't been very available," Jupe pointed out. "Now, the conspirators won't let you walk out or drive out, Mr Barron—not until they get what they came for. I'm sure you want to bring those people to justice, but you can't do it without proof. And you can't find out who is the spy on your staff until they make their move. Mr Barron, you have to give them room so they can trap themselves."

"Perhaps," said Barron, "but in the meantime, I'll arm myself."

He got up and went into the house. A few minutes later he returned to the veranda.

"Someone has gotten into my arsenal," he said. He kept his voice steady. "There must be a duplicate key. The lock wasn't broken, but all the ammunition is gone. We are trapped. We're prisoners! And there is a traitor! One of the people I chose for my staff. I have been mistaken in one of my own people!"

"Yes, sir," said Jupe, "and now we'd better find out which one it it."

16

The Aliens Return

IT WAS AFTER NINE that night when Pete and Konrad stole up the lane and made for the meadows to the north of the ranch house.

"I do not understand," said Konrad. "If it is all a trick, why does Mr Barron go to the meadow to meet a spaceship? How can he meet a ship when no ship is coming?"

"They tricked Mr Barron and now he'll trick them," said Pete. "It's all Jupe's idea."

"Jupe has good ideas," Konrad said, "but why does he not come with us?"

"He wants to watch the people at the ranch," said Pete. "He wants to see what they do after Mr Barron leaves."

"I wish he was with us," said Konrad.

"So do I," Pete confessed. "Never mind. All we have to do is hide on the upper meadow and keep quiet. Then Mr Barron will get the drop on the crooks and you and Mrs Barron will go out over the cliffs to get help."

"Mrs Barron will climb up the cliff?" said Konrad.

"She says she will," Pete told him. "She says she can do it. I'll bet she can."

Pete held up his hand for silence. They had reached the edge of the field below the dam. The moon was up and the grass looked silver grey in the wan moonlight, but there were deep shadows under the cliffs. Pete and Konrad kept to these shadows and worked their way around the field. Then they climbed past the dam to the higher meadow.

Fog carpeted the meadow with a thick white cloud. Pete groped forward until he found a clump of scrub brush. He and Konrad crept behind it and settled down to wait.

It seemed hours before there were voices on the field below the dam. Pete sat forward and strained to see through the fog. There was a flash of light and a clatter of stones, and Barron and his wife climbed over the rocks at the east end of the dam. The two passed within feet of the place where Pete and Konrad were hidden. Pete could see that Barron carried a bulky package under his arm. Mrs Barron walked quietly beside him, and she also carried a package. Hers was bulkier than Mr Barron's.

The Barrons paused after they had gone ten metres into the meadow. They stood still, the fog swirling around them.

"Suppose they don't come," said Mrs Barron loudly.

"They'll come," said Mr Barron. "They promised."

Suddenly the meadow was alive with blue-white brilliance. The Barrons started, and Mrs Barron stepped closer to her husband.

The cliffs were on fire. The flames seemed to shred the fog into bluish wisps and send it whirling on the night air.

Pete heard Konrad gasp. Something round and dark was settling towards the valley. It came from above and it moved as silently as a cloud. For a moment it blocked out the light from the blazing cliffs. Then the flames shone silver on its surface.

"It is the spaceship!" whispered Konrad.

"Shhh!" warned Pete.

The great ship touched the ground, and suddenly the flames on the cliffs dwindled and went out. For a moment nothing moved on the meadow. Then two figures came out of the darkness and the fog. They were clad in gleaming white spacesuits and they wore helmets. The one in front carried a light that looked like a blue torch.

Pete hardly dared to breathe. The aliens paused near the Barrons.

"Charles Barron?" said a voice. "Ernestine Barron?"

"I'm here," said Barron. "My wife is with me."

"Are you ready to leave?" said the spaceman with the light. "Have you brought everything you wish to take with you?"

"I've brought the only thing that can't be replaced," declared Charles Barron. He held his package out towards the astronaut. "*Blight!*" he said.

"What?" said the alien.

438

"*Blight!*" Barron repeated the word. "It's the title of the book I'm writing. It's about the flaws in the American economic structure. Perhaps on Omega I'll have a chance to finish it at last."

"Is that all?" said the spaceman. Pete had to hold himself to keep from laughing. The man from Omega had developed a shaky voice.

"That's all I've brought," said Barron. "My wife has her own treasures."

Mrs Barron stepped forward. "I've brought the latest pictures of my two sons," she said, "and my wedding dress. I just couldn't leave it behind."

"I see," said the spaceman. "Very well. Come with us."

The aliens retreated the way they had come and the Barrons started after them. Pete stood up, suddenly afraid. The Barrons were no more than indistinct shapes moving through a dream landscape of fog. In a moment they would vanish completely.

But then the aliens stopped. The one who held the torch stepped to one side, and the second one spun around to face the Barrons. His arms were raised stiffly, pointing toward Barron and his wife. Pete realized that this was a stance he had seen thousands of times on television. The spaceman was aiming a gun!

"Okay, Dad!" said the man. "Don't move."

The man with the torch waded through the fog to the great saucer-shaped thing that was moored on the meadow. He bent and fumbled with something, then moved and bent again. Suddenly the cliffs blazed once more and the saucer drifted upward. At first it rose slowly, but then it went more and more rapidly until it disappeared into the night above the cliffs.

The flames died and the meadow was silver in the moonlight again.

Charles Barron spoke. "I presume they will see that display of fireworks at the ranch below—and on the road. My people will believe I am gone, and those pitiful imitation soldiers will now feel free to invade my property."

The man with the gun removed his helmet with one hand. He was quite an ordinary-looking young man with longish dark hair. "You should have brought the loot with you, Pops," he said. "But don't worry. We'll get it in the end."

He moved close to Barron and thrust the gun almost into the millionaire's face. "Of course, we don't want it to take too long," he said. "We've put too much time into the job already. Now don't give us a hard time. If we have to search the whole ranch, we will. But if we do that, believe me, it will be over your dead body!"

Mrs Barron let out a frightened gasp.

"Be kind to yourself," said the gunman. "Be kind to the lady here. Tell us where you stashed the gold."

Barron sighed. "The existence of my gold appears to be an ill-kept secret," he said. "Very well. It's pointless to die for money. The gold is under the floor of the basement in the big house."

440

The gunman stepped back and the second man vanished into the fog. After a moment there was a ringing sound, like the jingle of a defective doorbell.

"Aha!" said Barron. "A field telephone!"

The gunman didn't reply. He stood watching the Barrons, and from the darkness came the voice of the second man.

"He didn't bring it with him," said the second man. "It's buried under the floor in the cellar of his house."

The man with the telephone paused for an instant, then said, "Right."

When the man reappeared, Pete realized that the field telephone must have been hidden behind one of the boulders at the base of the cliffs.

"The gold had better be there," said the gunman to Barron. "If those guys dig up a cellar and don't find it, they're going to put *you* under cement!"

"We shall see," said Barron. He swung around towards his wife and shoved her so that she stumbled away and fell to the ground.

For a split second, the man with the gun turned towards Mrs Barron. In that split second there was a spurt of flame and the sound of a shot. The gunman screamed and dropped his weapon.

"Don't move!" snapped Charles Barron. His arms were outstretched and he held a gun. "Ernestine," he said, "would you pick up that man's weapon?"

Mrs Barron already had the gun in her hand. She handed it to her husband as she got to her feet. The man who had threatened Charles Barron sank to his knees. He held his injured hand close to his chest and sobbed.

"Where'd you get that gun?" demanded the man with the torch as Barron searched him for a weapon.

"My father's pistol," said Barron. "I always keep it under my pillow. Your accomplices overlooked it when they looted my arsenal today."

Barron raised his voice. "Pete!" he called. "Konrad!"

"Here, Mr Barron." Pete started across the meadow with Konrad coming behind him.

"I think these must be the only two here," said Charles Barron. "If there were others, they would have shown themselves by now." He turned to his wife. "Ernestine, are you quite sure you will be able to climb that cliff?"

"As soon as I've bandaged this man's hand," said Mrs Barron. "You have a clean handkerchief, Charles. May I have it, please?"

Barron sniffed, but he handed over his handkerchief, and Mrs Barron knelt in the meadow and bandaged the gunman's hand. As soon as she finished, Pete took the torch and went in search of the field telephone. When he found it, he yanked coils of wire from the instrument and bound the two men.

Mrs Barron took her husband's torch and

tucked it into her belt. Then she held out her hand to Konrad. "We'll go up over the cliffs and walk out to the highway," she said to him. "I hope you're wearing comfortable shoes. We'll get the police, and my husband and the boys will attend to things here. We won't be back for at least two hours. Shall we go?"

Konrad nodded, and Mrs Barron began a careful ascent of the cliff. Konrad followed her cautiously in the dim moonlight, moving as she did, putting his feet in the places where she had put hers. Barron and Pete watched the two go up. It seemed to Pete that it was hours before they reached the top of the cliffs and disappeared into the wilderness above the ranch.

"There!" said Barron. "A remarkable woman, my wife!"

Leaving the 'spacemen' tied up on the meadow, Barron started towards the lower fields. "Come along, boy!" he said to Pete. "We don't want to stand here all night. I'm sure there's no end of excitement at the house!"

17

The Treasure Hunt

THE MAN WHO called himself Lieutenant Ferrante stood in the driveway near the ranch house. He pointed a rifle towards the sky and fired.

"Back to your homes!" he shouted. "Step on it! Move! Anybody who's still outside two minutes from now gets his big toe shot off!"

The ranch workers who had come into the lane to stare at the blazing cliffs retreated. The doors of the cottages closed behind them, and locks turned.

Ferrante stamped into the ranch house. The staff was gathered in the kitchen, together with Jupiter and Bob. The man Bob had seen outside the tent—the man named Bones—was there with a rifle. He sat on a straight chair between the table and the door, his gun across his knees and his eyes alert.

Ferrante stared at Elsie Spratt and Mary Sedlack, who sat at the table, hands folded in front of them. Hank Detweiler leaned on the back of Elsie's chair, and Aleman and Banales sat across from the women. They looked angry and tense. Jupe was at the head of the table with Bob beside him.

"Wasn't there a third kid?" said Ferrante. He scowled at Jupe. "Where's your pal?" he demanded.

"I don't know," said Jupe. "He went out a while ago and he hasn't come back."

The lieutenant looked hesitant, as if not certain whether to believe Jupe.

"The kid's not here," said Bones. "Al already looked upstairs. Want me to check the sheds?"

Ferrante made an impatient sound. "No," he said. "It's not important. He can't get far. Just keep them covered." He nodded towards the group at the table. "If the kid shows up, we'll nail him, too."

Ferrante went out. He paused for a moment in the drive to speak to a second armed man who stood guard there. Then he disappeared through the outside entrance to the cellar of the Barron house.

Jupiter Jones looked at his watch. It was almost half past ten. The cliffs had exploded into flames twenty minutes before, and Jupe knew it would not be reasonable to expect help before midnight. It would be a long, nerve-racking wait.

Jupe leaned back in his chair and listened. He heard smashing and thumping from the basement of the big house. Ferrante had come with three other men, in addition to Bones and the guard in the drive, and Jupe knew that the four of them were now hauling crates across the cellar floor and manhandling trunks out of the way. Jupe put up his hand to cover a smile. It would take them a long while to complete their treasure hunt. They would eventually move the woodpile, and in time they would even shovel out the contents of the coal bin and dig up the floor there.

The thumping, scraping sounds ceased, and there was a crashing which Jupe assumed was the cement of the floor being broken with a sledgehammer. It went on relentlessly for five minutes, then for ten. At last it stopped and the staff heard shovels turning the earth.

It was almost an hour since the cliffs had burned.

The man with the rifle shifted in his chair and looked up at the kitchen clock.

The men in the cellar stopped digging in the ground and began to move the woodpile. Logs hit the remains of the concrete floor and bounced away. Again there came the sound of concrete being broken, and again the scrape of shovels in the earth.

It was an hour and a half since the cliffs had burned.

The men in the cellar attacked the pile of coal. They shovelled and then smashed more concrete and shovelled again.

And it was almost two hours since the cliffs had burned.

Lieutenant Ferrante climbed out of the cellar. His shirt was sweat-stained and dirty and split across the shoulders, and his hair hung down over his eyes. One gloved hand rested on the gun at his belt. He came up the ranch-house steps in a dash.

"They tricked us," he said to Bones. "It isn't there. It never was there. I'm going up to that meadow and old man Barron will talk to me—and talk straight."

"You never take off those gloves, do you, Lieutenant?" said Jupiter. He spoke quietly, but there was a mocking certainty in his voice that made Ferrante look towards him almost in fear.

"It must be rather uncomfortable to wear gloves in this weather," said Jupe, "but it's very important, isn't it?"

Ferrante made a move as if he would leave, but Jupe went on and Ferrante did not leave. He listened.

"Yours is really a most artistic crime," said Jupe. "It required a great deal of imagination. Of course, the raw materials for the plot were already here. You had a woman who believed in friendly space voyagers, and so you constructed a spaceship. You had a man who was preparing for a disaster that would destroy our civilization, and so you fabricated a disaster. You jammed the radios. I imagine you used CB transmitters in the hills around this ranch and you broadcast noise to block the signals from the commercial stations that are usually heard in this area.

"After you jammed the radios, you cut the television cables and telephone wires and power lines. The ranch was then isolated, and the stage was set for the appearance of a company of soldiers."

The man with the rifle stirred nervously. "Hey!" he said. "Time's awasting!"

Ferrante made a move as if to go to the door.

"Are you going to take off your gloves, Lieutenant?" said Jupe.

Ferrante stopped. His eyes went to Jupe's face, searching, calculating.

"You've given a terrific performance," said Jupe. "You were a man frightened almost out of his wits by strange events. You pretended to be a stutterer, terrified of Charles Barron, but bravely resolved to follow orders and not to let anyone off the ranch and out on to the road.

"And wasn't Mr Barron obliging? He posted sentries along his fence. He warned his employees about going off the ranch. He helped create the climate of fear.

"Then the spaceship took off from the meadow after the cliffs burned, and Simon de Luca, the herder, was found unconscious with his hair singed. The spaceship must have been carefully planned and constructed. A helium-filled balloon stretched over a framework, I imagine. De Luca's appearance on the meadow surprised your men at first, but they decided to take advantage of it. They knocked de Luca out, singed his hair with a cigarette or a match, and left him to be found, supposedly the accidental victim of rocket fire. The illusion was to be completed by the appearance on the meadow of a person in a spacesuit—the one who kept me and my friends from leaving this morning.

"You hoped that Mr Barron would be convinced that rescuers were coming to take him

448

away, and eventually he was. You hoped that he would try to take his gold with him, and he did not. How disappointing for you!"

The lieutenant was like a statue, a deadly cold statue. His lips were a thin line and his eyes were hard. "Gold?" he said. "What do you know about gold?"

"About as much as you do," said Jupe. "Barron distrusts banks and the government, so he has to trust in gold, and he has to keep his gold here on the ranch. This is his fortress. Anyone could deduce that much. But to know all of the other things about the Barrons—those things that you have found so useful in preparing your drama—you needed a spy. You needed someone on the inside who could study the Barrons and report to you—let you know what was going on. It was someone very close to you, wasn't it, Lieutenant? It was someone who used the same homey expression you used—a rattlesnake in a rainstorm. Someone who has a deformity on her hand, very much like the one you have on yours—except you hide yours by wearing gloves. It was your sister Elsie."

There was a surging, electric quality to the silence in the kitchen. Elsie Spratt leaned forward and glared at Jupe. "I'm going to sue you!" she said.

"No, you won't," said Jupe. "You won't sue anybody. You're going to be too busy trying to defend yourself. Of course, you won't be alone. The lieutenant is so well informed because there's a field telephone on this ranch. It must be very well hidden. Could it be in the stall of that stallion who is so dangerous that only Mary Sedlack can go near him?"

Jupe smiled at Mary. "In time we'll probably find that it was you who suggested to Barron that the radio be monitored," he said, "and not Barron who asked you to listen. It was your radio, wasn't it? And there was a tape recorder hidden in it. The message from the spaceship was on tape, just like the President's message."

Mary's air of competence had deserted her. She seemed almost in tears. "I don't know anything about it," she insisted.

"Yes, you do, Mary," said Jupe. "You and the lieutenant are friends—good friends. Elsie has a picture in her room. It's a picture taken at a New Year's Eve party. There is a dancing couple in the background—a young woman with long, fair hair is dancing with a bearded young man. You cut your hair before you came here, Mary, or I'd have recognized you instantly. And Lieutenant Ferrante, alias Spratt, shaved off his beard."

"You want me to shoot this kid?" asked Bones.

"You shoot Jupe and you've got to shoot everybody in this room," said Hank Detweiler grimly. "If you want to be tried for a mass murder, well . . . " He made a gesture as if to say that he did not greatly care.

Then he turned to look at Elsie. "You really are a find," he said. "I should have had my head examined, getting you the job here."

"What did you expect?" she cried. "Am I supposed to be grateful for a chance to cook and scrub and worry about leftovers for the rest of my life? And watch Jack grow old in that rotten little shop, making a nickel here and a dime there? We were meant for better things!"

"Like what?" roared Detweiler. "The women's prison at Frontera?"

"Don't say that!" wailed Elsie. She stood up, her face frantic. "We've got to go, Jack," she said to the lieutenant. "Get out of here. It's late and . . . and we've got to . . ."

She stopped. There was a distant sound of cars on the drive.

"Someone's coming!" said Bones.

Jupe looked past Bones and through the side window. He saw a lithe, muscular shape dash from behind a clump of bushes to the big house, grab the cellar door, and slam it shut over the stairwell. The person then sat down on the door and watched as Charles Barron marched from behind a corner of the big house. Barron faced the guard who had been left in the drive.

"Don't try any violence," Barron warned. "My wife will be here at any moment with the police."

Barron had scarcely uttered the words before two cars from the sheriff's department roared up the drive. They stopped with screeching tyres just beyond the ranch house. The back door of one car opened and Mrs Barron leaped out.

"Ernestine, be careful!" cried Charles Barron. "You could be killed doing that!"

"Yes, dear," she said as she ran over to him.

The armed guard by Barron sized up the situation. He dropped his rifle and put up his hands.

There was a thumping at the cellar door and Pete leaped aside. The door flew up and Ferrante's three men started out, then froze where they were at the sight of the cars. The sheriff's men were tumbling out of the vehicles with their guns drawn.

Barron gestured toward the men in the cellar doorway. "They're all tired out from digging for treasure," he told the deputies. "You'll find two more tied up by the dam. And there are a couple more in the ranch-house kitchen, where my youngest guest Jupiter Jones has been keeping them entertained. I don't think they'll give you any trouble. Jupiter has probably convinced them that it would do them no good."

He began to chuckle. "There may be hope for us yet," he said. "We have some very fine young people today."

18

Mr Sebastian Asks Some Questions

ON A BRIGHT AFTERNOON about ten days after they returned to Rocky Beach, the Three Investigators set out on their bikes. They passed the beach community of Malibu, then turned off the Pacific Coast Highway on to the rutted side road called Cypress Canyon Drive.

At the end of the drive lived Mr Hector Sebastian, a friend of the boys. They had met him not long ago when they were working on a bank-robbery case. Mr Sebastian had once been a penniless private detective. A bad injury to his leg had forced him to change careers. Now he was a rich and famous writer, and the only mysteries he solved these days were the ones he dreamed up for his books and movies. But he still took a professional interest in the detective business.

Mr Sebastian had recently purchased a ramshackle old building which had formerly been a restaurant named Charlie's Place. He was slowly converting it into a residence. When the boys wheeled into the parking area outside the place, Mr Sebastian was there, leaning on his cane and contentedly watching an electrician perched atop a ladder. The man was working on the neon tubing that ran around the eaves of the house.

"Hi, boys!" Mr Sebastian grinned and nodded towards the man on the ladder. "I'm enjoying my new life of comfort and ease," he said. "Once, I'd have been up on the ladder struggling with the wires myself. Today I get to supervise. Actually, I only get to watch. That man is a master electrician, and he doesn't take kindly to supervision."

"Are you having the neon taken off the house, Mr Sebastian?" asked Bob.

"No," said Mr Sebastian. "I'm getting it fixed so that it works properly. Then, if I'm expecting company for dinner, I can turn on my neon lights and my guests can find me."

Bob looked startled, and Mr Sebastian laughed. "I know," he said. "Neon isn't the usual thing to have on a house. But think how handy it will be on a dark night for somebody who doesn't know the neighbourhood. Now come on. Let's go inside. When you called this morning, I told Don you were coming. He's been out in the kitchen rattling pans around. I don't know exactly what he's cooking, but the place smells terrific."

The boys followed Mr Sebastian up on to the rickety wooden porch of Charlie's Place, then in through a lobby which was rich with the odours of baking. Beyond the lobby was a huge room which had once been the main dining room of the restaurant. The floors there were polished hardwood, and huge plate-glass windows looked

454

out over trees to the ocean. The room was almost bare of furniture, there was a low, glass-topped table with several patio chairs beside it. At the other end of the room, partially screened by a bank of tall bookshelves, sat a big desk and a typewriter table. Papers were scattered on the floor around the desk, and there was a sheet of paper in the typewriter.

Mr Sebastian nodded towards the desk. "I'm having trouble settling down to work here," he said. "I write a hundred words or so, and then I have to go roaming around my estate to make plans for the things I'm going to do here. Like the terrace."

Pete looked around. "What terrace?" he said.

"I'm going to have a terrace right outside these windows," said Mr Sebastian. "I don't understand why the people who owned Charlie's Place didn't think of it years ago. I'll have a couple of the windows taken out and sliding glass doors put in, and I'll have a concrete terrace running across the front of the building. I can sit out there in the afternoons with a cool drink, and maybe Don can learn to make cocktail snacks."

Mr Sebastian raised his voice then. "Oh, Don!" he cried. "They're here!"

Almost immediately a smiling Oriental man appeared in the lobby. Hoang Van Don was Mr Sebastian's Vietnamese houseman, a refugee who was enthusiastically learning American ways. He had plainly gone to great trouble to prepare for the visit of the Three Investigators. He held a tray loaded with food.

"Here is best for good friends," Don said. He set the tray down on the glass-topped table. "Grandma's Graham Cookies," he announced. "Brownies made with Friendly Farms Fudge Mix. Happy Daze Ice Cream and Uncle Hiram Root Beer with nature's sparkle."

"Amazing!" said Mr Sebastian. "You've outdone yourself!"

Don's grin became even wider, and he bowed himself out of the room. The others seated themselves around the table.

"I am trying to interest Don in a social club that meets in Malibu the third Tuesday of every month," said Mr Sebastian. "It's a dinner club for newcomers to the community who want to meet other people. I keep worrying about what will happen to my digestive tract if Don keeps on composing his menus out of things he sees in television commercials. If he met some real live Americans in their homes, he might discover that in this country we do have food that isn't pure sugar—and that isn't pre-mixed, frozen, or preserved in plastic."

Jupiter chuckled and bit into a brownie. He said it tasted fine. Eying Jupe's waistline, Mr Sebastian guessed the stocky First Investigator wasn't fussy about what he ate.

"Now, boys, what's up?" asked Mr Sebastian. "You said on the phone you'd been trying to keep someone from being done out of a fortune. I assume you've been on another case."

Bob nodded and handed a large Manila envelope across the table to Mr Sebastian. "Here are our notes," he said. "We thought you might like to have the inside story on what happened at Rancho Valverde."

"Rancho Valverde?" said Mr Sebastian. "You were there? What luck! The newspaper reports were fragmentary. I certainly *would* like to have the inside story."

Mr Sebastian opened the file folder that he had taken from the envelope, and began to read the notes that Bob had typed up on the mystery of the blazing cliffs. He did not speak again until he had finished. Then he closed the folder and leaned back in his chair. "Good night!" he said. "I'm worn out just reading about that scheme. Surely there could have been a simpler way to go after that gold!"

"Almost anything would have been simpler," said Jupiter. "But Jack Spratt and his friends are frustrated actors, and they couldn't resist the temptation to make a big production."

"I've noticed that myself," said Mr Sebastian, "in the short time I've been acquainted with Hollywood. Some actors can make a production out of anything."

"And all the elements for grand drama were there," said Jupe. "There was Charles Barron's well-known distrust of the world, and there was Mrs Barron's belief in the rescuers from another

457

planet. Perhaps Spratt and his friends knew about Orson Welles' broadcast of *War of the Worlds* and were inspired to create a drama about the end of our own world. They must have had a good time dressing up in army uniforms and spacesuits."

"The costumes were from the Western Costume Company," said Pete. "The telephones were army surplus that Jack Spratt and his pals bought. They stole the army jeep."

"We aren't sure where they got the flying saucer," said Bob, "but we think they probably built it. After they released it from the meadow, it floated off and it hasn't come down to earth anyplace. Probably they made that crazy-looking metal thing that was found on the meadow, too. Some experts have looked at it, and they all say it doesn't do anything. It's strictly window dressing. It's pewter, and Mr Barron is going to use it as a paperweight. We have to guess about some of the stuff because nobody is talking. They all clammed up and started yelling for lawyers the minute the sheriff showed up."

"Naturally," said Mr Sebastian. He held up the file folder. "There are some gaps in the story," he said. "For instance, the success of the scheme depended on isolating the ranch totally for a few days. How did the crooks keep traffic off the road that ran through the valley?"

"Easy!" said Pete. "They just put up some 'ROAD CLOSED FOR REPAIRS' signs at either end. The road is used so little that they figured no one would bother to investigate. Nobody did."

Mr Sebastian nodded. "An acceptable risk. Now, who was it that attacked you boys when you tried to cross the meadow and leave the ranch? Had Spratt posted guards there? Was the person who smelled like horses Mary Sedlack?"

"We think so," said Jupe. "We think that Mary saw us leave the house that morning, and that she used the field telephone in the stallion's stall to call the soldiers on the road. Spratt then alerted his men on the cliffs, and they were waiting for us. Mary followed us, we think, to make sure we didn't get off the ranch, and she attacked Bob as two other people attacked Pete and myself. Then she went back to the ranch and took her regular morning shower. That's our assumption, because she didn't smell of horses any more when Mr Barron brought us back to the house. I doubt that she knew the odour would be noticeable in the first place. She was around animals so much that she wouldn't think of it herself."

Mr Sebastian smiled. "Horsey people do tend to have an aroma," he said. "So you found a field telephone in the stable, did you?"

"Yes, we did," said Jupe. "It was rigged so that Mary or Elsie could call out to the road, but no one could call in. Spratt didn't want anyone to hear the ringing the device makes on an incoming call."

"Jack Spratt must be a whiz at fixing things," said Pete. "He rigged the field telephones, and he fixed Elsie's radio with a hidden tape recorder so that she could play the speech that was supposed to be from the White House at a time when everybody would be listening. He fixed Mary Sedlack's radio, too, so she could play a tape of the message from the spaceship. Once Mary convinced Mr Barron that it would be a good idea to monitor the radio, she just sat in the dining room and waited for an audience, and then she played the message. We turned out to be the audience."

"The radio and the tapes will be hard evidence for the district lawyer," said Jupe. "So will the field telephones and the fog machine on the meadow."

"A fog machine?" said Mr Sebastian.

Jupe nodded. "They had to have fog. The fog hid the equipment at the foot of the cliffs—the tanks of gas·and the mechanism that ignited the gas and made the cliffs blaze. The tanks were lowered down the cliffs with ropes, then lifted up again so that no one on the ranch would know that they had ever been there. The flying saucer must have had long lines, too, so that it could be allowed to lift off the meadow, or it could be hauled down and tethered close to the ground."

"The crooks hoped that Mr Barron would bring his gold when he came to meet the spaceship," said Bob. "They thought they'd just grab it and run. They probably believed Mr Barron wouldn't make too much fuss about it because he'd feel like such a dunce. Imagine telling the cops how you lugged your gold out to a mountain meadow so you could take it to another world in a flying saucer!"

"It would make poor Barron look like an idiot, wouldn't it?" said Mr Sebastian. "Well, thanks to you boys, it didn't come to that."

Jupe frowned. "We should have realized sooner what was going on," he said. "I should have noticed sooner that Elsie and the lieutenant were both using the same highly individual expression. Once I noticed that they both talked of rattlesnakes and rainstorms, everything else fell into place. The lieutenant's gloves became significant, and I recalled that it was Elsie who turned on the radio to get the President's message. It was also Elsie who subtly prompted Mr Barron to isolate himself. She planted the idea that the ranch was to be a refuge for government officials, and then worried about cooking for a crowd of visitors. Barron picked up the cue and told her that she wouldn't have to, and that he was posting guards to keep strangers out. She was playing on his dislike and distrust of government interference."

"What made you suspect Mary?" asked Mr Sebastian.

"The message from the flying saucer," said Jupe. "I thought of it while we were in the kitchen and the men were digging up the cellar. If Elsie had been responsible for the fake message from Washington, I knew that Mary might be responsible for the message from outer space. Then I remembered the picture I'd seen in Elsie's

461

room, and I realized that the couple dancing in the picture were Mary and Spratt, and the puzzle was solved. But it was like a jigsaw with too many pieces."

"Complicated, but interesting," said Mr Sebastian.

"There was a police lieutenant talking on television the other day about confidence games," said Pete. "He said if swindlers worked as hard at something honest as they do at con games, they'd all be rich."

"Probably all too true," said Mr Sebastian. "I've seen some industrious crooks in my time, but they don't seem able to be honest. Maybe that's why we call them crooks. They aren't straight. Or they just don't see things realistically."

Jupe nodded. "Elsie probably didn't plan to rob Mr Barron when she first went to work at the ranch, but she and her brother felt that they hadn't been treated right by the world. They thought they should have gotten better breaks, so it would be all right for them to even things out by taking Mr Barron's treasure."

"Life isn't fair, is it?" said Mr Sebastian. "We kid ourselves when we expect that it will be. And what about Mary? Why did she get involved?"

Bob shrugged. "All we know is that she needed money for vet school. Maybe she couldn't pass up the chance to get it fast."

"Ambition got the better of her? Could be," said Sebastian. "Now, did you ever find out where the gold was hidden?"

"Mr Barron won't tell, but we can guess," said Jupe. "The lawn furniture was made to order, and it had slots that were similar to those you find in coin vending machines. I think Mr Barron bought his gold in the form of coins and dropped the coins through the slots into the hollow places in the furniture. I think his chairs and tables were filled with gold!

"I also think the gold is someplace else by now. Elsie and her brother got too close to the treasure. I'm sure Mr Barron has taken steps to see that no one else does so again. And perhaps someday he'll regain some trust in banks or ordinary investments. In the meanwhile, Mrs Barron hasn't lost her faith in the Blue Light Mission. The convention will be held at the ranch this summer, and Mrs Barron is having a speaker's platform built on the upper meadow. Tanks of butane will be installed there so that the cliffs can blaze on cue whenever she wishes them to."

"Great!" said Mr Sebastian. "I love it. That makes the neon tubes on my house seem positively restrained!"

"Now there's one thing we need to know," said Jupe.

"What's that?" asked Mr Sebastian.

"You introduced our last case for us, after Mr Hitchcock died and couldn't be our sponsor any more. We thought that if you liked this one, and if you weren't too busy with your own work . . ."

Mr Sebastian held up a hand. "Say no more. I'll be honoured to introduce the case. It's fascinating."

Mr Sebastian absent-mindedly ate a brownie. "You know," he mused, "that scheme was really foiled by Mrs Barron's sense of hospitality. If she hadn't asked you to stay for dinner, you'd have been off the ranch by the time the hoax started. There's a lesson there."

At that moment, Don put his head in the room to see how the food was.

"Fine, just fine," said Mr Sebastian. "Keep up the good work, Don. Who knows? Someday you may foil a robbery with a plate of chocolate brownies!"